HELEN DUNMORE

A Spell of Winter

PENGUIN BOOKS

PENGUIN BOOKS

Published by the Penguin Group
Penguin Books Ltd, 80 Strand, London WC2R ORL, England
Penguin Group (USA) Inc., 375 Hudson Street, New York, New York 10014, USA
Penguin Group (Canada), 90 Eglinton Avenue East, Suite 700, Toronto, Ontario, Canada M4P 2Y3
(a division of Pearson Penguin Canada Inc.)
Penguin Ireland, 25 St Stephen's Green, Dublin 2, Ireland (a division of Penguin Books Ltd)
Penguin Group (Australia), 250 Camberwell Road, Camberwell,
Victoria 3124, Australia (a division of Pearson Australia Group Pty Ltd)
Penguin Books India Pvt Ltd, 11 Community Centre,
Panchsheel Park, New Delhi – 110 017, India
Penguin Group (NZ), 67 Apollo Drive, Rosedale, North Shore 0632, New Zealand
(a division of Pearson New Zealand Ltd)
Penguin Books (South Africa) (Pty) Ltd, 24 Sturdee Avenue, Rosebank, Johannesburg 2196, South Africa

Penguin Books Ltd, Registered Offices: 80 Strand, London WC2R ORL, England

www.penguin.com

First published by Viking 1995
First published in Penguin Books 1996
This edition published 2007

007

Copyright © Helen Dunmore, 1995
All rights reserved

The moral right of the author has been asserted

Printed in England by Clays Ltd, St Ives plc

ISBN: 978-0-141-03358-7

www.greenpenguin.co.uk

Penguin Books is committed to a sustainable
future for our business, our readers and our planet.
This book is made from Forest Stewardship
Council™ certified paper.

'I saw an arm fall off a man once,' said Kate. She turned the toasting-fork to see how the muffin was browning, then held it up to the fire again. We stared at her.

'Yes,' she went on, 'it was in my grandfather's house in Dublin. They were bringing my uncle Joseph down the stairs. Narrow, twisty stairs they put in houses where they'd given no thought to the living or the dead. You couldn't get a coffin up them. But my grandmother had kept the body too long in the house. She was mad with grief, she didn't want him to go. She kept putting more flowers in the room, shovelling flowers in on top of him to hide the smell. Then she'd be sitting with him all night long.'

'Was that your grandmother O'Neill?' I whispered to the flames.

'Who else would it be? You know my daddy was the eldest of the twelve. But this one, Joseph, was his next brother and the favourite. If there was meat or meal, it would be Joseph got the meat.'

'Did you know him before he was dead?'

'Who's telling this story? He was twenty-six when he died with a kick from a cart horse. How could I not know my own uncle?

'Well now, Joseph must have been up there a week or more, with my grandmother lighting fresh candles round him and saying prayers enough to wear out the saints. No one else's prayers were good enough for Joseph, only hers. I remember the talk in the house. We were giving scandal. It was the middle of summer, and hot. My mother wouldn't go near the house in her condition, and the smell had driven everyone

I

but my grandmother from the room. That was when it was decided that they would force her to have him brought down and taken out of the house for burial. She wouldn't even see the priest, so it was my father had to go up and talk to her. But she wouldn't listen. In the end four of them had to take her by the ankles and elbows, kicking and screaming to wake the dead. They shut her in the scullery until it was done.'

'Did they lock her in?'

'There was no lock on the door. My aunts sat in with her and there were two men set to guard it so she couldn't burst out. But the noise she made was terrible. So it was left to my father to bring Joseph down, with only Dodie to help. That was his next brother after Joseph.'

We nodded. We knew about Dodie, who never held a job or went out of the house if he could help it.

'They were bringing him down the curve of the stairs,' said Kate. She laid the muffin down on the hearth and showed us with her hands how the men eased the body round the narrow top of the stairs. 'There we were, all of us looking from the kitchen.'

I saw them in rows, Kate with her bold eyes staring the most.

'And the noise of my grandmother from the scullery, with her shawl thrown over her head though that didn't muffle the screeching at all. And then there was a smack where Dodie stumbled. I heard my father curse and the wall shook as the pair of them fell to their knees trying to get their balance and keep poor Joseph from falling. And we heard a terrible soft sound like the leg being sucked off a cooked chicken, and there was Joseph's arm bouncing down the stairs to the floor below. It lay on the floor in front of our very eyes,' said Kate.

'What did it look like?' asked Rob. His voice had gone growly with excitement. I said nothing. I stared at Kate, and

2

I saw white strings like roots coming out of the arm as it bounced down the wooden stairs.

'It had a silver shine on it,' said Kate, 'like the shine on money. But underneath the flesh was puffed up and purple. And the hand was swollen bigger than any hand I'd ever seen.'

'Did they pick it up?' I whispered.

'Oh yes, they had to do that. You can't be burying bits of a body here and there. But for a long while no one moved, and the only sound was my grandmother drumming her heels against the flags in the scullery. Of course she knew nothing of what was happening, nor ever did, for no one told her. Not even the youngest child that was there that day.' Kate held her empty toasting-fork up to the flames, forgotten.

'It was my aunt Kitty who picked up Joseph's arm. She took one of the white baking cloths from the drawer and went forward and laid it over the arm. Then she picked it up wrapped in the cloth like a shroud and took it out of the house. As she went past us we saw a stain seeping through the white.'

'Was it blood?' asked Rob.

'It was black,' said Kate. 'Black like tar.'

We sighed deeply. There was no sound but the puckering of the flames. The muffins were singed and dry, but who would want to eat them now? Then I thought of something.

'But where was your grandfather, Kate? Wasn't he in the house to make them bury Joseph before his arm fell off?' I knew that all twelve of them were afraid of their father, Kate's grandfather. I could close my eyes and see him plain from what Kate had told me. A little, wiry, jockey of a man. He should have been tall, but he grew up in famine times when there was no food for a child to grow on, said Kate. His tall sons and daughters stood over him and he lashed them with the whip of his tongue as if they were slow horses.

'He was away,' said Kate. Her face closed up and we knew she would tell us no more about where her grandfather had been. 'They got Joseph out of the house as quick as they could, and into his coffin. I heard Aunt Kitty say it was God's mercy he didn't fall to pieces entirely, there on the stairs. He had a quick burial.'

'How old were you, Kate?' asked Rob.

'Oh, eight or so. A little younger than you and a little older than this one,' she said, tapping my head. She leaned forward and poked the fire. 'These muffins are like leather. Away down to the kitchen, Cathy, and ask Mrs Blazer for fresh.'

I hesitated. 'Kate . . .' I wanted to ask more, but I didn't know what questions to ask. Was she going to tell Rob, when I was out of the room, because he was older? And besides, there was the long flickering passage, and the dark turn of the stairs to go down . . .

'Well, are you going or not?' she demanded impatiently. 'It's you that's eating these muffins, not me.'

I moved slowly to the door. I looked back at Kate and Rob in the circle of firelight. A cold draught felt at my ankles. Kate's strong white arms speared the dead muffins and tossed them unerringly into the wastepaper basket. She looked so sure and brave, even though she was the one who had seen the dead arm with her own eyes, when she was just my age. I wondered if I would be as sure as Kate when I was older, when my skirts were down over my boots the way hers were. I would wear stays then, like Kate, and have a shape that went in and out and made you want to put your arms tight around her waist to feel its narrow springiness. I was Cathy and she was Kate. We had the same name really. I was Catherine and she was Kathleen, but no one had called her that since she was baptized at two days old.

Mother was gone, and Father was away. There was Kate to look after us, and Eileen in the sewing-room, and the kitchen warm and humming with people. There was Grandfather in London. There was nothing to be frightened of here. The fluttering shadows only startled me because they were sudden, like moths' wings.

'What's wrong with the girl?' snapped Kate at the fire, and it snapped back a slim tongue of flame, as sharp as hers. I went.

One

It is winter in the house. This morning the ice on my basin of water is so thick I can not break it. The windows stare back at me, blind with frost. Inside my nest of quilts I am warm, and Rob's coat presses down on me like two hands. I huff out my breath and watch it smoke.

I can see nothing through the frost flowers on the glass. I wonder if it is snowing yet, but I think it is too cold. It will only take a minute to rake out last night's fire and build up a fresh pyramid. There is always enough wood. All I have to do is walk out and gather it. There are five years of rotting trees and fallen branches which have been left to lie in the woods.

The coloured cloth spines of our childhood books look at me. Grimm, Hans Andersen, *At the Back of the North Wind*. But to get something to read I'd have to skate across the icy sea of oilcloth between me and the bookcase.

I kneel up in bed and put on Rob's coat. Its thick, stiff wool is becoming supple again from the heat of my body night after night. I put the sleeve to my face and sniff. The smell is still there, undiluted. The coat crushes my nightdress to my body and prickles my breasts. I button it up the boys' way and feel about on the floor for my slippers.

The paper is dry. I put paper and kindling by the fire last night, so it will light with clean blue and yellow flames as soon as I put a match to it. I coil the newspaper sheets into little balls without reading a single word. They are old newspapers, covered in long, thick columns of names. I never look at them. Then I make a pyre of coils and balance the kindling into a tent around it. I was always the best at making fires. It's an instinct, knowing where to lay the flame of the match so that it catches the draught and flares up against the rough, flammable cheeks of white kindling.

I hold my hands to the flames as they begin to jump. There is no wind at all in the chimney, and this has always been an awkward grate. The flames lose heart and shrink back into the wood. I spread out a double sheet of newspaper and hold it over the grate to make it draw. The paper sucks in and I plaster it tight against the edge of the fireplace. In a couple of minutes the fire stirs behind it and begins to roar. I wait until it glows big and yellow behind the paper, singeing the newsprint brown. It would be so easy to read what was written, but I don't. Not one word. My fire is roaring like the big range down in the kitchens, which is never lit now. It has hunched there for months, dusty as winter soil. No one has blackleaded it.

I put down the paper, sit back on my heels and open Rob's coat. The flames are strong and they make yellow shadows on my white nightdress. The milky cold of the room is beginning to thaw. Soon the windows will grow little circles of plain glass.

I am getting hot. Rob's thick coat tents the heat. The smell is coming out more strongly now. Wool and sweat. Although I've brushed the coat I have never cleaned it. The earth smell is still there, like the smell on a bundle of tramp's clothes you find in the woods.

Little prickles of heat run down my sides. I feel my face flushing, and I push back my heavy plait. I kneel up and wriggle out of my nightdress under the coat, the way we used to do when we were undressing on the beach at Sandgate, while Nanny knitted and watched. It is decent to dress and undress beneath a tent of bleached cambric. My nightdress slides into a small white heap. I tug Rob's coat close around me. A row of spare buttons in the side seam presses into my hip. They will leave a mark on my flesh that will last under my clothes all day, secretly. He never needed to change the buttons. They are still held on with strong dark thread, the way they were when the coat was bought. The label scratches the top of my neck and the first bone of my spine. I remember how cool the air felt against the nape of my neck when I first put up my hair. I wore a white dress which I hated, and Rob came up behind me and touched the skin I had never seen.

'It's so white,' he said. 'It's never had the sun on it.'

Then I twisted away from his fingers and picked up the skirts of my dress and ran down the staircase like a girl who could not wait to get to the party.

Now I move my body inside Rob's coat, so all my skin will touch the lining which has touched him. My breasts tip forward, catching on the hairy wool of the coat's opening. My fire dances and grows strong, stronger than the worn brown oilcloth, bought for hard wear, stronger than the iron frames of our two beds, stronger than the chain of the gas lamp over the table. I prop two dry logs into the flames and sit cross-legged, naked to the heat of the fire and the heat of the coat. I listen to the scuff of mice in the attics above me, the creak and settle of long rows of rooms beneath me, the cry of rooks beyond the frost-bound windows.

I never wear Rob's coat out of the house. I put on my thick navy-blue wool skirt with red braiding, and my black squirrel jacket. A big red sun hangs above the trees, catching in their spiky branches. I walk up the rhododendron path and through the Spanish chestnut grove. I climb over the gate into First Field. It should have been ploughed by now so that the frosts can break up the big clods of earth into sweet-smelling, crumbled spring soil. There is an awkward turn here by the hedge and the plough always swings out in a curve and spoils the clean line of furrows flowing up to the horizon. In a frost like this I could have walked on the wave-like crests of the furrow without crumbling them. The earth is iron hard, the frost a week deep. But no one has ploughed. The Semple boys are gone. Next year it will all come right, old Semple told me, spitting out of the side of his mouth as he's done since he'd had his stroke. He will plough the field himself, he said, rather than see the land go to waste. But I know he never will.

The field is lumpy with half-remembered patterns of cultivation. It is fine soil, well-drained and rich. This is where we stood to shoot the pigeons that took the grain. They came out of the woods, never seeing us or remembering the deaths of a previous season. We must have shot hundreds over the years. Rank heaps of weeds blacken in the frost. The rabbits are bold enough to take the gun from your hand now, said old Semple. It will take years to root up the corn-cockle and poppies. We don't need to call him old Semple any more, I think suddenly. There are no young Semples any more. George went first, then Michael, then Theodore. The Semple boys never had their names shortened, even when they were children in big boots kicking up the dust on their way through the lanes to school. They did not go to church with the other families in the village: they walked three miles across the fields to a tiny chapel where the same six families met week after week to share their passion for the Lord.

I think of the spittle running down the side of old Semple's mouth and hanging in his rough beard. The beard is greyer than the hair on his head. It is a dirty ash grey, and bobbles of spittle tremble in it with the trembling of old Semple's body. He has always been clean-shaven, but he will not let his wife shave him now.

This was where Rob shot the hare. It was bad luck to shoot a hare, they said in the kitchens even as they took it from us and exclaimed over its size and the fine roast it would make. He didn't kill her cleanly. She came like running water over the rise in the field, her ears flat to her body, her big legs bounding in great sure leaps. We had only been after rabbits. Rob swung up his gun and shot her. We ran to where she was lying, big ripples running through her flesh as she felt the wound. She was hit in the back legs and there were white bits of bone bubbling in the dark mess of blood. She didn't seem to know where she'd been shot and her body quivered all over as she struggled to make her legs run. Her lips were drawn back over her teeth.

'I'll shoot her again,' said Rob.

'Don't, she'll come to pieces,' I said. 'Hit her on the back of the neck like a rabbit.'

I took Rob's gun and he got the hare by her ears and swung Grandfather's blackthorn stick. She gave a buck in his hands then she was still and her eyes began to film at once, though blood dripped steadily out from the hole in her thigh.

'You've got all blood on Grandfather's stick,' I said. I thought of the hare's form we'd come upon once, when it was still warm. I'd put my hand in it and felt it.

'She wouldn't have young at this season,' said Rob, as if he was arguing with someone. I thought of leverets lying still as death, waiting for their mother to come home. He bent down and pulled up a tuft of grass, then wiped the stick carefully with it until there was no trace of blood left.

'No,' I said, my mind full of the blind, skinny leverets, 'she won't have any young. It's the wrong time.'

'Do you want to carry her, Cathy?'

I knew that the hare sickened him. She was a bagful of blood, dripping, not the beautiful thing she had been. 'All right. Give it to me.' I took the hare by her front paws. She was heavy, and warm. Much heavier than I would have thought, from the way she leapt down the field. My arm ached as we walked back to the house, and the hare banged against my legs. She would be staining my coat, but I didn't look down to see. It was black, and the blood wouldn't show. Rob carried my gun as well as his own. Two of the Semple boys were working in the woods with their father. Theodore and Michael. They were planting young beech where Grandfather had had to take down an oak that was rotten to the heart. It might have been there a thousand years or more, Rob said. When it came down we'd count the rings, we said, but we never did, and it was soon sawn up and carted away for firewood. The Semple boys were twelve or thirteen then, a couple of years older than Rob. A short while ago they'd been children like us, but now they wore working clothes, like men. They stopped digging to look at the hare.

'Give it to Mrs Blazer, she'll hang it and roast you a fine saddle of hare for Sunday,' said old Semple. Theodore looked intently at it, as if he were imagining what it would taste like. We often gave them rabbits, but hare was richer, different, darker meat.

I thought of it hanging in the pantry, with blood coagulating in a white china dish under it. It was always cold in there, because the pantry faced north and there were big, chill marble slabs on which meat rested. Wire mesh covered a small window which looked out to a bank of earth. There was always a faint, iron smell of blood. You had to know how long to hang each creature. So long for a piece of venison, so long for a pheasant or a hare. Grandfather knew everything about hanging animals. But you didn't call them animals once they were shot, you called them game. Like you called people corpses.

I walk up the frozen field. I cannot damage the earth, or anything that is in it. The rooks circle low, flapping their big wings emptily. Cold stings my cheeks and I walk faster, tucking my hands under my elbows to keep them warm in the squirrel fur. I should have brought my fur gloves, too. At the top of the field I stop and look back at the house, where one thin plume of smoke goes straight up into the sky. It is my fire. All the other chimneys are cold. Later Elsie Shell will come up from the village and light the kerosene stove in the back kitchen and cook my dinner. She will bring butter and eggs in her basket, and a new loaf. I told her I didn't want fancy food. I am used to plain. When Elsie has gone I will tear off the crust of the loaf and spread it with sweet yellow butter and eat it walking from room to room, with Rob's coat round my shoulders. Elsie shudders exaggeratedly as she goes away in the early December dusk.

'I shouldn't care to be on my own in this great place all night, the way you are,' she said to me yesterday, planking down my mutton cutlet and gravy with her big raw hands. She wants to come and live here again, with Annie and Mrs Blazer and the others, the way it used to be. But I won't let her. It is never going to be the way it was. I tell her she ought to think of getting a job in the new drapery at Over Loxton. There is money there. They are setting up the shop in a big way, hoping to catch trade from half the county. Elsie could sit in a black dress behind the counter, waiting for the little cylinders of change to whizz back along the wire. But would they want Elsie with her kitchen hands and easy way of talking? And Elsie likes coming here.

'I know the ways of that range like nobody else,' she says, looking at it as if she sees it pulsing with heat again, the blacklead on it glistening like tongues in hellfire.

'It doesn't worry me, Elsie,' I say. 'I like the kerosene stove. And I like being alone.'

I am going back into the silence my grandfather came from.

You have to keep on with a house, day after day, I think. Heating, cleaning, opening and closing windows, making sounds to fill the silence, cooking and washing up, laundering and polishing. As soon as you stop there may as well never have been any life at all. A house dies as quickly as a body. Soon the house will be as it was when my grandfather first came here with my mother still a baby. He had imagined the way it would be, with lights burning, and fires, and people moving to and fro, and births in the bedrooms. Everything had stopped when he stopped being able to imagine it any more. I should have asked him more questions when he was alive. If I shut my eyes I see him now, with my mother in his arms, wrapped in a long coat and tramping round the house he was going to buy, the future he was going to buy, the life he was going to buy.

'The man from nowhere.'

'Convenient place, nowhere.'

I ought to have made sure I knew more. He'd had a past, a geography of silence. None of us had ever mapped it.

My feet are beginning to hurt with the cold that strikes up through the soles of my boots. It is not a day for standing still. In summer you can't see the house from here, only a thick waving frame of green. But now through the black limbs of the trees I see the country of its tiles, where we sat and baked in the valleys on simmering hot summer days, where we hauled ourselves up through skylights, kicking wildly, where we clung to chimney stacks as we felt for the next foothold. I see long rows of blank, staring windows. I am too far away to see the paint curling on the window frames, the marks of damp and rot. When Grandfather was alive the struggle to keep out water and wind went on and on. There was never enough money for the army of workmen that was needed. One of the Semple boys would be taken out of the fields to slosh paint on to window frames, or scaffolding would be cobbled together and a man sent up on to the roof to pour liquid tar on to the worst leaks in the valleys. Grandfather would go round the house with Rob, showing him where a patch of brickwork was crumbling, or the streak of a hairline crack was beginning to race and widen. All these things were like symptoms of a disease that could never be put right, only kept at bay for a year or two.

Grandfather never took my arm and pointed it up towards a missing tile, though I knew as much about the house as Rob did. More. I watched it, and he never did. I knew where its walls trapped sunlight and fed it back to you when you leaned against them after dusk. I knew where the pears ripened first against the kitchen-garden wall, and how to reach inside the apricot net, twist out a rose-freckled apricot and cover up the gap with leaves. I knew the long white rows of attics where Kate and Eileen slept, reflected in their spotted looking-glass. I knew the yeasty smell of the cellars where beer was brewed for the house. I put my finger into the head and sniffed hops and malt and once I turned the spigot and drank thin new beer out of my hands until the cellar walls spun round me. I slept all afternoon under the mulberry tree, and when Rob came to find me my dress was splattered with black mulberry juice. I knew the icy gush of pump water on a blazing July afternoon when Rob and I took turns to work the handle and let the water pulse out over our arms. It was my house, too. I had the smell of it in my clothes and on my skin.

The sky is not going to clear. Mist rises off the ground and mixes with the thickening grains of cold in the air. The sun is fading. Perhaps it is going to snow.

It is winter, my season. Rob's was summer. He was born in June, and I was born in the middle of the night, on the 21st of December. My winter excitement quickened each year with the approach of darkness. I wanted the thermometer to drop lower and lower until not even a trace of mercury showed against the figures. I wanted us to wake to a kingdom of ice where our breath would turn to icicles as it left our lips, and we would walk through tunnels of snow to the outhouses and find birds fallen dead from the air. I willed the snow to lie for ever, and I turned over and buried my head under the pillow so as not to hear the chuckle and drip of thaw.

I look at the house, still and breathless in the frost. I have got what I wanted. A spell of winter hangs over it, and everyone has gone.

Two

Rob's season was summer. August. The shade as black as wet walnuts. The birds silent in the heat. Rob was nine, I was seven, and Miss Gallagher was coming at eleven o'clock. We were dressed ready, told to go nowhere until she came. My sleeves were too tight, not enough to hurt but enough so that I couldn't forget that I was wearing my blue travelling dress and not my everyday pink summer poplin and my white pinafore. And my gloves were crushed and crumpled already. Rob looked cross and scratchy in his Norfolk jacket. Grandfather wasn't coming. He had come into the nursery very early, and given us sixpence each, and told us that he would send the trap for Miss Gallagher at half-past ten. We must be ready at eleven, and mind not to keep Miss Gallagher waiting.

The stable clock struck the three-quarters. It was hot already. Wisps of straw lay baking between the cobbles, and there was a steady *clang clang* of John's bucket as he swilled out the stable floor. Then his boots tramped across the yard to the pump. He did not look our way. On a normal day we would have taken the big whisk broom and chased the straw round the yard, or I would have sat on the mounting-block while John lifted Princess' great tufted hooves to check them for stones. But everyone knew we were going to see Father in the sanatorium.

'Let's go and wait for the trap at the top of the drive,' said Rob.

'Why?'

'Kate and Eileen will be looking out of the window.'

I thought about this. They'd been talking this morning

while Kate brushed my hair. Eileen had come for the slops. Nanny didn't get up with us in the mornings any more, because she was too old. She had been our mother's nurse too, and she was very tired. Soon she was going to live in a cottage by the sea with a girl to do for her. She'd been all right until Mother went away. Now she just looked at us with misty, surprised eyes and called us by the wrong names when we went to say good morning to her. They were the names of children she had looked after years ago. Kate and Eileen were whispering about Father. When I got back I knew they would ask me lots of questions, looking at each other over my head and nodding. Kate's bright dark eyes would snap messages too quick for me to see.

'But they won't know where we've gone,' I said to Rob now.

'Course they will!' said Rob scornfully. 'They all know we're going in the trap with Miss Gallagher. And she'll get out and talk to Kate, you know how she is.'

Kate didn't like Miss Gallagher, nor did Eileen. But they would listen with still, respectful faces, drawing her on to say more than she meant to. The way Miss Gallagher wanted everyone to know she had a secret soon stripped her secrets from her. Kate and Eileen would make mincemeat of Miss Gallagher. Kate was cross anyway, because she had found Rob's baby field-mouse in a box under his bed. He had been keeping the mouse alive with milk from the rubber inside of a fountain pen, but its eyes were stuck up with yellow stuff and the milk ran out as fast as Rob dropped it in. Kate said it was a nasty thing and she would put it on the fire, though we knew she wouldn't. It was just her temper.

I thought I heard the horse, but then there was nothing but the empty lane and all the noises we never thought of or counted, because they were always there. Rob had a stick and he swept it along the ditch, slicing off heads of cow-parsley as cleanly as if the stick was a sword. He turned his wrist and a blade flashed in the sun. Rob was teaching me to bat. Before this summer I'd had to bowl all the time so he could practise. Time hung, and stopped. I would be here for ever, I thought, watching the dust spurt under Rob's boots, hearing the chunk of an axe in the woods, listening for the stable clock to strike eleven, and the sound of the trap.

'Rob,' I said, 'do you think Father knows we're coming?'

'Course he does. Grandfather told him in a letter.'

'But sometimes . . . when Grandfather goes, Father won't see him. Eileen said so when she was talking to Kate in the night nursery.'

'Eileen! What does Eileen know?' said Rob scornfully, mashing at the broken stems in the ditch. 'I'd like to see Grandfather tell Eileen anything.'

I looked up, comforted. Rob smiled. His face was like a warm brown speckled egg. I wished I had hair like Rob's, conker-brown and shiny. He and Father had the same hair, but Father put stuff on his to make it lie still, and Rob only used water. I had rough, springy black hair that crackled when Kate brushed it at night. When there was a storm coming the hairbrush made sparks.

'Irish hair,' Kate said.

'Just like the mother, I've brushed it many a time and watched it flare up to the brush like that,' added Eileen in a low voice over my head. We were in the night nursery and Eileen was beating up the pillows on Rob's bed. She liked beating pillows. Sometimes she would pretend they were people she was beating.

'Who?' I asked.

'That's for you to ask and me to know.'

'Oh, *Eileen*!'

Rob came to bed later, when the nightlight was half burnt down. Eileen stared into the gas lamp as if she saw Mother sitting at her dressing-table, with the heavy silver brush making long sweeps down her wild hair.

Rob and I never talked about Mother downstairs, in case anyone heard. Only when we were in bed and Rob's legs made a tent which threw huge shadows over the opposite wall, and our voices met and mingled in the darkness, saying anything they liked. Sometimes I got out of bed and pattered across the oilcloth to squeeze in next to Rob. Our beds were so narrow that it was only the tight way Kate tucked in the bedclothes that kept me from falling out. Rob was always warm, and I was always cold. Kate thought it was bad for us to have the nursery fire kept in while we slept, unless we were ill. If we were ill at night she would lean over us and hold her hand on our foreheads to feel if we had a fever, and if we had she would go and fetch a shovelful of red coals and set the kindling to it. It was part of the ache and dazzle of fever to see Kate's big shadow and the glowing heap of fire she held out at arm's length in front of her.

'She's coming,' said Rob, 'I can hear the trap.'

In a minute I heard it too. The clipping of hoofs in warm dust, the squeak of the springs, the clink of the harness. It was Semple driving Miss Gallagher today.

'Don't ask her anything about Father,' hissed Rob. Semple crossed the reins and climbed down to help me up the little step, though I didn't need him. I remembered when he used to swing me up, holding my waist tight. Close up I saw the crinkling of his burnt brown face, where the lines were deep enough for an ant to walk in. He smiled at me but he didn't say anything. He never talked to us when there was anyone else there. Miss Gallagher patted a place for me, close beside her.

'Spread out your skirt, Catherine, we don't want Father to see you all creased and crumpled, do we?' she said. She fingered my skirt. She always fussed over my clothes, even though she had on the same things every time we saw her. A hard, prickly, dark navy-blue coat and skirt. In winter, an umbrella with a yellow knob. In summer a dark-blue parasol. Miss Gallagher could make a sunny day look like a funeral.

She darted a glance at Rob and pursed her lips. Her little eyes were shiny under her hat. Miss Gallagher didn't like Rob, but that was only because she didn't like boys and never spoke to them if she could help it. If I made her have to say something to him I scored a point, but if Rob did he scored two, because it was harder for him. When I was there it was easy for Miss Gallagher, because she could talk to Rob through me.

'And have you heard from your dear mother?' she asked me, leaning close as the trap began to jounce along the lane. On the other side of us Rob scowled, and I knew he was wishing he still had his sword and Miss Gallagher was a dried-up stalk of cow-parsley in the ditch.

She was not supposed to ask us about Mother. No one was. But Miss Gallagher didn't care.

'She's quite well, I hope? Not suffering too much from her hay fever this year?'

There was no hay fever where our mother had gone. Once I asked Nanny and she told me. Mother was in a beautiful country with flowers like yellow feathers which made arches over your head. The country was by the sea, and almonds grew there too, green almonds, not like the ones we had at Christmas. The sea there didn't go in and out like our sea at Sandgate, and it was dark blue.

'So warm you'd think you were swimming in milk,' Nanny said.

'Did you swim?' I asked, staring at her.

'I paddled up to here,' said Nanny, showing me the place on her leg. 'Mackintosh bloomers, we all wore.'

Nanny had been there years ago, with her old children.

Our mother's house would be glittering white, she said, so white it hurt your eyes. I thought of the yellow feathers tickling our mother's face, and the way she would shut her eyes and laugh.

'Mother doesn't have hay fever any more,' I answered. I moved my feet as if my boots hurt.

'You can take those off in the train, Catherine,' said Miss Gallagher. She was always wanting me to take things off so she could help me put them on again.

It was two miles to the station. The platform was perfectly still, and the signal was down. The porter came out to look if we had any bags, then he went back to his place in the shade by the wall and screwed up his eyes, staring into the dazzle of rails. Rob put a penny in the chocolate machine on the platform and bent the bar of chocolate backwards and forwards before taking off the silver paper and giving half to me. He didn't even look at Miss Gallagher. Big stains of chocolate sprang on to my gloves. I wondered if Father would notice them. I thought he would, but perhaps since he was ill he would be lying down and all he would see would be my face leaning over him. I could keep my hands down by my sides.

'Will Father be able to sit up?' I whispered to Rob.

'Course he will, idiot,' said Rob. I rubbed my gloves together but it made them worse. The chocolate was like mud, growing the more I tried to get it off. The signal jerked and the wires by the line sizzled. The porter peeled himself away from his cool place and put his cap straight. Miss Gallagher seized my hand as our train gave a far-off 'Whooooo'. We knew from the sound that it was going through the cutting, and in less than a minute we would see first the smoke, then the engine as it rushed out on to open track again and into the station.

A fat lady lurched out of the Ladies compartment and

dropped her three brown-paper parcels on to the platform. Miss Gallagher gave Rob a look which meant 'Pick them up!' but he took no notice of her. The fat lady scrabbled, catching hold of the strings. Her face was purple and she had white hairs coming out of her chin. They sprouted in a little bunch. I wondered why she didn't have them pulled out. Perhaps it would hurt her. Those hairs were the kind of thing Miss Gallagher would have on her face, though in fact she did not.

'Really!' said Miss Gallagher to the air, pushing me ahead of her into the compartment. It was hot and smelly. First of all there was the smell of train dirt, then under it a smell of violet cachous. Miss Gallagher seized the strap and banged down the windows. The train started and I fell hard against the cushion so that dust flew out.

'We'll have something to eat,' said Miss Gallagher, sitting back against the seat and putting up her veil. We stared as she took a paper out of her big black bag. There were three hard-boiled eggs and a twist of salt, nothing else. I had never eaten eggs without bread. She gave one to Rob and one to me. I held mine tight until brown chocolate from my gloves started to come off on to its white shell. I pressed the egg too hard and tiny cracks rippled out from my fingers, then bits of shell began to break off. Underneath it there was dirty white egg with green-blue marks on it, like bruises. A cloud of smuts flew in at the window as the train began to gallop around the bend. Rob leaned forward and took my egg out of my hand. He looked at Miss Gallagher then he put his arm back the way he had taught me at cricket and threw the egg straight out of the open window. Miss Gallagher stared. A sharp patch of red burnt into her cheeks and she opened her mouth as if she were going to break her rules and speak to Rob.

'She doesn't like eggs. They make her sick,' said Rob. His own egg had vanished. I wondered if he had eaten it while I looked at mine, but I didn't think so. We were learning conjuring out of a book, but we hadn't got very far yet, certainly not far enough to vanish an egg. I wondered if the eggs had flown through the air and landed in a nest, a skylark's perhaps, or a nightingale's, some bird that nested on the ground. But then it was August –

Miss Gallagher poked her face into mine.

'Are you feeling sick, Catherine dear?'

I nodded. She pulled down the opposite window and warm air flapped round us, making so much noise no one had to speak. I leaned on the corner cushion and shut my eyes.

Later on there were houses, sprinkled on the country and making it messy.

'We're coming into the outskirts,' said Miss Gallagher. I thought of Miss Gallagher's hard, prickly skirt, and the way she twitched it tight round her when she walked up steps. Sometimes Miss Gallagher said 'underskirt'. Or she laughed and said, 'Queen Anne's dead, Catherine.' That meant my petticoat was showing. The train was rattling and shaking. A thick, different smell poured in through the windows and Miss Gallagher banged them up again.

'Next stop,' she said.

We walked down a small quiet path, not even as wide as a lane. But there were houses ducked down behind the trees everywhere. I had the feeling of the houses pressing on us, hidden by thin veils of green, pretending to be country. Rob walked close beside me so I could feel his shoulder moving against mine. His Norfolk jacket was rough and safe through my sleeve.

'There's the park,' said Miss Gallagher. 'This park is famous for its deer, Catherine.' She nudged me, showing her long, strong yellow teeth, 'Look out for the deer, dear.' Her teeth hawed at me then she folded her lips back over them quickly.

24

I stared through the trees but I couldn't see anything. We had deer at home, and Rob and I used to see them very early in the morning, feeding. They were fallow deer and we would track their rumps, flicking through the long grass. Their white spots were camouflage when light moved over their brown skins.

I knew from the way Miss Gallagher was walking that we were close to where Father was. Her steps were quick and hungry. There was only just room for the three of us on the path, but ahead it widened and ran across a little green towards a pair of gates.

'Here we are,' said Miss Gallagher.

We looked at what was written on the gates.

'*The Sanctuary*,' Rob read aloud. Later on I'd ask him what it meant. I remembered not to ask Miss Gallagher anything.

It was a big, staring, tiptoe house. The path was new yellow gravel, not old grey gravel with weeds trying to push up through it, like at home. The doors had two lions crouching by it, one on each side. They had no moss or soft places on them, like our stone pillars which were worn away by frost and lichen so that you could rub your fingers in and out of the tiny valleys and mountains. The lions' teeth were new and sharp, ready to bite. Rob went ahead so I could walk right up the middle of the steps, as far away from the lions as possible.

In the entrance hall there was a woman in a dark dress sitting behind a heavy desk, with a little brass bell on it. From where she sat she could watch everyone who came up the drive. She had a pile of papers in front of her, and a big pen-stand full of sharp, shiny pens. She stared ahead as if she had been waiting for us.

'Stay here, children,' said Miss Gallagher, and she marched straight up to the desk. She put her head right over the desk so that it was close to the dark woman's, and then she whispered so we couldn't hear anything. All we could see was the back of her hat nodding. A hard shiny beetle bobbed on the end of her hatpin. It was Miss Gallagher's scarab.

'I never take it off, Catherine. I always have it somewhere about my person. The scarab is a bringer of good fortune.'

Since she'd told me that Rob and I had always looked for the scarab somewhere about her person. Did she wear it at night too? She was always wanting to stay the night with me, but Kate and Eileen had a string of reasons why she never could. I knew Miss Gallagher would wear a huge flannel nightdress with the scarab stuck in it like a dagger. It would wink and glitter while I was asleep like the eye of a nightmare.

'She'll make you say your prayers aloud with her,' said Rob.

'I don't want that one here poking and prying,' said Kate.

'Father won't let her come,' I said. Father had never liked Miss Gallagher. But now Father was gone, and Miss Gallagher was taking us to see him.

Miss Gallagher came back and took my hand without saying anything. I was afraid the chocolate would get on her gloves, so I tried to pull my hand away, but she only held on harder. Suddenly the woman at the desk stood up and smiled. Her voice poured like treacle across the shiny wooden floor. 'He may be in the garden. It's such a perfect day,' she said to Miss Gallagher, as if it were their secret.

'Oh *yes*,' cried Miss Gallagher. 'What a summer we're having!'

'The roses – I never saw the like.'

'And such ducks of little clouds,' said Miss Gallagher wildly. Her face was flushed. She never knew when she had said enough. The woman looked at her as if she was used to this sort of thing. Rob lolled against the door, staring out, making himself separate from us. He watched the sky which burnt as if it had been hammered.

'We're very fortunate,' said the woman behind the desk, and put her lips together. She picked up one of her pens and began to stab the paper with it. Miss Gallagher looked round for me and Rob. Her eyes were watering, the way they did when she was excited.

'When are we going to see Father?' asked Rob flatly, counting the row of bells on the wall as if it didn't matter whether she answered or not. 'I thought that was what we were here for.'

Miss Gallagher squeezed my hand.

'This way, Catherine,' she said. 'Not far now. I expect those little legs are tired, aren't they?' she added, smiling at me. I drew my hand out of hers and walked stiffly beside her through the double glass doors.

Three

There were closed doors all along the corridor. The bare polished floor disappeared. Thick carpet swallowed the noise of our boots. The carpet had dark-red roses on it, as big as cabbages, and the roses were the colour of boiled beetroot, or the blood that oozed from the butcher's parcels left on the slab for Mrs Blazer. They made me think I could smell old meat and cabbage, but all I really smelled was polish and Miss Gallagher's skirt shushing along next to me. None of us said anything. The corridor seemed to have swallowed up our voices, too. Once the corridor bulged out into a half-moon space at the side, like a room with a path running through it. Someone had set spindly chairs there, and tables with flowers on them. I wondered if anyone ever sat there, and what they did. But there was no sound except a humming deep in the house, like the hum of a furnace.

'I know the way, I've been here before,' said Miss Gallagher proudly. Rob looked at her, but he would not ask her when. Miss Gallagher had no right to have seen our father before we did. She had been here before, talking to our father, carrying back stories of him which we had not been told. Rob was angry.

'Don't be frightened, Catherine,' said Miss Gallagher. I had not been frightened before, but now I began to be. If only she would walk ahead, and let me walk with Rob.

'Here we are,' said Miss Gallagher.

There was a small brass number 17 on the door, and a little flap like a letterbox under it. Rob touched the flap. He was going to lift it. I saw the mist from his warm fingers on the brass.

'Don't touch!' hissed Miss Gallagher. He had done it. He had made her speak to him. Two points. Rob lifted the flap and I squeezed up close to him so we could both look through, while Rob's warm rough jacket rubbed my arms. We saw a white space, perhaps a wall, or sky. Nothing was moving in there. It was the kind of room where there might be an animal hidden in the corner which would jump out on you.

'Is Father in there?' I whispered.

'I think so. He knows we're coming.'

'How does he know?'

'Grandfather will have told him,' said Rob confidently.

Miss Gallagher rapped on the door above our heads. I heard something move but no one answered.

'We'll go in. He may be resting,' said Miss Gallagher. When she put out her arm to turn the doorknob tiny raised dark hairs prickled all over her wrist and the back of her hand. I wondered how far the hairs grew, under her clothes. Perhaps they grew long, and thick. The doorknob clicked and Miss Gallagher's body filled the space as the door opened, then she moved into the room. I saw a bed like a raft on the pale shiny floor, and on the shipwrecked bed there was Father, lying on his back, staring at the door. His eyes moved a little and he looked at us. First he looked at Rob, then he looked at me. He smiled like a weak sun.

'Kitty cat,' he said, 'come on in.'

No one called me Kitty cat now. I was too old. I felt strange, as if I were suddenly the wrong size for Father.

'And how's the boy?' he said, crinkling up his eyes at Rob. The real smile had gone but he was trying to hold on to it. The wide shiny floor between us and Father was like a deep sea. They did not put any carpet in here, although at home it was only in the servants' rooms that there was no carpet. I had hold of Rob's hand and he tugged me forward, our feet

29

slipping and squeaking across the floor. Rob went right up to the bed so that he was nearly touching Father. Father did not even look at Miss Gallagher. She had gone over to the window and she stood there staring out, fiddling with the blind cord. The back of her looked lumpish and sad, as if it were saying 'I know when I'm not wanted.' I had heard her say that once, when Mother was still at home. I slid my feet forward so that they matched Rob's.

'Who gave you the roses?' I asked. They were dark, fresh ones, with little drops of water curling inside the petals. There were none of Father's things in the room, not even his razor or the stuff in a little green bottle which he put on his face after he shaved.

'Someone puts them there,' said Father. He screwed up his face a bit as if he were trying to remember. 'Every morning,' he sighed. The thought of the roses seemed to make him tired. His hair was combed flat in a new way, and it wasn't shiny any more. It looked as if Father had been put out in the rain and left there. I thought of how Father always came in from the rain with quick, fresh steps, holding his gun under his arm. He had a fine mist of rain all over him and he smelled of air and the fields and sometimes of blood from the birds he had shot. Rob said he couldn't smell the blood, but I could. I would stand on the fifth step and jump to Father and he'd catch me up tightly into his arms, and wrap me in his smell and the warm touch of his cheek with the bristles coming through because he hadn't shaved since morning. The rain would come off in patches on to my pinafore and make me smell of the fields too.

He would go into the drawing-room without changing anything but his boots, and he would let me toast his muffins at the fire, and butter them. Rob was the one who always spread the Gentleman's Relish, which was really called Patum

Peperium. We all liked it, though only Father was allowed to have it. But on these days he would give us a quarter of a muffin each on the end of his knife, and I would push the Gentleman's Relish into the buttery surface of the muffin with my tongue, then suck it out.

I toasted muffin after muffin. When I turned round from the fire with the toasting-fork the windows would have changed from dark blue to black and it would be suddenly night, with the rain coming thicker, blowing in gusts against the panes. I would give Father his next muffin and think of how he was safe in here with us, and not out in the wild wet dark, walking over the fields.

'I shot two rabbits on Monday,' said Rob. 'A buck and a doe.'

'We'll make a gun of you yet,' said Father. He smoothed the counterpane down over his legs. There was still a wrinkle. He smoothed it again, trying to make it quite flat, his face twitching as if a fly had landed on it. I tried to remember if I had ever seen Father lying in bed before. Perhaps he had always pulled at the bedclothes like that, and frowned, as if the straightness of the sheets was more important than we were. I watched the shape of his legs under the bedclothes. Were they thinner, and was that why he was lying down? There was a boy in the village who got pushed round by his brothers and sisters on a cart. It was like a long tray with wheels on it, and the dust blew in his face in summer. His legs were wasted away so that you could put your hand round one of them and touch your fingers together, even right up at the top of his thigh. If you gave his brothers and sisters a penny they would fold back the blanket and let you put your hand round his leg. He was called Sammy Hucknall and Nanny told us he wasn't like that when he was born, it was because of an illness. Illness could make your legs shrivel up like dead flower stalks, so you could never walk again.

That was why Kate came in and out all night when one of us had a fever. What kind of illness had Father got?

'Can you walk, Father?' I asked.

'I could climb a mountain,' said Father in a loud, firm voice. 'But I must polish my boots before I go out.' There was a drawer in the table next to his bed, and he leaned over and got out a cloth and a tin of polish. He didn't even have to look, because he knew where the knob of the drawer would be. It was as if he was used to doing everything while he lay in bed, just as Sammy Hucknall was used to the dust and the trolley and the blanket being peeled down so that people could feel his legs.

'You ought to put your boots outside the door for them to polish, Father,' said Rob. He sounded angry. We'd never seen Father do anything like polishing his own boots. What Father did was put them in the boothole and shout if they weren't shiny enough the next morning. I was sure he wouldn't know how to polish.

But Father bent down again and hooked up a pair of boots from under the bed. They were shiny and clean. Miss Gallagher turned round and stared brightly at us. 'Such roses in the garden!' she exclaimed. But no one answered. We watched Father's hands going round and round as he worked on the leather, feeding polish into the grains. The backs of his hands were pale, and there was a deep purple mark on one of them. I wondered how it had come. Smears of polish rubbed off on the bedclothes, but he didn't seem to notice. I smelled the polish, and a dry yellow soap smell, like the smell of a clean kitchen floor.

The door opened and a tall rustly nurse came in without knocking. She stood with her hands folded and looked down at Father. She must have seen the marks on the sheets, but she kept a small smile on her face, as if she was pleased about something.

'*We're* keeping busy today,' she said, looking at Miss Gallagher. She balanced on her toes, rocking lightly backwards and forwards. Her stiff white veil bounced on her shoulders. 'Dr Kenneth will be coming round in quarter of an hour,' she said to no one.

'We may be in the garden,' said Father.

'Very well,' said the nurse. '*Ve*-ry well.' I waited, but she did nothing. She stared out of the window, past Miss Gallagher's scratchy shoulder to the glaring summer sky, looking even more pleased than she had done when she came in. Then she wheeled round and crackled out of the room. Father rubbed at his boot with the cloth. He went in circles which grew smaller and smaller until the cloth wasn't moving at all. His fingers were gripping it so tightly that his knuckles were stretched and white. The smell of polish and roses was beginning to make me sick. Father polished and polished. There was sweat on his face, all over, like mist on a window.

'Can we go out?' asked Rob.

'Of course we *can* go out,' Miss Gallagher said triumphantly. 'We aren't prisoners. The question is, *may* we? Hadn't we better wait for Dr Kenneth and see what he says?'

'Come on,' said Father abruptly, shoving the cloth into the drawer. 'Let's cut along and see the garden.'

He pulled back the bedclothes and swung down his legs. He had all his clothes on in bed, even his socks. It made it look as if he was only pretending to be ill. Perhaps it was all a joke. In a minute he would tell Miss Gallagher he was taking us home. I watched his legs as he got out of bed, and they looked just the same as they had always looked. Rob was watching too. We both saw how his feet fumbled their way into the boots, like an old man's feet.

The garden was a dull pale square of lawn, cut by paths and clumps of trees. There were long white chairs set out in the shade, and people lay in them with their eyes shut. Some people were walking about but there was nowhere to walk to, except around the same trees and chairs, over and over. The people had cloudy looks on their faces, as if they could not see anyone else. But they never bumped into each other. No one spoke to us. I wondered if Father knew any of these people. They did not look at all like people he would choose. Father stood in the middle of the grass, looking around as if he did not know where to go.

Then it was all right. A lady with a little black dog under her arm waved at us from the shade of a big oak tree. She got up from her chair and swam towards us, her big smiling face tilted up to the sun like a plate, her eyes half-shut. One of her hands was held out as if she were meeting us at a party, and her white dress was just like the dresses Mother used to wear when people came to tea on the lawn. But it flopped a little on the lady, as if it did not belong to her. She had a white parasol too, with blue ribbons threaded through it. Her hair was a fine heap of shiny fairness, as pale as straw. She smiled at us welcomingly and I thought perhaps this was the owner of the house, the one we should have met in the hall instead of the pen-scratching lady. She walked across the lawn as if it belonged to her.

'And so these are the children. What perfect pets,' she said, and she laid two white fingers on Father's sleeve. Her eyes were smiley and swimmy and she kept them fixed on Father as much as she could, drawing him under the wavery shade of her parasol where her pale cheeks glimmered and her crown of shining hair tumbled down like water. She didn't look at us. The hard eyes of the dog glared at me from the crook of her arm. I stared back, because I knew that a dog will always look away first. Then I nudged Rob.

'Look,' I whispered. 'Look at the dog.'

It was a toy. It looked so real that I thought that the lady had just had it clipped, but now I saw that the stiff tufts of fur were false. The dog's head bobbled as the lady rocked it, but it didn't really move. She handed her parasol to Father and he held it over her while she cradled the little toy dog and stroked its fur.

'Does he want his dinner, does he? I'm most frightfully sorry,' she said, putting out her hand to Father, 'I shall have to go. He's terribly impatient, poor darling . . .'

He bowed, handed back the parasol, and we watched her beautiful skirts brush away over the grass.

'Shall we have tea?' asked Father. 'How about meringues? Still fond of meringues, Kitty cat?'

A maid was walking around the garden, setting out tea things on little tables. Father seized some chairs and pulled them up for us round one of the tables. Miss Gallagher flumped down in front of the teapot, and began to fuss with the hot water. Then she pulled angrily at her bodice.

'The heat!' she said crossly. Half-hoops of sweat had soaked through her dress shields on to the dark-blue cloth under her arms.

'And there aren't enough cups,' she snapped. 'Only three.' Father looked worried. The maid was over at the other side of the garden, with her back to us. When she turned with a pile of plates he crooked his finger as if we were in a restaurant, but she did not come. Now I saw how pale he was.

'I don't want any tea,' Rob said quickly. 'I hate tea anyway.'

'Jolly if they had lemonade,' muttered Father. No one was taking any notice of what he wanted. I felt my face grow hot. There was no shade near our table, and all the places under the trees had been taken. People sat in the dapply shadows and stared out from their safety as if we were on stage. Nobody else had children with them. There were thin slices of pink-and-white cake on a plate in front of us. Rob took one and munched it, although he hated sponge cake. I looked for the meringues, but there weren't any.

'Angel cake,' said Father. 'Their sponge is first chop. Have a slice, Catherine.'

My hat had slid down on to my neck, and the elastic was digging into the soft place under my chin. Father reached out and stroked back my rough, heavy hair from my forehead. 'Catherine,' he said, smiling. I smiled back, but in a moment his smile broke up into flecks and disappeared. His hand still lay heavy on my head, as if he didn't know it was there. I looked at Rob, but he went on eating his cake right up to the icing, keeping the icing till last. Miss Gallagher poured out the tea noisily, clinking the cups and tutting into the hot-water jug. Father kept stroking my hair, not looking at me, as if I were someone else. He had forgotten about me, as well as the meringues. And it wasn't fair to keep on saying 'Kitty cat' and never 'Robbo'. I bent down as if the lace of my boots had come undone, and his hand slipped away. When I wriggled upright again he had put a slice of the cake on to a plate for me. I didn't want it, but he kept watching all the time. I took a mouthful of tea to swallow down the cake, and choked. 'Catherine, really!' said Miss Gallagher, and the tea burnt my throat. Father looked away as I crumbled the cake while the sun beat hard and hot on our heads. Three men were walking round and round the garden with their arms linked at the back, criss-cross. Sometimes, at dusk in the summer, Father walked round the lawn arm in arm with someone who had come to dinner, both of them smoking cigars. We watched them out of the night-nursery window. Then Mother would come out and call them in, her pale skirts like moths against the shadowy grass. Once she came right out because Father called to her that a nightingale was singing in the magnolia tree under the terrace.

The three men did not speak to one another. I wondered if

Father knew them, or if he would like to walk round the garden like that with someone. They were coming round again when one of them said in a loud voice, 'Tea time!' and the others broke away and began to snatch up slices of cake from different people's tables. Miss Gallagher's tongue clicked again.

Suddenly a shadow crossed us.

'Dr Kenneth,' said Father. We looked up. Dr Kenneth was a tall black pillar against the sun, and we couldn't see his face. He was leaning back against the blaze of the sky, his thumbs in his waistcoat pockets. His shadow fell on Father's head like a hand.

'Mmm,' he said, looking at Rob and me. 'Mmm.' He frowned and stared as if he were looking through our clothes to find out what illness we had. I clenched my hands into fists so he wouldn't see the chocolate on my gloves.

'Mmm,' he said again. 'Jolly little beggars.' Then he reached over and put two slices of cake on to Father's plate. 'Cake,' he said. Father said nothing. 'But where's the milk, where's the milk?' boomed Dr Kenneth. 'Didn't I give orders about the milk?' He turned and the maid came over to us as if she was being pulled on elastic which Dr Kenneth held in a secret pocket. 'Milk,' said Dr Kenneth. 'One glass mid-morning. One glass before luncheon. One glass at teatime. One glass before bed, warm or cold.' He ticked the glasses off on his fingers until there was only his thumb left.

'Yes, sir,' bobbed the maid.

'Fetch it now, girl, fetch it now. No time like the present,' said Dr Kenneth, and he watched the maid scuttle towards the house. His big meaty face turned on Father. He looked as if he had been half-cooked, then taken off the range.

'Milk,' he said. 'Milk. That's the ticket.' I squinted up my eyes to see if he was smiling, but he wasn't. He took a watch out of his waistcoat pocket and held it in front of him. Then he nodded, and said again, 'Milk. That's the stuff.' Father sat absolutely still. They had cut his hair so that it slipped down over his forehead and made him look not like Father. Dr Kenneth put one hand on my head and one on Rob's and pushed down hard, as if he were testing how far our necks bent. Then he was gone. A moment later the maid bobbed back across the lawn and slapped a glass down in front of Father. She looked hot and cross with us. It wasn't fair, because she should have been cross with Dr Kenneth.

'We shall have to be going,' said Miss Gallagher, wiping her moustache. But Father sat heavily in his chair as if he hadn't heard. His head was sunk forward. There were drops of sweat hanging in the fine hair above his forehead, and I watched them crawl like tiny transparent insects. Suddenly Rob stretched across the table and took the glass. Very deliberately he lifted it, held it high and turned it over until a slow and careful arc of milk ran from the lip of the glass to the hard lawn. I watched it fall, make a blue-white pool, and begin to vanish. Soon there was only a skim of whitish grease on the grass. I wished I had done it. Slowly, slowly, Father's lips creaked into a smile.

Father said goodbye to us in the corridor. He kept yawning, even when he was shaking Miss Gallagher's hand and saying goodbye. I thought for a moment he was going to shake Rob's hand, too, and even when he hugged us it felt more like a push. And then he was gone, and all the things we hadn't told him vanished, too.

'Poor Father is tired, Catherine,' whispered Miss Gallagher loudly. 'It's the heat.' All the doors were shut again. For a moment I thought that I would run back and find Father's door and catch him before he got back into that bed, and make him stop. But already we were walking along the corridor. Miss Gallagher slowed down as we went past the desk in the entrance, but this time the dark lady was scratching hard on her pile of paper, and she did not even look up at us. Rob had taken a bit of string out of his pocket and he was making a special knot in it as we walked along.

The path we had to take wound back through the rose garden. Roses grew high on both sides, nearly as high as my head. They were drooping their big, soft heads in the heat. As we brushed them, hanks of petals fell on our sleeves, on our boots, on the path. There were brownish-white petals, and apricot ones, and deep dark red, like the ones in Father's room. But the dew had dried and the roses would be dead by the end of the day. They smelled old and sweet, like the rose-petals Mother used to put in the silver bowl in the drawing-room. I watched patterns of sunlight on the hard earth, and my feet in front of me, walking and walking. Nothing but petals, and boots, and the rasp of Miss Gallagher's skirts, and the blurry shapes of roses everywhere, and the smell of roses strong enough to choke us.

We came round a bend in the bank of roses and there was Father. He was breathing in long whistly breaths, as if he'd been running and was trying not to gasp for air. He was waiting for us. He must have found another way and run to get there first, just as if he was playing hide-and-seek with us in the woods at home. Perhaps he's coming back with us after all, I thought. But Miss Gallagher pulled me close to her with bony fingers. Freckles were standing out on Rob's face, the way they did when he was ill.

'Toffee,' said Father. 'Forgot about the toffee.' But there was nothing in his hands. He began to search through his pockets, and I waited for the little sky-blue and silver packet to appear, the way it used to do when Father magicked it down his sleeves for us. Father was the only one who ever bought us that toffee. And sometimes he bought nougat instead, in a long light wooden box which slid open. The nougat was wrapped in rice-paper which melted on our tongues. Now there were just two pockets left, and they were flat, empty. Father looked at us like a conjuror whose trick had not worked.

'It doesn't matter, Father,' said Rob hoarsely. He cleared his throat and said, 'I expect you left it in your room.'

'Yes, of course!' said Father. 'That'll be it. What a chump. Never mind, I'll make it up to you next time. Which shall it be, toffee or nougat? Kitty cat?'

'Toffee,' I tried to say, but my voice wouldn't come out right. The roses dissolved like Father's washed-away face. I shut my eyes and turned towards Rob.

Father pulled me against him. He pulled me hard against the roses. There were petals all over the ground and the crushed smell hurt my eyes and my nose and spilled down my face in salty gulps. He was holding me too tight, he was hurting me –

'Father,' I cried. We were shaking and I didn't know if the shaking started in him or in me. He was burning hot, even through his clothes. He kissed my hair and kissed my head with quick, hot, clumsy kisses. But it wasn't me he was kissing. His voice came thick and hot by my ear as he crouched down and clutched me to him. 'Cincie,' he said. 'Cincie, Cincie, Cincie.' I wriggled and twisted but I couldn't get away from his voice. Miss Gallagher was shouting but the words were all jumbled up in my head with 'Cincie, Cincie, Cincie', and Father's hot breath blotted out everyone.

Then there was a thud which went through me though it didn't touch me. Father's arms fell, and Miss Gallagher pulled me away. The side of Father's head was flowering with bright, fresh blood. It ran fast and shallowly down his face, over his eyes and round to his ears. I saw Rob standing with a twisted branch in his hand, his face white, staring at the place where he had caught Father with the torn end of the branch. He looked as if he were going to be sick. Father put up his hands to his head then drew them down with a sticky web of blood on them. He looked at Rob and almost smiled.

'Damn it, Robbo,' he said, but as if it were a small thing Rob had done.

'Leave my sister alone,' said Rob in a breath of a voice.

'Why, Kitty cat,' said Father. 'I'd never hurt my Kitty cat.' He faced us and we stared back. Then in a quite different voice, Father's voice, he said, 'That's enough now. Cut along,' just as if we'd been playing a wild game in the corridors and landing by the night nursery and it had got too rough and ended with me crying and Rob angry, the way it did sometimes on winter evenings when we hadn't been able to get out all day.

But it was summer and the smell of roses licked at us like the tongue of an animal. Miss Gallagher's fingers pecked at my back. She was a huge crow which had settled on me, wanting to drag me away.

'Cincie!' she panted. Her hands were stiff with rage. 'He'll soon send you the way of his precious Cincie.' I had never heard her talk like that, her voice thick and coarse as if she hated us all. Her hands batted at my dress, swiping off rose petals. Her words snaked into my ears and clung there, stickier and stronger than Father's desperate kisses. I twisted out of her grip and there was Rob, his white face bent as he finished the knot in his string. He had dropped the branch. He looked at me and I took his hand and he held on hard as we walked away down the sunbaked path together, leaving Miss Gallagher and our father to tidy away what had happened.

Four

The door opened. I knew it would be Kate, so I didn't move to cover myself.

'What are you sitting here in the dark for?' she asked from the door. Her shadow sprang out on the opposite wall, big and comforting.

'It's not dark. There's the fire.'

I spread out my hands to the rosy tissue of flame. I had kept my fire in all afternoon and its heart was molten and bright.

'And you in your chemise. You ought to get dressed. It's dinner at eight and everyone's upstairs, changing.'

I looked round at the glow of Kate. The house was full, and she was in her element. This was what she thought life should be like. She had had enough of our long, quiet, visitorless days, and she'd told me so often since I began to grow up and to be the one who held the key that could open our house to light and music and dancing.

'It's only right – he'll do it for you, if you ask.'

He was my grandfather. It was true, he would do as I wanted, though it never fooled me into thinking I was anything in his heart compared to Rob. I was too like my mother, and so he couldn't love me. He'd given my mother everything, even the fine slender upright Englishness of Father. But my mother had shown her true colours and she'd given everybody the slip, even her own children.

It was because of Kate that we were having our dance at last. Kate was the one who had made all these lights pour out, softly golden, from the rows of upstairs windows. They splashed down on to the terrace stone, and the house hummed with voices, the clink of hot-water cans, the slap of doors and hurrying feet. Young men with cold bright cheeks had been fetched from the station and now they were wrestling with too-tight collars in front of every mirror Kate could find. Clouded, silvery looking-glasses, propped up where the light was good. The trap had met each train since one-thirty. The girls had come the day before, to give their complexions time to settle before the dance. It was so cold that some of them had arrived with their faces blotched candle-yellow and purple. Then there were pretty girls in furs, their heads dark and sleek as ash-buds and their noses pink from the cold. They pulled off their gloves and laughed and bent down to sniff the tubs of white hyacinths in the cold hall. Later they'd go exploring the edges of the woods, and the spiky geometry of the rose garden. I went with them, but they always wanted to turn back before we were out of sight of the house. There was always someone playing the piano, and whoever it was it sounded the same: hesitant, faulty phrasing, then a rush and ripple of notes. There was always someone winding the gramophone in the conservatory. It played until my head ached: 'Bye-bye Daisy' or 'Solitude'. But they were all the same tune. That was why I'd come up to my room after tea, thinking I'd go down soon. Grandfather would be looking round the room and asking where I was. But Rob was there, that was enough. He was the one who had dragged the gramophone into the conservatory, and they were wearing in the soles of new dance slippers on the cold black-and-white tiles while the gardenias gave out more and more perfume as the air grew warm. Rob had scratched the soles of Livvy's slippers with his penknife, fine criss-cross scratches to stop her from falling.

Everywhere smelled of lavender polish, gardenias and the tubs of forced hyacinths old Semple had brought in two days ago so their flowers would open, perfect for the day. And there was a smell of warm, excitable flesh. I caught the note of each body. There was Livvy's cool, greenish-blondeness, nearly as scentless as water, the Avery twins' blend of *papiers poudrés* and their own sharp foxiness, the dark Ellenby boy who smelled of warm brown paper. Rob was a mixture of new bread and gun smoke. Even today, he'd been up and out into the woods with his gun as soon as it was light. I looked out of my window and saw his steps go black as the frost softened.

Everything was ready. Our life was put away so it would not spoil the party. The dark wicked spikes of Grandfather's cacti had been pushed back so they would not catch on the girls' dresses and tear them.

I looked at Kate's strong white arms, bare to the elbows. She'd been running up and down with hot water since tea.

'Have they got everything they need?' I asked. 'Did you remember to put out the violet soap?' Kate held up her hands to me and I smelled the violet on them. Her hands were rough but in this light all I saw was their broad shapeliness. Her hair had gone into close damp curls from the steamy water she'd carried. She was near and I breathed in the familiar Kate smell of cotton and soap and sweat. My Kate. She was twenty-nine now. I had grown up and Kate was no longer just a pair of powerful, pummelling arms, a warm, wide lap and a rustle of half-understood gossip and sweet names and slaps. She was a woman.

Eileen had gone. Her mother had had female troubles after the birth of her last child. She couldn't walk, or lift, or turn the mangle for the washing. I was thirteen when Eileen went. It got mixed up in my mind with the griping pain of my first monthlies and the certainty that everyone knew and could trace the bulge of stitched rags under my skirt. I didn't want even Rob to know. But Kate made nothing of it. She whisked away my rusty bundles to boil clean in the laundry, and brought me a vile-tasting cup of raspberry-leaf tea to ease my cramps. She stood by the bed, arms folded, looking down to make sure I drank it all, with the ironic, impersonal expression she always had when she was outwitting illness in either of us. Pain floated in my stomach like a tight hand suddenly unclenched.

'Kate,' I said, sipping the stuff slowly to keep her there, 'what happened to Eileen's mother?'

'Well, now. It's her female parts paining her, a bit the way you are at this moment. Only she's had eight children, and she was getting too old for it. She should never have had this last one, but catch Eileen's Da leaving her alone for five minutes.'

'Eileen said she couldn't walk.'

'No,' said Kate, 'what should be held inside her has slipped and it keeps her from her walking.'

I waited, but she gave me no more details. I thought of the tight, springy cleft of my own body and I tried to imagine it loose and sagging. I lay there under the thick white sheet and loved the feel of my own body, hurting but undamaged. I would never have eight children like Eileen's mother, never let myself be lame and limp for anyone to catch. I would run fast.

I knew where babies came out, but how they did it I could not imagine. I knew the pain was terrible, like with a cow when the calf got stuck. I had seen John plunge his arm up to the elbow into a bellowing cow to turn the limbs of the calf twisted up inside her. I had seen the bloody streaks and strings from the cow running down his arm. I tried to imagine someone doing that to Eileen's mother. The thought of it made me squirm sideways and squeeze my legs tight together.

'Yes,' said Kate sardonically, 'you'll have no troubles, if you keep like that.'

'Can't they – put it back again?' I whispered, out of the huge curiosity brimming in me.

'Oh, with cutting and stitching they could do it, I dare say,' said Kate in her usual bold voice. 'But would you let a man do that to your own flesh and blood? No surgeon'll take his knife near Eileen's mother. 'Eileen will nurse her – anyway, she's worth ten of any doctor. If her mother binds herself up tight things'll go back as they should. Only she'll never be able to do for her family again, and so we've lost Eileen.'

She said it like that, 'we've lost Eileen', tasting the drama of it on her tongue the way Kate always did, even though I knew she really felt it too. She had cried when Eileen went, up in her attic when I was supposed to be in bed. But I was listening at the bottom of the attic stairs, rubbing the rough drugget with my bare foot, caught there, knowing she wouldn't want me, not now. Where would Kate be without Eileen to sleep with in their white attic, and sit with over the fire after we slept, and go out with on their half-days? How would she trim her hat without Eileen to look and judge; how would she choose new ribbons from the pedlar to thread through bodices and petticoats without Eileen to tell her when a pink was too harsh or a blue drained the colour from her lips? They kept the pedlar in the kitchen drinking tea while they turned the heap of ribbons over and over, choosing. But no one was ever going to see them, I thought . . .

When Eileen left I couldn't imagine what the house would sound like without the constant running-water ripple of Kate and Eileen calling, talking, ordering, reminding one another of things they had forgotten. And the night-time murmur of their gossip, like water clucking over stones. We got used to it, of course. Kate talked to me more. I was growing up, as she said, and Rob was away at school, so there was just the two of us. For years Kate was my ally against Miss Gallagher, who still came to teach me French and Geography and watch me with her small, hot eyes, cannibal eyes. Miss Gallagher had a bicycle now. 'My trusty Pegasus', she called it, patting the saddle. She sat bolt upright, pedalling so slowly the front wheel wobbled. The sight of her coming up the drive drove Kate into a frenzy.

'Will you look at the sight of her. And that one skirt she wears all draggling there in the dirt.'

Kate's scorn made her almost ugly. If she'd had Eileen there they would have blotted out Miss Gallagher with their laughter. I never defended Miss Gallagher, although I knew how she still loved me. Her love frightened me. She would have wrapped herself round me like a rubber mackintosh and kept off the rest of the world, if she could. It was a great day for her when Rob was sent to school. But there was always Kate, fresh as a summer night after a thunderstorm, twitching the clammy shelter of Miss Gallagher away from me. I never forgot how Kate raged and shook me when she caught me once praying with Miss Gallagher, both of us on our cold knees on the oilcloth, trying not to sneeze because of the fluff under the bed.

Miss Gallagher had talked of nothing but the dance for weeks. She had pored over patterns and swatches of silk, taking off her glasses to peer for flaws in the weave even though I told her they were meant to be there. She had wanted to be there when the dressmaker came to fit me.

'She's coming up tonight, to see me when I'm dressed,' I said to Kate, standing up and smoothing down my chemise and petticoat. I loved myself half-naked, and the way the fire shadows made a rich tunnel of darkness between my breasts. If I could have gone down and danced like this now, it would have been worth while.

'Who?'

'Miss Gallagher,' I said, knowing Kate knew already.

47

'I thought you were to call her Eunice,' said Kate, 'now you're seventeen and you're a young lady.' I smiled at the wealth of disbelief Kate put into the last two words. At my age she had been working away from home for five years.

'Eun–i–ke,' I said, 'not Euniss. It's Greek.'

'That's what she tells you, is it? The Greeks would turn away their eyes for shame at the sight of that one. Well, if I were you I'd put something decent on yourself before Yewneekay gets here, then. Where's that dress?'

'Hanging up, where it was. If it hasn't fallen down. It's so slippery.'

'You don't deserve to have nice things,' scolded Kate, 'the way you treat them.'

I shrugged. 'I'll never wear it again after tonight,' I said.

'Don't you be so sure of that. The money this is costing we'll all be walking naked by next winter,' said Kate. 'And now I'll get your hot water. Mind how you wash your arms and shoulders. And under your arms. Think of him breathing in when you put your arms on his shoulders in the dance.'

Firelight warmed the fine down on my forearms while I waited for her to come back. Thank God I did not have thick dark hairs on my arms, the way Miss Gallagher did. If I had, I would have got Rob to singe them off with a match-flame, no matter how much it hurt. Though Kate said you could melt a puddle of wax and spread it on your skin and once it was hard it would bring off the hairs with it. She knew a girl who did that before her wedding-night, because she had hair all over her legs, like a monkey. Thick, black, silky hairs. Beautiful if they hadn't been on her legs. And then she had to go on destroying the hair in secret, all her married life. Imagine that, said Kate.

In a minute she would be back with the water. I was late. Everybody would be ready except me, and I was supposed to be there to welcome them in my rose-pink dress, first at dinner, and then at the dance. But it felt far off, and the lapping of the fire was more real than anything.

It was Rob who came in, not Kate. He was dressed but for his collar, which flapped loose.

'I can't get at the studs, Cathy, do it for me.'

He had mangled the stiff collar, trying to force it.

'Haven't you got another one?'

'I had three. This is the last. You can make something of it, can't you?'

I stood up, pushed the collar into shape with my fingers and fixed the studs. It was all right unless you looked closely, the way Livvy would look with her cool, fastidious eyes. I held him back and stared at the unfamiliar black-and-white column that shaped his body instead of shaping to it like his soft everyday clothes. There was a red raking line on his neck where he'd dug the collar into the skin, but it would fade. He put up his hand and fingered the collar uneasily.

'Is it spoiled?'

'It's fine. No one will notice.'

I picked a speck of white cotton from his jacket and turned him round. He was perfect. He smiled suddenly, forgetting about the clothes. At once they began to look right on him, the way Rob's clothes always did.

'Aren't you going to get dressed?'

'Kate's bringing my hot water.'

'My eye, *you'll* be late,' he said gleefully, as if he was ten again. Then his face changed. I felt his look move over my breasts and shoulders, where the firelight polished my bare skin. I stepped back a little. The door tapped as Kate pushed it with her elbow, the way she did when she was carrying the heavy water cans.

'You'd better go down. One of us ought to be there. Grandfather –'

'Yes.'

49

Kate was studying him, judging the effect of black and white against his brown skin. He had parted his hair in the centre and it lay flat, close to his head, but I knew after ten minutes' dancing it would spring free, or else he'd forget and run his hand through it and the careful parting would be gone. Kate nodded. He looked right, not like me.

'Quick and wash now.' She turned to me. 'We'll have our work cut out with that hair of yours.'

'Why should she put it up?' said Rob, to provoke her. 'Isn't it better the way it is?'

Kate looked at me and laughed. She was seeing the rosy light on my bush of hair and half-nakedness. She always said to me that I didn't pay for dressing. I would catch a husband better with my clothes off; the pity was that things didn't work that way. Or else I needed better clothes than I had ever had. The way my skirts and blouses came back from the dressmaker made my breasts and hips look lumpish, like something big and soft packed into parcels and dented with string. I used to wonder if the Miss Talbots had got the measurements wrong when they cut out the pattern; they made all my clothes. But Kate said, 'It's not the measurements, it's the way they cut the cloth. They've no eye for the hang of it.'

The Miss Talbots hadn't been let near my rose-pink silk. I had gone up to town for the fitting, and the dress came back in a white, flat box full of tissue paper, to be shaken out by Kate and tried on me in the glare of a sunless winter day. I only looked in the mirror once. The dress was not part of me. It hung like something pegged out on a line.

'A pity there hasn't been a death in the family,' said Kate. 'With your skin you'd look like a queen in black. Black velvet,' she repeated, eyeing me, 'and a black velvet ribbon round your neck. And then something in your hair . . . diamonds maybe . . .'

But the light rose silk hung off me like a frill on butchers' meat.

'You want something moulded, like this,' said Kate, showing me with her hands. 'It should be tight round your breasts. After all, you aren't a piano.'

I laughed. The pleated silk bodice did look exactly like the pleating on the back of a piano.

'If we had a death, we wouldn't be having the dance,' I pointed out.

'Well,' said Kate, 'at least wear black velvet in your mind. That way you'll hold yourself better.'

It was time to get dressed. I turned to the wash stand and picked up my sponge. I swept the warm violet-scented water down my arms and let it trickle into the folds of my elbows, then washed my neck, ducking down so that water would damp the corkscrew curls at my nape. Rob lounged by the fire, spreading his hands to make them into red starfish against the flames. Kate brushed past him,

'You'd better be getting yourself downstairs,' she said, 'or someone else will be taking her in to dinner.'

Kate didn't like Livvy. She never used her name if she could help it, only 'her' or sometimes, mockingly, 'Miss Olivia'. She thought Livvy was sly. It was just the way Livvy looked, her greenish-blonde flesh, her coils of hair that were bright like the moon, not the sun, her pale, slanting eyes. Kate had never bothered to get to know Livvy.

'If that's beautiful, you can call me a kettle,' she said.

Livvy made me think of hyacinths. She was waxy, like they were, with the kind of scent that you could not get out of your mind once you had smelled it. She was cool and perfect. Her furs were like the dark sheath of earth from which the white hyacinths grew. The real, clodded earth of the fields and woods never came near Livvy.

Rob got up and stretched, making wild shadows on the

ceiling. Kate ducked under his arm, giving him a push towards the door.

'Get on with you, I've her hair to do yet, and that dress to get on.' The draught flickered between my shoulder blades as he shut the door behind him.

'Sit down so I can get at you,' instructed Kate as she pulled my hair loose for brushing. The brush would never go through unless she lifted my hair and swept it through from underneath.

'You'd think the black would come off on your fingers,' Kate grumbled. It was hard to make my hair shine, though the fire brought out glints of red and gold in its blackness. The strong, sure tug of the brush in Kate's hands was almost the oldest thing I remembered. And the blue sparks in the dark nursery at night.

She rubbed in some pomade to soften it, and brushed again. There would be no sparks tonight. The violet pomade masked the smells of hair and skin, as the violet soap had done. I wanted to wash it off.

'It's going up beautifully,' said Kate in triumph, as her quick fingers twisted, knotted and pinned. I felt my head grow heavy, and the cool air struck my neck. The knot of hair pulled my head back. Kate fluffed curls loose on my forehead, wetted her finger, ran it round the inside of a curl so it would lie as she left it.

'Look at yourself!' she told me. I saw the rich slope of my shoulder, the heavy, cloudy knob of hair, the line of my cheek and jaw.

'It's a crime to put that dress on top of it,' said Kate, but I stood and lifted my arms and she slipped the silk over my head, holding the dress like a tent so it would not touch my hair. There was a brief moment of pleasure as the cool stuff slithered down me, then it settled and Kate twitched at the folds, fastened the neck, pulled the skirt straight. I stood still, not bothering to look in the mirror. I knew Kate was looking for me.

'Hmm,' she murmured disappointedly.

I glanced and saw how the rose-pink drapery bulked out my breasts and made the mass of hair above it look suddenly too dark and clumsy. The skirt was not right either.

'It's the devil of a dress,' exclaimed Kate, looking as if she would like to tear it off me.

'It's what they all wear, it doesn't matter,' I said.

'Think of black velvet. If they'd even put some black velvet ribbon, say here, across the neckline . . .'

'It would only make it worse. The silk is too light. It would bunch it up even more.'

'Yes, you're right. Now if Eileen was here . . .' said Kate in frustration. Eileen was the one for clothes. She would have done something about the silk, if only to make sure it was never bought. Kate could do anything with hair, but though she could see in her mind's eye just how the black velvet of her imagination would look on me, she could not cut out and sew the way Eileen could.

'Grandfather will like it, anyway,' I said. Kate smiled back. For once I would look like Grandfather's version of the young girl growing up in his house.

'And Miss Gallagher will be in raptures,' I added.

'God, girl, you're right. Get yourself down to the company before she comes creeping up the back stairs to paw you.'

The fire shuffled softly as the coals collapsed inward.

'Put more coal on, Kate, I'll want it later.'

'You won't want it. You'll be dancing till dawn.'

'Oh yes? With the piano tuner?' I said, smoothing the raspy pink pleats. I caught hold of Kate's hands.

'Waltz!' I said. Kate often danced with us when Rob and I practised with the gramophone. She took the beat and lifted me into it, and we were off across the floor of the night nursery, breaking up firelight and shadows in a waltz that became a gallop and ended in a dizzy stop by the door.

'Down those stairs. Now!' ordered Kate, pointing, and I went.

Five

I looked down into the pool of the hall and saw the dancers flicking like white carp under water. There was Livvy. She saw me and called up, 'Catherine!', turning her mermaid face to me and half-smiling the way she did.

'You look lovely,' she said, but she wasn't thinking about me.

'Are they going in to dinner?' I asked.

'Yes, your grandfather was looking for you.'

There would be a partner picked out for me, to take me in and sit on my right hand and make me talk and smile. I knew who it would be: Mr Bullivant. I would find myself placed close to Grandfather, where he could hear what I was saying and make sure I wasn't making a fool of myself. He had never trusted me. That was why he had his eye on Mr Bullivant. Mr Bullivant was new in the neighbourhood and he had money. He was not like the others round here, who were so proud of being the same as one another and just the same as they'd always been. He was like Grandfather, but richer, younger and I think even hungrier, though that was deeply hidden.

No one cares what they say in front of children. We'd known we were different. It was in the gossip at children's parties, wafting over my head while I struggled with a lump of sweet cake.

'He's getting to look *exactly* like an old pirate. All it needs is the patch.'

'You wouldn't remember when he first came, would you? His hair was black as the inside of your hat.'

'Quite Spanish.'

'And the way he used to carry that child everywhere in his arms!'

'The man from nowhere, d'you remember? That's what we used to call him.'

'Poor Charlie.'

'Like a lamb to the slaughter.'

Charlie was my father. The slaughter was being married to my mother.

'Someone should have said something to him.'

'Yes, but you never *know*, do you? These things take time to come out.'

'The little girl's awfully like her, isn't she?'

'Awfully.'

There was never enough money. We had the land Grandfather had wrested from God knows where, and we sat on it as if it were an island. Mr Bullivant had bought land too, three times as much as my grandfather. He too had no connection of blood with this place. He would ride over and ask my grandfather's advice and they'd sit drinking stone-dry sherry together and drawing plans in the library. Or, rather, my grandfather talked and Mr Bullivant drew plans, and the one had no connection with the other. Mr Bullivant wasn't a friend, because Grandfather had no friends, but he was always welcome in our house. If he married me I would be taken care of, close but out of the way, as Grandfather preferred me to be.

I stared at Livvy. She was wearing white satin and she had no colour at all, from her pale, close-coiled hair to her white slippers. There was a sheen on her like the inside of an oyster shell. She was what every girl here hoped to be, but no one else would ever look like Livvy. She put two fingers on my arm and I felt their coolness through my gloves.

'Are you going in with Rob?' I asked. She hesitated.

'Yes, I suppose so,' she said. If she had not been so beautiful her childish voice would often have grated on me. Her eyes, that never quite fixed on anyone, swam wide as she turned away, showing the perfect shallow curve of her cheek and jawbone. Suddenly she smiled. Her cheekbones lifted. Another door opened on another room of Livvy's beauty. But that was an old trick of hers. She would make you catch your breath.

'Isn't this fun, Catherine?' she asked.

I wondered if she really thought so. Once Grandfather gave me a porcelain vase, so delicate that the fine strokes of colour on it were like veins in skin. It was for violets, because I had brought him a bunch of cold, white sweet violets twined with ivy, and he had been pleased. It was Rob who had the gift for doing things like that, not me. I'd been afraid to bruise the violets with my hot fingers when I had found them, a white splash in the bank, sweeter than common violets. I kept the vase for a long time, until one morning my looking-glass swung forward and swept it off my dressing-table, so that it smashed on the floor like an egg and showed the brown water stains inside it.

Grandfather leaned over the table and gripped my wrist. I started, and realized that he had been talking to Mr Bullivant while I sat silent, staring down the table at Livvy next to Rob. Mr Bullivant smiled at me. I heard the echo of the words I hadn't listened to, and realized he'd been inviting me and Rob over to Ash Court. He had a new billiard table and perhaps Rob would like to play. Yes, he had money and everyone knew it. In the four years since he had bought the estate he had poured out thousands on it. I wondered if he knew how people talked and judged, or if he cared. He did not look as if he cared. He sat at ease, not bothering with most of the neighbourhood beyond politeness.

Grandfather had a pile of shells on his plate and a little heap of white, plump Kentish cob-nuts. He had cracked them for me. I knew why he was doing it now, showing me attention, showing that I had value so that Mr Bullivant would value me more. Tonight I was his granddaughter and he would prove to the world what he was doing for me. This dance was mine, even though I didn't want it and it cost too much. He smiled the tight, cornered smile that was all I ever got from him, and I thought of Kate's grandfather and the man whose body came apart as he fell down the stairs, then I held out my gloved hand and took the nuts. I wondered if he had cracked nuts for my mother when she was a child. However hard I looked at my grandfather I never saw my mother there. I was looking for the wrong things, perhaps. Mr Bullivant was talking of planting a cherry orchard. There would be Morellos for preserving, and Whitehearts, and he had a scheme to net the young trees in a new way against bullfinches. Perhaps Rob and I would come over and look at the plans he had prepared.

I never saw my father again, after that one time at The Sanctuary. He fell under a horse. Perhaps it was a cart or a dray and the great hairy hoof of the cart horse swung out and caught him on the temple. It could happen like that. *Never walk behind a horse, Catherine.* They told me that as soon as I could walk. I saw the hairs on the horse's fetlock and the sharp yellowy edge of its hoof, and the metal shoe glinting. Or it was a carriage horse, high-stepping, with a wide wicked eye in spite of its harness. Its hoof would flash and my father would fall and the next horse would be caught in the traces and my father would go down as the horse rolled on the ground, crushing him as it struggled to find its feet, and its hoofs struck sparks from the air. Or perhaps it was just one horse, stepping out airily on a summer morning, its rider thinking of nothing, touching its flanks lightly with the whip, breathing in the damp blue air collected under the limes, when my father . . .

Nobody told us. There has been an accident, Grandfather said, his face crumpled. He looked even worse than he'd done when our mother had left. An accident with a horse. Father had lived for two hours and then he had died. We didn't go to the funeral.

'You had chickenpox, Cathy!' said Rob. I remembered the itch of the pox, like wool next to my skin in summer, and the way Kate dabbed calamine all over me while I lay bare on a white sheet. Powdery dust of calamine came off on the sheets, and Kate said she would tie my hands if I didn't leave the scabs alone. But I was sure that was later.

'You did. It must have been then, or we would have gone. You know Grandfather. He would have made us,' Rob insisted.

But I knew I'd been well when my father died. For a while I forgot his face but I still felt his hand as he pushed back my hair which was like my mother's hair, flaring up to the brush like hers. I smelled medicine and roses. I was back in that day when I took Rob's hand and we walked away from our father, leaving him on the path with Miss Gallagher. We did not turn round even when we heard the little whining noise he made in his throat.

I had seen him so often in my dreams, as often as I saw the dead man with his white-rooted arm bouncing down the stairs. Once I dreamed that white violets grew out of his arm and I picked them to give my grandfather. I felt the hairiness of violet stems between my fingers. But the mark of the hoof was in my father's flesh. It was embedded in his forehead and it moved when he smiled at me. 'Tuesday, perhaps?' asked Mr Bullivant. 'Yes,' I said. I didn't mind seeing the plans for his cherry orchard, if Rob would come too. I would make him. The long white table glittered and flashed. All down it people were lifting their silver knives and peeling their fruit. Our fine William pears had been unwrapped from the brown paper which let them sweeten without rotting, and now they fell into grainy yellow slices on the plates while the juice ran down on to the napkins. Only a silver knife would cut the fruit without browning it. Each golden pool of sweet white wine shuddered in a crystal glass. Voices tapped and rang and I saw Livvy's beautiful shoulders arch above the white satin that looked greenish under the candelabra, as if she had water pouring from her.

'Yes,' I said again, 'I'd like to see them,' and Grandfather tumbled another handful of cracked nuts into my hand. They tasted like white meat. Grandfather and Mr Bullivant smiled at one another, but their smile was about me; it did not include me. In the next room band music dipped and swooped excitedly, waiting for us to open the double doors of the dining-room and stream out in our couples, our hands warm and sweating from the wine we'd drunk and our bodies looser than they had been, ready to mould to one another. They were playing 'Solitude' again. Before I could sleep there would be hours of dancing.

'More kidneys?' Rob asked, lifting curls of bacon and tonging them on to plates. Coffee smoked against the light. There had been a hard white frost again and the skin of ice on the lake was thickening. If this went on we would be skating by the end of the week. I wanted to go down and test the ice to find out how it was bearing, but I would wait until the house was empty or I'd have a crowd of them, eager and red-faced in the frost, streaming out of the house behind me like hounds, talking of skating-parties and ice-picnics. It was ten-thirty and our guests were still coming downstairs, their faces small and

wan in the daylight. The men looked as if they had just
dipped their heads in buckets of water to get the wine out of
them. They jostled politely by the sideboard, spearing kidneys
and sausages. Kate came in and out, slapping down pots and
stirring the porridge where skin had formed. She put down a
jug of thick yellow cream, wrinkling her nose as if to say,
'You can eat it. I wouldn't.' She stood there, fresh and
strong, with her arms folded, looking as if she were laughing
at them all. I longed for them to be gone and us to be alone
again, the way we were.

'Cheer up,' Rob whispered, 'they'll all be gone by the
12.40.'

They were leaving already. Grandfather had ordered the
station fly and John was coming round with the trap. A
group of the young men had volunteered to walk across the
field paths, while their bags went in the fly. The ground was
so hard they could have walked in their evening shoes without
spoiling them. Grandfather organized everyone, telling the
girls to wrap their furs close, offering rugs for their knees and
brandy for hip flasks. He was buoyant, in his element, his
desire to have his house to himself again sheathed in an
elaborate display of courtesy. An apple-wood fire flared in the
hall as the door swung open and shut, and the sharp smell of
apple-wood smoke blew out on to the icy terrace. We might
not often open our house like this, but when we did there
would be extravagant flames and flowers and hours of dancing. None of them would suspect the coldness at the heart of
it as my grandfather waved to the girls' rosy faces, turning to
the house, misted by plumes of horses' breath. I longed to
have the house empty. Mr Bullivant had slept on the leather
sofa in the library for a few hours and ridden home at first
light. I half-envied him.

'Where's Livvy?' I asked Rob.

'I haven't seen her,' he said briefly. I wondered if the night

61

had been a success for him. I'd seen her revolving in his arms, dance after dance – or, at least, for exactly as many dances as was correct, because that was Livvy's way. But she was the kind of girl who could have her breasts touching a man's shirt front and his hand on her waist and seem farther from him than ever. I thought how she might leave an ache in Rob, like the ache in your arm from stretching up to touch fruit just out of reach.

'She's tired from dancing, I expect,' I said, with a false reassurance in my voice that went against the grain of the more complicated things I felt about Livvy, and Rob and Livvy.

'Tired!' he said. 'She's always tired, whenever –'

He would have tried to kiss her. Maybe in the conservatory where he thought the heavy perfume from the hyacinth tubs and the half-dark would soften her. I knew just how she'd say it, 'Oh Rob, I'm tired. I must go and say good-night to your grandfather. Didn't I see Catherine go up half an hour ago?' The words would have dropped like small, cold pebbles, not the fountain spray Rob dreamed of when he thought of Livvy. He wanted to bathe himself in her so he would come out dripping and newborn, the way Kate said a man could feel after he'd been with a woman. I didn't know what Kate knew, but I guessed there was rock in Livvy under all that pearliness, and Rob would break himself on it before he really knew it was there.

'You've got to come to Mr Bullivant's with me,' I said.

'Why? What is it this time?'

'He wants to show me the plan for his cherry orchard.' Rob laughed. 'You ought to take Miss Gallagher. She'd soon scare him off for you.'

'Say you'll come. I told him we'd come tomorrow. He'll give us lunch.' No one we knew had food like Mr Bullivant's. He had a cook from Italy who made pasta like kid-gloves, slippery with meat juice. Some people laughed at his food but I loved it. In the summer Angelo made a lemon ice so tart it was like biting into a plump ripe lemon and getting the spray of zest in your mouth.

'But you've no idea what it tastes like when Angelo makes it from lemons which were growing on the tree an hour before,' said Mr Bullivant. The lemons hung lamp-like behind flickering dark leaves, in the lemon house of Mr Bullivant's villa in Italy. The earth was dry and in the winter there was the smell of the oil stoves which kept the frost from burning the lemon trees. The people there sent his lemons to England, packed in tissue paper in long wooden boxes. I had seen them and helped to force out the nails that held the lids shut on the fruit.

'I'll come,' said Rob.

'And you're not to go off and leave us, the way you did last time when Mr Bullivant was showing us the wine cellars.'

'The way you rushed on, there wasn't time for a fellow to look at anything.'

'Because you kept stopping to taste the wine.'

'He said I could. Why do you think he had that tray with the glasses brought down, and the wine biscuits?'

'You should have seen your eyes when you came up the cellar steps into the light. Black and swimming, like frogs' eyes. And then you nearly fell up the last step.'

'If you call *that* drinking – ' said Rob scornfully. He always had that card to play. I'd been nowhere and seen nothing.

'We'll go at ten. If it's like this, we'll walk,' I said. I wanted to stride out across the field paths, not trundle along the lanes in the trap. I would wear my thick-soled new boots, and feel the swing of my heavy coat and the strong beat of my blood. I would hook my arm through Rob's and lengthen my step to his. On the path the mud would be packed and frozen flat.

Six

When they had all gone the fire in the hall died down. Ash blew across the rugs as doors banged open and shut. Grandfather had gone out and Kate, Elsie and Annie whisked about the house, tidying and polishing and moving back the furniture which had been taken out of the drawing-room for the dancing. The Semple boys came up from the village to move the piano and the heavy chairs. Little icy draughts teased my skin. My eyes stung from tiredness as I emptied flower vases and piled up heliotrope and white lilac for the compost heap. The flowers had wilted overnight, from the heat of our bodies and the fires. And then they'd been forced. Forced flowers never live long. They put on a show to deceive you. But there was a vase of early Lent lilies just opening. I touched the petals: they were cold, veined purple and green. I knew where they grew in the garden. If it snowed they would bud under its blanket, hidden, then with the thaw the flowers would stretch wide to the sun as if it stunned them.

Rob had his jacket off and was heaving at the piano with the rest of them. They were all laughing, their teeth white. How red their mouths were. Where was Livvy now? I wished she could see Rob laughing as he hauled at the piano, not thinking of her.

'Steady on! She's tilting. Let her swing round.'

A dull jangle came from the piano.

'This 'ull want tuning,' said Theodore, slapping its deep-polished side the way he would slap a girl behind a barn or in the warm sweet-breathing dusk of the milking parlour. Their chapel-going soon peeled off those boys, once they were out of their father's sight.

'Tickle 'er up and tune her,' George joined in. ''Cos she won't make her sweet sounds 'less you treat her right.'

They all laughed, their faces red and shiny with sweat. Rob laughed like the rest of them. They hadn't seen I was there.

I walked away, into the conservatory. Outside the day was thickening to a dull yellowish twilight. Three o'clock. The dead stillness of frost had eased and I saw a flicker of wind cross the tops of the elms. It would be like this to the end of winter. The dark coming a little later each night, and the stubborn pushing of bulbs at the soil. My mother was walking on a long bright promenade by a purple sea. She did not write to us. Was her hair turning grey now? Was age putting a check on her blitheness? Did anybody love her any more? I saw her wind her hair in a white silk scarf, and then the breeze from the sea unwound it, coil by coil. She would stand and face the water: there would be a frigate, far out and lit up. The air would smell of salt and orange blossom. She would never come back to dig Lent lilies out of the snow and drag her skirts in the ash that blew across our hall.

Now there was a figure standing beside my mother, dark and upright. He took her arm, turned her to him, gently fastened the scarf about her hair while she smiled past him.

'My angel!'

'Rodney . . .' But she spoke absently. Rodney; no, the name was wrong. The sky faded. It was all rubbish, anyway. She only wore the scarf so that the loose skin of her throat was hidden. Soon the flesh under her chin would begin to wobble. In a year or two she would start to wear palest pink, never white, and she'd always sit with her back to sunlit windows. I'd got to grow out of seeing her as I'd last seen her, always victorious and sweet-scented, always going somewhere else and leaving people behind as if that was part of her triumph. They were just a man and a woman, two insects squeaking to one another in front of the long mouth of the sea, where foam showed like teeth. She was a fool, a fool who ruined other fools. That was what Grandfather said when he sat drinking after my father's funeral. He looked at me as if he hated me and told Kate to plait back my hair and not let it fall in my face like a street child's.

'Tight! Tighter than that! Can't you make the child look decent, even in mourning?'

There was something about my eyes that was wrong, and the way my hair grew. I had eyes that were put in with a dirty finger, Kate said. I should have had eyes like Livvy's, clear and pale like collected water. I was too like my mother. My face made people think of the things men and women did together in the dark.

When my mother left I saw Father cry. It was because a dress she had had altered came back to the house in a long flat brown-paper parcel, addressed to her. He tore it open and the grey folds of the dress blew round his face like cobwebs. It was an evening chiffon which we called her ghost dress. He scrubbed the fabric against his face, snuffing up the smell of it, which was the smell of her body. I watched him and knew exactly what he was smelling, because whenever I went past her bedroom door I tried the handle. Usually it was locked but sometimes I got in. It was just as if she was coming back any minute. I climbed into her wardrobe and rubbed my face against her skirts: the slither of satin, rasping wool, fine cotton lawn. All round me there was the smell of her body, bringing me home. It made me cry, so I knew why Father cried.

Grandfather came into the hall.

'Charlie,' he said, seeing Father, but Father didn't seem to hear him, or anyone. Grandfather went over to him and drew the dress out of his hands. He put his arm round my father. I had never seen him so gentle. They were like that for a long time, my father sitting with his head down and his arms

66

hanging loose at his sides, my grandfather bent over him. I wished I was one of them. My grandfather kicked the grey chiffon under the bench with his boot, and I never saw it again, though I looked everywhere. I did not dare take anything out of my mother's wardrobe, but the chiffon, perhaps, I could have had, since nobody wanted it. I'd take it to bed with me and wind it round me in the darkness.

They'd stopped moving the piano. The Semple boys must have gone. My forehead had a ridge on it from leaning against the pane, not seeing what was outside the windows. I couldn't see the elms any more, the air was thickening, whitening –

'Rob! Rob! It's snowing!'

It was falling fast, the first flakes sticking to the terrace stone, joined by others. In a few minutes it was thick enough to make a footprint. Rob wound his arm over my shoulder and I smelled his sweat. He was panting.

'Cath, let's go out in it.' He wrenched at the bar fastening of the conservatory door and the air blew in, carrying snow.

'No, wait!'

I looked round. The conservatory was filling up with white light. We were both inside and outside. I looked up and saw the furry flakes tunnel down and settle in a pelt on the glass.

'Shut the door, Rob, let's get some candles.'

I ran to the kitchen for a box of household candles and saucers to put them in. Rob fetched the oil lamp. We'd set them around the edges of the glass, where the flames would shine through the plants. Kate followed to see what we were doing as I knelt to light each wick, dab wax on the saucer, fix the candles upright. The flames sprang out and turned the snowy sky dark blue outside the glass. I set a candle by the orange trees my father had planted when he was a boy. He had planted twenty, and these four had survived and grown into trees. He'd brought them with him when he married my mother. Every summer they went out on to the terrace, and they were brought into the conservatory again before the first frosts. My grandfather saw to it still. I lit the candle and at once the sour wizened oranges that the trees bore shone out like treasures. Their dark dusty leaves made pointed shadows on the floor. Rob lit the oil lamp and hung it up so it spilled yellow light like petals. Already the warmth of the candles was drawing out the perfume of hyacinths. Rob knelt on the floor, dragging out something hidden against the wall.

'The gramophone! Wind it up, Rob, we'll dance.'

I'd dance now. I felt like dancing. There was our stack of records in their cardboard sleeves, ready to play. He pulled one out, balanced the record on a finger, twirled it like a conjuror's plate.

'Give it to me, you'll smash it.'

I held it while Rob wound up the gramophone. It was 'Nile Journey'.

'Come on, Cathy, we'll have much more room if we push the tubs back.'

We shoved back the heavy tubs, the orange trees and the hydrangeas and the camellias, pushing them against the snowy glass.

'Mind you don't leave them there for the frost to scorch,' Kate warned.

'It's all right just for now –'

More and more of the black-and-white tiled floor appeared. I tapped my foot and heard the ring of my toe against the cool surface, sweeter than the pock of a dance slipper on polished wood. Candle shadows leapt from my foot across the tiles. Rob held out his hand for the record. The needle wobbled, settled into the groove, and started to spin out sugar.

'Up – on the NILE
in the bright moonshine –
will you be mine
or the crocoDILE's'

bawled Rob, drowning the words.

'God, that's desperate stuff,' commented Kate. 'Imagine, he was paid to write it.'

'Perfect tripe. Let's find something else.' He lifted the needle but it bumped down again, scoring the wax. Kate stood there, her skirt switching just a little, side to side.

'Is there nothing worth dancing to in all that lot?' she demanded.

'Depends what you call worth dancing to –' frowned Rob, shuffling through the records. 'Nothing much here – what happened to "Because", Cathy?'

'You danced it to death last night.'

'Mmm, come to think of it, so we did . . .'

'Because – you went away,
Because – you said goodbye . . .'

he hummed, sitting back on his heels with the spoiled record in his hand. Kate stirred the pile of records with her toe, lightly, contemptuously.

'Here – there's this waltz –' said Rob. He put it on. It was thin and plaintive, like music from far away, snatched by an icy wind. It matched the falling snow and the sour smell of oranges on my fingers. Rob stood up, shoved the records out the way and held out his arms to Kate. She moved forward lightly, smiling. She tapped her foot twice then she moved off in the curve of his body, on the beat of the waltz.

Kate didn't dance like Livvy. There was part of her that went out of herself, into the music, into the touch of the man holding her. How light and elastic she was as she danced.

69

Kate lived in her body, not like the girls of the night before who carried their pretty bodies around with them as if they didn't know they were there. Not like Livvy, who was always half elsewhere. Kate's waist swayed. She took Rob's hand and her white freckled arm shone against the darkness of her blue dress. I saw his eyes half shut, smiling down at her. Kate's white arm, Kate's dark-blue dress. She was not just Kate any more, our strong Kate with her jugs of hot water and her flashes of temper and sadness. I saw it didn't matter that Kate was twenty-nine, not really young any more. Her long sliding eyes, the strong white line of her throat, her red mouth: they hadn't changed and they wouldn't change. Kate was beautiful. Another flurry of snow funnelled down to stick and slide on the glass while the twilight lost its grey and became as dark as the sky between stars. I would keep it like this for ever. Snow stitching its pattern, whirling down and furring the white windows. The little bitter oranges my father had planted, glowing in the light from the oil lamp, and the perfume of hyacinths all around us, teasing then yielding. I wiped orange oil from my fingers and knelt on the cold tiles by a tub of white hyacinths and watched them dance.

The music stopped.

'Wind it up, Cathy, let's have it again,' said Rob.

'No,' said Kate. 'Why would the poor girl want to sit and watch the two of us dancing all night? Come on, Catherine, I'll dance with you.'

'What about me?' Rob asked.

'You'll play the music for us,' she ordered him.

I was used to dancing with other girls. It was the way we had learned when we were little, before we were let loose on the boys at dancing-school. I put my hand on Kate's waist the way Rob had done. My hand fitted into the soft warmth of her the way my whole body had once curled into her lap. Suddenly I remembered what it had been like to burrow my head into Kate's breasts and hear the deep, quick thump of her heart. Her heart was hers but I could hear it when she could not.

'We can't both lead,' said Kate. She was laughing. Her face was very close to mine. Her sharp white teeth showed in her red mouth. I felt clumsy, bumping and fumbling against her. We couldn't get started. I would never be able to go through the waltz with her, the way Rob had.

'No,' said Kate, 'not like that.' She took hold of me the way she'd take hold of a dress that was hanging the wrong way, creasing itself. She would shake it out with one brisk shake and put it back so that it hung, smoothing itself by its own weight. Suddenly I was at ease, letting her hold me. I remembered Kate and Eileen folding sheets in the attic, holding the corners, bringing them together, cracking the linen hard as they pulled it straight. They made it like a dance. Rob lowered the needle and it started again, the pale sound of the waltz. I moved off with Kate, smelling the sharp fresh sweat of her day's work and the faint scorched smell of her newly ironed dress. I shut my eyes as our skirts brushed the white hyacinths, then the dark-blue ones that leaned over the edges of their tub. I felt one snap and I knew how its juice would trail from the glutinous stem on to the tiles. We would break more flowers as we turned and swooped, but I didn't care. Kate was closer to me than the darkness behind my closed eyes.

'My turn,' said Rob. He took my hand and my waist and I danced out of Kate's arms into his. He spun me faster so that the snow whirled outside and the little oranges trembled on their stems as we brushed the trees. Kate wound the gramophone while we danced without music, and she brought the waltz back to us so we didn't miss a step.

'Now!' said Kate, and she cut in across, took Rob from me, danced him to the ice-cold door which led out to the terrace, danced him back and left him, and in two steps I was Kate's again. Whatever she'd done to the music it seemed to go on and on now without anyone winding the gramophone. It ached in me like the cold settling slowly through the dome of snow. The waltz caressed me under my clothes, touching my breasts and all the white warm flesh which was so much more myself than the face I showed. Rob was watching us, his face yellow from the oil lamp. I felt the pump of Kate's heart, beating fast from the dance.

'Kate,' I said. 'Kate,' and I laughed without knowing what there was to laugh for, and she smiled back, the corners of her mouth curling as they did when she sang me to sleep on songs of girls dying from betrayal and young men leaving the country where they were born.

The conservatory door smashed open. I felt the jar before I saw her. She stood there in her black mackintosh coat with snow heaped on her shoulders. On her it looked dead as scurf. She glared at me out of her pinched and raging face and the music wound down slowly until the needle hissed into silence. I saw that the black-and-white tiles were mashed over with hyacinth flowers. It was a wonder we hadn't fallen. The little oranges had split and rolled to the corners of the room.

'Are you mad, Catherine? Are you completely mad?' demanded Miss Gallagher. She wouldn't look at the others, only at me. I thought how she'd seen me with my eyes closed, leaning back in Kate's arms. How long had she been standing there, waiting to burst the door open? Now I felt the flare of colour in my face and the way my hair stuck to my forehead. In spite of the oil lamp and the heating pipes it was cold.

Rob turned his back on Miss Gallagher, whistling through his teeth, dismissing her. She would like to kill him, I knew. She'd always wanted to wipe him out, make him not be my brother. I knew the murderous edge of her love for me. She would like to blot me out too at this moment, because of what she'd seen. She would wipe out Rob, and Kate. She would wither the fruit and flowers and blast the snow so that there was nothing left but hard brown earth. It would be better for us to be destroyed than to sin. But she could do nothing except stand there. She was ugly in her long coat with the snow starting to drip off it on to the floor. The wind outside had polished her nose to purple, and at the end of it a drip gathered to match the dripping snow. She looked ridiculous and I saw Kate thinking her ridiculous, shrugging her shoulders slightly as she picked up bells of crushed hyacinth from the floor. Kate could always play the servant when she wanted. Kate was on her knees and bold, and I was cowering upright. I was bad at anger; I'd always been bad at anger. There was something pitiful in Miss Gallagher which muddled me. It made me crisp my fingers inside my fists and I could not share the hostility which burned clear in Kate and Rob. I was afraid of Miss Gallagher because she loved me and I had always feared she sensed some affinity between us which I couldn't yet see. It made me fear that other people pitied me as I pitied her.

'Look what you've done. It was your precious father who planted those orange trees,' said Miss Gallagher to me. She was panting and it thickened her voice so it could have been a man's voice.

'We know,' said Rob, tinting his voice with boredom. She was scarcely human to him.

'You know! You know nothing, none of you!' she raged. 'But you will know. You'll find out. You'll drive your sister the way her mother went, and then you'll find out. Look at her! Look at her face! You fool, can't you see what blood she's got in her?'

She knows something, I thought in a panic. She knows something we don't know and she's going to say it now

73

unless we can stop her. I saw Rob sharpen, his eyes narrow on her. In a moment she'd say it and then it could never be changed or taken away. But Kate was there first.

'She has her mother's eyes,' said Kate, her voice a light flick of assurance across Miss Gallagher's fury.

'And what would a piece of Irish filth know about it?' asked Miss Gallagher. Then she gasped and her high colour shrank into red patches while her throat gulped. She was afraid. She hadn't meant to say that.

'Was that meant for the mother too?' asked Kate easily. It was a minute before I realized she was talking about *our* mother. I saw how Kate could hate without a blow or a word. I had seen women fighting in the village once, two of them clawing at a third. When she fell to the ground they kicked her in the side of the head, then one of them jumped on her face with her heavy boots so that the marks of the nails in the soles sprang out in blood. She twitched and jerked and they waited each time until she was half out of the mud and cow dung before they kicked her down again. Her face was slimed with blood and snot where they had broken her nose. No one stopped them. It was a fight over a man, the husband of one of them.

But Kate used different weapons. She stared at Miss Gallagher until Miss Gallagher had read in her face everything that Kate thought of her mackintosh and her love for me and her ravings about my father. Miss Gallagher began to cry. She turned away from Kate with her shoulders hunched as if Kate had hit her, and she blundered back to the door. She skidded where the slime from the hyacinths had coated the tiles like a snail's trail. She would escape through the house, and then she would have to tell the story of this afternoon to herself over and over until she could make a different shape from it to comfort herself. All alone in her house she'd make herself believe that everything had happened differently. That

I'd been glad to see her, had welcomed her even. She would make herself believe that I was grateful when the candle flames shrank into nothing and the snow was just snow. Then she would dare to come back. Kate had beaten her again and it had been too easy. I couldn't bear those mackintoshed shoulders with the snow drizzling down them. She was shaking. But Rob looked at me and smiled.

Seven

'The fountain,' said Mr Bullivant.

But snow had covered everything up. It clung in clots and folds, wiping away the scars of raw earth where Mr Bullivant was digging, landscaping, restoring. He knew how the park would look one day, when the torn earth had healed over and the trees had grown. He knew how the skin of the lake would crinkle under a summer breeze, and strands of weeping birch would touch the water. I looked down towards the low, frozen swamp where Mr Bullivant's imagination sailed. I wished I could look forward, as he did.

'What's wrong with the pair of you?' I heard Kate say. 'You live backwards, as if there's no tomorrow.'

No one else thought much of what Mr Bullivant was doing, but because he was rich they went along with it even though they didn't understand the vision that drove him. He was money. He brought masons and joiners and carpenters down by train, each the cream of his trade, but there was work for local men under them. Then there was feeding the men, and furbishing up a couple of cottages for them to live in while the work went on. Fires had to burn in every room in Ash Court night and day, to dry out the new plaster. A chimney place was opened up and the skeletons of a dozen starlings came tumbling out of the black, blind space. The sticky black soot had to be swept, and every bit of the wood panelling covered in dustcloths until it was done.

There was digging in cartload after cartload of manure where the rose beds would be, and preparing the ground for a new orchard. Where the old turf had grown coarse with mares' tails, dandelion and fat hen he was planning a new brilliant sheet of green. He saw sun rippling on the blossom of full-grown cherry trees, while we saw only trampled ground and little stubs of new timber wired round against the deer. There was mud everywhere. I'd never seen so much mud and machinery.

'This is my battlefield,' said Mr Bullivant, when half the seasoned oak for the treads of the new staircase arrived in swilling rain and got stuck in the churned-up drive. He went out in his rain-cape to stand at the horses' heads, urging them on as they steamed and strained and mud sucked at the wheels. In the village the men said how he'd looked, rain streaming off him, showing his teeth as he laughed. He was a mad bugger, but he knew what he wanted.

He knew what he wanted and he knew how to carry on wanting it, even when the house and park looked worse than they had done before he ever touched them. I had never wanted anything that much.

'Do you want to see the statue? I'll fetch a broom and knock off the snow.'

He'd been clearing away the tangle of scrub and brambles himself, he told us. He'd seen enough of the sculpture to guess at its quality, and he didn't want the workmen knocking it about. There were only a couple of people in the country with the expertise to restore it –

'I'll have them down in the spring. The whole pumping system will be clogged with earth. I've tried to find out how long it's been left to rot like this, but no one knows.'

'I've never heard of there being a fountain here,' said Rob.

'It's been here a hundred years, I'd say. My best bet is that someone saw it on the Grand Tour and took a fancy to it. I've been looking up the records. I haven't found anything yet, but it'll be recorded somewhere, in the accounts or the steward's books. I doubt if they ever knew what they'd got hold of. They'd have sent it by sea from one of the Italian ports. Trieste, perhaps. A lot of stuff came through Trieste. It'll take a while to get it properly dated.'

He went off to fetch the broom. Rob stamped his boots; we'd been standing in the snow.

'Think he'd mind if I went off to the stables?'

'Rob, you promised you wouldn't leave me with him.'

'Yes, but you like this sort of thing. Am I supposed to stand around all afternoon while he scrapes snow off some old statue that's been buried for a hundred years? And a good thing too if it has.' He dug his hands in his pockets and looked at me with a teasing smile, the way he always did when he wanted to make me do something. Rob had to get his own way, no matter how small the issue. Mr Bullivant had a new hunter, brought home two weeks ago, and Rob hadn't seen it yet. He couldn't wait to go and torture himself with the sight of what we could never buy.

'Mind if I go and have a look at Starcrossed?' he asked when Mr Bullivant came back, carrying a broom and a soft handbrush.

'No, of course not. You go. Tommy will tell you all about him.'

'It's just that I've heard such a lot about him already.'

Rob was putting it on again. Eager, boyish, apologetic. In another minute he'd be calling Mr Bullivant 'sir', I thought, irritated. Anything to get what he wanted. But horses were just things Mr Bullivant had because he needed them, and he had Starcrossed because it would never occur to him to buy anything but the best, whether it was brick or horseflesh. He'd never go down to the stables after dinner and spend hours saddle-soaping tack, just to be within the smell and touch of the horses, and to hear the sudden clattering stir of their hoofs. Mr Bullivant rode in the same way as he organized his stables; competently, without much interest. He wouldn't love the nerviness of the horse as Rob would. He wouldn't dream of flying over fences, or the way the horse danced on the cobbles with its ears pricked forward.

I thought of Kate's phrase. *If I had the arranging of things . . .* she'd say, and tell us how the world would run differently and better then. If I'd had the arranging of things, Rob would have had Starcrossed, and left Mr Bullivant to his fountain. Things ought to go to the people that could love them, I thought, though I should have known better.

Every time I came over to Ash Court I thought about money. The way Mr Bullivant had money, and the way we had money. We couldn't afford things, but of course we had money: we'd known that since we were sitting in Kate's lap. Kate made no secret of what she thought. We ate white bread while the world ate brown if it was lucky. How could it matter what the neighbours thought of my grandfather, compared to the facts of eating or not eating? But along with our privilege there was foolishness, almost childishness.

'You don't live in this world,' Kate said. 'Fair enough, but you don't even live in your parents' world. You live the way your grandfather lives.'

'We don't stay here all the time. Rob's been away to school,' I'd say defensively.

'School! What sort of a life would you call that? They don't see a soul but themselves from one end of the three months to the next. It's worse than a barracks, that place, for at least a soldier gets his pay. But they'll never make a soldier out of your brother.'

She'd never seen Rob's school, but she knew enough from what we told her. She didn't think it was a hard life, in spite of Rob's spectacular tales of beatings and early runs and brutal, silent fights at night in the dormitories. After all, they had plenty to eat and enough energy to play games morning, noon and night. She just thought it was stupid to send a boy

79

to such a place, and as for paying for it, my grandfather must be mad, especially when there was work needed on the roof.

'I have three buckets in my bedroom, full up every time it rains,' she informed us, 'but then your grandfather never goes to the top of the house.'

There were no buckets at Mr Bullivant's. No water closets that ran dry and stank in hot weather, and froze in the winter. At home we had fires that mottled our faces when we were within a few feet of them, and beyond them an icy wilderness of draughts. Mr Bullivant had put in the latest underfloor heating. Hot air blew up sweetly through square vents in the corners of rooms. There was a network of piping under the floors, and a huge furnace that was fed like a juggernaut, day and night. I imagined there was one boy to tend it, bare to the waist, sweating as he loaded his shovel, tossed it into the roaring red heart of the flames, bent to load it again. When the hall door opened you were lapped in waves of soft, flowery heat. There were always bowls of dried rose-petals, and fresh, out-of-season flowers. I think the flowers came down from London, wadded with cotton-wool against the frost. This time there were narcissi in every room, drifts of them, white and sherbet-scented with small, intensely gold hearts. Their scent pricked the air like tiny needles. They brought the delicate chill of spring with them. There was no slavery to the seasons here. I imagined waking in the morning, stretching out in the steady, even heat, peeling off my nightdress and walking naked to a bathroom where water spouted, reliably steaming, from huge brass taps. I wondered if I would miss our alternations of roasting and shivering, which were as natural to us as the squeeze and swell of our hearts.

The sun had melted a thin crust of snow but now as it sank the air was freezing again, blue in the shadows. Mr Bullivant was watching me.

'Here,' he said, handing me the soft brush, 'you take this. Shall we clear the snow so you can see it?'

I stood by him, my shoulder nearly touching his arm. He took my hand, guided it, plunged it through the snow. I touched metal. But it was blunt through my glove and I couldn't get the feel of it. I pulled my gloves off and reached in again through the coat of snow. I was touching a finger, the metal so cold it burnt me. I brushed, and it appeared, a pure, dull green. It was a hand, grasping a pouch of arrows.

'Bronze,' said Mr Bullivant. He began to brush the snow off in long smooth sweeps of the broom. The hand became an arm, the arm gave way to a shoulder. But I stood back, letting him reveal what was there.

'Here she is,' he said. 'Diana huntress, chaste and fair. Wait, in a minute you'll see her hounds.'

The dogs strained towards me, slavering. The woman had a bow in one hand, and her quiverful of arrows in the other. Her bronze face was fierce, the face of a huntress seen by her prey. There was dirt in the deep sockets of her eyes, and her mouth was half-open, urging the dogs on towards us.

'See their mouths? That's where the water comes out. I've found some of the piping. But the pump won't be working, not after all this time.' He took the soft brush from me and worked gently at her eyes. But the dirt was frozen in.

'Her left arm's damaged,' he said. 'Look where she holds the arrows.'

It looked as if someone had done it deliberately. The bronze was badly dented, spoiling the smooth swell of muscle and fall of cloth the sculptor had planned.

'It can all be restored,' said Mr Bullivant. 'Stand back, then you can see her properly.'

We crunched backwards over the snow. The brushed bronze gleamed strangely. Diana's head was up, the hair bound back hard from the beautiful brow. The dogs hung there, caught in mid-leap by her command.

'There,' said Mr Bullivant, 'what do you think of her?'

His face was closer to mine than it had ever been. I'd never noticed the difference in the colour of his eyes before. The right one had a stain of brown in its green. It was only the heavy lids that made his eyes look sleepy. They were sharper than the smell of narcissi, the pupils pinpointing as he looked at me against the whiteness of snow. We were much too close.

'You're cold,' he said, noticing my shiver. 'We'll go into the house.'

'No, I'm not cold. I like it here.'

'You like the snow, don't you? It suits you.'

'Yes.' I looked around. The sun was small and red now, hazed as if there was more bad weather coming. The trees were black as rooks. As soon as we went indoors night would leap to the windows, blotting out everything beyond. Out here it would stay half-lit by snow for hours, while rabbits and deer limped through the icy garden and gnawed bark from the young trees.

'I always think of you outside, in the woods or in the garden,' said Mr Bullivant.

'Do you?'

'Yes, why do you sound so surprised?'

'I suppose – I don't believe that people think of me, when I'm not there.'

'That's rather sad. Why wouldn't they? Thinking of people when they're not there – it's one of life's great pleasures, isn't it? You must do it?'

'It's not a pleasure for me,' I said instantly. I hadn't known I was going to say that. Our parents were rarely mentioned by our neighbours now. They had been fed enough fictions to fill the silence. My mother was abroad for her health, in the south of France. My father had died in a sanatorium. Conveniently, my grandfather could not bear to speak of either of them. This certainly avoided the risk of questions. My grandfather had turned my parents into shadows, and, as far as I knew, everybody had agreed to it.

Mr Bullivant looked at me and his face changed. 'I'm sorry. Call me a clumsy idiot. I forgot about your father and mother.'

'Oh! I wasn't thinking of them.' I stared at the cold graininess of the statue. A garden in winter, no scent, no flowers. But in my head there was the sickening smell of roses. It made me not able to breathe. I had my father's arms around me, squeezing.

'Tea,' said Mr Bullivant. 'D'you like Lapsang Souchong? And muffins with crab-apple jelly? And there's a chocolate cake for Rob.'

There was a fire lit, as well as the central heating. It was a pale, shining fire and the shadow of its flames flowered on the Chinese carpet. There were three bronze looking-glasses on the walls, and in them the room was secret and brilliant. It was quiet apart from the little shift and stir of the coals. I didn't feel like talking. It was enough to sit and breathe the warm, sweet, pent-up air. Outside it was growing dark, but Rob was still in the stables.

'I'll send a message,' said Mr Bullivant, and he stretched out his hand to the bell but did nothing. Warmth crept through us, flushing my face. I watched his hand. The nails were cut square, very strong-looking and smooth. I had taken off my things in the hall and I thought how dull my dress was against this room. The watery green silk that covered the sofa was finer than anything I'd ever worn. I wished I wasn't sitting opposite a looking-glass. Every time I looked up I caught sight of myself, with that flat, startled look in my eyes that people have when they have to sit too long to be photographed. When the tea came I would have to pour it out, and the teacups would be delicate. My hands holding them would be big and red. Livvy's hands would look just right, though they were the only part of Livvy I disliked. They were white, and their tapering fingers had a slight fleshiness, like the meat in a crab's claw.

'Ah, here we are. Tea!' said Mr Bullivant. The girl placed the tray in front of him and set out the cups. They were big, shallow, white china cups with a rice-grain pattern in them.

'I hope you don't mind,' he apologized. 'I can't bear fiddling with dolls' cups.'

'No, I like them.'

He smiled. 'I rather thought you would. You don't strike me as a fiddly person.'

'What are the sandwiches?'

He pointed. 'Egg and anchovy – my passion. Don't feel you have to share it. Cucumber. I thought we ought to have cucumber. And potted beef for Rob.'

There were almond tarts too, and a dense, nearly black fruitcake with its top covered in glazed cherries, angelica and walnuts. There were the muffins he had promised.

'Would you cut me some of that?' asked Mr Bullivant. 'Another weakness, I'm afraid; I eat it with Wiltshire cheese. Look the other way if you like.'

I cut a big wad of the cake and a piece of the crumbly cheese and watched him pack them together and eat them. The tea was pale gold and fragrant. I thought of Kate's black tea. Without its kick in her stomach she'd never keep working from dawn to midnight, she said. The heat of food and fire spread down to my finger-ends. I sighed.

'Have you had enough? What about more of these sandwiches – they're very good.'

I took a piece of the fruitcake. It was moist and shiny, and

84

much lighter than it looked. I bit into a piece of crystallized ginger.

'We'll fetch Rob in a while,' said Mr Bullivant. 'No need to drag him away from the horses. We'll have fresh tea later. Come on, we'll have a look around. There's a room finished you haven't seen. My study.'

My idea of a study was a dark-brown, leathery, smoky room, with light flattened by half-curtained windows. Grandfather had such a study, though it was an affectation: he was much too restless to read. But I was ready to be polite. Everything would be new, at least, and I loved the smell of new leather. We went down a half-finished corridor. The floorboards had just been laid. Everything in this wing had been rotten, he said, it had all had to be torn up. But there was no dry rot, thank God.

'Though of course you can smell that as soon as you step over the threshold. I would never have bought the place.'

'Mmm.' I thought vaguely of the smell in certain parts of our house. Was that dry rot? If so Mr Bullivant would certainly have diagnosed it. Better not ask.

'Here.' There was no door handle, but a piece of rope wound round the door kept it from closing. The rope was pale, like ship's rope. He pulled down a switch and the room sprang into light. It came on in a soft flood and there were pictures everywhere, bathed and glowing. There was no harsh central light, no glare. The walls were a warm, living white. A very pale, slightly worn rug lay on the floor. Tiny unicorns ran on a background which was the colour of woods in April as tree after tree lights into leaf. In front of the long windows there was a chair, quite small and finely made. No rows of books, no tobacco smoke, no studded leather.

But there were the pictures. They were so alive that they

seemed to vibrate on the walls. You could not have had books and heaps of paper in here, because the pictures would have cancelled them out and made them look like dead things. And you couldn't turn your back on pictures like these to stare at a desk. The wall on my left had two enormous paintings on it. One was taller than the other, almost from floor to ceiling. It was a painting of a wood in winter: at least, I thought it was that. But not a wood like our woods: the light was quite different. The bright leafless trees shone as if they had been polished. The strokes that made up the painting were thick and very noticeable: it looked as if you were meant to be able to see how the paint had been put on. I was used to paint which blended immaculately under shiny varnish, so that it would look as real as possible. This painter had had a different idea of reality. The sky was so pale it dazzled, and behind the wood there was a heap of hills, purple as damsons. The other painting was square. It was painted as if from high above a town, in the burning heat of July or August. There were almost no shadows; it must have been not long after noon. The sun was so intense it had bleached out much of the colour from the tiled roofs and deep crooked streets that ran between them. The roofs tipped against one another, irregularly shaped, like dominoes toppling crazily. The houses were pale as squares of harvest wheat.

'Who painted them?' I asked.

'A man called Richard Tandy.'

'I've never seen pictures like these.'

'No. Not many people have.'

'It's not England, is it?'

'No. It's in the Pyrenees, in the forest above Pau. That one's Italy, where I live.'

'Is your villa in it?' I asked, stepping close to the picture. He laughed.

'No. That's the town, where the market is. My villa is about four miles outside the town.'

'Do you know him, then? Richard Tandy?'

'Yes, I've known him a long time. I've been buying his pictures for years. He doesn't sell many, you know. People don't want them.'

'Don't they?' I asked. In a way I could see why. You could not have these paintings in a room and get on with eating and drinking or quarrelling, as if they were not there. I could understand why there was nothing but the carpet and chair in Mr Bullivant's study. The paintings disturbed the air. It was more than a vibration: the colours were as exultant as angels. I thought of the trite sweetness of the few flower studies we had, or the relentlessly detailed portraits of dying animals which had come with the house. Richard Tandy was painting in a different language.

'I like this room much better than your drawing-room.'

'Do you?' He was looking at me attentively, warmly. 'Yes, you're right, of course. I am happier in here than anywhere else. My place in Italy is like this. Nothing on the walls except pictures. The plaster's a bit irregular, you know; you could look at it for ever. You can see how it's been put on. And then the floors are tiled. Tiny black-and-white tiles; quite cold in winter. But it's never winter for long.'

'Why don't you make Ash Court like that then, if you prefer it?'

'Oh, you couldn't do that here. The climate's against it.' He stared at the pictures. His face was heavy from this angle, set. I wondered if the climate was the only thing that was against him, here. I turned back to the pictures. I re-entered the wood in winter and the burning town. He had turned too, and we stood together for a long time, not speaking. There was the faint sound of our breathing. I drew closer to the painting of the roofs. I wanted to touch them, feel the brushstrokes. Even the shadows looked as if they would give off heat. I traced the dense terracotta line of a roof, my fingers not quite touching the canvas.

'Touch it,' he said.

I touched. The ridges and grooves of the paint felt familiar, like the whorls on my own fingers. I was in that baking heat, in that pure, acrid smell of sun.

'Come back,' said Mr Bullivant. I turned and smiled at him.

'I thought I'd lost you,' he said.

'No. Not quite.'

'I'm glad you like them. I thought you would.' He pointed to a small lozenge of dull, deep red. 'There's a colour that would suit you.'

'It's exactly the same colour as dried blood,' I said.

'All the same, it'd suit you.'

I turned aside, letting the sunburn of his look rest on my cheek.

'You are very like your mother,' he said suddenly, as if surprised.

'How do you mean? How would you know?'

'I've met her.'

I stared at him. 'You can't have done. She'd left long before you moved here.'

'Not here. In France.'

'But you don't live in France. You live in Italy,' I said stupidly. He sighed, 'I don't know her, Catherine, not really. I've met her, that's all. In Antibes one winter. She's quite a figure there . . .'

'Quite a figure – what do you mean?'

'People know who she is. She's very – remarkable,' he answered, thoughtfully, as if he'd only just now realized what my mother was.

'She can't be all that remarkable. After all, she's forty.'

He smiled. 'Oh yes, she's got grey hair. That kind of hair goes grey early. You've the same hair yourself. But she seemed quite happy with it.'

I couldn't even begin to picture it. 'Did you talk to her?'

'Not for long. Half an hour perhaps.'

'What did you talk about?'

'Oh – other people, I think. She made a lot of jokes. Good ones, too. There were people we both knew.'

There were people we both knew. He talked about her as if she was in the next room. She made jokes, she knew people, she was remarkable. She simply couldn't be related to the beautiful figure of guilt and silence we'd grown up with. There were so many things I wanted to ask that they silenced me. And I was angry, too. He had talked to her when we had not. My own mother.

'Why did you never say?'

'You don't talk about her, do you?'

'That's no reason. We don't talk because there's nothing to say.'

'I should have thought there was a lot to say. Too much, perhaps.' He was watching me carefully.

'Well, what did *she* say then? Did she talk about us?'

'No. I told her I'd bought Ash Court and she said she knew the house.'

'I don't suppose anyone even knows she has children.'

'If they don't, it's not because she's trying to hide anything. She's not that kind of person,' he said.

His confidence enraged me. 'How would you know? You've only spent half an hour with her.'

'You've spent half an hour in front of these pictures,' he said, 'and you know they're different from anything you've seen before. You know *them*.'

'So she pretends she hasn't got children.'

'No,' he said slowly, 'if it's anything, it's that she doesn't want to make an easy story out of you. Plenty of people would be glad to hear it, I'm sure.'

He had liked her, I could hear it in his voice. And I didn't want him to have liked her. I wanted him to be on my side, seeing the past as we saw it.

'I can't imagine how she ever lived here at all,' said Mr Bullivant, as if to himself, as if he had forgotten me. 'I simply can't picture it.'

'She might have been happy, how would you know?'

'She might, I suppose. But I don't think so.'

'And is she happy now?'

'Yes,' he said. 'Yes, I would say that she seemed happy.'

'You see. We're nothing to her any more.'

'You don't believe that, Catherine. I should say that there isn't a day when she doesn't suffer because of you.'

'You can't know that, from half an hour.'

'No,' he said. 'No, you're right. I went back. You've always been told, I suppose, how she left you and no mother who loved her children could ever have done it.'

'Because it's true.'

'But when you meet her – when you know her – you begin to see that there could be other reasons. That it could have been like ripping herself in half, but she had to do it.'

'Did *she* say that?'

'No. She said nothing about you at all.'

She said nothing about you at all. The colours in front of me vibrated faster and faster. The room was cracking open like an egg. There were possibilities I'd never dreamed of, stories I'd never been told and had never told to myself.

'I must go,' I said.

'We'll go down,' he said at once. His voice was quick and warm. 'I'm sorry – I didn't mean to upset you.'

I said nothing. I was fairly sure that he'd done what he meant to do.

'Rob will be wondering where we are. He'll be wanting his tea,' said Mr Bullivant, and he flicked off the lights, extinguishing the pictures.

But Rob wasn't waiting for us. He'd be with the horse, still, I knew, talking to it, helping groom it, as absorbed as we had been in the painted landscapes. Mr Bullivant rang the bell for fresh tea and a message to be sent to the stables. I knew Rob wouldn't want to be brought in, and when he stood in the doorway he was frowning, stunned by passing from the drowsy animal warmth of the stable to the iciness of the yard. He brushed past me, carrying a sheath of winter air around him, then he stood by the fire to warm his hands.

'We'll have to be off soon, Cathy,' he said. 'There's more snow on its way. I felt the first flakes.' He glanced round the silky room, critical and impatient. But Mr Bullivant looked at the window and said, 'It won't come yet. Sit down and have your tea.'

Rob sat beside me on the little sofa. He was usually so right in every movement, but in here he was awkward. He sat forward, as if he were in a waiting-room.

'Potted beef?' offered Mr Bullivant.

Rob took four sandwiches and piled them on the delicate plate. He spread his knees out and grinned, showing his teeth. He posted the sandwiches into his mouth one after the other, then sluiced the tea down, sucking slightly at his teeth. They might have been the cheese doorsteps and the metal flask of Kate's boilings which he took for a day's shooting. I saw that where Rob had been indifferent to Mr Bullivant, he was now hostile. It was the horse, I told myself. The sight of Starcrossed in Mr Bullivant's stable had been too much for Rob.

'More tea?' asked Mr Bullivant.

'No,' I said, 'Rob's right, we ought to go. It's a long walk.'

'Someone can drive you.'

'I'd rather walk,' I said, looking down at my boots planted on the carpet. They were sturdy and sensible. I needed to put some time between this house and our own. It was too beautiful; it made me uneasy, prickling me like the scent of narcissi and making me hungry for things I hadn't got. No, it was even more disturbing. It was like the drifting scent of flowers in a room where there are no flowers. It set me searching. I didn't care so much about the Chinese silks or the looking-glasses and china. I was on the wrong scale for them, and clumsy. But I couldn't forget the room with the pictures. I could see how I might belong there.

Rob shot me a small, approving smile when I said I'd walk. He thought I was choosing between him and Mr Bullivant: that was the way Rob thought. It was always like that in our house. If you were not on one side then you were on the other.

'Or,' said Mr Bullivant, 'you could stay. It's very cold out. I can get a message to your grandfather.' He had a telephone. He could arrange for a telegram to be sent. It would be no trouble. Everything could be found for us.

'A hot bath first? And then dinner. I've a claret you might like, Rob. And perhaps you'd take Starcrossed for a hack along the lanes for me in the morning. He wants exercise.'

'I want my exercise now, I'm afraid,' Rob said smoothly, 'and a telegram would alarm our grandfather.' He wasn't boyish any more, he was an adversary. I wondered if Mr Bullivant saw that as clearly as I did, and understood why it was so.

There might never be another time. This was perfect: the snow, the night closing in on us. The bathwater would be hot, deep and scented. There'd be no question of rationing because Kate could only carry so much hot water up the stairs, and Rob hadn't had his bath yet. No shivering in a shallow skim of water that was lukewarm by the time it was poured. And the sheets on his beds might be silk. What a pity it was impossible to ask. Or if not silk, then linen so thick and glassy that getting into bed was like slithering into a cream-laid envelope. But Rob would spoil it. There was no point staying if I was on edge all the time, waiting for what he might do or say. I remembered how he'd struck our father with the branch. I'd always wanted Rob to be with me so much more than I'd believed he could want to be with me. Now I hardly recognized the new sensation of wanting Rob not to be here at all.

'So I can't tempt you,' said Mr Bullivant. 'Well, at least let me lend you a lantern, so I can think of you having some light on your way back.'

Thinking of people when they're not there – it's one of life's great pleasures, isn't it?

He stood up, looking down at us. Most of the sandwiches were uneaten, in spite of Rob. They'd be thrown away, along with the dinner we might have had. Suddenly I knew that he would have ordered it to be prepared, just in case. *The waste of it*, Kate harped in my head. But nothing was less important than money in this house. For a moment the thing that might have happened was as clear and real as the thing that was going to happen, then we got up from the sofa.

Eight

Rob stopped on the path. I'd been treading in his footsteps, using the shelter of his body like a coat. Walking had become dreamlike, one foot after another. Mr Bullivant was in my mind. George Bullivant. I saw him reach up to sweep a layer of snow off Diana's arm, then I saw him pouring out for me a thin golden stream of tea, and buttering a muffin to put on my plate. He had seen my mother, stood beside her and talked to her. I could have gone on walking all night, not feeling the cold, letting pictures rise in my mind. I have always loved journeys, because they absolve me from action. But Rob stopped and we were nearly home.

'Let's not go back yet,' he said. His voice was eager, conspiratorial. It was the voice of our childhood and here in the snow it was time out of time. Rob was in the same dream as I was. I wondered who came rising up into his mind, over and over. The lantern made blunt gold splashes on the snow in front of us. The wind was getting up and it blew piled snow off the branches on to our coats. I looked at the footsteps behind us and the blank page ahead. No one had come this way but ourselves.

We were just a couple of hundred yards from the house. We had walked back between the shelter of the hedges, our boots squeaking, our lantern light filling the hollow of the lane. We were the only creatures out in the night. The birds were roosting, fluffed up behind ramparts of snow. I peered through the hedgerows as we passed, half expecting to see stoats changed to ermine, and the white-tipped tail of a fox, but there was nothing. The cold air sighed around us, stinging my cheeks.

We were by the orchard. On our left was the close lacework of the trees, their branches striped black and white like the skunks' tails in Rob's *Picture Almanack of the World*. Just here was the place where the wall had collapsed into a pile of soft yellow stone years back. This was the oldest part of the orchard, where a thicket of burly apple trees grew close together, unpruned, bearing fruit on their highest branches. We used to scramble through the gap in the wall to fill a sack with the big, winey apples, easily bruised. They never kept. They were always furred white before we could eat them all. We dared each other to dig our fingers into their rottenness.

These trees were not picked any more. It wasn't worth a man's time, with the business of setting up the ladders. Leaves and branches fell where they would, and fruit clung on through autumn until the frosts. Even now, in the middle of winter, finches fed on a few wrinkled yellow apples.

The orchard lay still in its sheath of white. Rob's breath puffed towards me and clouded the glass of the lantern.

'Come on, let's go this way,' said Rob. His face glistened as he pointed into the trees.

'It's not a path. It doesn't go anywhere,' I said.

'Yes it does. Come on. We're going to make a snow-house. This snow's perfect for it – we'll never get it like this again.'

I remembered. Years ago there had been three warm winters. The first one began just after the terrible summer when we went to see Father. Everywhere we went in the house, doors squeaked shut against us. The house was restless with the lies we were telling our neighbours. Grandfather led the campaign, and Miss Gallagher was enlisted to add her voice to the rise and fall we could hear from the cold halls and passages. We were barred and left outside to swallow whatever story we were given. But if they knew how to talk, we knew how to listen. We would find out what had happened.

Rain spattered against the windows like a disappointment,

and there was an epidemic of whooping cough in the village so we were forbidden to go there. On our own day after day we lolled in the window seats and longed for snow. We planned what we'd do when it came, as it was sure to come. We'd harness Jess to our sledge and ride her to the North Pole. We'd take supplies: dried meat, stoned raisins, cocoa. And when we got there we'd build a snow-house and stay until spring came. Rob had a book about Eskimos with coloured illustrations that showed small squat men, faceless in fur hoods, cutting blocks of packed snow and laying them together like bricks, circle over circle, closing to a small round hole at the top to let the smoke out. The next picture showed an Eskimo family. The wife was chewing sealskin to soften it so she could stitch it into shoes. The baby lay in a papoose, wound tight as baby Jesus in his swaddling clothes at Christmas. Outside, in the breathless silence of Arctic nights, the husband crouched by an ice-hole, spearing fish. We stared at their lives, so purposeful and so different from our own.

'That's what you'd have to do, Cathy,' said Rob, reading the text, 'chew off the blubber.'

'What's blubber?'

'Pure fat,' said Rob, knowing I cut away every shred of fat from my meat. If Kate was in a bad mood he would eat it for me. 'It says here it's the same colour as candle wax. Think of that, Cathy, thick strips of yellow blubber to chew whenever you feel hungry. I wonder what it tastes like.'

I made drawings of our snow-house. They were neat plans, showing where we would eat, where we would sleep, where we could carve out the space for our entrance tunnel. We never called the house an igloo, because it would have removed it too far. Igloos were distant and exotic and no longer our own, but a snow-house sounded possible.

'A green winter makes a full churchyard,' everyone said.

The sky stayed dull. We stopped hoping as warm rain leaked out of the overfull clouds, day after day. In the night a hushed splatter against our windows masked the voices downstairs.

We went half-heartedly to the woods and built a dam instead, but Rob smashed it before it was done. I remember how sad I was that year when the first celandines opened flat to the sun and I knew winter was nearly over. It was hard to believe it would ever come back.

Father would never come back. He had consumption. He went to a sanatorium but it was too late. All the doctors in the world couldn't do anything for him. All the King's horses and all the King's men . . . that was one story. We gagged on it as we'd have gagged on yellow blubber.

I knew about the stories we told to other people, and the stories we knew. My father had held me close in the rose garden, and kissed me. He had cried and a doctor had told him to drink milk as if he were a little boy. Rob had hit our father with a broken branch and made the side of his head bleed. It didn't need to be talked about to be remembered. If I told that to a girl like Livvy, how would she ever understand it?

In the end we agreed that the snow would never come. Our life was dull, like the sky. 'You live in the past,' Kate said. 'You live in your grandfather's time.' But she was wrong. The past was not something we could live in, because it had nothing to do with life. It was something we lugged about, as heavy as a sack of rotting apples.

'We'll have to use our hands,' said Rob.

We floundered over the wall. My coat skirt was heavy, its braid clogged with snow. 'You know where there's the little clearing?' I said. We held the lantern high and shadows flared and ran backwards into the hollows under the trees.

'Just here,' said Rob. He reached up and hung the lantern

from a branch. Light steamed up faintly from the white ground.

'We'll have to stamp the snow down flat first,' I said, remembering the book. We paced out a circle and began to tramp the ground with our boots, crushing the bramble stems, grass, dried Michaelmas daisies and cow-parsley stalks which had made tents of snow for themselves. We swept up armfuls of snow and scattered them, then packed it all down to make a level, icy floor. It took so much snow.

'We'll never be able to make the walls,' I said. 'Look how much it takes just to cover the floor, once it's packed.' We'd never achieve that glassy, perfect brickwork.

'Doesn't matter,' said Rob. 'We can build up the walls with branches. There's all this fallen stuff we can use.'

We uprooted fallen branches and brushwood from their sockets in the snow. Snow showered in my face. It stung for a second but I was hot with the work, so hot that I peeled off my gloves and dug out the branches with my bare hands. Rob was laying down the first outline of the walls, branch on top of branch, brushwood stuffed in between the layers, snow packed in the crevices.

'If there's another fall, it'll cover all the gaps,' he said. He banged down stakes of wood into the frozen earth to support the horizontal branches. The thud and shock echoed out into the frozen night. I was working as hard as him and my body felt light and invincible, as if I could dig for ever, find anything under the snow, build all night long. I wasn't even out of breath.

'Look, Cathy, the moon,' said Rob. He sat back on his haunches and looked up at it. It was pale and unclear, surrounded by flakes of cloud, but the night sky was breaking up and its light would grow stronger. The coming storm must have blown out before it reached us.

'We shan't get our snow.' The swollen half-circle of moon

shrugged off cloud as we watched. Soon it was riding high, bright edged. Our lantern shone less clearly and the whole orchard began to swim into focus in the moonlight.

'Doesn't it look as if something's just going to happen,' I said.

'It always does,' said Rob slowly. 'Then you wait . . . and nothing happens.' He turned back to packing the snow with his hands, plastering it against the thatch of twigs. We had ruined the smooth white of the orchard floor. Moonlight dragged on its rough surface.

'There,' said Rob, standing up. He clapped his gloves together and snow flew off. The walls were nearly waist high, and vertical. 'Now all we have to do is lay more branches across the top, for a roof.'

All we have to do is . . . I smiled. How often I'd heard Rob say that when we were making bows and arrows out of holly wood, or climbing over the roof lashed together with washing-line, or building a tree house, or shooting squirrels, or taming wild kittens. *All we have to do is* . . .

'You go first,' said Rob. I crouched down and peered inside. When I had imagined the snow-house I had thought of entering it through a tunnel of ice, with blue light glowing through the walls, but this house was dark inside, and it smelled of earth and rotting wood. I bunched up my skirts and coat and crawled through the gap. The floor was freezing. Surely it was much colder in here than outside: a dull cold that worked through my clothes and made me shiver.

'Are you in? What's it like?'

'It's dark. Pass me the lantern.'

But there was no waxy glimmer of ice, even when Rob gave me the lantern. We had plastered our house with snow on the outside, but inside there was the rough surface of branches and twigs. There was mould on the branches where they had lain on the earth. The smell was mushroomy. Rob's head and shoulders filled the entrance.

'Move over, Cathy, I'm coming in.'

I moved aside, tucking up my legs. There was just room for us both. Rob turned like a dog turning in its basket and faced me. The lantern shone on his face. His nose wrinkled.

'Smells a bit, doesn't it? Must've been foxes in among that fallen wood.'

'I think it's just the mould . . . but isn't it freezing?'

We stared at each other. For a moment mutual deception held us with its old grip. Ten years ago we'd have kept it up, never let one another know how disappointed we were. It had been a point of honour never to say that the messes we cooked over camp fires were burnt to glue, or that our bows and arrows wouldn't shoot straight, in spite of a day's patient whittling with Rob's pocket-knife. But we were grown-up now. Rob looked at me and his face quivered with laughter.

'In fact, it's pretty disgusting in here, isn't it?'

'Perhaps if we had something warm to put on the floor – How do you think Eskimos can bear to sit on the ice?'

'Oh, I'm sure they don't, not really. How we used to think all that stuff in the book was gospel, though!'

He was wriggling out of his coat. 'There you are. Sit on that. If you move up, there'll be room for both of us.'

'You'll freeze –'

'No, all that digging's made me warm.'

But I opened my coat. There were yards of material in it; it would nearly wrap around both of us. Rob shuffled up close to me, and a spasm of shivering ran through my whole body.

'It's a good thing you don't still get your chests,' he said. 'Kate would kill me for having you here. Come here, I'll warm you up.'

I felt his voice rather than heard it, like a vibration passing straight from his body into mine. He drew the coat tight around us both, putting his arm round my shoulder and pulling me close. The warm, familiar smell of his skin drowned the dankness of our snow cave.

'It's getting warmer.'

'Yes.'

'It's quite nice in here, really, isn't it?'

'Mmm.'

'Are you glad we didn't go home?'

'Yes.'

His arm was tight on my shoulder. I could feel each separate finger, and its pressure. 'Cathy?'

'Yes?'

'What was he talking to you about all that time?'

'Oh, nothing.'

'He must have been. All that time I was with Starcrossed, you were with him. I came in once but there was nobody in the room. Just the tea things, so I went back out to the stables.'

'We were only looking at his paintings. It didn't take long.'

'I shouldn't have left you alone with him.'

'I didn't mind.'

'Yes you did. You asked me not to.'

'I know, but that was before.'

Rob was silent for a moment. Then, 'Before what?'

'Oh, nothing special. Only, I know him better now.'

'Better? Just today?'

'Well, you know how you get to know people. A day can change things. Like it did with you and Livvy, last summer.'

I needled him, seeing how far I could go. His breathing changed.

'That's different.'

'Why?'

'Livvy's your age. And she's a girl. Bullivant must be – what? Nearly forty.'

'He'd need to be, to have made all that money,' I agreed maliciously.

'You know what I mean.'

'Yes, I do. And I can't think why you're being so pompous.'

'You're my sister. I don't want to see some Bullivant making a fool of you.'

'It's not like that. Did you know, his name's George? George Bullivant.'

'It would be. Just the sort of name he would have.'

'Don't be silly, Rob.'

I thought of Rob dancing with Livvy, dancing with Kate. Now I was dancing. But when he next spoke Rob's voice was different.

'It's not so bad after all, this little house. Are you warm enough now?'

The tickle of his breath was on the side of my neck. I was warm enough now, and the ends of my fingers were tingling.

'You know, Cathy, we oughtn't to marry.'

'I'm not thinking of marrying.'

'Yes, but you will. Someone'll ask you, and then you'll think of it. Some brute of a Bullivant.'

'Oh, Rob.' I smiled to myself in the dark. For once I felt immeasurably older and wiser than my brother.

'Yes, but you do see, don't you? Why we oughtn't to?'

'No, I don't. No more than anyone else.'

'Because of our children. Look at their grandparents. One mad and one bad.'

'You can't say that.'

'Why not? Why not say it? It's true, isn't it? Is that what you'd want for your children?'

'Rob, is any of this, any of what we've had, what anyone would want for their children?' I was angry. My words spurted out as if they'd been waiting years to be said. There was more, I knew it, a hot angry jet of it. What were we doing? What sort of life had we? And now here we were playing some ridiculous game in the snow in the middle of the night, in the middle of winter, when I could have slept in one of Mr Bullivant's silken beds. Did other people have this insane drive to destroy what was best for them, and cherish what was worst? Was that what our father had given us?

'I hate him,' I said. It was one of those things you say before you know you are going to say them, then find as soon as they are said that they are true.

'Who?'

'Father.'

My anger and hatred boiled in me. If it could take shape it would be a fire that would melt the snow-house to a puddle.

'Why did he have to do it? Why did he have to leave us with all this – mess and greyness? Grandfather and Miss Gallagher. If he hadn't gone – if he hadn't done it – just because Mother left –'

The back of my throat ached with tears. I was gagging on what hadn't been said. 'She wasn't worth it!'

The beautiful phantom I had made of her shrivelled like a pricked toy balloon. Her hair was grey, her white skin raddled. Her lovers were bored with her, glancing at their watches as she told stories of her past. The lukewarm Mediterranean slopped at her feet. She had given us up for this smell of cigars and mimosa, for a voice at her ear and someone to put her wrap around her when the night breeze strengthened. She was a spoiled, stupid, pettish woman who thought less of her children than the cat does. I would not listen to what Mr Bullivant thought of her. I would hug her to me like a disappointment.

'She just couldn't stay, that's all,' said Rob. 'There's no right and wrong about it.'

His voice was cold and sad. The story of my parents

shrank away under the touch of it. They'd loved one another, but not very much and not for very long. There wasn't enough there to make a tragedy.

'It's all right,' said Rob. 'Don't think about them. They're not what matters. But we mustn't make that kind of mistake.'

His finger curled behind my ear, stroking and searching. 'It's all right, Cathy,' he said, to the rhythm of it. 'It's all right.'

I'd seen a baby in the village whose mother had died of fever four days after it was born. A neighbour was trying to feed it on sops of milk and sugar, but it wouldn't take them. Old Semple came up to the house to ask my father if he could obtain a proper feeding bottle for it from the town. The baby was crumpled and puny and it cried all the time, a thin, creaking cry. One old woman said in its hearing that she didn't think it would live. It shrieked and deep round creases sprang from its mouth to its eyes. Its skin flushed purple and the scream rattled in its throat. The woman holding it touched its cheek and it turned blindly to her, its mouth rooting in air, its eyes squeezed tight over tiny shaken drops of real tears. It was silent for a second, rooting for the touch of its mother's nipple. Then it broke down again into desolate screaming.

My mouth was like that baby's as I turned to Rob. I didn't know what I was feeling for. The smell and touch of it were beyond my imagination. It was like looking for the memory of a happiness I might have experienced once.

We met with our wet, searching, open lips. Everything I had seen a thousand times I now learned by touch. The graze of his skin against my cheeks because he hadn't shaved since morning. The taste of his saliva, the shape of his mouth arching to meet mine.

The smell of the walls. Mould, damp and penetrating iciness. The smell that Rob said was fox but which might have been the seeping juice of a three-days-dead rabbit. The cold rough plaiting of branches at my back.

'It's like a grave,' I thought as Rob let go of me. We couldn't move away from one another because there was no room, but he was suddenly as far from me as he'd been close a few seconds before, his mouth straining on mine, his teeth biting my lip as I cried out. As for what had happened between our bodies, I hadn't got the words for it. My legs ached where he had forced them up and apart. But something else had happened too. In the middle of it I'd felt myself give way, warm and liquid, opening my legs wider and wider so that he could plunge into me again and again, each stroke making me shiver. That was after the first panic when he was forcing himself against me and I was small and tight and dry and he couldn't get inside me, and I panicked more, hearing his desperate breath in my ear. If we hadn't been in the cage of the snow-house I'd have bitten and fought and shoved him off. I'd have run. He wasn't Rob then, he could have been anyone. And the words he used had nothing to do with me, nor had the frantic kisses and snatching at my breasts and my hair. He couldn't get near my breasts anyway, they were so well wadded in my stays and my thick winter bodice. It was easier to drag my skirt up. But when he was inside me he was Rob again, my brother, remembering who I was. We'd gone too far then to do any pretending.

'Cath – Cathy, Cathy – are you all right, am I hurting you?'

It was like when we cut our wrists and rubbed the blood until it mixed and no one could have told which was his, which was mine. But we cut too deep and there was too much blood, dripping in heavy dark drops on to the nursery floor. It hurt then, but I said it didn't, and I suppose he did the same.

When Rob was inside me he groaned as if I were hurting him, and knotted his fingers in my hair. I was half turned on my side and my hip ground into the icy floor. We had slipped off Rob's coat and I didn't know where the door was. The snow-house seemed suddenly huge, ballooning around us, stabbing us with pangs of freezing cold which were so sharp they might have been flames.

Then it was all over. We weren't Rob and Cathy any more. We were two cold, aching lumps of flesh, crushed together and wanting to be separate. His weight hurt my left arm and I felt something slow and sticky trickle out of me and down my leg. He sighed and rubbed the back of his hand over his face. For a moment I thought he was crying. How were we going to get home without speaking to one another, because if we once started to talk about this what more would be uncovered? How were we going to throw words across the gulf of what had happened? It had gone too far. That baby in the village: I couldn't remember if it had lived or died.

'I'm hungry,' said Rob. I laughed aloud in relief.

'You're always hungry!'

'Yes, but now I could eat anything. I could eat Miss Gallagher.'

It was an old fantasy of ours. How would we cook her to make her edible? Long, slow roasting after a judicious period of hanging in the game larder? Or should she be cut into small blocks of flesh and casseroled in the ashes overnight? And how should she be flavoured? We could never decide how she'd taste.

'Like a mackintosh when it's been rolled up and put away wet.'

'Like the sweat on cheese.'

'If we had a fire, we could cook something,' I said.

'If we had something to cook, we could make a fire. You're cold, Cathy.'

'Yes.'

'You're shivering.'

'Not because I'm cold.'

'I know that. I know everything about you. Even the way it says in the Bible. I told you we ought not to marry.'

A pang of fear went through me. Had all this happened because of that? Because of Mr Bullivant, and the way Rob had watched us standing together at the fountain? Because of the empty room when he came in from the stable? Had he thought something needed to be stopped?

'And I told you I wasn't thinking of marrying Mr Bullivant.'

'Oh, I wasn't thinking of him,' said Rob, in a voice of pure surprise. I hesitated, wanting to ask more, then I let him convince me. We were so alone now. If I couldn't even believe Rob then I'd be bricked up on my own with what we'd done.

I know everything about you. He knew more of me now than anyone, and I knew more of him. More than Livvy, more than Kate. It left us alone together, a shipwreck with our secret that dragged at us like treasure. The flame in Mr Bullivant's lantern was guttering. Time to go home.

Nine

But we had to bring home what we'd done. That was the difficult part. The snow-house and the frozen orchard were time out of time, separate. What happened there could be hidden. But as soon as we came indoors I got frightened. I'd never felt that kind of fear before, except when I woke up after a bad dream, my nightdress cold with sweat and my heart hammering in my throat. When I climbed the stairs I thought that I was shedding clues like drops of blood. Anyone could track me down. If Rob came and sat by me on the oak settle in the hall, the way we'd always sat, roasting ourselves at the fire, I thought we were too close. I kept seeing us together as if I was a third person, watching, spying, guessing.

The brush of a shoulder, the touch of his hand, his whistling. There was no barrier of skin or space between us. I felt myself flush and sweat. My heart made my blood hiss in my ears. I thought it was over as soon as it happened, sealed away in the musty silence of the snow-house. But now I couldn't make it stop happening, and Rob didn't want to.

He came to my room, not the first night but the second. I was in my nightdress in front of the looking-glass, plaiting my hair. It was much warmer and I'd been listening to snow thinning to watery soup and running down the drainpipes. It was a dark, thick night, with no stars. Kate had gone to bed early with a bad head and a cup of ginger tea. Grandfather had gone over to dine with Mr Bullivant, and he'd be back late after a game of chess. These days he often talked to me about Mr Bullivant, watching my face, raking my body with his bright, hooded dark eyes.

'Cathy,' said Rob. He was behind me, leaning over, playing with the pins in my shell box. I looked into the glass and saw him smiling there. Our two faces were side by side. Suddenly I saw why people said we looked alike, in spite of the difference of colouring and sex. Mirrored we looked out at the world in the same way. He had always come in and out of my room like this, fiddling with my hairbrushes, perching on the side of my dressing-table, flinging himself full-length on my bed. Behind us in the looking-glass there was the bed, oblong and tight-tucked. It looked as if it were floating between the floor and the ceiling.

'Cathy,' he said, putting down the pins and watching my reflection. I saw his mouth move. He was smiling.

'Why shouldn't we always live here?' he asked, his voice soft and wheedling. 'We could be like Harry Callan and his sister. We could have a cottage like theirs on the edge of the village.'

The Callan cottage looked out on the fields and the woods beyond. Nobody could peer in through their windows. No one was ever asked to cross that threshold. Harry Callan would not even have another woman in his house to nurse his sister when she had pneumonia and he had to sit with her day and night until the crisis had passed. Perhaps he was right. Liza Callan got better, and the doctor said not many could have brought her through it the way Harry did. I thought of the Callans walking to church, Liza dumpy in her good black, Harry parched and fierce.

'I don't want to be like them,' I said, and watched my lips make the words. I looked stiff and foolish.

'No,' said Rob, 'not *like* them. But they're happy, aren't they?'

'I don't know. How can you ever tell, with other people?'

'She could have left. She could have married. She was pretty once, you can still see that.'

'It's not enough to be pretty. You've got to be –' I couldn't think of the word.

'Ready,' said Rob.

'Yes, I suppose so. Free, perhaps.'

'She's better off with him.'

'How can you be so sure?'

'He knows what she likes. They're like one person.'

'Isn't it more that they can't be two people any more?' I asked, thinking of how Harry Callan would stand silently, bent and black, as Liza spoke to people after church. His hands were folded behind his back; he cracked the knuckles with a small, sickening sound. They'd grown together, as if their sides had been opened and the bloody wound pressed together until it healed. 'Would you want to be one person with anyone?' I went on, my eyes meeting his mirrored eyes.

'I don't know,' he answered slowly. 'But I want to be able to think my own thoughts. With some girls –' He broke off. Now it was not my reflection he saw; it was Livvy's. With some girls you're thinking of them all the time. You can't get free and be yourself.'

'I expect that wears off,' I said. 'Look at all the married people we know.'

'Not always. Take Father, the way he was about Mother. He could never get free of her. Don't you remember how he'd come in to the nursery and walk about but he wouldn't play a game or read a book or even talk to us? I thought it was something we'd done wrong, but it was him tearing at himself with thoughts of her. She came between him and everything. She drove him mad.'

'No,' I said, 'no one could have done that. It must have been in him.' *You're so like your mother, Cathy. Isn't she the image of the mother. That hair now – I've never seen stuff like it except on the mother.* But I wasn't. Abandoning, betraying, powerful, she had filled our dreams as she would never have done if we'd had her living presence. They were confused dreams from which I woke with an ache of guilt. I hadn't loved her enough. If I had loved her more, she would never have gone. I had saved half my bar of nougat for her but then I had eaten it.

'One day,' said Rob abruptly, 'before he went to that place, The Sanctuary, I'd been out before breakfast and when I came back I saw him on the drive, crouched down, picking up stones. He had two heaps of them beside him and he was poring over every stone, holding it up to the light before he put it on one pile or on the other. I said, "What are you doing, Father?" because I thought maybe he'd like me to help. He looked up and pointed to one pile and said, "These are the saved." Then he put a pebble down on the other pile and said, "These are the damned." Then he laughed. He said, "It's easy, isn't it, Robbo? Come and have a go."'

'Where was I?'

'Kate was washing your hair. I remember that because when I came in you were sitting by the fire and the room smelled of rosemary. You know how she used to give your hair a last rinse in rosemary water to make it shine.'

'What did you say to Father?'

'I didn't say anything. I sat on the drive next to him and started picking up stones and putting them on the piles for him.'

'I couldn't have done that, I don't think. I'd have been frightened.'

'He was feeling round for more stones as if he couldn't see them. You know how blind people touch things as if they're much more precious than they really are? I couldn't just walk off, could I? Besides, I was afraid he'd do the whole drive if I left him on his own. What if Grandfather had come out and seen?'

'He must have seen something like it in the end. Or else they'd never have sent him away to that place.'

'He'd have gone on shutting his eyes to it,' said Rob. 'He loved Father. Only something happened one night. We must have slept through most of it but when I woke up I heard feet running and then a banging noise like fists on a door. It went on and on but I didn't want to wake up, so I mixed it into a dream and in the morning I forgot about it.'

'I wonder what happened.'

'He had a knife.'

'Who, Father? How do you know?'

'Grandfather told me.'

'Grandfather told you! He can't have done. He'd never tell us anything like that.'

'It was when I said Father would still be alive if Grandfather hadn't sent him to The Sanctuary. Then he said there were worse places. The doctor wanted him to go to the Royal Bethlehem Hospital. He said it was the best place for Father, they'd have the right treatment for him there. But Grandfather said no one was going from his house to be shut away in Bedlam. He thought he'd done the right thing, that's why he told me about the knife.'

'What did Father do with the knife?'

'Oh, nothing really,' said Rob. 'That's what was so stupid. I mean, when you think of all the guns in the house and what he could have done with them if he'd wanted. He was just shouting and waving the knife around, as far as I know. A bit pathetic, really. But the servants saw some of it, and then the doctor came and there was such a row that I suppose Grandfather had to do something. He sounded quite mad, you see. Father, I mean.'

'Is that what Grandfather said?'

'No, it was Kate. She was sorry for him, she said it was a

fit and it would have passed off if they'd let him alone. They should never have sent him away.'

'*In my opinion* – did she say that?'

'Yes of course. You know how she does. But she'd have kept Father here and looked after him herself if Grandfather had let her.'

I thought of Kate saying 'In my opinion', making 'owe' of the first syllable, making it sound like an opening door. With Kate, opinions meant action. Why hadn't Grandfather let her?

'I suppose it had gone too far. Too many people knew. If anything had happened, he'd have been blamed.'

'He wanted to keep it quiet,' I said. 'That's what it was. Before everyone started talking.'

'No,' said Rob, 'it's not as simple as that. Don't you remember how he was with Father?'

I thought of his arm around my father's shoulder.

'He got the servants to say nothing,' said Rob. 'Do you remember how Tommy Linus left around then? And Susan?'

'I don't remember Susan.'

'She worked in the kitchen. She hadn't been here long, and Grandfather felt he couldn't trust her to keep her mouth shut in the village, so he got rid of her. Tommy Linus had to go because he'd actually wrestled the knife off Father, and got a cut on his arm. Grandfather couldn't bear the sight of him after that. He found him a job the other side of the county.'

'He never told you all this.'

'Some of it. And Kate told me the rest.'

'And you never told me any of it.'

'It was only last year I found out. I thought you'd ask too, when you wanted to know. When you were ready.'

'It was hard on Susan,' I said. Rob laughed.

'Hard on Susan! She's the last person I'd have thought you'd care about. What about Father?'

'No, it was hard. People get dragged in — it wasn't her fault. She couldn't help what she saw.'

'That's what's so restful about you, Cathy,' said Rob lightly. 'You're not always seeing things and asking questions.'

'Only because I don't dare.' It felt like the boldest thing I'd ever said. My looking-glass face flushed over the cheekbones as I held Rob's gaze.

'Do you suppose,' said Rob thoughtfully, 'they ask questions about the Callans in the village?'

'No,' I said. 'The Callans are respectable. Liza Callan does her washing when she should and you could measure Harry's bean rows with a ruler, the way they march up and down. But if Liza dressed in sky-blue and Harry grew nothing but lilies the village would tear them to pieces.'

'There's hope for us then,' said Rob. 'Make yourself dull, Cathy.'

It was easier to talk to the mirror than to one another. Our words rose and hovered in the room, and what we didn't say joined them and became part of the conversation.

Harry knows her, the way I know you. I know what you like. I can make you happy. Come here . . . let me touch you . . .!

He was touching me. One of us must have been the first to touch, and I was not sure who it was. My hand strayed willingly up his sleeve. His mouth on mine was firm and warm, like the apricots that hung on the wall, the ones I knew how to find and eat without anyone knowing I had eaten them. I could nibble an apricot behind my hand, sucking its juice in secret and spitting out the stone. Now I was the one who reached up and hooked my arm around his neck and pulled him down to me. The glass watched but I stared it down.

There was no lock on my door. I never thought of that.

The house seemed to be sleeping, but it wasn't late. The outer doors were not yet locked. I'd forgotten how Miss Gallagher had come upon us when we were dancing.

Rob was asleep, face down, his breath stirring against my shoulder. I lay carefully still. The bed was too narrow for both of us to relax, and anyway I wanted to stay awake. The drip of the melting snow came almost in the rhythm of Rob's breath. This time it hadn't hurt, not much. And it hadn't been a blind thing done in darkness either; we'd both known what we were about. This time we'd acknowledged it. When Rob was inside me he smiled down as he began to push. It felt familiar.

I shifted his head a little, on to my shoulder so we would both be more comfortable. I was sleepy now. I stroked one shiny conker-brown strand of his hair, and touched it to my lips. The flesh of his shoulder was white, not like the speckled-egg brown of his face. It was very white and fine and smooth to touch. I wondered if anyone else had touched it, but the thought felt distant and unimportant. For a while I counted his breaths the way I used to count numbers for the sake of it, a hundred, five hundred, a thousand. The room folded away into silence as my eyes drooped and I welcomed the rushing sound of sleep.

I have often wondered when she came in. Had we been sleeping long? Had Rob sighed and shifted his position, or turned away from me? Were our mouths slack with sleep, spittle forming at the corners of our lips? When she came in, did she see at once that there were two people lying on the bed, or was it at first just the wrong shape, a distortion of what she expected? She had come to see me. Perhaps it wasn't the first time. People do steal in to watch those they love when they can't be watched back. Lovers raise themselves awkwardly on one elbow and brood over the body of the one they love until hand and arm go numb, prickling with pins and needles. Mothers creep into bedrooms at night to tuck up their children, and stay to watch them. I'd watched Rob.

My mother never did, of course. She had other things to do at night. Sometimes she'd come in to turn a white shoulder in the looking-glass and fan the perfume of lilies of the valley across our beds. I can't imagine her tiptoeing in to inhale the smell of our sleep. But Miss Gallagher knew the house so well. She knew where to put her feet on the stairs to avoid the boards that creaked. She knew that my door handle needed a half-turn and then a little tug before it opened. She knew that it was light that would wake me, not noise, and so she taught herself to feast in whatever dregs of light came in from the landing or the gaps between the curtains.

We used to talk about eating Miss Gallagher, but it was she who ate me. It must have taken a long time before her hungry eyes were satisfied. She kept coming back for more. That was how she found out, found us.

Of course she didn't leave a trace. If she'd had any sense of style, Rob said afterwards, she'd have left that scarab hatpin plunged into the sheets.

'Or into your heart,' I suggested.

It wasn't until much later that she let us know what she knew, and by then we'd grown greedy as well as confident. I went to bed earlier and earlier. Rob would stay up another quarter of an hour, talking to Grandfather, his eyes straying to the clock, before he followed me.

'Good-night,' I'd say. 'Good-night, Grandfather, good-night, Rob,' and a pang of excitement would cut through me as he lifted his eyes for a second from his book or newspaper, or from the chessmen, and said carelessly,

'G'night, Cath.'

Every night the excitement again, every fibre of my body taut for his footfall. Every night his homecoming plunge, like a swimmer into familiar sea. Every night the pain less and the pleasure more. I never plaited my hair now. I let it wash and tangle around us, and my nightdress was a white rag kicked down to our feet. In the looking-glass I wasn't the Cathy I knew any more.

'Put your hair back. I can't see your face.'

'I can always see yours. You can't hide.'

'I know.'

We lay still while the room grew cold around us. We didn't want to dress. I watched his semen dry into stickiness on my stomach while I learned the words for what we were doing. He ran his hand over my ribs.

'We're like Adam and Eve.'

'Why?'

'Well, they must have been brother and sister, mustn't they? Made out of the same flesh.'

'I've often wondered about their children,' I said.

'What?'

'Well, they married one another. And yet they say the children of brothers and sisters are monsters. That would mean the whole human race was descended from something monstrous.'

'You don't need to worry,' said Rob. 'We shan't have a child. I've made sure of that.'

I looked down my body. Its heavy white curves were waiting for something. *I've made sure of that.* The trail of semen glistened but it led nowhere. There was no creature hiding at the end of it.

'D'you think she minds?'

'Who?'

'Liza Callan. Not having children. The – the barrenness of it. The two of them in the cottage and no one else ever coming.'

Rob didn't answer. His hand slid home across my thigh.

*

Daytimes fled by. I caught sight of myself sometimes, my eyes startled and smudged round with sleepless nights. A light nausea of tiredness, not unpleasant, followed me all the time. I felt powerful and beautiful. It didn't strike me for a few days that I hadn't seen Miss Gallagher. Then I noticed vaguely that she hadn't visited us for nearly a week. This was unheard of, unless she was ill. But she wasn't ill, Kate said, she'd been seen pedalling furiously along the lanes as usual, from cottage to cottage,

'Doing good,' added Kate. The greatest drawback of sickness or poverty, to her mind, was that it laid one open to visitations from Miss Gallagher, with her greasy pots of chicken soup and her advice. I dropped the thought of Miss Gallagher from my mind.

'It's going to be fine tomorrow,' said Rob. 'What about a long tramp and a picnic, Cathy? Just us two?' he added boyishly, flicking half a glance towards Grandfather. The snow and frost had gone and we'd had a run of those soft, blooming January days that sometimes fool the birds into brilliant singing. There were snowdrops out, and fat white Christmas roses where heaps of snow had been.

'God knows who else you think would have the time to come,' said Grandfather. 'We've all got work to do. If you've got to walk, why not go shooting?'

It was fine. I woke early while it was still dark, and dressed as it grew grey. After I'd lit the fire I wrapped a shawl around me and sat at the window looking out. I love the colourless look of winter gardens from a distance. Then when you are walking in them there are hundreds of tiny changes of grey and green, bright orange lichen on the walls, and golden shreds of half-eaten crocus under the oak trees. I was full of excitement. I wanted to walk miles and come home with my whole body aching.

I saw something move in the shrubbery. It would be a

deer, I thought. But it was a fox, alert to the pale morning light, its ears pricked. It stood still, looking towards the house, scenting the air, for there was no wind. It was only for a minute or two that it stood there, but it seemed longer. Then it turned and trotted away across the grass, its paws making deep pad-marks in the overnight skim of frost. Rob would be up now. I must go down to the kitchen and find our picnic food.

'Sausages,' said Rob. 'We'll make a fire and cook them. And what about some of that cold game pie?'

He packed the food into two canvas bags which we could sling over our shoulders. He was much quicker and neater at this sort of thing than me. He could make better sandwiches, too. I was clumsy and my sandwiches always fell apart. If I'd lived alone I'd have eaten fruit and cheese at every meal rather than think of what to order each day.

'Apples?' Rob asked, weighing one in either hand.

Mrs Blazer was stoking the range, keeping an eye on us as we stripped the larder. She smelled of days of sweat as I brushed by her. 'Not too much of that game pie now,' she warned. 'Your Grandfather likes that.'

'And this seed cake,' said Rob, pouncing on it. 'Is there any greaseproof paper, Cathy?'

'If you'd a waited, I'd a made you up a passel of tongue sandwiches,' said Mrs Blazer. 'Off that tongue I pressed yesterday. It's ready to cut now.'

'We'd rather the sausages, thanks . . . Any mustard? And is there a jar of those pickled walnuts?'

'Not a whole jar, you're not going to take,' said Mrs Blazer flatly.

'Can't carry them otherwise. Got to have the jar, or they'll make the sandwiches soggy. Look, you've a dozen at least. You'll never miss one.'

'They've to do till the end of next summer. And what'll

you have to your cheese after dinner if there isn't a pickled walnut?'

'Right, we'll just take this little jar then.'

I found some stuffed prunes in paper shells, left over from Christmas, and a packet of Muscatel raisins. It was these odd sweet things I liked. Mrs Blazer wiped Grandfather's breakfast kidneys with a clean cloth, split them open and skewered them ready to grill. Kidneys and roast bone Mondays, Wednesdays and Thursdays, bacon and eggs Tuesdays, Fridays and Saturdays, and devilled chops on Sundays. Grandfather had to have meat in the mornings. He did not eat breakfast with us, ever. All our childhood he'd been up and out at five-thirty, back to oversee our porridge at eight, then he would eat his own breakfast while we started our lessons. The wafting fragrance of his bacon drove Rob mad.

'Grandfather's a hog, guzzling bacon while we get nothing!'

But Grandfather believed in a low diet for children, with meat no more than once a day. 'We had bacon when Father was alive,' said Rob, but I looked back and couldn't remember. I didn't like bacon anyway.

'Meat's for men,' said Kate.

'Why?'

'Because they're wild wolves. Look at their eyes.'

Her voice set the wind howling. Under their hoods Grandfather's eyes gleamed strangely, piercingly –

'Kate!'

'There now, what's the why of all this caterwauling?'

'I had a bad dream.'

'We'll blow it away then.' She held her palm out flat in front of her and puffed. 'There! It's gone. Now go to sleep in two minutes or I'll spifflicate you.'

Rob buckled up the straps of our bags. I was in my walking

skirt and heavy plaid wool jacket and cap. We looked at each other. 'Ready?'

Last night he had curled sideways to suck my nipple. His first suck had sent sensation in a thin bright line down through my breast to my stomach and between my legs. I jerked, then lay still, watching the dark top of his head. I could see just where the hairs sprung and parted. We'd learned to manage in the narrow bed so that we got the best of it. I'd put my hand down and touched his hair, then stroked it. It was like being on a boat at anchor far out on a summer's day, lying with the heat of the sun soaking into the length of our bodies, feeling the knock and ripple of water under the hull. If we'd been other people, not Cathy and Rob, brother and sister, it would have been so easy to say 'I love you'. But of course we did. We were brother and sister, weren't we?

There was a fine pale mist as we set out, but the sun was growing stronger. It was a perfectly still morning, full of the sound of rooks.

'Where will we go?'

'Somewhere high. I know. Isley Beacon.'

Ten

They used to light fires on Isley Beacon. When Boney was going to invade there were tinder-dry heaps of brushwood ready to flare up from hill to hill. Or so they said. There were no marks of fire on the close-bitten turf. The soil was thin and poor, no more than a skin over white bone. But the pasture was beautiful with flowers when you looked close: tiny speedwell, rock rose, kidney vetch and wild thyme set in the turf, nibbled by sheep which left their tarry droppings all over the hill.

We flung ourselves face down. The early frost had melted and the hilltop was drenched in sun. We were hot from the climb, sweating. I took off my coat and lay on it, staring up into the sky, which was a fine, glazed blue. It might have been summer but there were no larks singing. The sheep ran away from us, their horny hoofs hammering the turf so that it echoed dully when I put my ear to the ground. But in spite of the sun a deep chill struck up through the ground, and I left Rob lying there and walked along a smaller flinty track to the edge of the hill. The ground fell away steeply there. Our track wound up, following the ribs of the hill, a pale ribbon of exposed chalk. Below me the land stretched out for miles, half in the shadow of the hill, half bathed in sun. I could see our woods and fields, and the bulk of the house, almost hidden by trees. Behind the trees Grandfather would be overseeing a couple of men hired for the day from the village while they cut turnips out of the clumps and chopped them for fodder. Then they were going to repair a length of fencing which had gone in the October gales. If I'd had a telescope I could have seen the tiny figures bending and stretching over their tinier burdens. The air was absolutely still and clear. Everything looked so ordered from up here. I couldn't see the mud in the lanes, the choked hedges, the gates sagging on their hinges. Everything was asking for money, the kind of money Mr Bullivant had.

I glanced behind me. Rob lay flat on his back, eyes shut. He had chosen the highest point, the flat slab where the fires were lit. Or so they said. There was a bronze-age fort here once, when the land below was a sea of forest lapping the flanks of the hill, full of bears and wolves. They made fences of stakes around their huts and watched for their enemies. I saw their enemies mounting the hill like shadows, moving from hiding-place to hiding-place so that their movement was like the rippling of the wind. No sound, no hint of their presence until they were on you.

I walked across the turf to Rob. My feet made no sound but he sensed me coming and looked up.

'I surrender,' he said.

We opened our bags of food and ate greedily. The pickled walnuts puckered my mouth but I ate them one after another, staining my fingers. Rob brought a white paper bag out of his pocket. Sugared almonds. He laid a trail of them between us. Comfits for weddings, or christenings. I bit through the hard crust to the nuts, eating my way towards Rob.

He spread out his coat and we lay together, not really touching, our faces to the sun. Red worms of sunlight wriggled behind my eyelids. His hands were dry and warm. From the side his lips looked as if they were smiling, though I knew that they were not. The sheep bleated as they came close again, gaining courage from our stillness.

'What if there's a shepherd with them? Whose are they?'

'These are from down below – look at the marks. He wouldn't come close if he saw us. He'd think it was some lad with his best girl.'

'He might recognize us,' I said.

'Not he.'

But I'd never really thought before of how careful we would always have to be. No twining together in warm summer lanes. No dancing close to the tolerant smiles of the middle-aged ladies sitting at the sides of the ballroom. No public love, ever. No weddings, no christenings. There was a time when secrecy was exciting, when it was like a warm fire burning inside me. *We are the only ones who know.* I held my breath as my bedroom door creaked open and Rob slipped in. No one else knew. But there was always that unspoken 'yet' to terrify me. What was happening between me and Rob might be growing towards its own discovery. We could see everything from up here and no one could see us, but we couldn't spend our lives on Isley Beacon.

The thought passed. We watched the shadows of cloud-shreds move over the fields. It was not quite so clear now. The days were short. Already an evening blueness stained the more distant fields and woods. But the sun was still on us.

'We'd better be going,' said Rob.

'Oh no, not yet. Let's stay a bit longer.'

'Aren't you cold?'

'No. Not in this sun.'

I was always the cold one, but not today. Rob sat up.

'I'm going to run to get warm,' he said.

He ran from a standing start. He ran from where I was as if he were being spooled away along an invisible thread. His head was thrown back, his arms high at his sides. He set a pounding pace that always crumbled after a few hundred yards. But he could sprint. His shadow fled away behind him on the grass, growing huge. His boots drummed the ground and it echoed hollowly, like a memory of the beat of horses' hoofs.

It was late. I felt the cold now, standing up. He was still

running, away from me, small in the distance against the rim of the hill. He looked as if he were going to run off the edge of the world.

'Rob!' I called after him, but he still ran. 'Rob!'

There was a darker patch of turf under my feet, as if the chalk below had been burnt. I'd found it at last, the place where they lit the beacon. When I'd looked straight at it I'd missed it, but out of the corner of my eye it showed up like the shadow of a scar. The brushwood must have crackled as the buried flints split their way out of the chalk. That long flare of red tonguing out into the night.

Rob had dwindled to a pinpoint on the long spine of the hill. I shouted again, louder and louder, frightened, seeing myself left alone in a darkening world.

Eleven

Her bicycle was by the front steps. Upright, ugly and insistent. Usually she'd wheel it round to the stable yard, out of the way.

'Give me your bag,' said Rob. 'I'm going in through the kitchen.'

'I'll come too.'

'No. She'll be waiting for you. She's your person. You deal with her.'

There was mud on my boots and I would need to brush the braid round my skirt. My hair had slipped out of its knot in the long lolloping run down the track from Isley Beacon. All I wanted was a bath and then dinner and a drowse by the fire, my mind blank from the day in the air, my body slack. Even the black spokes of her bicycle looked accusing. She had been sick and I hadn't visited her.

She was waiting in the hall, wearing her new yellowish dustcoat and her felt hat. The coat flopped around her, long and lean as a washed-out banana. Why did she persist in wearing the thing all the time, when she never drove anywhere? Her shoulders were hunched as she strained forward, devouring the fire. She always made me feel that the blaze was too high and the flames too luxuriant, though all we burned was wood brought in from the estate. She heard me and turned.

'So you're back,' she said, 'and where's Robert?'

There were two heated spots, one in each cheek. They did not burn clear; they were a dull hectic red. Her glance slithered over me and away.

'He's gone round to the stables,' I said.

'You've been out the whole day, Kate tells me.'

It was like being a child again. For years now she hadn't dared assume her rights over me so openly. But first we'd had the scene in the conservatory, and now this. She was pushing for lost territory. She could always sense when I had something to hide.

'It was good to get out of the house,' I said. 'We don't often get a day like this in the middle of January. It was beautiful, we walked right up on the top of Isley Beacon,' I went on, offering up our day to her and hoping it would satisfy her. She would pounce on it and smear it.

'It was cold enough. But I dare say you kept warm, the pair of you.' The malice in her voice frightened me. *The pair of you.* How she'd always hated us being a pair. She'd never acknowledge it. The most she'd yield to our relationship was a cold, grudging 'your brother'. She could say the name Robert as if it were a punishment.

I dare say you kept warm. I looked at her and she looked back at me, her face full of narrow triumph. Her lips were parted over her long teeth. She was excited, and there was something sly and childish in her excitement. We stared at each other too long, until I felt my stare become an admission. When I spoke my voice was over-friendly, and I knew even as I asked, 'Have you had tea? Shall I ask Kate to bring some?' that I had lost ground.

'Kate has other fish to fry, I dare say,' she answered. *I dare say.* It came across with ugly boldness. She was admitting things too: how Kate had never liked her, how she wasn't really welcome in this house, how the love she'd tried to pour out on me had been thrown away like waste water.

'All the same, let's have some. We'll go and sit down.'

But she wouldn't leave the hall. She must have been thinking it over beforehand, imagining the scene, painting it in the colours she wanted. She was like a child colouring neatly between the lines and hoping for masterpieces.

'No, thank you, Catherine. I'm not staying.'

But she wasn't going either, and I was stuck there with her in my dirty boots and muddy skirt, wiping loose hair out of my eyes. She looked me up and down. How she always exaggerated everything. Her life was theatre, bad theatre. Her trusty steed, her scarab pin, her love of secrets behind closed doors, her little way of pursing her lips over words that had almost slipped out. What a liar she was. I had had enough.

I wanted to tell her to shut up, let us alone, get out. She knew nothing. Nobody had ever touched her or wanted to. I'd had enough of her sliming her trail over our lives. She stood there rocking slightly from heel to toe like a huge, useless doll, and I wanted to push her, see her keel over and knock her head on the hard stone hearth, singe her hair in the flames. I wouldn't help her, not if she had her head in the red heart of the fire. I knelt down and pushed the poker between the logs, dislodging a shower of sparks and the smell of apple wood. The last load of wood had come from two James Grieves we had lost in the gales. I breathed in the smell of the smoke. Of course she didn't know anything. How could she? On Isley Beacon we'd been higher than anything but a hawk. It was just her old jealousy. She was sick and yellow with it. I jabbed the poker in hard and levered two logs apart until they sent up new bright flames. I thought of how she'd held my hand and led me through The Sanctuary to where my father was, and I shivered with revulsion. She'd enjoyed that too. I remembered her fingers rearranging my petticoats, tucking in, scrabbling at the lace. Thank God I was out of that long tunnel of my childhood. She had had her time.

I glanced up over my shoulder and caught her looking at me. She was drinking me in, and she went on boldly even when she saw me looking back. She'd got me at last, she thought, and I belonged to her now. Everything had changed and I was where she'd wanted me all those years. She put out a long hand and touched my hair.

'Catherine . . .'

I shrank away from her. I would have knocked her hand off but I didn't dare. Yes, she knew. Somehow she'd spied and watched and she'd got what she'd always wanted. She could hold me where she wanted now. You are dirty, her eyes said, and I shall make you pure. The most frightening thing about her had always been the lies she told herself.

'It's not right for a young man to be hanging around at home. Your grandfather ought to send him away to work for his living,' she said. 'He needs knocking into shape. He ought to go to sea,' she added wildly. Visions of the future she could visit on Rob rose like goblins in her eyes. Storms at sea, a ship rounding the Cape of Good Hope, Rob clinging to the railings — a wave breaking over the decks, a sickening lurch, a cry no one heard, the ship sailing on while a tiny figure tosses in its wake, growing weaker and weaker . . . She could do it now, she believed. Through me she could get rid of Rob, the way she had always wanted.

'Why on earth would he want to go to sea? None of us ever has.'

'Oh no,' she said, with heavy satire, 'of course not. It's good enough for the finest men in the land, good enough for my second cousin the Admiral, but not good enough for you. You'd rather go elsewhere, like your precious father.'

She had always been sentimental about men in uniform. Her nonsense was making my head ache.

'Your father,' she said, '*he* went somewhere, didn't he? Did you know they wanted to send him to Bedlam?'

'I don't know anything about it,' I said, 'and I don't want to.'

'Oh yes, they did. But your grandfather stopped it.' Her words dropped on me like little balls of spittle. She spoke quietly and conversationally, and no one passing through the hall would have guessed what we were talking about. I didn't feel like laughing at her now.

'Your father was a moral lunatic,' said Miss Gallagher. 'Do you know what that means, Catherine?'

'God knows!'

She paused, torn between her automatic desire to defend the Redeemer's name ('She treats God like a pawnbroker,' Rob said) and her hunger to move on to better meat.

'I had hoped, Catherine, never to have to speak to you on the subject, but I know my duty now. I should never have kept the truth from you all the time,' she continued, with an involuntary smile of pleasure. She would have got her phrases out of one of the novels she loved, tales of virtue rewarded and the flowering of beauty in plain, poor women. I saw her rolling the words over on her tongue in her narrow bedroom, rejoicing because at last she'd made her chance to use them.

'I knew about that, anyway,' I said.

'Did you, Catherine? I wonder,' she said, looking at me with amused pity. She would have rehearsed that too. Then she poked her neck forward with a jerk, ugly but effective, like a blackbird stabbing at the head of a worm as it emerged from the wet soil. Her eyes pinned me. 'Have you ever thought what happens to a servant who gets herself into trouble?'

'She gets married, I suppose.'

'Oh, you innocent!' she trilled, letting it hang between us that innocent was certainly the last thing I was. 'Not always, Catherine. The asylums are full of such girls. They are moral idiots, not fit to live among decent people. They need to be taught the difference between right and wrong. I visit one such place quite regularly, you know. Of course I have never talked to you about it.'

But now you can, I thought.

'Not many people know about them,' she went on, 'but

charitable people contribute funds. The inmates wear a uniform. I helped to design one.'

'What's it like?'

'Really, Catherine, I should hardly have thought that was significant. As long as their bodies are covered. Though I flatter myself that I know something about clothes.'

I looked at her long swathes of dustcoat. You are a monster, I thought. How she would love insinuating herself into any institution, sipping tea with the matron and gently recommending further punishments. How she would love walking up and down among girls who might have been pretty once and were now on their hands and knees scrubbing flags with big chapped hands.

'The matron of St Agatha's is a particular friend of mine,' said Miss Gallagher. 'Moral idiots,' she repeated, with light, particular emphasis.

'That doesn't mean anything to me,' I said.

'Oh, doesn't it? I thought it might. Your grandfather would know what it meant at once, after his terrible experience with your father.'

Chill was licking at my heels. No matter how much wood we piled on, all we ever achieved in the hall was a blaze on our faces and a desert of cold behind. She knew and she was going to tell our grandfather.

'You don't look well.'

'I'm tired. It was a long walk. And I haven't changed.'

'Oh yes, Catherine, I think you have,' she said, looking at me with her head on one side. Then she became practical again, the friend of the family. 'You must have perspired and it has given you a chill.' She looked at me as if she could see the pores of my skin and smell my sweat. 'Shall I ask Kate to fetch hot water for your bath?'

'No, not yet.'

'I could stay while you have it.'

'I'm sorry, Miss Gallagher,' I said, and I smiled appeasingly, 'I'm not feeling awfully well.'

'*Eunice*. How many times have I got to tell you? After all, you are grown-up now. We're both women. Eunice. Perhaps it is one of those times? Have you got your visitor?'

I felt as if she were running her hands over my body.

'Oh you silly girl! You don't need to be shy with me.'

She had creaked into horrible playfulness. We were girls together, talking about female intimacies.

'If Rob *does* go away,' she said, lingering over the idea deliciously, 'I could come and keep you company. I'm sure your grandfather would not object, if you asked him. And you need someone to help you with your clothes, if you're going to have all these parties and gaieties. Won't it be fun?'

We were in the future tense already, not the conditional. I knew all about how language was put together from hearing Rob's Latin as he struggled to learn his tenses and declensions. I could feel my way to the right answers swiftly, as if a path lay between them and me. She was so sure of herself now. Stupidly sure. She really thought it had been that easy and it was all over. I would give in and Rob would go like a lamb. Oh, she'd juggle us all. Yes, she'd frightened me, but now her big face was silly with the prospect of happiness.

'I must go upstairs. I've got a pain,' I said. She looked at me with maternal satisfaction, like a mother who loves her child the more when it is sick and scabby, hidden away from other eyes. Then she reached out the back of her hand and stroked it down my cheek. I jerked sharply away and rubbed my flesh where she had touched it. Her hand fell down to her side and she looked at me with tiny hating eyes.

'Touch pitch, and you shall be defiled,' she said. 'You're filth, Catherine. You are walking in the darkness. It is the evil spirit in you that makes you turn from me. But I shall rescue you in spite of yourself, Catherine. I know my duty.'

She was rapt. I had given her more happiness than she had ever imagined. The prospect of my redemption glowed before her face, brighter than the fire. It was perfect: she could hate the sin, and love me. She scarcely saw me go out, leaving her there.

'She knows,' I said, and watched the pupils of Rob's eyes shrink to pinpoints.

'How? How can she?'

'I don't know. She just does.'

He sat back on his heels on my bed and whistled softly through his teeth.

'The old devil. She's been after you since you were born.' Sss, sss, sss, went his whistling, and he actually smiled, his cheekbones rising mockingly.

'She's a monster. You don't know half of it. You're to go, and she's to move in with me and help buy my clothes.'

'*Help buy your clothes!* That'ud be the worst of it. Do you think she'd find you a nice coat like hers?'

'It isn't funny, Rob. *She knows.* She's going to tell Grandfather.'

'Keep your hair on, Cath. She wouldn't dare. He'd get rid of her the way he got rid of Susan and Tommy Linus. Besides, he wouldn't believe a word of it.'

'Wouldn't he?'

'Of course not.'

'She says he would, after Father.'

'Did she actually say that? Threaten you?'

'No, not quite . . . but it's what she meant.'

'Mmm.' He was frowning now, tense. 'I always said she was mad.'

'We're moral idiots, that's her line. She could get me put away for it.'

'That's absurd. She can't do that.'

'She could. There are asylums for it. Father nearly went to one, why not me?'

'You don't believe she could, or you wouldn't be talking about it like that.'

He was right, of course. Just by talking her over between ourselves, the way we'd always done, we were weakening her. We'd annulled her between us many times.

'But it's different this time. She really means it. She is mad, or half-mad, anyway. That's why she's dangerous.'

We'd always laughed at her. Her clothes, her scarab pin, her long teeth and her cloying love for me. But all that mockery hadn't changed anything. She was still here, as durable as rubber, and she came and went in our house as she wanted. She hadn't changed. In her grotesque way she had the same power to want as Mr Bullivant had, and to go on wanting long after anyone else would have given up. We had never taken her seriously.

'She's the hare and the tortoise,' I said.

'She can't be both at once.'

'No, we are the hare. We think we're so far ahead of her. We're young, we've got everything. We bound off for a bit then we lie down in the sun and shut our eyes and forget about her. But she won't be forgotten. She just keeps going, plodding on her track.'

'Funny things, tortoises,' said Rob, 'the way they move. If you watch them all the time they don't seem to make any progress. But if you go away then come back after a while, they've always gone out of sight. And they're the devil to catch in the long grass.'

'Yes, that's it – that's what I mean. She's like that.'

'So what are we going to do about her?' He said it lightly, as if it was a game.

'Make her go.'

'Make her go? And how do we do that?' Hazel flecks swam

in his eyes. I could see every grain of colour and the way it thickened into patterns, raying out through the iris like a dandelion clock.

'I'm sure there's a way.'

He laughed. 'She's not the boy in the wallpaper, Cath.'

The boy in the wallpaper had lived in a narrow frieze of pattern until nightfall, when he came out and slipped between the bars of my cot-bed. He had gone on coming for years. At first I liked him, but his stories ballooned bigger than shadows and I couldn't control them any more. He told me about the burned ladies who always wore veils of deepest mourning over their faces. And when they drew them off, slowly, there were no faces at all, only greasy knobs of melted flesh with two eyes sitting in the middle. There were the Noink-Noinks who squeaked whitely, like mice, only high up. At night they all came to me, flocking and twittering.

I was six when Rob killed the boy in the wallpaper. I'd woken again, sweating and grovelling at the bottom of my bed. My nightdress clung to me in urine-soaked folds.

'I'll kill him for you,' Rob promised. 'I'll wait for him tomorrow night and when he comes I'll kill him.'

'How will you?'

'I mustn't tell you. You'll have to hide with your head right under the blankets and promise you won't look out. If you do he'll win and he'll kill me.'

I cowered under the blankets. They were hot and scratchy and I had no sheets: it was a punishment for wetting my bed. I heard the squeak and shuffling begin. They were coming, peeling off the wall, dropping lightly to the bed, scampering across the floor. Then there was a thud, a cry. Silence. A long pause.

'Rob?' I did not dare peep out of the blankets.

'It's all right.' His voice, curt and muffled. 'I've got him. But he's done my arm.'

'Can I come out?'

'Yes. He's dead.'

He was dead and gone. Rob sat on his bed, rather pale, holding his arm.

'Ouch! Don't touch it, Cathy. That's where he hit me with his nightstick. If I hadn't been quick he'd have done worse.'

I stared respectfully at Rob's nightshirted arm where he clutched it.

'You won't wet the bed any more,' Rob told me. 'Kate will put your sheets back.'

I listened for the boy in the wallpaper, but his teasing voice was silent. He had gone, and the wallpaper was only wallpaper.

No, Miss Gallagher was not the boy in the wallpaper. Footsteps tapped down the corridor and we sprang apart.

'Has that one gone yet?' demanded Kate. 'I'm late with your grandfather's coffee for keeping out of her way, and now he's raging. Why he can't drink tea in the afternoon like a Christian soul, I can't think.'

'Nothing very Christian about tea . . . nothing very Christian about Miss Gallagher, come to that. Kate, you'd know – is she a witch?'

'I'd know, would I? Well, as it happens, I can tell you. She's much too stupid to make a witch. Any broomstick she had would never get off the ground. Now out of the way and let me see to this.'

She knelt, building a wigwam of kindling. Somewhere a bell rang furiously.

'He wants his coffee, the old devil,' she muttered as if to herself.

'I'll do that,' said Rob.

'You will not. You make a terrible fire.'

'We can't sit here like a pair of stuffed owls while you do everything.'

'Why not? Isn't that what you're for?'

'Touché.'

'Too-shay yourself. Do you think I don't know French? At least push the damper in after a quarter of an hour. *If* you remember, with all you've got on your mind.'

'What's that supposed to mean?'

She looked at him with her long bright eyes and shrugged. 'You don't usually stop talking when I come into the room.'

'No more we do. Sorry, Kate.'

'Oh, I'm not complaining. Just observing. I've enough to do making all these fires up and putting clean linen on your beds.' She gave another long oblique look that included us both, lifted the basket of kindling, kicked open the door with her heel and was gone.

'Yes, she's got to go,' said Rob, as if we hadn't been interrupted.

'It's all right saying that, but how?'

'I'll think about it. And you do too. My best ideas come in the middle of the night, I find.' He grinned at me and the burden lifted. It was all play.

But he didn't come to my room that night and I lay awake, alone. I didn't think of Miss Gallagher. I thought of my father and how they had taken him. Had they grappled his arms behind him, pinioned him, made him walk between two indifferent men who'd been brought in knowing nothing but that there was trouble? Had they been rough with him? Or had he crumbled already, compliant as he'd been in the hospital?

If he'd been himself he'd have stung that doctor into silence. Instead he'd sat there with his glass of milk in front of him, and reached out his hand to lift it obediently to his lips. But Rob had taken the glass and poured the milk in a long arc to the ground.

My father had stumbled in and out of the rose garden,

looking for us. There would have been thorns in his hands. They had been able to take him and do what they liked with him. 'A moral idiot'. The flesh had hung from his face, slack and heavy. He was fatter than he had been, stripped of house and wife and children and gun. I wished he had still had his gun. He would never have hurt anybody.

'When I'm out of sorts, a day's shooting soon puts me right.' Had he said that, or was I imagining what I wanted to remember? The beads of moisture on his shooting jacket. The battered cap he always wore. The way a hare or a pair of rabbits would swing from his hand. And the cold touch of the skin, the warm flesh beneath, the smell of rain and tobacco and cologne when he swung me up and kissed me.

'Moral idiocy,' her doll-like voice tapped at me. I twisted in my bed. How I hated her.

Twelve

In the middle of the night I gave up trying to sleep, sat up, wrapped the counterpane round my shoulders and settled to wait for morning. The house creaked like someone turning over in their sleep. How quickly I'd got used to Rob's warmth beside me, and the strawlike smell of the bed we shared. Kate had put on clean sheets and there was nothing left but a bland smell of soap.

I hadn't forgotten. The memory of it was in my body, not in my mind.

Soap flannels my ears. Water runs in and blocks them so that Kate's voice booms like a deep-sea diver's. I shake my head, trying to get rid of the sound.

'Stand still, Cathy. My God, you could grow a crop of potatoes in here. Stand *still*, will you, you're not going out with your father looking like that.'

Kate seizes my head and crams it between her knees. She's in a bad mood today, cuffing me about as she gets me ready. Where is Rob? I don't know and I don't think of him. My whole imagination is set on the expedition with Father and I hold out one leg and then the other, indifferent as a doll, while Kate garters my woollen stockings. She rakes my hair with the comb and begins to plait. I don't know how long it is since Father promised me this day with him. I have taken it to bed with me, shaped it in the dark. I am hungry for it but it is a satisfying hunger, as if I can already smell the meal that has been prepared for me. Father never takes me out on my own. It is always Rob on his left hand and me on his right. We call these hands our hands. Rob must not touch mine and

I must not touch his. I swing Father's right hand possessively, and sometimes I put my face against it, quickly so he will not see, and turn it over to kiss his palm. I do it very lightly and he never notices it is me.

Today I'll have both hands if I want. We are going to walk over to Silence Farm because there is a horse we might buy for ploughing. It's not really called Silence Farm, but we've called it that for so long I can't remember the proper name any more. At Silence Farm they'll give me black tea, and a nip of something stronger for Father. The darker and more bitter the tea, the prouder I am to drink it. My tea comes in a china bowl with bands of flowers on it, not in a cup.

'There,' says Kate, tipping me off her lap, 'that's you done for today. Mind you don't go over the top of your boots in the mud.'

It's been raining for weeks but today is fine. There is a wind and the ground's drying fast, but there are big, mud-slopped puddles too. I always go in puddles. I start at the edge and shuffle in very slowly, watching the skin of the water lap my boots. Sometimes I get right to the middle, sometimes there is a snatch and a slap and I am whisked up and dumped back on the dry earth.

'And don't go raising the dead with those boots outside your mother's room. She has a headache.'

'No, I won't,' I say, but half-way down the corridor I notice that my boots make a much more satisfactory noise now that they have been away to town and had little steel tips put on at sole and heel. I click my heels like a pony and shy at my mother's closed door, tossing my head. But the next minute Kate whisks out of the night nursery, sweeps me up and whooshes me to the top of the stairs. She kneels down in front of me and hisses into my face,

'Now get yourself downstairs and no more noise out of you. You'll be late and he won't take you.'

Her long eyes sparkle danger. I don't always know with Kate whether it is real or not, so I put my lips tight together and nod obediently.

'Good girl.'

She's right, Father is waiting for me in his cap and jacket. But he makes me swallow a plateful of toast first, his own toast with thick marmalade on it, cut into triangles. We are never allowed toast, only porridge, but today I'd rather go with an empty stomach and be sure we were on our way, out of the house and together. On the other hand it would be nice if Rob was there to see me eating the toast. I keep my eyes on Father all the time to make sure he doesn't suddenly remember something he has to do. And then, just as I've bitten a little door in the last piece of toast, he does.

'Wait here, Cathy, I must go and say goodbye to your mother.'

'Kate says she has a headache. She wants to sleep. She said no one was to go in her bedroom in case it hurt her eyes.' I go on, inventing feverishly. I know all about my mother's headaches. I would tell him she was dead if I thought it would keep him down here with me, but I am pretty sure it would not. 'Oh.' He hesitates. 'One of her sick headaches?'

'Yes. Kate said so.'

'Better not go in then. She might be asleep. I'd hate to wake her . . .' he says quietly, as if to himself. I think of my mother's white, shut face in her cloud of pillows, and how she always turns her head away towards the window when one of us creeps in through the door.

'She said not to wake her,' I repeat.

'Oh well, in that case . . . we'd better cut along. Finished that toast?'

I crunch the last triangle and lick butter off my fingers. 'Finished, Father,' I echo obediently. I am sleek with virtue and butter.

Father is taking a gun. I like its dull shine, a bit like the gleam of the range. It is a shotgun. I would like to stroke it, but I'm not allowed to touch. Touching a gun is the one thing that will make Father shout and slap me. He doesn't care at all about puddles. But the backs of my legs itch, remembering the sting they got when I put out my finger to the gun barrel where the sun was licking it. Lucy's puppy races at Father's side. As we walk the puppy skids to a splay-footed halt, runs back, snaps at his shadow, races to catch up with us again. He runs three times farther than he needs. He's going to make a useless gun-dog, John says, but when I say this Father tells me, 'He's young, Cathy,' and slaps his side to make the puppy come.

The stubble is wet, the soil heavy. My boots clod up with mud and they are heavy to lift.

'Don't drag at my hand,' says Father, and I let go and hop over the caked ruts in the field path. My skirt is dirty already. I might as well go in lots of puddles on the way home. Father is walking fast, with the puppy dancing effortlessly at his side. I must keep up. I stumble and grab at whatever's there, but it's a hoop of sharp-clawed bramble and it tears my palms through my gloves. As long as I keep my gloves on I won't see the blood. Father's even more ahead now. The sunlight bounces off his hair and the cotton-wool swathes of old man's beard which loop the hedges. I was going to collect some to make tiny eiderdowns but there's no time.

'Come on, Cathy!' he shouts back. I pick up the sides of my skirt and jump a puddle. The mud is over the top of my boots now, and squeezing down into them. It spatters up into my face. Father has stopped, looking back for me, and next moment a big white handkerchief is scrubbing at my face. It smells of cologne. I am going to smell the same as Father.

'Try and keep to the dry side up by the hedge.'

I stare round. Is there a dry side? It all looks the same to me. But Father's boots aren't even splashed. We are coming to the top of the field. I know the way from here – through the field gate, straight across the next field down to the lane, then all the way along the lane to Silence Farm. No one else lives here. The lane is full of birds and rabbits that don't bother to run until you are nearly up to them. I always try to catch one with my bare hands, creeping up on them softly and talking to them.

I know the way, but Father seems to have forgotten. At the top of the field he leans on the gate, waiting. But I'm already here, and Lucy's puppy is squirming under the lowest bar of the gate. Father ought not to let the puppy loose here, because there are sheep. But he doesn't seem to notice. I pull very gently at his sleeve.

'Father, the sheep.'

He looks at me as if I'm another person. His eyes are empty.

'Oh. Yes. The sheep.' He reaches down, grabs the puppy's collar and holds it. The puppy strains its soft neck against the collar. Its eyes stretch as it tries to butt its way free into the air. Father gets a leather leash out of his pocket and ties it on to the collar. The puppy runs to the end of it, jerks hard, falls back. It runs again, falls back and whimpers. Father is quite still, looking away over the gate, while the puppy keeps throwing itself against the air. But he must be holding the leash very tightly because his hand is bunched on it and the knuckles are white. The puppy yaps and whines loudly. Suddenly, as it begins its run again, Father pulls the leash up sharp with both hands. The puppy paddles in the air, caught by its throat. The noise changes. The puppy's face hangs by mine, and I shrink back. I don't know what Father is doing. He always knows what to do with puppies and dogs. Father jerks hard again then drops the puppy. It sprawls on the ground, coughing, and its legs go all ways. Father rummages in his pockets and gets out a white paper bag.

'Like a humbug, Cathy?'

Father likes humbugs, and so do I. But I look at him doubtfully and don't take the sweet. The puppy is making a funny noise, as if it can't breathe properly.

'Here, take two,' says Father, shaking them loose in the bag. They always stick together. I pick a humbug out of the stripey mass, put it in my mouth and suck hard. The puppy is getting up. I'm sure he's all right now. But I wish we could go on to Silence Farm. This journey is too long, and I need to go and there's nowhere here. If I was with Rob we'd both go on the path, seeing how big a puddle we could make together. Father takes my hand and swings the gate open. He ignores the puppy, but it creeps along behind us, close to the ground. I wonder why it still wants to be with us, but perhaps it can't think of anywhere else to go.

We are in the middle of the field when Father stops. His hand holding mine is suddenly wet and I want to pull mine away, but I think of the puppy and I don't. Father looks back the way we've come, then quickly ahead. His hand tightens on me. 'Quick, Cathy. See how fast we can run to the hedge.' His voice sounds as if he's pretending it's a game, but I know it isn't. He runs with his head down, dragging me stumbling over tussocks of grass, scattering the sheep. In the shelter of the hedge he crouches down panting. His face is all covered with sweat. I am standing between his knees and he is holding both my hands. Far back across the field I hear the frightened whine of Lucy's puppy. He can't find us.

'The puppy's lost,' I say, but Father doesn't take any notice.

'I'll tell you what we'll do,' he says. His voice is tight and quiet. 'What we'll do is we'll just walk a little way along this hedge, it's not very far, and then we'll get to the gate and over it, then it's only down one more field and through a bit of the woods, then home. That's not very far, is it? We can manage that. Oh God. Help me. It's all right, Cathy, I'm all right. Wait a minute. We'll just get our breath. Father's out of puff, that's what it is. Oh no. Oh no. Not very far. Nearly home now. Over the field. That's all. Just keep going straight on.'

But we aren't moving. Father sinks slowly into the tangle of wet, coarse grass under the hedge. I can't see his face any more, only the top of his head. Then he lets go of my hands and covers his face. He wraps his arms tight round his head and curls up in a ball, as if he is going to sleep. He is making strange noises, like crying or laughing. Behind me I can hear the puppy getting close. I turn round and there he is, pushing his way over a tussock of grass. He needn't have climbed over it, he could have gone round. He is shivering. I pick him up and hold him close to me. He curls up like Father and tries to lick at his neck, but he can't reach it properly. His body keeps giving little jerks in my arms.

'It's all right,' I whisper in his ear, 'don't be frightened. We're going home in a minute and your mother will look after you.'

In a little while the puppy feels better. We start playing a game where I stroke his head and he rubs his ears up against my hand. He likes that. Then out of the corner of my eye I see the gun where Father has dropped it. It is pointing at us.

> Never never let your gun
> pointed be at anyone.

I ought to move it. Even Father would want me to move it, I argue with myself, but when I glance at him he's very still. He won't even know. I stand up with the puppy in my arms and tiptoe towards the gun. I tiptoe in a careful circle until I am behind it. Then I put the puppy down on the grass.

'Keep still!' I tell him. 'Guns are dangerous.'

I kneel down in the grass and slide my hands underneath the butt of the gun, making sure it is pointing away from me.

There is the trigger. That is where the shot comes out. Very gently, very quietly, I lift it. After all I'm only going to turn it round so that it is pointing into the hedge. I'm not doing anything bad. It is very heavy. I can't hold it at all the way Father does. I brace myself and lift the weight of the gun on to my shoulder.

But my back is to the hedge. The gun is pointing not at the hedge, but at Father. I shift it. It is slipping on my shoulder, hurting me. I'm afraid I'm going to drop it. The puppy wriggles round my feet.

'Cathy!'

It's the breath of a voice, no more. I've been too busy trying to control the gun to notice Father. But he's up, uncoiled on his hands and knees staring at me and the gun which is pointing straight at him. I'm going to swing it round, only it's so heavy. Father's face is white, streaked with mud.

'Cathy! Don't move now. Keep perfectly still. I'm coming round to you.'

I stand perfectly still. The sun glints on the gun, the puppy wriggles warmly against my ankles, and my arms tremble with the weight. Father edges very cautiously round the grass, watching me all the time. Then he is at my shoulder, lifting the gun. There is a sharp, fierce smell coming from him.

'I've got it now, Cathy,' he says. 'Step aside.'

I step aside.

'Are you all right now, Father?' I ask.

'Yes,' he says. 'I was ill for a bit, that's all. Like your mother and her sick headaches. But I'm better now. And what in God's name were you doing with this gun? How many times have you been told?'

'It was pointing at me,' I say, beginning to cry, 'and you were asleep and you always told me −'

'What did I tell you?'

'Never, never, let your gun . . .' I sob and hiccup. But I can't finish it.

'Pointed be at anyone,' says Father, and he swings up the gun and points it at a cloud in the bright autumn sky. 'There now. Watch this.' The gun kicks his shoulder and the bang comes, splitting the sky into thistledown. I shut my eyes and ask,

'What did you hit?' but Father laughs. 'Nothing. I was only pointing at the air. Come on now. Let's go home.'

'What about Lucy's puppy? He's not very well.' And father looks at the puppy just as he usually does.

'Poor little beggar. He's played out. You can carry him if you like.'

I glow with pleasure. I'm not usually allowed to carry the puppy, because he hasn't been wormed yet. But, 'Aren't we going to Silence Farm, Father?'

'Oh – Silence Farm,' says Father as if he's forgotten all about it. 'No, Cathy, not today.'

I think of the bitter tea and the dark parlour with its slippery chairs, and the rabbits in the lane.

'No, Cathy!' says Father. His voice is beginning to sound funny again. Quickly I take his hand, holding the puppy cradled in my other arm.

'I don't really want to go there anyway,' I say. We walk quietly most of the way home. Father helps me over the ruts, and at the end of the muddy part he wipes my boots clean with grass.

Just before we come to the wood he says casually, glancing down at me,

'No need to tell anyone we didn't go to Silence Farm, Cathy.'

'No, Father.'

'We'll forget about it.'

'Yes, Father.'

I know he means all of it. The puppy and him curling up under the hedge and me holding the gun. Already I am not quite sure if any of it has really happened.

'This little fellow's cut his paw,' says Father, 'we'll get it bound up before Lucy sees it.'

I smile. Lucy is the fussiest bitch, John says, it's a wonder she can bring herself to bear a litter of puppies, still less do what she has to do to get them. I squeeze the puppy and he looks up at me anxiously, his puppy-grin showing white needle-sharp teeth.

It was cold inside the counterpane. How many other days had dropped clean out of my memory? What had I lost? He told me to forget, and I forgot, not because I was obedient but because I was afraid. My shoulders were hunched high and my breathing was tight.

'Cathy will do as she's told.'

'You didn't see what happened.'

'You didn't hear that, did you, Cathy?'

'We'll forget –'

'Yes, we'll forget . . .'

'. . . all about it . . .'

My body trembled, as if it knew things I didn't know.

Thirteen

I'd had two hours of sleep after the dawn came, and my head ached. When I drew the curtains my eyes stung. In the mirror they were small, washed out as if I'd been crying in my sleep. The winter light was harsh this morning and my clothes were scratchy as I pulled them on, shivering. Rob shouldn't have left me alone. We had to be together now. When his face on my pillow twitched with dreams, I could almost read them. They were my dreams too, my nightmares. I was entering him, going through the walls of skin between us. I thought of the inside of his brain like honeycomb, pale golden. I was a bee crawling through the chambers where he thought, my wings clogged with honey. We used to pretend to remember a life before we were born, when we played in our mother's womb together. And how I was sad when he left before me, leaving too much space, forcing me to grow without him. I almost remembered seeing him swim away over the threshold without me. I grasped his heel but he was slippery. He was gone.

We had to be together now because there was nowhere else to go. We needed to drowse together, fitting one to another and lapsing in and out of sleep. My heartbeat slowed to the pace of his, and I seemed to feel a larger heartbeat enclosing us both.

But he wasn't at breakfast. There was a half-eaten fried egg in his place, and a cup of coffee he hadn't even touched. His chair was shoved back. He'd be down again in a minute. I poured tea for myself and watched the stream of it wobble with the shaking of my hand. The hand looked like someone else's, not mine. I could not predict what it would do next. I was very tired, that was all it was.

Kate came in and started to bang plates together.

'He hasn't finished,' I said. 'He hasn't had his coffee yet.'

'He won't be drinking it,' said Kate. 'She came to fetch him. They're going riding.'

'Who?'

'Livvy Coburn, who else would it be that could make Rob go off without finishing his breakfast?'

'Have they gone?' I asked, my hands clumsy, knocking my tea so it slopped. His coffee was still warm.

'You might catch them,' said Kate, eyeing me ironically, 'if you run.'

'It's just there's something I needed to tell Rob . . .' I wouldn't run, not in front of Kate. I walked to the door, stiff, my thighs rubbing against one another, my face set in a little smile.

They were on their way out of the stable yard. The sun was on them as they sat big and powerful on their horses. They stretched down their necks and looked at me as if they were part of another race, Livvy on her beautiful cosseted mare and Rob sitting on a horse I didn't know.

'It's Starcrossed,' said Rob. His face turned to me, a glitter of evasion which I couldn't read. 'Mr Bullivant sent him over for me to exercise.'

He belonged there on Starcrossed, his back straight but not stiff, his thighs against the powerful muscle of the horse. The two of them shone.

'When are you coming back?' I asked.

He looked at Livvy, and she said, 'I must be home for one o'clock. There are people coming for luncheon. But my mother wants you to come too, Rob. Starcrossed can go in our stables. Isn't he an absolute angel, Catherine?' she asked, and she laughed and leaned over to pat Starcrossed's neck. Her touch was slow and caressing, and she glanced over her shoulder at Rob, her laughter still bright in her face. She was blonde, pink-tipped, immaculate. I wondered if she knew why she suddenly wanted him. No, she acted on instinct. She might look remote, but Livvy was as intuitive as a fox. She knew when her belongings slipped out of her grip.

'Stand back, Catherine,' said Livvy in her thin sweet voice. 'She strikes out with her heels.'

But I wasn't going to let them go like that. 'Rob,' I said, 'what about Miss Gallagher? You said you'd do something about her.'

'When I get back,' said Rob. 'It's all right, Cathy, forget her. She's nothing to worry about.'

'Oh, she's a sweet old thing really,' said Livvy, 'but quite batty, of course. You don't mind her, do you, Catherine? She likes *you*, you know.' She smiled at me kindly, offering me Miss Gallagher as if she were worth something. Or did she believe that Miss Gallagher was all I was going to get, because deep down where Livvy could see and I couldn't, we were alike?

Livvy's mare skittered, her hoofs flying, and I backed into the stable doorway. Released, Rob touched Starcrossed with his heels, and the two of them turned to go, the sunlight flowing on the horses' flanks like water.

There was a drip drip from a tap someone hadn't quite turned off. In the doorway dust curled slowly up a beam of sun. The stable floor was matted with dirty straw. It ought to have been swept out, but John was ill and Rob had left it. He should have been working here, not out riding with Livvy. There was too much to do and the place was falling apart. I was sick of it suddenly, sick of the way we lived and of my own passivity. My body itched with impatience and I seized John's broom and began to sweep. I heard the sound of hoofs behind but I wouldn't turn. He couldn't see me from the yard, he'd have to come in, ducking his head and losing the advantage of being on horseback. I knew it would be

Rob, come back to make things right with me so he could enjoy his day with his mind at ease.

'Cathy!'

'Mmm?' I said, sweeping so hard that a cloud of sour dust went up in his face, 'What?'

'Stop it, I can't talk to you when you're whisking about like that.'

'It's got to be done. This place is a pig-sty. You ought to have done it.'

'All right, I know, I know. Listen, I've only got a minute. I told Livvy I'd forgotten my whip. Listen. Don't be like that, Cathy. I had to go when she came over specially. It would have looked strange if I hadn't.'

'Yes, of course. So you had to go. Why did you come back, then?'

'You know why. Because I –'

'Because you?'

'Because I had to.'

I glanced up at him as I swept round him. 'Mind your feet. So you went because you had to and then you came back because you had to. That's very interesting but where does it leave me?'

I was hot, sweaty, exhilarated. With the broom in my hand I felt strong.

'You'd better go,' I said. 'She'll wonder where you are. That stuff about the whip won't fool her for five minutes. Go on, go to her. You know you want to.'

I had never felt so powerful. He stood there not knowing what to do. I felt my smile stretch across my face. 'Go on. I don't care.' And I didn't. I was big and coarse compared to Livvy but I was strong. When there was a job to do I could do it. I could clean out these stables and more besides.

'What about her?' he asked, hesitating in the doorway. I knew he meant Miss Gallagher.

'I'll deal with her. You'd better go, Livvy doesn't like waiting.'

No one else came to interrupt me. I kilted my skirt into my belt and heaped the dirty straw in the yard. Winter flies crawled slowly, almost asleep. They looked blind. If we'd let that straw lie much longer there'd have been maggots in it. I forked it on to a barrow, then wheeled load after load to the midden. I fetched John's zinc bucket and swilled down the cobbles with clean shining arcs of water. I put fresh hay in the mangers and spread new straw for bedding. When it was done I leaned in the doorway. The thin January sun felt warm. Wisps of new hay blew about and the wet cobbles glistened. A wood pigeon purred on the roof as if it were summer and I stretched myself until my bodice creaked. There was a burning ache at the base of my spine.

I'd had an ache like that the day I came back from the hay field with Rob last summer, so late the moon was up. Rob had been working with the men. Kate and Elsie carried heavy tin cans of tea, and I took a basket of plum cake with a white cloth tied over it. I wore my old blue cotton and I'd stuck marguerites and yellow poppies into the ribbon of my straw hat. I didn't care about anything that day. I was at ease in my body, and forgetful. The sun flickered on my face through tiny holes in the straw brim, and a little breeze blew over the standing grass and made it shiver. They had cut all but the square in the middle of the field, and they'd be done by night. The breeze dropped and the sun struck hot on my arms through the cotton. The men were resting in the shade under the hedge. Rob lay on his back, staring straight up at the sky, nibbling the juicy end of a grass stem. His hands were folded behind his head and there were patches of sweat under his arms. He'd been in the field since early morning, when the dew dried.

The men saw us coming and there was a shout, the kind of

shout they'd give girls from the village: I don't think they recognized me. Rob sat up too and I saw how he would look if you didn't know him, his teeth gleaming in a burnt face, his eyes narrow. I pulled back the cover of my basket and walked from man to man, offering them the cake. I knew Rob was watching me all the time.

'Is that tea Kate's brought?' he asked.

'Yes.'

'We ought to have beer for the men. It'll be dark by the time we finish.'

'Ought we? I'll ask Grandfather.'

'You ask him,' said Rob. 'The way you look now, he'll give you anything you want.'

The smell of the hay was sweet. I drew my skirts under me and sat on the grass, next to Rob. *The way you look now.* I felt the glow of it all over my body as I looked down into the minute world of stalks and insects. The stalks bristled where they had been cut, and the insects ran about purposefully, lugging invisible crumbs of food. I dropped a currant and watched two ants wrestle with it. The sun was low now, its light warm and jelly-like. I looked out and saw that we were all gilded, more beautiful than we had ever been or ever would be again. I wouldn't go back to the house and ask about the beer. I would stay up here and help with the hay-making.

All that long light evening we worked to get in the hay. My big open-pronged rake dragged on the uneven ground. At first I was clumsy with it, then I caught the trick of swinging my whole body, not just my arms, as I pulled the loaded rake towards me. I didn't think of anything, only the heaped hay, the swing of the rake, my slow progress across the field. Kate was working a few yards from me but we didn't speak, except once when she said I had got the hang of it fine. She might have grown up in Dublin but she'd spent every summer with an aunt on a townland not far from Cork. She had a terrible life, the aunt.

'I'll tell you now, Cathy, it was a warning never to marry on to a farm. All the men arguing over the land year in year out while the women work themselves to death and have a baby a year.'

My hat was in the way and I took it off and threw it into the ditch. The flowers in its ribbon were wilted already. The sun was lower and less burning now. The air grew thick, blue as rosemary in the distance with columns of gnats whining as they rose and fell. Queen Anne's lace showed in the hedges like phosphorescence. I raked and raked, stooping until my eyes swam in the near darkness.

There was another shout when John came up with the beer. Grandfather had thought of it after all.

'Here, Cathy,' said Rob when the can came round for him to dip in his tin mug. He held the mug to my lips. I was thirsty and I drank it straight down as if it were the cold tea we'd had earlier. He tipped it higher, too high, and beer ran over my lips and down my dress.

'Steady, Cath, you'll smell like a brewery.'

But I drank down to the end of the mug before I handed it back to him.

We walked back together, a little behind the others. The wagon had gone down from the next field already. Another day or two to dry off the hay we had just cut, and we'd be finished. I'd go up again tomorrow to help turn it in the heat of the day. The shorn fields smelled sweet. An owl coasted low behind us, looking for baby rabbits. All the men had gone off with a rabbit or two. It was as easy as picking daisies to get them when they were dazed with fear, making for the ditches. They were mostly young ones. We linked arms and swayed from tiredness as we walked. Rob was whistling, a bit flat as he always was. There were dog roses in the hedges, the white ones like tiny flat lamps lighting our way. It had been perfectly clear all day and now dew was falling, bringing out the smell of cut grass and the smell of heated dust as we kicked it up with our boots. I hadn't bothered to find my hat. Somewhere there was an old cotton sun-bonnet I could wear tomorrow. It didn't matter what I looked like. I was light-headed from beer and the sun, leaning on Rob, feeling the stored warmth of the day come out of his skin. He turned and smiled and I knew he liked to have me there, as close to him as he was to himself. The others were nearly out of sight, but they could have turned and called back some joke or greeting that sprang from the hours we'd all spent in the field together. They would have thought nothing of the way Rob and I leaned together. We were brimful of weariness and happiness, we were brother and sister, that was all.

'That's a good job done,' said Mr Bullivant. I jumped. He was standing by the mounting-block, smiling at me.

'Don't come too near me,' I said. 'I smell like a stable. I must go and change.'

'You look fine to me.'

I looked back at him and smiled. I felt fine. I wasn't tired any more. The stable was clean and the long confused unhappiness of last night seemed to have melted away.

'I can't stay long,' said Mr Bullivant. 'There's a picture framer coming by the 3.14. But I brought something for you. Here.'

He had put down the box on the ground. It was made of pale wood, nailed roughly together. Just a packing-box, to keep safe whatever was inside it.

'I'll need something to get these nails out.'

'Shall I go and look?'

'No, I'll use my pocket-knife.'

He knelt down and began to lever out the nails that held down the lid. They came out easily, the wood splintering round them. He lifted the lid and there was a layer of white crumpled tissue paper. He looked up at me.

'Come and feel. See if you can guess what's in it.'

Under the paper were round lumps, firm but not hard. I didn't want to guess: it was always embarrassing to guess at a present, in case the guess revealed that I had expected too much.

'I don't know.'

'Yes you do. Smell the box.'

I leaned forward. It smelled of cheap soft pine, and then, inside, sharp and unmistakable enough to make my mouth water –

'Lemons.'

Our faces were close as we knelt one on each side of the box. He reached in and took off the top layer of tissue paper. Under it there were rows of lemons. Twenty, each one wrapped separately in coloured tissue paper. In between the lemons there were long dark-green leaves.

'Take one out.'

They were tightly packed together so as not to roll and bruise. I eased out one fruit. Under the paper it was plump and gleaming, a clear yellow streaked with green.

'I asked them to pick these just before they were ripe,' he said, 'there are five layers. A hundred lemons.'

'Where do they come from?'

'From the lemon house at my villa in Italy. Tommaso writes that they've had snow there, it's very unusual. They've had to keep the braziers in the lemon house burning all night.'

The fruit was not quite ripe. There was an acid edge to its lemoniness, which it breathed out through coarse, gleaming pores. The lemon was chilly in my hand, as if it had been travelling for a long time through the winter. I thought of the long train swaying its way north, whistling as it plunged under the alps. Mr Bullivant had written to his villa in Italy and asked them to pick a hundred lemons for me. I wondered what Tommaso was like, the man who'd opened the letter and gone out to the lemon house with his basket, and picked the fruit. He had looked for lemons which were still a little green, so they would arrive perfect.

'They are full of juice,' said Mr Bullivant, 'and quite thin-skinned. Let me show you.'

He took the lemon from me, laid it on the cobbles, pulled out another blade on his pocket-knife.

'You don't mind?'

I shook my head. 'Of course not. They're yours, really.'

'Oh no. I've given them all to you. You can do as you like with them.' He slit the skin of the lemon. There was a spurt of aromatic oil, then he cut the lemon in half and a bead of juice welled to the cut surface, flattened and began to drip.

'Three days ago these were growing on my trees,' said Mr Bullivant. I put my finger on the cut fruit and tasted the juice.

'I'll make lemonade with them,' I said.

'It's good for you, in the winter. You look tired. You ought not to do so much.'

I laughed. 'I don't do this every day. If I'm tired, it's because I'm tired of doing nothing. I ought to do more.'

'You could read? Or study – a language perhaps?'

I shook my head, remembering French lessons with Miss Gallagher. Those endless yawning afternoons, with Miss Gallagher rolling her 'r's over the smothered sounds of her digestion. 'I don't like that sort of thing.'

'I know. Very tedious, that sort of thing,' he agreed, while his different-coloured eyes laughed at me. 'But you might try Italian, in case you ever came to my house in Italy.'

'That's not very likely. We never go anywhere.'

'Catherine –' he began in quite a different voice.

'What?'

'Why do you just – *accept* things like that?'

'But you gave me the lemons,' I said. 'I accepted them because you offered them.'

'No, of course I don't mean that. I mean how can you accept so little? How can you say that you never go anywhere as if it doesn't matter?'

'I don't see that it does matter so very much. Lots of people never move from where they're born.'

'Your grandfather did.'

I looked at him sharply. How much did he know?

'That was different. He had somewhere to leave. Somewhere he wanted to leave.'

'And your mother,' said Mr Bullivant, 'she left too. She speaks French, and Italian. She speaks better Italian than I do.'

'She's had plenty of time to learn it. I don't suppose she's got much else to do.'

'She struck me as someone who would always have things to do,' said Mr Bullivant.

'Very likely,' I said. 'But I don't take after her.'

'Nor after your grandfather?'

'No.'

'It's strange, because you are so like her to look at. And not at all like your father – at least, to judge from the photographs I've seen. Whereas Rob is very like his father. Even the way you move is like her.'

'I might look like her, but it doesn't mean I am like her.'

'I don't know. I think it's very important, the way someone moves. The gestures. The way you turn your head. They flow from something inside, don't you think?'

'All the same,' I said, 'I'm happy here, in this house. I'm half English. She isn't English at all.'

'But wouldn't it be safe to take a little journey somewhere, just to find out?' he asked.

159

I began to unwrap the fruit, laying it so that each plump waxen body pointed the same way. I thought of my mother leaving. There'd been nothing dramatic about it. It was just a holiday, away from the children and the terrible winter. There was a story about how she'd never really recovered from my birth, although between her sick headaches she crackled with dangerous health. Then the holiday stretched and became a season of absence.

'You're very fond of your brother,' he said. My heart jumped. I turned over a lemon. Now the row was perfectly straight.

'Yes, of course.'

'But he'll go away himself. It's bound to happen.'

'No, he'll take over here. When Grandfather —'

'He might,' said Mr Bullivant, tapping a lemon, 'but he might not. Times are difficult.'

Grandfather talks to him, I thought. Those long nights, playing chess. What slips out? The unmended fences, the poor prices, the borrowing of money and plough horses. Kate's buckets beneath the holes in the roof. The bravado of our party in the middle of it all, outfacing the neighbourhood. But Grandfather would cling to the house whatever happened. He would be one of those corpses that cannot relax its grip: you have to break the fingers.

'So you won't count on it, will you? Rob being here, the house being here. Don't let it make you turn your back on everything else.'

'If there is an everything else,' I said.

'Of course there is,' said Mr Bullivant. 'Why, you don't have to go as far as Italy. In London, even —'

'I've never been to London.'

'Good God,' said Mr Bullivant. 'Good God. The railway runs not two miles away, and you've never been to London. Where's your curiosity, Catherine?'

'Where's my money?'

'That silk dress you wore to the dance would have bought a few railway tickets.'

'It was cheap,' I said, 'couldn't you tell? I'm sure you could.'

'It certainly did nothing for you,' he agreed instantly, as if he could see the dress in front of him. But it was dead and buried, rolled into a ball in the bottom of my wardrobe.

'Never mind,' I said, 'you won't be seeing it again. Didn't you say you have a picture framer coming?'

'Yes, I must go.' He stood up and brushed the dust from his knees.

'Thank you for the lemons,' I said.

'I shall build my own orangery at Ash Court,' he said, 'and I'll ask you to come and pick the fruit there, if you won't go to Italy. We'll eat our dinner under the orange trees.'

'They take a long time to grow,' I said.

'I can wait.'

We said goodbye, and I stooped to pick up the box.

'Let me. It's too heavy for you.'

'No,' I said, 'it's nothing,' though the box was awkward in my arms. I should have asked him into the house, given him something to eat and drink. It was exhilarating to be deliberately ungracious to him, to play against the grain of my liking for him. He made me see those orange trees kindling with fruit, sweet-scented in a velvet night. As I walked away from him into the house I felt myself smile.

Fourteen

I didn't turn when I heard the door open. Let him be the first to speak. But it wasn't his voice.

'Catherine!'

It was Livvy. I'd never seen her dirty before. There was mud on her face and the front of her riding-skirt. And something darker, rustier —

'Rob!'

'Cathy, there's been an accident.'

Even then part of my mind registered that she called me Cathy because he did. She had no right: it was what my family called me. Then her words sank deep into the space that had always been waiting for them. Of course he was dead. I got up slowly, looking away from her. My hands stuck out in front of me, pointing like signposts.

'I'll go and tell Grandfather,' I said, 'you sit by the fire.'

'What do you mean? I haven't even told you what's happened yet.'

'He's dead,' I said, 'isn't he? Isn't that what you came to tell me?'

'No, of course he isn't dead. Really, Cathy, you do make things difficult. He's had a fall.'

She was in charge, and strong. '*You're* the one who ought to sit down, Cathy. You look awful. He put Starcrossed at a hedge and he shied. Something ran under his hoofs. I think it was a stoat. Horrible little beast.'

'Did you jump it?'

'For goodness' sake what does it matter? They're bringing him home on a gate, he'll be here in half an hour. You'll have to send for Dr Milmain.'

'I'll tell Grandfather,' I said again. She was tugging off her gloves, finger by finger, looking down. Had she jumped off the mare, forgotten about herself and run to him? The rust on her dress was where his blood had fallen. Had she laid him in her lap and cradled him to her? I went out of the room to find my grandfather, but he was already coming down the stairs. Livvy's news had flown round the house. He brushed past me and went straight to Livvy. He put his hand on her shoulder and she lifted her face to him, letting tears come now, letting them hang and not fall so that her wide pale eyes were more beautiful than ever. He wiped a smear of mud off her forehead.

'Poor child,' he said.

'His leg's broken,' said Livvy, 'the bone came through his skin,' and a little shiver went over her face like wind on water.

'John's already gone for Dr Milmain,' said my grandfather. He took no notice of me at all. His eyes were fixed on Livvy, attentive, hard, considering.

'They had to shoot Starcrossed,' said Livvy. 'His leg was smashed.'

'We shan't let them shoot Rob,' said Grandfather. 'We'll have him as good as new for you.'

He spoke to Livvy as if she were his daughter. There was no space for me in that room, and I didn't want to be there. Livvy smiled up at my grandfather. You fool, I thought, can't you see it means nothing. You're money Rob might get hold of, that's all. Don't think you've charmed him. But she was bound to think it, since it was what she always did wherever she went.

He said, 'Catherine will take you to her room. Get Kate to bring up some hot water, Catherine. And something to drink – brandy? Do you take brandy?'

'No,' she said.

'Try some. It will do you good. Think of it as medicine.'

How she softened herself to him. That smile. Had I ever smiled like that, could I ever smile like that? No. And I didn't want to.

'I can't be looking after Livvy,' I said. 'I've got to get things ready for Rob.'

I stared at him and he stared back. I knew who he was seeing.

I shan't stay here. You can't make me. Nobody can make me.

'I'll be out by the stables,' I went on. 'They're bound to bring him round that way. I'll show them up. They can put Rob in my room and I'll nurse him.'

'Kate can nurse him.'

'Kate hasn't the time. She has her work to do.'

'Kate has always nursed you.'

'That was when we were children. *I* shall nurse him.'

He stared at me with his half-hidden eyes. We took no notice of Livvy but we hadn't forgotten her. He might have hit me if she hadn't been there. He had hit me once but I'd dodged and he struck the table. His hand had swollen so he had had to wear it bandaged for a week.

'How can you nurse a broken leg? He'll want lifting. You're not capable of it.'

'Dr Milmain will give me directions, and Kate can help.'

I saw what he saw: my set, sullen face, my big hands. I was capable and I knew I was. I could inflict my will on him. Livvy watched us, taking in everything, the bitterness and the likeness between us. I didn't care what she saw. She had taken Rob away from me on Starcrossed and look what had happened. Now it was my turn. What if my grandfather was hard? – he'd always been hard. His face was clamped tight, fixed in on itself. He was hard but he liked soft things, and he thought Livvy was soft. She would be no trouble to him in the house if Rob married her, or so he believed. But she was like water, that trickles through your hands but wears away a cliff.

'They'll be bringing him,' I said again. 'We'll have to have the bed made up ready.'

I didn't go straight to the stables. I went to my bedroom first and met Kate coming along the corridor with an armful of linen.

'I've taken off his good sheets, they'll only be spoiled,' she said. She had the old sides-to-middle ones in her arms, soft with wear. 'These'll do fine for now.'

'He's going in my bed,' I said, 'and I'll have the truckle bed put in beside him. I'm going to nurse him.'

'*She's* not staked her claim, then?' asked Kate.

'She'll go home,' I said, 'and change her clothes for dinner, and she'll eat it too. She'll just be a bit paler than usual so that everyone asks her why.'

'You're right,' said Kate. 'She has a fine appetite, I've noticed it before. She's one of those girls who can put away a good plateful, and then look as if she lives on fresh air and water.'

'They've shot Starcrossed.'

'Isn't it a shame to feed a creature like that to the dogs,' she said perfunctorily. And then, her face lively, 'And what's your Mr Bullivant going to say?'

'He won't say much, he doesn't care about horses. And he isn't mine. Anyway, that's Rob's business. Mr Bullivant knew well enough we couldn't pay for the horse when he lent it. The money's nothing to a man like him.'

'He could be yours if you wanted him.' She laughed at me with her long eyes, the bundle of linen drooping from her arms like a baby at a christening.

'Rob's hurt,' I said, to stop her. 'Livvy said the bone was sticking out through his skin.' I wondered how I could say those words and feel almost nothing, only the faintest prickle like life crawling back into a dead limb.

'It won't be as bad as she says,' said Kate confidently. 'She's a long streak of misery, that one.'

It was delightful, the way Kate cut mysterious Livvy down to size. We smiled.

'Give me the sheets,' I said. 'You light the fire.'

Livvy was wrong about the bone. It hadn't come through the skin, but it thrust up under it, sickeningly askew. He was colourless with pain, his hair dull where he had sweated into it. He smelled of blood and sweat and dirt. There was dirt in a deep cut on the side of his head, but it had almost stopped bleeding and Kate thought it was best to leave it until the doctor came.

'He's late. He should be here by now,' Grandfather kept saying. We could not get him out of my room, although I knew Rob wanted him to go. He was sick with pain, dizzy, holding tight to the sheets as if he thought he would fall off the side of the bed. We had hooked the sheets and blankets up over a basket to keep the weight off his leg, but he had to be covered. He said he was cold, and long shudders ran down him.

'It could be a lot worse,' said Kate. 'Once it's set, he'll be better.' And she stirred up the fire until sparks snapped up the chimney.

'Brandy,' said Grandfather, 'get him some brandy, Kate.'

'I'm not sure I should if Dr Milmain's coming with chloroform.'

'It won't hurt him. Brandy never hurt anyone.'

Rob felt for my hand. 'Darling,' he said, 'darling.'

'He's wandering,' said Kate. 'He thinks you're his best girl.'

'He hasn't got a best girl,' I said. 'He's tired, Grandfather. It wears him out to talk. Why don't you go down and see if the doctor's here? I'll sit with him.'

'I'll get that indiarubber sheet to put under him,' said Kate.

'He'd be better if he'd take some brandy. It'd put heart into him,' said Grandfather. 'He needs nourishment. What about beef-tea, Kate?'

'Go down and give it to Livvy,' I said.

'She's gone,' said Kate. 'A groom came for her.'

'Good,' I said, and looked across at my grandfather. Those hooded eyes full of his black temper could not frighten me today. I could say anything to him with Rob's body between us. Rob's hand was pale on the sheet, each tiny dark hair distinct, as if it were growing from wax. He was never pale, but now his freckles looked like dirt on his skin. He was curled a little away from Grandfather. I knew he was shrinking from him, afraid he would try to touch him. I felt inside myself how Rob's flesh cringed from the jar of Grandfather's hands. But Grandfather hung over him and couldn't leave him alone. He touched Rob's shoulder with awkward tenderness.

'We'll soon have you right again,' he said, but Rob was too tired to answer. He lay with his head flung back as if to separate himself from the broken bone and the tent it made under his skin. At least Livvy was out of the way. In the end she was a poor thing, I thought. I would never have left him, either by that ditch, or now.

'I'm sorry,' I said to Rob when they were gone. 'I couldn't get him to go. But it won't be long until the doctor comes.'

'He means well,' said Rob. 'I felt sorry for him. All that about brandy. I'm all right.'

'Yes, you're all right.'

'Don't let them muck me about.'

'No, I won't.' I squeezed his hand very gently. My feeling of protectiveness towards him was like a passion. He was quiet for a while, and his colour was so bad that I began to wonder if he was hurt somewhere else, inside, where we couldn't see. Then he sighed.

'It's just I'm so tired,' he said as if he were explaining something politely to a stranger. 'I'd be all right if I could go home and sleep.'

'You are at home,' I said, but he'd lapsed into a quieter, distant place where he didn't hear me. I wanted Kate back. Suddenly it was frightening to be alone with him. I looked at the door and she was there like an angel, flapping her yellowed indiarubber sheet in front of her.

'He's only wandering,' she said, coming quickly to the bed. 'He had a bit of a blow on the head, that's why. Tomorrow he won't remember anything, it'll be just as good as getting drunk. And Dr Milmain's here, wasting his time talking downstairs to your grandfather.'

'What's this, what's this?' asked Dr Milmain jollily, rubbing his hands like the parody of a physician. Rob smiled warily. The doctor looked eager as ever to get his hands on one of us. He was stripping off his coat already, rolling up his sleeves.

'Nothing serious,' he announced after a few minutes' examination. '*Noth*-ing serious. We'll have you up and about by the middle of next week, eh? And what's this? Blood? Nothing to it, Kate'll have that washed and dressed for you in three minutes, won't you, Kate? But first we're going to have to do a bit of basket-work here . . .' he went on, all the time feeling up and down Rob's leg, gently and lightly. He was no fool. His hands moved as if they had knowledge of their own, and liked what they did.

'Now some doctors'ud have you off to the sawbones for this,' he muttered, 'but *I* shan't. Why trouble trouble? No, all it needs is a little bit of patience − easy, Rob − and a bit of common sense and chloroform − steady on, there's a good chap, Kate's going to hold the pad for me. I want you to close your eyes and think of angels while I count to seven.

There you are, lucky number. Breathe deeply. Bet you won't get to eight. How much do you bet me? Not that I'm a betting man –'

But Rob had gone. He was out of it, he didn't feel anything I told myself as Doctor Milmain's hands grew fast and fierce. 'Now hold his ankle. There,' he ordered me. 'Bring your weight down so it can't move. And Kate, keep that knee quite still.' He felt at the place where the bone had broken, his fingers nervous and exploratory as butterflies. Then his face changed. He seized hold and pulled once, twice, hard. I thought I heard the ends of the bones grate.

'There now, that's done,' said the doctor in quite a different voice. 'A bit tricky, but he'll do.' He was splinting Rob's leg, winding on a quick mass of bandage.

'I'll be here every day,' he said. 'The thing to watch is the colour of the skin. Any change at all, especially below the ankle, you send for me. Pain? Oh he'll have pain. But the head's nothing. Wash it with iodine. And get him to wiggle his toes, Catherine. It'll heal twice as fast. Four times an hour and every time he thinks of it. You're going to be the nurse, I take it? He's to drink as much as he likes and do nothing. That means bed-bottles. Hold that bowl, Kate, he's about to be sick.'

He was coming round, his mouth squaring into a retch. Then there were long strings of vomit running between his mouth and the dish. I wiped his mouth when he had finished and helped him to lie down.

'Just the chloroform, nothing serious. Give him a bit of dry toast at five o'clock and as much sops as he wants.'

'You're going round,' Rob said in a hoarse voice. 'I can't see you.'

'No more you can. But you'll have enough of my ugly mug by the time we're through with this. Now be a good chap and go to sleep. If you want anything your sister's here. I'll just wash my hands.' Kate poured in the hot water and he soaped them carefully, finger by finger, whistling under his breath, not glancing into the looking-glass.

'Were you with him when he did it?' he asked me abruptly.

'No. No, it was Livvy – Olivia Coburn. I was here at home.'

'You'd have been safer with your sister, Rob.' But Rob didn't hear him. He was already asleep.

Pain? Oh yes, he'll have pain. Kate could soothe him better than I could. Her shadow on the ceiling seemed to quieten the whole room. I wanted to be there, in that room, nowhere else. I grudged fifteen minutes for swallowing some soup and a chop downstairs. I did not need food. Rob had a fever and for two days Dr Milmain came twice a day, then one morning he was suddenly cool and still in the bed, watching the faint trace of winter sun grown distinct, smiling.

'Rob? D'you want some barley water?'

'No. But Cathy –'

'Mmm?'

'You were here in the night, weren't you?'

'Yes.'

'I thought so.'

It was a small kingdom but it was strong. Kate serviced it, bringing up coals and hot water and jugs of barley water, taking away Rob's bed-bottles and bed-pans. No one else was allowed in. Of course Grandfather came, but he was a stranger and I think he felt himself one. The talk snagged, the rhythm of our life was lost when he tapped at the door. Once I heard Miss Gallagher's voice somewhere far off in the house, talking loudly. I would not think of her. She was out of the way and powerless. The things that were important were Rob's beef-tea and the daily glass of port he was allowed, the way his

skin itched inside the splint and wadding, the punctuation of
Dr Milmain's visits, the building and dying down of the fire.
Kate was with us when she could be, and it was better when
she was there, as if the presence of a third person were not an
impediment but a shaping force. We were more ourselves
when she was there.

There were a couple of long, raw grey afternoons when we
were just the two of us. We played two-handed bridge, and
chess, and I read aloud to Rob from *The Prisoner of Zenda*. We
didn't touch. Livvy had sent messages and a basket of cold
russet apples, but she hadn't visited. Russets were his favourite
apples and we ate them together, six in an afternoon, biting
away the sweet, nutty flesh and leaving the cores lying on the
bedclothes. He was sitting up now. Tomorrow he would be
allowed out of bed for the first time. Everything would
change. He flipped the cards down, dealing our hands.

'Let's not play any more.'

'All right. What d'you want to do?'

'I don't know.' I stood up and walked to the window. It
was the blank, lifeless end of a January afternoon. There was
no frost.

'Can you see the snowdrops?' asked Rob.

'No, there aren't any.'

'You're not looking. Under the acacia. There,' he said, as if
he could see them, as if he were pointing at them. And there
they were, white tiny stains in the gloom that grew sharper as
I looked at them.

'It hardly seems worth having flowers now, does it?' I said.

'It'll be spring soon,' said Rob. I felt a pang of anxiety. I
was safe here, with everything banked down and predictable.
Rob's illness was like a second winter. We had our rituals,
our drawing of curtains and lighting of fires. Spring would
be too strong a light, showing up the dust everywhere.

'I'll be out of here long before the spring,' he went on.

'You might not be.'

'Of course I shall.' He looked at me. 'It's not so bad being shut away like this in winter, but once the spring comes . . .'

Not so bad. 'No,' I said, 'it's not so bad.'

'I mean, I'm very grateful and all that,' he said quickly. 'You and Kate have been marvellous, don't think I don't know that.'

'But,' I said.

'Oh well, there are always buts. Aren't there?'

'I don't know. Not for me,' I said slowly. My jaws ached as if I were getting a cold. My chin hurt. Something was wrong. It was hurting the way it did when I was going to be sick –

I slammed up the sash and leaned out. The air was cold and tasteless, like water. It was all I wanted. Sweat had come out on my forehead and I shivered as it dried.

'Are you all right?' asked Rob. 'You look awful.'

'I'll be all right in a minute.'

There was a thick, hazy thudding in my head. I folded up and sat on the floor by the window, leaning my cheek against the wall. Cold air washed deliciously around my head.

'I'll ring for Kate,' said Rob's voice through the clamour in my head.

'No, don't.'

I was coming back to myself. I felt him watching me.

'It's all right now,' I said. 'I'll get up in a minute.'

'You've spent too long in this fug with me,' said Rob, 'and aren't you eating? You don't look right.'

I thought back. 'I did eat something this morning. Porridge.'

'It's four o'clock, Cath. Here. Have some of these grapes of Livvy's.'

'No, I'll get some tea in a minute.' I got up carefully and crossed the floor to Rob's bed. He took my wrist in his hand.

'You're cold. You aren't well. Stand up a minute, Cathy.'

I stood up.

'Pull your dress tight round you. There, I thought so. You've got thin.'

'Thin? Of course I'm not.' I'd never been thin.

'Have you looked at yourself in the glass lately?'

No. For the past two weeks I'd been scrambling my clothes on and off by candlelight. If my face looked different, I thought, it was from tiredness.

'I ought to have seen it before,' he said.

'I'm all right,' I said. If I wasn't careful I was going to cry. Now he told me, I could feel my own weakness. I couldn't even begin to want to eat.

'Go on,' he said, 'have a grape. Open your mouth.'

He held the purple grape against my lips, but I shut them tight.

'I don't like them.'

'You do. You like grapes. And they're such good ones. Open your mouth.' I shook my head, but he rubbed the grape against my lips, first gently, then harder, until the skin of the grape burst and I felt the wet, sticky juice sliding down my chin.

'You've got to eat it. I'll make you.'

I was sealed against him, like a cell closed with wax.

'It's running down your dress. I shan't stop.' He held the bunch of fat, bloomy grapes in front of my eyes. I closed my eyes and felt thick, burning tears gather behind them. But I wouldn't cry and I wouldn't open my mouth.

'Cath. Cathy. Cathy darling, what's the matter? Are you ill?'

I twisted sideways, pulled my wrist out of his grip and stood back from the bed.

'I don't want to eat her grapes. And don't call me Cathy darling. What if someone hears? What'll they think?'

'They won't think anything,' he said. 'You're my sister.

That's how I think of you.' He said it simply, as if it were the truth.

'We've still got her to think of. Miss Gallagher.'

'Oh, she's forgotten the whole thing already,' he said easily.

'You can't possibly believe that.'

'As soon as I'm back on my feet I'll deal with her.'

He would be back on his feet any day now. He'd be as strong as ever in a week or two, with only the pale chip of a scar under his hairline.

'I feel like John the Baptist,' I said.

'What?'

'*He must increase, and I must decline.*'

'Rubbish. You must eat. Then you'll increase, too.'

But I knew that the engine of sickness in me was like a fire, banked down so as to spring up stronger the next day. I felt it, but I didn't understand it. I'd always been at home in my own body and now there seemed to be no room for me in it. It had been taken over by something more powerful than I was, with a mind of its own. My sickness swept back over me and I shut my eyes.

'I want Kate,' I said. The meagreness of my voice in my own ears frightened me. I was shrinking everywhere, dwindling until I could not find myself. Soon there would be nothing left. Through the turbulence in my head I heard Rob ring the bell, once and then again and again, more urgently.

Fifteen

The room was dark and quiet. Kate had gone. I was sleeping in Rob's bed.

'It's happening at last,' I thought, 'we're turning into one another.'

His bed smelled different from mine. The sheets were slightly dirty, and smooth. Kate had not bothered to change the bed since Rob had had his fall. There were his heap of pennies and his little tin of lead shot on the bedside table. I was alone for almost the first time in two weeks.

I lay and looked down my body. He was right, I'd become thin. I needed looking after. My legs were long and white and useless looking, and my hipbones jutted. But my stomach was still soft and round, and my breasts were even bigger than they had been. Blue veins wriggled across them. I wondered what Rob would think of them when he touched them. I touched them. They felt hot and taut. My heart was beating fast as if I'd been running, but I'd been lying still for hours. Kate said I was to stay in bed for the rest of the day and she'd bring me a glass of port with an egg beaten into it. I couldn't eat it, I said, it was disgusting to think of strands of egg floating in dark red wine. All right then, she would bring me the port on its own.

'A glass of port is good for you. It builds up your blood.'

My blood needed building. It needed to be thickened and slowed. It was running too quickly around me and burning me up. At night when I wanted to sleep I was kept awake by the bumping of my heart.

Say you'll believe, O say you'll be true
to a heart which beats only for you.

That was love. It was what everyone wanted. But I didn't want the beating of my heart inside me, like an animal padding up and down, up and down. I lay awake staring into the hours between midnight and morning, and when the morning came I was too tired to eat. Even the smell of Rob's coffee nauseated me.

Kate came in with the glass in her hand.

'Shall I light the lamp?'

'No. My head aches. I only want a candle.'

She put it on Rob's bedside table, and the glass of port next to it so that a thin red rim shone around the dark liquid. It looked exactly like blood.

'Mind and drink it,' said Kate. 'Oh, and she's here. Euniss. She wants to come up and see you.'

'Tell her no. Tell her I'm ill.'

'I told her that but she's still here waiting. She's been talking to your grandfather, telling him you need looking after. She'll be digging your grave for you if you aren't careful.'

I had a brief vision of Miss Gallagher spading clods of earth out of a raw clay grave. The earth was as greasy as her mackintosh, and the sky so wet it squeaked. *Talking to your grandfather.* 'Did you hear what she said?'

'Why would I want to listen to her?'

'But did you?'

'It was only the usual old nonsense. Lie down now. You won't get well if you don't rest, and I can't have the both of you on my hands.'

'Help me drink the port. I get dizzy when I sit up,' I said, to keep her there. As long as Kate was with me Miss Gallagher could say nothing, even if she came in, and I didn't think she would unless I was alone.

'Let's get you up then. Dig in with your heels and push yourself up the bed. That's it. I've got you.'

I felt her strong hand knuckling my back. She wedged me in with pillows until I was half-sitting and then lifted the glass of port. But as the smell of it came close to me my lips puckered with nausea.

'Take it away. I can't drink it.'

'Course you can drink it.' But she didn't insist. Kate had the kind of tact in her body that would never let her force anything on anyone. Already she had put the glass down on the table.

'What's the matter with you? Tell me now.'

'It makes me feel sick. Everything makes me feel sick.'

She sat back, rimmed by the candle. I couldn't see her face. Then there was her voice with a laugh in it. 'If it was another girl and not you I'd be worried by now.'

'What?'

'Sick. Dizzy. Thin as a stick except for those big buzzies. There could be a bad reason for all of it.'

Her meaning struck me and I almost laughed back. Then it hit me again. She was still talking.

'But I can't have the pair of you taking to your beds, and me running between you. Should we put you in the one bedroom the way we used to do?'

I stretched my face into a smile. 'No need for that. I'll be better by tomorrow. I'm not really ill.'

'Oh God, and here's Euniss coming. Lie down, shut your eyes and I'll get rid of her for you.' We listened to the flat slap of Miss Gallagher's footsteps. I slitted my eyes and saw her poke her head around the door. There was a frill of light round her big shape.

'Only me!' she trilled. 'How's our invalid?'

'She's asleep,' said Kate.

'Is that so? And I could have sworn I heard voices as I

came along the corridor. Never mind. I'll sit with her for a bit, Kate, and you can go and attend to Robert.'

'She's best left quiet, after going off like that.'

'Of course. Quiet company, that's what she needs. She's been too much with her brother. It isn't good for her.'

'What could be better for anyone than their own flesh and blood? Though of course you've no family yourself.'

'Allow me to know best, Kate. I think I may claim to understand Catherine.'

It was hopeless. I opened my eyes as if waking. 'It's all right, Kate. She can stay.'

'And who's *she*, I should like to know,' bridled Miss Gallagher automatically, plumping herself down in the chair where Kate had been. Her buttocks spread out sideways, straining against their harness of scratchy cloth. Her scarab pin winked at me, and the candle flame blew sideways, elongated itself then shrank down. She was here and there was no getting away from her. But it was time. I'd been tensed, waiting for this.

'It seems so long since we've had a chat,' said Miss Gallagher, 'just the two of us. It's quite cosy with the candle, isn't it? Of course, you've been very taken up with him, haven't you? Robert. Since he had that nasty fall. But it's the horse I feel sorry for. Why should a dumb beast suffer? Not that I expect you to see it as I do, Catherine.'

'No,' I said. 'What do you want?'

'Good gracious, as if I ever wanted anything. My wants are *very* few, Catherine. I've just come to keep you company.'

Most of her face was in shadow but I saw the shine of her teeth. She kept them spotlessly clean, she told me. Ten minutes' brushing, morning and evening. They had never been white, she'd told me: yellow was the natural, healthy colour of the enamel. Her lips were parted over something like a smile, but behind it there was the hungry acreage of her face, sucking at me.

'You know what I mean,' I said. 'I haven't forgotten, if you have. What do you want now?'

'What nonsense you talk, Catherine. But of course you're not well.'

'Why is it nonsense? It wasn't nonsense before.'

I stared at her. Oddly it made me bolder to be lying down and helpless. I could outface her with my illness. She made a sudden, awkward dab at the bedclothes over my legs, and gave me a pat on my knee like one you'd give to a dog with an uncertain temper.

'We've always been good friends, Catherine, haven't we? Why, when you were a little girl you wouldn't let me go home without saying good night to you in bed.'

I couldn't remember. It might have happened once.

'My Miss Gally, you used to call me.' Her voice dripped a fond treacle. 'You were such a dear little sprite, Catherine.' I watched her hands crisping as if they held a small paper doll called Catherine. For a little while it would dance its papery dance, then those hands that made it would tear it to pieces. 'Of course you were a motherless child,' she went on, 'that made us closer. A boy hasn't got the same feelings. I never heard Robert mention your mother's name from the day she went. Not from that day to this.'

'Don't talk about Rob like that,' I said. My power was swelling. I was going to meet her head-on. We were going to fight again and this time I was going to win. She was not going to hang over my life breathing her threats like sugar.

'Very well,' she said, 'the less said about *him* the better. To anyone. Don't you agree, Catherine?'

'I do,' I said.

'When you're well, you'll see things more clearly. We can have such happy times.'

179

'Happy times,' I said. 'I'll take you for a walk when I'm better. We'll go in the woods and I'll show you my secret places. The weather will change soon and it'll be spring. I know a clearing where there's a bank of wood anemones, just where the sun strikes down. There's a fallen tree and they grow beside it. They flower each year but no one else sees them. You know what they look like, don't you? White and tender, with tiny mauve veins in them when you look close. People call them windflowers because they're never still. Even when we can't feel the breeze the flowers are moving to it. The leaves aren't so pretty, though. I always think they're like claws if you look close. I'll take you there.'

'Oh,' she said. 'Oh, Catherine. I'd never hurt you. You know that, don't you?'

'Because you love me,' I said.

'Yes.'

I shut my eyes again. 'I'm very tired. My head aches so.' I knew she would go now. I did not have to open my eyes to see her timid, joyous face as she tiptoed towards the door. I'd silenced her for a while. Long enough for me to think about what I had to do next.

Suddenly I was putting on weight again. I could eat like a wolf. I woke hungry in the mornings, longing for eggs with dark yellow yolks which spurted when I dug in my spoon, new bread and salted butter. I poured cream on to my porridge and drizzled golden syrup over it. I ate all this and then I was still hungry for crisp, slightly burnt slices of toast with Gentleman's Relish. I dug my knife deep into the paste, already tasting the smokiness of anchovies. I came down to breakfast early and sat over it late, drinking fresh tea, shutting my eyes and basking in the pale flood of winter light through the windows.

'Good girl. You're looking better,' said my grandfather

one morning as he passed me in the hall, but he didn't touch me.

Rob could walk again. I lay in bed each night waiting for his slightly irregular footfall. The first night he came again he hurt me when he lay on top of me and drove into me. My breasts were tender and all I wanted was for us to lie still and close. He knew it straight away. I never had to explain things to Rob. There were other things I could do for him. He showed me and I showed him. It never mattered who knew first how to touch and where to touch.

In the middle of the night I was always hungry. He crept downstairs to the kitchen and brought back a wedge of cold apple pie or a rice pudding. I broke its stretchy skin with my tongue and lapped up the delicious cold creaminess of it. It was cool because it had been kept on a marble slab in the larder.

'You'll get fat,' said Rob. 'Look, you're getting fat already. We needn't have worried about you. Did you know Miss Gallagher told Grandfather she thought you had consumption? Of course he didn't take a blind bit of notice. What a perfect fool that woman is.'

'I feel better than I've ever felt in my life,' I said. 'I like being fat. And I don't feel sick all the time any more.'

'That was just nerves. It was her fault: I believe she really frightened you.'

'She won't give us any more trouble.'

'No, she's eating out of your hand these days, isn't she? I've noticed. What have you done to her?'

'Oh nothing. She's rather pathetic, really. Anyway she isn't important.'

'You'll need to be letting that skirt out,' said Kate. 'Look at the way the darts are pulling. It'll ruin the cloth.'

'It's all the food you've made me eat. I'm getting fat.'

'Yes,' she said. I was standing in the window, against the light. I looked down at the white points around the stitching of my skirt, where the cloth strained away from it. The seams creaked as I moved.

'Turn sideways,' said Kate, and I turned.

'Jesus,' she said. 'How long is it since you've had your visitor, Catherine?'

I had to think. I never liked to think about it since it first came and made me different from Rob for ever. It had stopped because I was thin.

'Not long,' I said.

'Are you sure now?'

'I'm perfectly well, Kate. Look at me!' I spread out my arms and felt the cloth tighten around my waist. She was right, it ought to be let out.

'Catherine, do you know how you look now? But no, of course it couldn't be.' I had never known Kate hesitate in anything she wanted to say. It irritated me. Why was she looking at me like that?

'What, Kate?'

'It couldn't be that you were going to have a child,' she said in a rush. Her colour was high and fierce, the way it was when she was angry, but this wasn't anger.

'Going to have a child? Oh no. It couldn't be that. He made sure of it,' I said, the words falling out of me like eggs. She stared at me.

'What did you say?'

'What did I say? Of course I'm not going to have a child. I can't. It might be a monster.'

She took hold of the top of my arms and shook me. 'You're not well yet, you don't know what you're saying. Have you been going over there, Catherine?'

I saw what she was thinking of. It was as clear as if it were written, like the sky explaining things to me.

'You mean to Ash Court?'

'Yes.'

I just looked at her and saw her believing it. Why had I
said that about monsters? But she wouldn't guess, because
that was too bad to be true. Kate was on her own trail and it
led to Mr Bullivant.

'I'll kill him,' said Kate. 'Couldn't he see you don't know
anything? Why did you let him? Did you know what you
were doing?'

'No,' I said, 'don't say anything. Nobody must know.'

'Everybody's going to know soon enough. Look at you.
It's only because they're not looking that they don't see it.
It's in your face too. My mother could tell when a girl was
pregnant just from looking at her face. It's in the eyes. Look
at you, look at those brown marks under them. You'll be
feeling it move yourself, it must be about that time.'

I felt a snake coil in my belly. It had a flat, inhuman face.
Nobody had seen it yet, but soon I would feel it. It would
rustle, then stir in its basket inside me where it now lay
sleeping. At last it would emerge and everybody would see it.
But what kind of creature would it be? How was it possible
that it could live? A monster, Rob said. He had made sure
this would never happen, but it had happened.

'Oh no,' I said. 'Help me, Kate. You've got to help me.'

It was moving. Now I thought about it I had been feeling it for days. It was blind inside me. I must not think of
a snake or I would want to tear at myself until I had
gouged it out. It was like a clothes moth fluttering in a
cupboard. That was better. But that night I saw snakes. I
felt the tiny stir of its tail and I knew that Rob was right.
We had made something that ought never to have been
made.

'It's a baby,' said Kate, 'a little baby.'

'You've got to help me. If you don't I'll do it myself. I'll find out how, you can't stop me. I don't care what I do to myself. I don't care if it kills me.'

She would help me, I knew she would. She knew things like that.

'I'll help you,' said Kate. Her face looked strange in the light, as if she was frightened of someone. But there was no one in the room to make her afraid.

The woman had been a nurse, Kate said. She knew what she was doing. She would meet us at the empty cottage at eight o'clock the next night. She had given Kate a list of what to bring. Kate kept it folded in her hand and did not let me see it.

'But it's not safe in the empty cottage,' I said. 'The ceiling's coming down.'

'We shan't be staying,' said Kate. 'It doesn't work right away. There'll be time to get you back here. It's just we can't bring the old woman into the house.'

'Someone'll see us.'

'They won't. Anyway, you've been ill. You had a fancy to go out for air and then you were tired and we sheltered in the cottage. Sick people have fancies.'

'You must keep Rob away from me. Don't let him come in to me.'

'I'll say I'm sleeping with you while you're ill.'

'Yes, that's good. And Kate –'

'Yes?'

'Will there be much blood?'

'There was with –' she stopped and I knew she had been going to say a name. I wondered if it was Eileen's, but I knew she wouldn't tell me.

'Then put old sheets on my bed. We can burn them.'

She looked at me.

'What's the matter?' I asked. 'Isn't that a good idea?'

'It is. Only I'd never have thought you'd be so practical.'

Her words hung over us.

'This time next week, it'll all be over,' I said.

'Don't wear that skirt again,' said Kate. 'Anyone can tell if they look.'

'They won't be looking. People only see what they expect to see.'

'That's true enough. Now get some sleep.'

'You'll help me.'

'I promise.'

I will tell you what the woman did. It was a crime. She made me lie down on the splintery floor of the empty cottage. Kate had brought a blanket to put under me. The woman made me open my legs. She had a rubber bag with liquid in it, and a syringe. It went up inside me and she squirted hard until there was flashing pain in my side and she stopped. Kate had gone to the door to look out. I must have screamed but there was nobody coming.

'It doesn't hurt,' the woman said, looking at me hard. We had made an owl hoot. The silence of the night rearranged itself.

'No,' I said. 'It was the shock, that's all.' Kate helped me up. I was shaking because of the cold in the cottage and the smell of dirt. I felt as if my insides had washed loose.

'If it doesn't work, send for me again,' said the woman. 'It's all in the price.' Kate counted the money into her hand. It was my money. The woman dipped her hand into the folds of her skirt and the coins were gone. I thought of her money-dirty hands entering my body.

'Are you all right?' asked Kate. 'Can you walk? We should be going.'

She was on edge, wanting to get us away from the empty cottage and the woman, but I didn't care. I might as well lie here and bleed in the dirt and make the owls hoot. I was all right. I was nothing. I could not even tell how I felt. If I hadn't been holding Kate's arm I wouldn't have known I had a body.

'Don't be frightened,' said Kate. 'This happens to lots of girls and you'd never know. They go on and get married. It was his fault, not yours.'

'I'm not frightened,' I said. I thought of my father, piling the stones into heaps on the drive, two piles, the saved and the damned. We picked our way back home over the snapping twigs, and I climbed the staircase to my room alone. I was not ill and nothing hurt me, but my feet felt heavy and it was an effort to keep climbing. To go up those stairs was as hard as to climb into a tower, but I knew I must. Kate had been clever, she had made my grandfather believe that another doctor should see how Rob's leg had healed. She had done it as if reluctantly, sorry for the money it would cost, and he had believed her. So my grandfather had taken Rob to see a surgeon in town, although he wouldn't be half as good as Dr Milmain, Kate said.

'Never mind, it's money well spent. We'll have the house empty,' she said, and she laughed.

I heard it in my head as I went up the stairs. Money well spent. Money well spent. I had only to get to my room and later Kate would come. I was at the top of the stairs now, and the darkness around me was beginning to sway, but nothing hurt. I would get there. I forced myself through a narrow tunnel of lights which sparked and fizzed in front of my eyes. I fumbled for the door handle and there it was, and although I could see almost nothing now I knew the way to my bed.

It began to work in my dreams. My dreams were hurting. I rolled over and there was Kate.

'Hush,' she said. 'You're making a noise.'

'It's started,' I said. There were big hands working at my stomach, squeezing it. It hurt but it was not too bad. I could get through this, I thought. Then a sharp white pain jerked into me. Kate put her hand over my mouth. I tasted the sweat on it.

'Keep quiet. They'll hear you,' she said.

I turned my face into the pillow. The pain snapped at me, then shrank away. The pain was the old woman's hands still in me, her dirty hands. It was coming again.

A long time later Kate was pushing at me. 'Lie still. Lie still. I've got to have a look at you.'

I felt myself bleeding. It was warm and wet and it came out whether I wanted it to or not. I tried to close myself up with my muscles but there was another helpless gush of blood.

'It's stuck,' said Kate. 'That's what's making you bleed. Try to push. If we get it out you'll be all right.'

She was pulling at me and my legs were shaking so much I could not keep still. My body thumped against the bed as if it was a fish someone else had landed. I was in my body but I could make myself go out and watch it. Kate had washed her hands with yellow soap and they were clean. I saw the pale half-moons of her nails, with blood on them. I sat up and felt the blood slide into a pool under me.

'It's coming, it's coming,' said Kate, and I felt it come through me in a slithering rush, and out of me. There was more blood, then nothing but quietness inside me. It was gone. I lay back and there was a round stain on the ceiling that matched a pattern in my brain. I must have been staring at it all the time, without knowing it. I lay there flooded with something like happiness, though it was not happiness. The thing was gone and I was alive. I turned my head and saw Kate standing over a bucket. There was a slow, creaking noise coming from it, as if rust had a voice.

'What's that?' I asked.

'Nothing. It's nothing,' said Kate, her face hidden from me as she bent over the bucket.

'Don't look at it,' I said. I didn't want Kate to see what it was like.

'It's nothing to be frightened of,' she said. 'It was a girl.'

The creaking noise had stopped. 'What do you mean?' I asked.

'A little girl.'

'Let me see. Show it to me.'

She stood between me and the bucket. 'Lie still, or you'll start yourself bleeding again.'

'Show it to me. Kate, show it to me.'

I wouldn't have known what it was if she hadn't pointed. Head. Arms. Legs. It was a curled up thing, top-heavy and dark as a skinned rabbit. It squirmed slowly, but that was only the movement of the bucket as it swung from Kate's hand. Slowly my eyes settled and the little creature became what it was. It was tied to a bloody sac but you could see its hands, its feet, its big, noticeable sex. It was a little female thing. It was not moving.

'You were further on than we thought. I'll take it away now,' said Kate.

She would not tell me where she buried it. When I was better I went looking for it, first of all in the garden, then farther afield, in the woods, the orchard, the quiet corners of the kitchen garden. When I saw fresh soil I crouched down and paddled my fingers through it, but it was only where John had been digging. I looked under the silver birches where we had buried our pet finches long ago, but Kate had been too clever for me and it was not there. I had to sit for a long time with my back against the cold trunk of the birch before I had the strength to go back to the house.

*

I did not let Rob come to me at night any more. The surgeon in town had given him exercises to do, to strengthen his leg, and I sat and watched him do them. He swung his leg up and round, up and round.

'Wasn't that farther, Cathy? Wasn't that farther than I got it yesterday?'

I nodded. The leg jerked as if it had a life of its own. I could not imagine touching my brother. He hopped and swung, hopped and swung. His leg would be as strong as a spider's soon.

'We'll have another dance!' panted Rob. His eyes were brilliant. 'As soon as I'm better. You and me and Kate, like we did before. You'll like that, won't you, Cathy?'

I sat with my hands folded. I was neither thin nor fat now; I was nothing. Blood seeped rustily out of me, into the wad of cloth between my legs. I thought I would never stop bleeding.

'Kate!' I whispered from the bottom of the stairs. It was moonlight. The light fell slant through the deep little window at the turn of the stairs, on to the drugget. I was barefoot. I whispered again but she didn't hear, and I could not bring myself to go up the stairs.

'Kate, where did you bury her?'

I would find her. I would kneel by the grave and eat the soil from it. I would make roses grow from the grave of my girl, but they would be slim, narrow-petalled yellow roses, not the fat red ones my father had spilled all over me.

'Kate, where did you bury her?'

I only whispered, but I heard footsteps. When we were little she had told us, 'Don't shout. You only need to whisper and I'll come to you,' and the big bag of the night had been full of whispering. She was at the top of the stairs now, in her long white nightgown with her plait of hair slipping forward over one shoulder. Her face was swollen with sleep, not my Kate's face.

'What is it? Are you ill?' she asked me.

She was here but now I could not ask my question. I stared up at her, at her feet curling on the edge of the drugget and the strong column of her body. She blocked the way up.

'Wait, I'll come down,' she said, and she pushed back her plait. She didn't want me to come upstairs. It was her place, and Eileen's, never ours. Behind her the floor creaked as if there were someone walking behind her.

'Is Eileen there?' I asked. 'Can I see her?'

'You're not awake yet, are you, Catherine? You're half in your dreams. It's years since Eileen went. Come on back to bed,' and she started down the stairs towards me.

'I can see her behind you,' I said. Of course Eileen was there. The night ruffled and parted, showed her for a second, then closed over itself like water. If I walked round the house I would see everyone. I would find my mother sleeping in her white room, on her pile of pillows. This time she would turn her face to me as I eased open the door. Her face would shine out from its cloud of hair. I was her daughter. She would not hurt me.

'She would never hurt her own daughter,' I said, but the darkness squirmed and I saw the little female thing in her dress of blood.

'Kate, where did you bury her?' I asked, but Kate was already going backwards as if a strong arm was pulling her up and away, away from me.

Sixteen

The next day Mr Bullivant brought over a letter for me. It was a thick cream envelope with unfamiliar black writing slanted across it. *Miss Catherine Allen*, it said. I love the sight of my name on an envelope. It looks so definite, so sure that I really exist. I fingered the envelope, wondering who had sent the letter and why it had been delivered to Ash Court. I'd open it later, when I was alone – but here was Mr Bullivant, planted as if he meant to remain. This time I'd have to ask him in, never mind what Kate thought. Every day the stepping stones I had to jump were wider apart. What did Kate think, what had Miss Gallagher seen, what did Rob guess? A forest of eyes watched me as I moved around the house, my body stiff with the stiffness of someone trying to look at ease. The stones rocked under my feet, half sunk in water which was rising fast.

Kate was feeding logs on to the fire as we went through the hall. She sat back on her heels and stared at us. She was seeing the man who had brought that long bloody night on us, not the one who really walked beside me. I thought of how we had made Mr Bullivant into a sort of ghost of himself, and wished we had not. I should have made her believe it was someone else. Her long eyes would have frightened me if they'd been turned on me with that look in them, but of course he knew nothing of what was in Kate's mind.

'A fine morning,' he said to her.

'I dare say. I've not been in it to find out,' said Kate.

He raised his eyebrows at me. 'What's eating her?' he whispered.

I felt myself colour as I looked back over my shoulder at Kate. I wanted to stay in the daylight world with Mr Bullivant. He had the fresh smell of morning on him from his ride, and I stood close to him, loving the smell which was like the smell of innocence. I was so tired. Kate stared straight at me, one of her hands flat on the floor, the other holding a log. I wondered what she saw. She was too sharp. Could you tell by looking at two people what lay between them? There was not enough between us, the air was thin. And there was Kate showing in her face that she remembered everything I'd said the night before.

'I wasn't really awake,' I wanted to say to her. 'I was imagining things, that's all.' But Kate believed in ghosts, and that they came when they were wanted. If I'd seen Eileen, it was for a reason.

I took Mr Bullivant into the conservatory. It was faintly warm, though the day was sunless, and the dusty smell of indoor soil was stronger than the smell of the orange trees.

'I'll ask Kate to bring you a glass of madeira,' I said, but he shook his head.

'I only came to deliver your letter.'

'Strange that it was sent to you. They don't often make a mistake, and it has my name written on it clearly.' I looked at the address again. The writing was certainly clear, and beautiful.

'Not really strange at all. There's something I should tell you. It was posted inside another letter, and sent to me on purpose. If it had arrived here with that writing on it, you would never have had it. Your grandfather knows your mother's writing.'

I was still looking at the black lettering with its smooth downstrokes and delicate slanting upstrokes. As I looked the strokes flexed themselves like the glossy wings of a blackbird.

It was my name, written by my mother. She'd sat at her desk in a window looking over the sea, an open window with flowers growing in it, and she'd blotted her sheet of paper swiftly, reached for an envelope, dipped her pen and written my name. She had written the word that was me, making my name as she'd made me long ago. I touched the ink.

'Why is she writing to me?'

'She didn't tell me what she was going to write. She just said she wanted to write to you, and would I make sure the letter reached you.'

'Why? What's made her write after all this time? Have you been telling her about me?'

He was crisping leaves in his fingers, not noticing that they were crumbling to pieces. It was dry here, the soil in the pots was dry as sand. 'Nothing you would mind.'

'You had no right. And nor has she — she has no right to know anything about me.'

'Hasn't she?'

'No. Not any more.'

'But at least read the letter. It may explain.'

'It's too late for that,' I said. I wanted the morning world which he'd brought with him, but it had gone. He was in with us now, dragged into the story. I was never going to get away from it. My fingers were sweating. The ink was blurred on the smooth cream-laid envelope. I itched to destroy it. But I would wait, and do it where no one could watch me. I'd given away too much already.

'She writes such good letters, too,' he said, half-teasing, as if I were a child.

'Does she,' I said. 'Well, I'll have to take your word for that.' Anger spurted down my fingers and I ripped the envelope across, then again the other way, and again. It was hard to tear because there were several thick sheets of paper inside, folded together, but I did it. I ripped up the black writing as if I were choking off a voice. Little pieces fluttered onto the black-and-white tiles and into the pots, and Mr Bullivant stooped down to gather them.

'Don't bother,' I said. 'I'll pick it up later.' I looked at the straw-coloured scattering of my letter. Some of it had fallen into a big tub where the earth was black and freshly turned. I touched it. It was moist. Someone had been digging in the tub.

'What's the matter?' said Mr Bullivant. 'You look ill. I heard you'd been ill. Come, sit down over here.'

'No,' I said. 'Pick the paper out of the tub. You do it. Please.'

'Do you want to piece it together? We could have a try, but it might be a bit tricky. Still, I'm your man when it comes to restoration. Here you are, these are all the bits, I think. No, hang on, there are more under that seat.'

'It's no good,' I said. 'Don't bother. It doesn't matter.'

'Of course it does. You look awful. Shall I fetch someone?'

'Not Kate. Get Rob.'

He was gone. I sat on the edge of the tub and closed my eyes. Kate had not gone out of the house that night. She had buried my baby here, where no one would ever look for it. It was here to feed the orange trees my father had planted. Next year they would have oranges on them like lamps. Fruit and flowers together, twining out of the bones of the little female thing. Grains of faintness hissed in front of my eyes and I heard voices swinging towards me.

'She doesn't look at all well.'

'We'd better get Kate.'

'No, it was you she wanted.'

I opened my eyes. There was fresh black soil on the edge of my skirt, like a mourning border.

'I've got you,' said Rob.

He had got me. The hunt was over. Our baby was just where we sat, as close to us as his arm was around my shoulders. If he looked down and ran his fingers through the soil, he would see it too. We'd made her, and Rob didn't even know she had existed.

'You mind that orange tree,' said Rob, rocking me gently. 'Grandfather's only just repotted it. He did it himself, you've never seen such a performance. Soil everywhere, Grandfather cursing, the roots up in the air. I'll be a Dutchman if it doesn't die on us.'

'That tub?' I asked stupidly. 'That one behind me?'

'Yes, of course. Can't you see it's fresh soil? Grandfather thought if the tree was in a larger pot it might fruit. But I don't believe he's packed down the soil. There'll be air bubbles and the roots will rot.'

'I thought it was Kate.'

'Kate? Catch Kate lugging these tubs about. She's got more sense. Of course it won't fruit. All it ever grows is those wizened little things the size of marbles. But you know how Grandfather's got a bee in his bonnet about these trees. All right now, Cath? You look better.'

'Yes, I'm fine.' He was talking to distract me, the way he did with horses when they shuddered all over, ready to shy. I knew it, but I liked it too, just as the horses did. My hands had gone slack in my lap. Rob was right, of course he was. It was my grandfather who had lifted the tree with its ball of roots and buried it in fresh black earth. The white roots – I shivered. Kate's story was there: it had never gone away. The arm. The roots of it where it came off. My dream of the arm, its roots flowering like white violets. Let me not think of it. Let me not think of bad things. But there they were, jostling to come in like night at a window. Rob would not let me be hurt. He loved me. He had killed the boy in the wallpaper for me when he came peeling from his frieze, leaping lightly on to the floor to stand and mock me. It was not our baby in the orange tub. The little female thing had gone.

'I am her mother,' I thought.

A poem danced in my head. It was about a woman whose baby died after birth. The baby was gone, but the mother who had also been born that night could not die.

A mother, a mother was born.

I wondered who had written it. Whoever it was they had known what they were writing about. Better not ask.

A mother, a mother was born.

But you could stop being a mother. My mother had done it, so she was the proof. And there was Mr Bullivant standing in front of us with the scraps of my mother's letter crushed up in his hand. He did not try to put his arm around me or touch me, because he was not my brother. Rob must have seen the scraps of the letter, but he asked nothing. Nobody could ask any of the questions they wanted to ask, and I was glad of it.

'I must go,' said Mr Bullivant. 'I hope you'll soon be well again.'

'I'll walk round to the stables with you,' I said suddenly. 'I need some air.'

'You ought to stay inside,' Rob argued, his grip on me tightening. The crease between his mouth and his nose deepened, the way it did when he wanted something. One day it would be a deep, deep line. How many days and years would it take to score that line as deep as it was going to be? How much wanting? I was going to be there to see it, I thought. All the changes of his body which were still hidden, like a map not yet unfolded. We could not help ourselves as we rushed on to find the meanings already hidden, printed in our bodies like those lines.

'No,' I said. 'There's no air in here, that's why I felt faint. It'll do me good to go out for a while.' For a second I thought he wouldn't release me, but of course he did. Our little group stood still for a second: brother, sister, friend.

'What shall I tell her?' asked Mr Bullivant when we were out of Rob's hearing.

'Was there a letter for Rob as well?' I asked.

'No. Only for you.'

We walked on slowly, side by side but not touching. 'I wonder what she wants,' I said, not making a question of it.

'Nothing. Just to get in touch with you.'

'That's wanting, isn't it?'

'Why don't you let her talk to you? Don't decide beforehand what she's going to say. She is your mother.'

'Mother,' I said. 'That doesn't have to mean anything. It's a word, that's all.'

'It's a powerful word.'

'Is it? Is it powerful to you?'

'Of course.'

'Because of your mother?'

'She's dead.'

'I see.'

'I doubt if you do.'

'Then you must tell me.'

'No, I mustn't. It's you we're talking about. This is your story.'

'Then it's not a very good one, I'm afraid.'

'That's because it hasn't started yet. It needs some action. So what are you going to do?'

'Don't tell her about me tearing up the letter.'

'Of course not.'

'When she asks, say it never came. To you, I mean. So you were never able to give it to me. If she writes again, I'll read it.'

'Will you?'

'Yes,' I said.

'She will write, you can be sure of that.'

We were in the yard. I picked my way over scattered, dirty straw.

'Time to clean out your stables again,' said Mr Bullivant. 'It's a beautiful day, isn't it?'

I looked up at the flat white sky and laughed, 'Do you call this beautiful? It isn't at all.'

'No? Well, perhaps not. But the thing is, it's promising.'

'You could say that. I suppose it can't get much worse.'

'Isn't that what promising means? But you must go in. You mustn't get cold.'

'I'm not cold.'

He looked at me. 'I don't know if I should say this, but you do look different. I can't quite put my finger on it. Older, perhaps. Is it because you've been ill? *Are* you really ill? Are they looking after you properly?'

'I don't know.'

'You ought to come away. This is no life for you, Catherine. It's not good for you to stay here and do nothing.'

Do nothing. I caught in my smile before he could see it, but he was quick.

'Oh, so you don't do nothing? What is it you do?'

'Nothing anyone else would like to hear,' I said. His particoloured eyes flicked at me. He was tense. What we said sounded like a game, but there was no joy in it. He was in the wrong place too; he ought never to have bought Ash Court. It would swallow him up, for all his money.

'Goodbye, Catherine,' he said. The light was strong in the yard, although the sun was hidden. I didn't want to go back inside the house, and I waited there in the yard until the trace of his horse's hoofs had become quieter than dust falling. There was a steady chink of metal from inside the stables;

harness-mending. I felt safe here, though I wasn't sure what I needed to be safe from. Myself, perhaps.

You always have to go back inside. Inside is what you have made and it waits for you. This time Miss Gallagher had come.

'Oh, Catherine,' she said, 'you look so pale. My poor child,' and she reached out her hand and stroked my forehead. Her hand was hot, and very slightly sticky. It smelled of rubber where she'd been gripping the handlebars of her bike. I pictured her pedalling her way to me, erect in the saddle, eyes fixed forward.

'Let's go out,' I said. 'You remember I said I'd take you walking in the woods? There are all sorts of places nobody knows.'

She flushed. I looked away quickly from her big, excited face.

'What luck I put on my stout boots,' she burbled, 'and here I was thinking I'd be sitting with an invalid. I heard you still weren't well.'

'I'm much better. Wait here while I change my shoes.'

I ran inside and fumbled in the boothole. There were Rob's boots, then mine, both clodded with mud. Never mind. My heart was thudding. I darted back through the hall. Nobody was about.

'Did you see Kate? Or Rob?' I asked casually as I stooped beside her to lace up my boots.

'No, there wasn't a soul to be seen,' she said gaily. 'Quite a morgue, Catherine. I could have gone in and out and no one any the wiser. But of course everything's safe here where we all know each other. And it was you I came to see. I've been worried about you, you silly girl. You need someone to keep an eye on you.'

'You don't need to worry. I'm fine. First chop,' I said, smiling at her.

'Oh, that dreadful slang of your brother's. Really, Catherine. But we shan't scold today, shall we? *What* an afternoon – isn't it perfect?' She screwed up her eyes and peered at the sky, which was no brighter than it had been when Mr Bullivant enthused over it earlier.

'Yes,' I said, 'it *is* nice, isn't it? So no one even knows you're here? How funny! Let's wheel your bicycle round the side of the house. We can leave it somewhere out of the way. I want to fetch something from the potting-shed.'

We went along the blind side of the house, away from the main windows. It was damp on this path where it ran close to the wall, and the sun never shone. We pushed her bicycle into the dry brown heart of a rhododendron clump. 'There, that'll be fine even if it rains,' I said. 'And look, when the branches spring back you'd never know it was there.' We laughed. 'I'll get the spade. I shan't be a minute – you wait here.' We were gay as two schoolgirls. I waved to her as she stood on the path, then I ducked round the corner and untied the twine that held the potting-shed door.

I loved the dry warmth of the potting-shed. There would be an old spade hung on a nail: yes, it was there. And a huge ball of twine, and rows of little pots, and labelled envelopes of seed. I had spent hours here on wet winter days when I was a child. It smelled of creosote, clean and safe. I could stay here now, writing labels, measuring lengths of twine to tie over the seed beds in spring. Those were good afternoons, when the rain poured steadily until it might have been a hundred years since I slipped out of the house, away from everyone. I still wore pinafores then. When I was tired I would throw my pinafore up over my head and suck my thumb until I went to sleep, curled up on a pile of sacks. Rob didn't like the potting-shed; he said it was boring.

But Miss Gallagher was waiting. I took the spade down from its nail. The handle was black-smooth with wear, but there was no rust on the metal. It was a good spade. I remembered using it in the days when I had my own vegetable patch. It cut clean, crumbling clods out of the earth, and when the soil was waterlogged it made clayey, shivering slices. But you weren't supposed to dig when the soil was wet.

'Good gracious! You can't carry that heavy thing, child! Why ever do you need it?'

'Grandfather wants a holly hedge,' I told her. 'He said if we saw any good specimens that had self-seeded in the woods, it would be worth digging them up and heeling them in somewhere until spring.'

'Surely it's the wrong time of year for digging up trees?'

'Oh no. Not holly. It's very tough. I just thought we might see some. I'll take these sacks to wrap round the roots.'

'Dear me, Catherine, you think of everything, don't you? Let me carry something.'

'No, you'll get tired. We've got quite a long walk.'

'Where are we going?'

'It's a surprise,' I said.

'Oh, this is rather a thrill! Doesn't it take you back, Catherine? Remember those treasure walks?'

I did, grimly. There had been miles of clues on drizzling afternoons, and the treasure was never worth having. A threepenny bit wrapped in brown paper had lit up a whole afternoon once; but it was Father who tossed that into her treasure box.

'I see I shall have to put my thinking cap on,' she said, delighted.

'Yes. Careful, this branch is going to spring back.' I held it for her and she ducked through so I was looking down on to the top of her hat.

'Where's your scarab pin?' I asked.

'Do you know, Catherine, it's so annoying but I've lost it.

201

I can't think where. Of course it's not really lost, only mislaid. I'm not superstitious, as you know, but I really do think of that scarab as my luck. But where on *earth* are we going, Catherine? I never even knew this part of the woods existed.'

Of course she did not. She was a woman of paths and gardens. For hours she had stood on the edge of the terrace, yoo-hooing hopelessly after me and Rob as we played deep in the woods in the melting twilight.

'We never heard you.'

'We didn't know you were calling. We're sorry.'

We were deep in the woods now. She did not know it but we were swinging round in a wide half-circle. Even in winter, with the leaves off the trees, you could not see far. There was the scrub of holly and rhododendrons, and long curtains of old man's beard hung, browning. It was a place for ivy and dark-leaved things which did not die easily. It was still and cold and the afternoon was ending. Our boots crushed brown oak leaves, beech mast and the husks of chestnuts dropped by squirrels. She slipped twice, clumsily, and caught her arm on the dry snake of a bramble branch. There were little beads of blood on her wrist, as bright as my own.

'Oh,' she said, looking at me, her hat askew, 'isn't it rather wild in here, Catherine? There's no path. Ought we to go any farther?'

'It gets easier farther on,' I said. 'Give me your hand. We're nearly there.'

We were nearly there. I used the spade to smash down the brambles. There were plenty of holly seedlings, but she didn't notice them. She was shielding her face from thorns. I knew what she thought, because they were the old thoughts about me that she had been lugging with her for years. *Catherine is wild. Catherine is a tomboy. If it weren't for her brother Catherine would be quite different. I do what I can.*

'Here,' I said, and we stopped. The crackle of our boots died, and we were no longer an interruption in the wood, but part of it. Ivy stirred by my fingers, where it hung loosely from a dead oak. The trees grew very close here, and they were killing one another as they strained for the light. It was only a tiny clearing.

'Just about room to swing a cat,' I said.

'Is this where the flowers are, that you were telling me about?' she asked, looking around, a little bewildered.

'No, they grow farther back,' I said. 'It's lighter there, and the sun comes through. There aren't any flowers here. Rob and I brought some white violets here once.'

'Did you? How nice! I love violets. I think they must be my favourite flower, but then it's so difficult to decide, isn't it?'

'Yes,' I said.

'Or roses – roses are the queens of the summer, aren't they, Catherine? Do you remember that poem I taught you?'

'I don't like roses.'

'No, you don't, do you? Fancy anyone not liking roses.'

But she was faltering. The dark wood was quickly getting the better of her jollity. We stood quite close together, looking up at the little patch of overgrown sky which seemed high up and far away. Suddenly a thrush sang out a few liquid notes as if the bird had turned over in its sleep, sung, then slept again. Farther away there was the long thick cawing of rooks.

'They're going home,' I said.

'What?'

'The rooks. Because night's coming.'

'Oh I see. Yes, it is getting rather dark, isn't it? Don't you think we ought to be getting back?'

'We've only just come,' I said. 'I haven't shown you the place yet.'

'Is there something special?' she asked brightly, humouring me. 'But then we must be thinking of home. I'm beginning to want my tea.' Her hair was wild. The woods had streaked and scratched her, and there was a long rip down her skirt. She smiled at me gamely, her teeth more pitiful than she knew. But I was pitiless.

'Which way do you think it is?' I asked her.

'Which way? Back to the house, you mean? Really, Catherine, I'm sure I don't know.'

'Guess.' I turned slowly, all the way round, and she watched me. 'This way? Or this? What do you think?'

'A guessing-game! Whatever next?' She appealed to an invisible onlooker.

My nose was fine. I would catch it as soon as it came, that first acrid thread of fear.

'Yes, a guessing-game,' I said. 'Guess what happened here.'

'Really, Catherine, this isn't such awfully good fun, you know,' she said. She was trying to be one of us, the way she used to try. Using our language.

'It happened a long time ago,' I said. 'Guess.' The light was thickening. She was quite clear to me, but I wondered how well she could see my face. I put the spade by my side and knelt down on the earth, beginning to brush away the dead leaves.

'What are you doing, Catherine?'

'Looking for something we left here.'

She was watching me with her mouth a little open. Ten minutes ago she would have asked if I was digging for treasure, but the heart was leaking out of her. 'It was around here that we buried it,' I murmured. She had to strain forward to hear me, but she heard me.

'What? What did you bury?' Her voice was sharp.

'The hare,' I said. 'We brought it here and buried it. Rob shot it in the field. Do you think the bones will still be here?'

'That's why you brought that spade,' she said.

'Yes,' I said. 'Partly. It's ill-luck to meet a hare, did you know that? It's a pity you haven't got your scarab pin.' She put her hand to her throat as if to fasten herself together. 'There's a poem Kate told me,' I went on. 'You have to say it when you meet the hare, to take away the ill-luck. We could say it when we find the bones. The hare has a hundred names, did you know that? You must call her by all of them. *Call him ditch-diver, broken-leg, black-on-the-ears, white belly, beat-the-wind* . . . We buried the hare just about here,' I went on, patting the ground. 'That's strange, it feels warm. What if the hare were to break out of the soil and leap past us? If I leave my hand here, do you think I might feel her kick at the earth? She would come out of the ground with her ears laid back, ready to run. She was big, you know, as big as a young child. Do you believe in ghosts, Miss Gallagher?'

'They are against my religion,' she said, as firmly as she could.

'Not against mine,' I said, 'I've seen them. Besides, if there weren't ghosts, who could bear anyone going?'

'They go to eternal happiness, Catherine.'

'That's lucky, then.' I brushed my hands and stood up with the spade in them. It made a clean, heavy shape, swinging of its own weight.

'You're not going to dig it up, are you?' asked Miss Gallagher.

'No,' I said, 'perhaps not. You've made me change my mind.'

She liked that. I felt her pleasure, though it was nearly too dark to see her expression.

'I told you a lie,' I said. 'It wasn't Rob who shot the hare. It was me.'

'Nonsense, Catherine, you couldn't shoot then. You were only a little girl.'

'Oh yes, I could. Rob taught me, but we didn't let anyone else know. I was a good shot.'

'We must be getting back, Catherine. It's much too cold to stand here talking.'

Her voice was brisk, a governess' voice. But she couldn't fool me, not any more.

'I like it here,' I said, hefting the spade a little. 'Isn't it one of those places that makes you want to stay?'

'I'm tired,' she said. 'I'm not feeling well. You're not well, Catherine. You should be in bed.'

'Really? Do you think there's something wrong with me?'

'You're pale,' she gabbled. 'You need rest.'

'You can't even see me,' I pointed out, 'not properly.'

'Catherine!'

'A moral idiot. Is that what you think? Say it again.'

'Catherine, stop it!'

'No one saw you come, did they?' I said. 'I wish I had my brother here. These leaves make a good bed. Wouldn't you like to sleep here, Miss Gallagher? Shall we lie down?'

She made a dive but the brambles caught her before I did.

'Sit down,' I said, and she flumped on to the leaves. She whimpered a little and I forgot for a moment it was her and felt tender, as if she were an animal.

'Hush,' I said, 'you'll frighten the hare. But I told you a lie. It wasn't a hare we killed. It was something else.'

She was crying now. If there'd been more light I would have seen the tears and slime on her face. '*The hill-leaper,*' I said, '*the dew-thumper, the ghost in the grass.* Do you believe in ghosts, Miss Gallagher? You made me kill her. If it hadn't been for you no one else would have known.'

I held the spade high. She saw it and burrowed down into herself, yapping with terror. Her hat was knocked off and her white bony neck gleamed under a thin knot of hair. The noise she made was thin and high and it went on and on. The thrush sang again, suddenly, startled.

'You frightened him,' I said, 'why did you do that?' The spade sliced down hard, into the earth. I felt the sing and shiver of it, and her noise stopped.

'It didn't touch you,' I said scornfully. 'Get up.'

She had keeled over like a doll and was lying sideways on the earth. She was pretending I had hurt her, but I knew that all I had done was frighten her. She was all right.

'Get up,' I said again, but she didn't move. Perhaps she had fainted. It was almost too dark to see, and I had forgotten to bring a candle. That was stupid. I bent down as close as I could without touching her. She was breathing in big, snoring breaths, and stuff was running out of the side of her mouth. While I watched she twitched suddenly, twice, her whole body jerking in its parcel of clothes, then the snoring stopped.

I stood, and picked up the spade and the sacks. It was dark, but I could find my way in and out of this wood blindfold. There was the feather touch of old man's beard blown against my face to guide me, and smooth holly trunks when I put out my fingers. The earth cupped my moving feet at each step. I would leave her there and slowly the hurt place would heal over. She would be ugly at first, but they would make her beautiful. They would all come out, the wood mice, the voles, the rabbits, the big spiders spinning out their stretchy webs. At first they would be frightened but then they would come closer, touching her cheeks and the hem of her dress. They'd walk around her until they had mapped the world her body made, then they would begin to climb. In the morning the rooks would rise boasting from their shaggy nests, and swirl above the clearing where she lay stiff with winter dew and starred all over with the points of spiders' webs. A cold fresh breeze would rustle through the undergrowth, and for a while the thrush I'd heard would sing.

Seventeen

They were playing cards.

'Two-handed bridge,' my brother said, 'Want to join in?'

'How can I if it's two-handed?'

'Share Kate's hand. Or mine if you like.'

Kate was wearing a new dress. I'd seen her sewing it but it looked quite different on her body. The colour was a dark, dusty rose, almost brown in its folds. Her face took a new soft colour from it, and she had twisted a tortoiseshell comb into her hair.

'You look beautiful, Kate,' I said, stroking a fold of her skirts. The cloth was very soft, and there was a sheen on it which I'd never seen on plain wool.

'It's cashmere,' said Kate.

'Cashmere!' It must have cost her a year's wages. I looked at Rob but he was smiling down at his cards.

'It's my afternoon off,' said Kate, 'so I thought I'd dress myself for a change.'

She had cut out the dress with a plain round neck and added a small lace collar. Kate had some bits of lace from home, collars and handkerchiefs, creamy and soft. She rinsed them in rainwater from the water butt, just as she rinsed her long hair in rainwater and splashed it on her skin in the mornings. *You should try it, Cathy. Better than any of those old lotions they advertise in the newspapers.* But I could never be bothered. The dress was simple because Kate could not sew to a difficult pattern, but all she needed was that warm-shadowed cloth moulding to her breasts and hips. The rose cashmere made you think of how it was touching her.

'Will you look at these,' said Kate, spreading out her cards so I could see them, 'what would you do with a hand like this?'

But it was a good hand, I thought. 'Play it,' I said.

'Mmm,' said Kate, staring down at the cards. She didn't even glance across at Rob; you wouldn't have thought she was playing with him. 'Oh well.' Then she glanced up at me. 'Hasn't she come in then? You got rid of her, did you? I made sure she'd ask herself back to tea. *I'm ready for my tea, aren't you, Catherine?*' she mimicked in Miss Gallagher's high, chivvying voice.

The imitation was too good: Kate's voice flickered over my skin, making it crawl. But I said woodenly, 'Who?'

'You know. Herself. Didn't she come in with you?'

Heat flashed up me. What had she seen? I looked down, shielding myself by scanning her cards again. 'I've only just come in,' I said casually. 'Who's been here?'

'I made sure she went out with you,' said Kate. 'I watched the pair of you going round the side of the house when I was up at the window. Did she go off then? I thought you were going for a walk.'

'Oh – Miss Gallagher. Yes, we did. But she left.'

'Was it a nice walk with Euniss then? Where did you take her?'

'Into the woods,' I said.

I felt Rob watching me. His eyes were dark, attentive pools. He was staring at me across the card table, but I wouldn't look back. I watched the cards, but the gas light glared on us and my face would not stay still. I never had a twitch but something was plucking at the corner of my mouth. They knew I had been with her.

She wouldn't be missed for a while. A whole day perhaps, if we were lucky. But when people started to ask for Miss Gallagher, Kate would know that she'd been here. It didn't matter that Rob knew, because that was the same as me knowing. I thought of Miss Gallagher wobbling home on her bicycle in the last light of the afternoon to make her solitary tea. Her house would be dank and quiet. She did not light a fire until evening if she could help it. Why? Coal was cheap, and we'd have given her wood. It was like her not to have a fire. Head up, legs slowly pumping up and down as the spokes ticked round and round. I heard the crunch of stones under her tyres and the tiny chatter of gravel inside her wheels. I had heard it so many times that I could not stop believing in it. Who was to say it wasn't still going on? Kate believed it was. Kate knew it was just an ordinary day. Here they were, playing cards, and only the sunrise of Kate's cashmere made the quiet scene by the fire at all unusual.

If we kept quiet it could still be a day like any other. Miss Gallagher had gone for a walk with me and now she was on her way home. There she went, her face shiny with the evening mist, her mouth closed over her big yellow teeth and her eyes open and seeing.

'Cathy,' Rob said, 'tell us what's happened.'

He was always quicker than me. He'd jumped ahead and seen what I hadn't. There was danger in the pretence I'd begun. He had taken it all in as quick as thought. We had to cut in first. Be open, Cathy, show things as they are. There is still just time. His thoughts felt at me, urgent as exploring fingers. *Don't try to hide anything.* And the spade was back on its nail in the potting-shed, having touched no one. Her bicycle was deep in the rhododendrons. There was nothing else. I had not touched her. Kate looked from one of us to the other.

'What's wrong?' she asked. 'What's happened?'

'She fell down,' I said. 'She was ill suddenly, in the woods, and she fell down and started breathing wrong. It was like snoring. I didn't know what to do. It was nearly dark. I couldn't carry her. I would have hurt her, dragging her back through the woods.'

'Did you try? Did you touch her?' asked Rob.

'No,' I said.

His eyes brimmed with something I couldn't easily read. I had never seen him look at me like that, and I knew all his expressions. He leaned forward and gripped my wrist, hard.

'Why didn't you tell us as soon as you came in?' he asked, and I knew it wasn't a real question, but a question asked so that Kate could hear it, and hear its answer. It was a line he was feeding me. If I followed it Rob would rescue me. He was holding on to the line and waiting for me, the way he always was. He would never let me fall. I tried to say his name but the other things came with it and filled my mouth like blood after a blow.

'It was the shock,' said Kate. 'Look at her face. Look at her eyes. She's been ill, she's in no fit state for any of this. Of course that one would be taken ill just where she could do most harm. Not that she's dead nor near it, so don't you think it, Cathy.'

'Then the noise stopped,' I said. 'I think she stopped breathing.'

'It was all your imagination,' said Kate. 'You know what you are. She'll have fainted, that's all. Just a little faint looks bad enough when you're alone. Unless it was a stroke – it sounds a bit like the stroke my grandmother had. Was her face twisted up at all, Cathy?' And she screwed up her face at me inquiringly. Kate could never describe anything without mimicking it.

'I couldn't see. It was too dark.'

The fire flared and the red-and-black faces of the cards looked up at me, composed and full of secret merriment. That Jack would lead you a dance, Kate always said when the cards were dealt. She and Rob would look after me. Perhaps it was not so terrible after all, since here we were talking. No one had sent the cards flying and fluttering around the room.

'A stroke,' Kate repeated, gaining belief as she spoke. 'That's what it was. That'll be it for sure. Still, poor soul, she wants help. Where's she lying?'

'She's deep in the woods,' I said, 'But I can find her.'

'You shouldn't go out again,' said Rob. 'We'll need men to carry her. And lanterns.'

'Send to the village for the Semple boys.'

'No need to tell Grandfather yet.'

'And a blanket – you'll want a blanket to wrap her in. Poor idiot, but you've got to feel sorry for her.'

'Brandy, Kate – and a hot brick for her feet. Get a bed ready. We'll have to have her here till she can be moved.'

'God above, if it's not one invalid it's another. You'll have to be getting a trained nurse this time.'

'What we'll need is Dr Milmain. Send for him first off, Kate.'

They had it organized, and there was no need for me to say anything. It was all happening so quickly now, voices in the hall, messages, boots clopping across the flagstones. Nobody liked Miss Gallagher but this was a surge of life in the dead time of winter. Suddenly the Semple boys stood there in stockinged feet, big and serious with excitement. They wouldn't walk mud into the house, they said, they had been cleaning the clogged stream that ran to the millpond, and they'd been in mud to their – waists, they said delicately, seeing me.

'You ought to have the doctor to her,' said Theodore, looking at me. 'She looks poorly.'

'He's been sent for,' said Kate.

'Ah yes,' said Mrs Blazer with satisfaction, 'he's been sent for. That's right. And who's to tell her grandfather?'

'No need for that yet,' said Kate. 'He's in his study, not to be disturbed.'

The Semple boys nodded. God alone knew what the old man got up to in that study of his, but everyone knew he had the devil's temper if he was disturbed there. There was drama enough today without it. What were we good for if not to spice the lives that laboured for us? Here we were with a death among us, or as good as, and maybe more to come.

'Can you remember just where it was?' Rob asked me again. It seemed we had to say everything twice. Like actors, we had to show that we'd rehearsed. It looks like a play, I thought, the way all those faces turn to me, waiting for me to speak. And Rob and Kate watched me like prompters, turning the leaves of their scripts over in their hands.

'She ran back, you see, to get help,' Kate said, her eyes snapping round the circle of faces. She glowed in her beautiful dress as she poured brandy against the cold. She handed out blankets, bandages and lanterns while I sat like a dead thing. She was that woman in my Bible, the dark one, graceful, holding her pitcher on her hip with one negligent hand. The woman at the well, that was it. How fast I was thinking. My thoughts leapt and joined, forming fantastic patterns. But I would have to stir now, I knew it, if we were to get to her. I'd thought I could leave her with the owls and foxes, but although no one loved her they wouldn't leave her outside as if she were an animal. Look how we were all gathered to bring her home out of the night. They'd find her and fetch her home.

I hadn't seen her eyes because it was too dark and she was lying face down. People said that when a man was murdered you could find the image of his murderer if you looked into his eyes before he was cold. Like tiny mirrors they would show the face of the last one who had looked down on him.

If Rob was there he would stand in front of them all and make sure nobody saw. It was crows that took the eyes of young lambs. I'd seen it. But Miss Gallagher was lying on her face. She could not look at me now and there would be no pictures in her eyes. The owl was watching her, sitting on his branch.

'There's no moon,' I said.

'It doesn't matter. We've the lanterns,' said Rob.

'I never touched her.'

'Of course you didn't. Anyone would have been frightened to touch her, the way she was,' said Kate briskly. 'I wouldn't have liked to myself, for fear of doing more harm.'

Her talk led them away from me. Kate was a liar like the mother peewit trailing her wing as she piped the predator away from her nest.

'But you'll never find her. I'll have to come with you.'

'You can't do that, you're not fit for it,' said Rob. 'Just be sensible and try to tell us where she is.'

How strange it was to talk to Rob like that, every word spelled out for others to hear. It made us like two new, different people. 'You don't know the place. I'm all right now, Rob. It was just –'

'The shock,' Kate supplied, 'and then running back all that way. You might have hit your head on a branch without knowing it. You looked terrible. I thought you were ill yourself.'

Everyone nodded, looking at me. It was right to be weak. They could almost love me for it. The Semple boys' rough springy hair was burnished bright by the lamps, and they looked at me pityingly, as if I were some hurt thing they'd found in the fields. They were known never to torment a bird fallen from its nest or a scattered litter of field-mice; it had been strange in them when they were boys.

'I'll have to show you,' I said, 'or you'll never find it.'
Words were beginning to loosen in me like the relief of fever
rising after the first sick, shivery aches of illness.

'We went past the horse-chestnuts, then deep into the
wood. She wanted to find the fountain.'

'What fountain? There isn't a fountain.'

'No, that was at Mr Bullivant's. We dug it out. But she
knew about it. You would never guess what was buried
under all that green. She wanted to see the windflowers.'

'They won't bloom for weeks yet,' said Theodore. 'Doesn't
she know nothing?'

'It was another flower, I can't remember it. My head won't
remember things. We went to the place of the hare. She
knows where everything's buried. She wants to see
everything.'

They were exchanging glances over my head, I knew it.
The words slid faster like a sleek of water pulled from
underneath as it comes to the lip of the waterfall.

'I mustn't say things,' I said. 'I can only do them. Let me
go with you.' I would fight the current. I pressed my lips
tightly together and turned against the current, letting it part
my hair like weeds. I swam harder and my face divided the
water like the prow of a ship. I saw rows of bubbles streaming
over my lips and I was silenced.

They let me go with them. I led them like an arrow,
though I had to stop and wait for them to fumble through
the trees with their lanterns. Rob was with me. He had to go
behind because there was only room for one to pass, and I
heard him breathing hard, harder than he ever breathed. He
was afraid. If we'd been alone I would have laughed at him
and told him there was nothing to be frightened of, but
Theodore was too close to him and then there was Dr Milmain.
I had to keep telling myself to slow down for them. The
wood breathed and crackled too, woken out of its sleep, but

its branches gave way for me as if they knew me, rolling back as smoothly as waves as I passed.

'It's like the Red Sea,' I said to Rob. 'Make sure you keep close to me.' Here were the silver sides of birches caught in lantern light. Holly threw shadows like pitch, and the ivy flapped close, wanting to wrap us to it. It was as still as the inside of a room which is out of use and sheeted over. The wood squeezed in on us, wanting to touch us and glad we had come. I didn't have to think about Miss Gallagher to find her. She was so close I could feel her.

'The thing about people when they're dead,' I said to Rob, 'is that you can't keep them in one place. They can go everywhere.'

'She'll be all right, don't worry,' he said loudly, for everyone to hear.

'It wasn't Miss Gallagher I was thinking of,' I whispered.

We churned up the smell of the wood with our boots. Dry sticks and lichen, leathery leaves, the dust that lives in tendrils of ivy. Each type of tree has a smell of its own if you peel back its bark. I thought of Mr Bullivant's new orchards bundled in straw against the frost. The flesh of his apples would be white and sweet when they grew. I had bitten my mother's arm once because it smelled of fruit when she leaned over me. Where I bit the creamy inside of her arm there grew a half-moon of red teethpoints. She did not punish me for it though it showed that night when she put on her silver dress.

'Little savage,' she called me, and she laughed. I saw the inside of her laughing mouth. 'Are her teeth pointed?' she asked Eileen. 'Does she file them like a cannibal queen?'

Behind me the lanterns tossed shadows against the trees and all around us the wood pressed in. We were coming to its dusty heart, where I had left Miss Gallagher. The wood opened to let me move.

'She's here,' I said.

She had turned on her back since I had left her. Our lantern light skittered across the big slab of her face and showed her eyes wide open. Dr Milmain shoved at my back.

'No,' I said, 'I must be the first to look at her.'

But she looked past me, at the sky where there was no moon. Her chin was up as if she had tried to say something; but then I saw it was only the uneven ground tipping back her head. Dr Milmain was too quick for me. He knelt at her chest, listening.

'Are they like mirrors?' I asked. 'Can you see anything in them?'

'What?' asked Rob.

'Her eyes.'

But Dr Milmain was putting his thumb on her eyelids, pressing them down. I could see everything. He pressed down firmly but the lids squeezed themselves up slowly each time he lifted the pressure of his fingers, and then he left her eyes as they were. There was nothing in them, I could see that now. There was no need to be afraid that I would find myself there.

'Heart,' said Dr Milmain, and he wiped his hands on his handkerchief. 'Some sort of seizure. We'll know more when we get her back, but I'll lay money it's heart. Nothing anyone could have done,' and he put his hand on my shoulder, the same hand that had pressed down on Miss Gallagher's dead eyelids. 'Nothing you could have done, so don't be thinking any more of it. She won't have suffered.'

The lantern shadows jangled as the Semple boys brought round their improvised stretcher in the tiny space of the clearing. They bungled her on to it somehow and tied her with lengths of crepe bandage. Their faces shone with sweat as they wound her coat tight to her sides. The rent was still there in her skirts. I thought it would have gone away. It seemed so long since she had torn it. And when they lifted

217

her there was dried mud crumbling from the heels of her boots.

'She'll do.'

'Got to ease her round.'

'Steady now, mind you don't tip her.'

'Hold still, boy.'

They called each other 'boy', the Semple boys, when they were working on a job together. They had got her safe and now they'd lurch her back through the trees to the house. They'd tied her neck so that her head wouldn't loll this way and that.

'Cover her face,' ordered the doctor. 'Here, have my handkerchief.'

'Case she gets scratched,' nodded Michael. 'Should've thought of that. Tie it nice and tight, boy.'

Rob and the doctor held up the lanterns to guide them. I was glad that Kate was not there. The brambles would have torn her cashmere to pieces and she'd never have been able to buy another. Besides it was better if Kate was not there with her long eyes flicking from face to face. She would be waiting for us with food and drink and a warm bed for Miss Gallagher.

'We must take out the hot brick before we lay her down,' I told Rob. 'We mustn't be like Kate's grandmother.'

There were other things Kate's grandmother had done, in the middle of all her praying by her son's dead body. She kept forgetting about his death and ordering hot bricks to warm him, but they wouldn't bring them. Once she had asked for a cup of tea to be brought up. Thinking that it was for her and it was a good sign, my aunt Kitty brought it, said Kate. Then through the door she heard her mother talking, telling her son to drink his tea before it got cold, with the price tea was these days it couldn't be wasted. When Kitty opened the door she was pouring it into Joseph's mouth. She hadn't let them tie his jaw decently closed, so his mouth gaped and the tea ran in and ran out again. I wondered if I would find myself bringing tea for Miss Gallagher. She liked sugar but she pretended she only took one lump. When no one was looking she would slip in another. No, I thought, she is dead. Her being dead was a bright certain space I must not lose hold of. I must not let myself think of bad things.

It was hard going back to the house. I felt like a swift which is safe as long as it stays in the air, cutting through air, feeding and sleeping on the wing. But they were slow carrying her, walking forward with their burden slipping about on the stretcher in spite of its ties, and I could not get past them. Rob had hold of my hand and I whispered to him that we could get back to the house a quick way if he came with me.

'No,' he said, 'stay with me, Cathy,' and so I stayed. I wished Mr Bullivant had been there, because I'd have liked to walk beside him.

'Did they send for Mr Bullivant?' I asked.

'No, why should they?'

'I'd like to see him.'

He was quiet, then suddenly he ducked down so his mouth was against my ear. 'You must be careful, Cathy,' he said. His breath tickled and I nearly laughed.

'You don't need to say those things to me,' I answered.

'She's dead. There are bound to be questions. Remember that you didn't touch her because you were frightened.'

'There's nothing to be frightened of any more,' I said. 'She can't do anything to us. She'll never open her mouth again, as long as they bandage her jaw.'

'Cathy!'

But Dr Milmain was on us, pushing between us.

'They'll crack her head against that trunk if they don't look out. Hey, steady there!' And the boys looked round startled, almost capsizing the stretcher.

'Steady, I said! It's not a dead pig on a pole you've got there. What a business, what a business!'

I felt the important huff of his breath. Theodore and Michael snorted.

'Heavy,' they said apologetically, but it had been a snort of laughter. The pig on a pole had made them laugh.

'She deserved it,' I whispered. 'She killed my baby,' but no one heard me.

When Kate knelt by the stretcher there was no doubt Miss Gallagher was dead. She crossed herself quickly. Against the rose cashmere the white dirty dead face did not change. There were burrs in her hair and scratch marks which had stopped bleeding.

'She didn't suffer,' said Kate. 'You can tell from her face. Look at the peace on it.' I looked but as usual Kate was quicker than me. I could see nothing but flesh and blood congealing into something else. If I hadn't known it was her I couldn't have recognized Miss Gallagher.

'Miss Gallagher,' I said, to make sure.

'Poor soul,' said Kate, 'to die with no one to call her by her christened name.'

'We'll get her upstairs now, and I'll make my examination,' said Dr Milmain.

Grandfather led the way upstairs with the long procession flowing behind him: Theodore and Michael with the stretcher, in their boots this time, flaking mud on to the floor; Kate with white towels draped over one arm and a jug of hot water as if someone were getting ready for dinner, and Mrs Blazer creaking upstairs in the leather slippers she slit at the side to give room to her bunions. Annie wasn't there. She could not bear the sight of a dead body, not even a bird. Except a table bird, of course. I stayed still, watching them go up.

Rob and I were alone in the hall. There was that look on his face again, the one I could not read.

'When Kate's finished I'll send her to you. She'll help you undress.'

'I'm not ill. I don't need any help.'

He stood near to me but not touching me. 'You're not yourself, Cathy. You must rest. Go to your room and I'll send Kate.'

'I don't want Kate. You come.'

'I'll have to talk to Dr Milmain.'

'Grandfather can do that.'

'No, Cathy. I need to get things clear with him.'

'She's dead, isn't she? That's clear enough.'

'You mustn't talk about it like that!' He took hold of both my elbows and held me facing him, our faces close.

'Like what? What do you mean?'

'You don't know how you sound. Listen, Cathy. Promise me you won't talk to anyone about it. Not even Kate.'

I looked at him. He was fresh and beautiful from the winter night. I smiled but he didn't smile back.

'Let go of my arms,' I said. 'What's the matter with you?'

'Go to bed, Cathy. You need sleep,' but his hands slackened and I pulled my elbows sharply down and sideways to break his grip, the way he had shown me when we were children.

'There!' I stood laughing at him. 'I'll go up, but you must come to me later.'

'I can't, Cathy. They'll be here half the night. Dr Milmain and everyone. They'll all be awake in the village. She's dead, don't you realize?'

'I realize,' I said.

My heart was as light as summer. It was all finished and gone and we could start again. I hadn't hurt anyone. It was a summer morning and mist was thinning over the wood. In a minute Rob would wake in the bed opposite me and we would throw off our bedclothes and run out without stopping to dress. My thick night-plait would thud between my shoulder blades as we ran down the long rough slope of the lawn. Our feet would leave wet black prints in the dew and we would scare the deer feeding on tender shoots in the rose garden. There was the whole long day before us: the cool shadows splashed across the garden thinning to the heat of noon, the long afternoon in the shade of the mulberry tree, the blue twilight in the woods. Rob would carry me on his back across the bog by the pond where everything simmered and grew juicily in a soup of water and green treacherous ground. He'd tread down water forget-me-nots and wild peppermint, and make tiny frogs shoot sideways like stars.

But Rob was looking at me. Very, very slightly, without moving, he was shrinking back and away from me. He had that look in his eyes again and this time it was not unreadable, though it was a page that I had never read before. Always before when I'd looked at him I'd seemed to see a bit of myself there, looked after and held in love, and now I looked and looked and couldn't find it. His eyes were open but they were closed to me.

'Rob,' I said, and he tensed, trying to guess his way ahead of what I'd say next. 'Rob, where did Kate get the cashmere for her dress?'

He didn't answer, but I saw a tiny contraction in his pupils. My brother was afraid of me. It was not for my sake that he wanted me out of sight, but for his own.

Eighteen

'It's never been my home,' said Kate. I was talking to the back of her head as she knelt, packing layers of clothes into her tin box.

'Wouldn't you like a trunk?' I asked. 'There's an attic full of trunks and we never use them. You could have one, I'm sure.'

'No, metal is better. The damp can't get in. There's always damp on a ship, because the salt draws it. And I'd like to see the rat that could gnaw its way into here.'

'Rat?'

'Oh, there's always rats. If you've a baby you keep it close.'

She stood up, rubbing her back, and kicked the corner of the box triumphantly. 'There, you brute. I'll be done with you soon.'

Her box was almost full. She had more clothes than I would have thought, and she had her own sheets too, which she had brought with her years before in case sheets weren't provided for servants. We had sheets for everyone, so hers had laid clean and creased, put away for years in a brown-paper parcel. Dried fragments of sweet woodruff fell out of them when she shook them out. Then there were the things my mother had handed on to her: an air-blue silk with one of its breadths scorched by careless ironing, a white satin petticoat and a close-fitting plaid skating jacket. Kate had been going to make over the silk for years, but she never had. Still, she'd take it with her. It was good silk. She had packed her working dresses and aprons, her Sunday dress and her lace wrapped in tissue paper.

'There's the pin-cushion I gave you!' I picked it up and

squeezed its fat softness. I didn't think she had kept it. It had her name embroidered on it in pink silk, and it was stuffed with sheep's wool which I had gathered from the hedges and washed, because everyone knew that pins stuck in sheep's wool would never rust. 'Too good to use,' Kate had said, and she had never used it.

The sunlight slanted in and showed up the bare patches on the oilcloth. There was a paler oblong on the wall where Kate had taken down her one family photograph. When I was a child she would bring it downstairs to show me when I begged her, and those stiff, set faces had become people to me, coloured by the stories Kate had told me so often that I almost believed they were my own memories. There was Joseph, alive and standing at his mother's side, arms folded. Behind them a waterfall streamed and willows wept over a little rustic bridge.

'Is that near where you live?' I had asked Kate once, tracing the curve of the waterfall through the glass, but she had laughed. It was a photographer's background, that was all, a painted cloth spread out behind the people on their chairs. You could choose the cloth you wanted. She remembered it well because there'd been an argument over whether they should have *My Rose Garden* or *Country Peace*. 'It was bad enough to get us all in the one room for that photograph, Cathy. But I thought Joseph and my grandfather would come to blows over that backcloth.' You would never have guessed it. The faces gazed out, empty and solemn, and I hardly recognized Kate.

'God, it's airless in here,' said Kate. She pushed back her hair, went over to the window and unhooked it. It swung back and fresh cold air poured in, filling the attic, smelling of rain and new things.

'You could tell with your eyes shut that it was spring,' said Kate. She folded her cashmere over and over, trapping it in layers of tissue paper.

'There, that's it. I've only to put in my last things.'

I looked through the swinging window at the landscape of the roof. The flaws in the glass made the tiles cockle up like seashells. Kate was going across the sea, back to Ireland. She'd find work there easily enough; indeed she had a place half-promised, she told us. She looked round the almost empty attic exultantly.

'You wouldn't know I'd ever been here.'

'Of course you would.'

I was tongue-tied. Kate was leaving and there was no arguing her out of it. She planned and packed with the rapid decisiveness I'd always loved, and I had to love the deft movements of her hands even now when they were acting against me. She had her railway ticket and her passage across the Irish Sea, and she would be met by her cousin, Aunt Kitty's son. This time next week she would be lining drawers with paper and unpacking her clothes in a room I'd never seen.

'I was sick as a dog when I came over,' she said, stretching up her arms and laughing. 'There was a woman with her children running wild on the ship while she called on all the saints to help her. I remember now those children's feet thudding past my head. They hadn't a pair of boots between them but their feet were tanned like leather. I wondered if they'd trample me, but I was past caring.'

'You were only fourteen,' I said.

'That's true. But I was a big girl. God, I can see it now, the tops blowing off the waves and those kids racing around the rails. Thank God we were up on deck. I'd have died below.'

The ship was real now, not us. She was still with us but we were going into the past, growing small like a country seen from a departing ship. Already she belonged to the rise and fall of the waves and the slap of the wind.

'No, it's never really been home. Well, you couldn't expect it,' she said again.

'I suppose not,' I said, smoothing down the neat oblongs of her packing. She would leave the lid of the box off for now. There was no lock, but she had a chain to wind through the fastenings, and a padlock for it. I stood up and walked over to the window where pale sun fell on my arms. I didn't know the view from here because Kate had never liked us to come up to her room, but now she didn't care. The room was nothing to her; it could be anybody's. Soon there'd be just her striped, lumpy mattress on its iron frame, the peeling whitewash, the oilcloth, a couple of hairpins on the floor and the smell of Kate, fading.

It's never been home. But when I said *Kate* I was saying *mother* or *sister*, I wanted to tell her. It was always you in that space. You can't go, because you're taking too much of me with you.

'You'll be all right, Cathy,' she said. Silence hung between us like a sheet we couldn't fold. We weren't easy with each other any more. She didn't come to my room to help me brush my hair and tell me the gossip by firelight.

'It was my mother's,' I said suddenly, 'wasn't it?'

'What?' asked Kate, so quickly that I knew I was right.

'The cashmere. It was my mother's, wasn't it?'

'You're not thinking that I took it. Your brother gave it to me.'

'I knew I'd seen it before,' I said. It must have been bought before my mother went away, when she thought she'd have a dress made up from it, and then it had been left behind with all her other things. I must have seen it in her wardrobe, folded and wrapped, and that was why I'd half-recognized it when Kate wore her dress. 'I don't mind,' I said. 'It might as well be used.'

'It's not for you to mind,' said Kate. She looked at me with an antagonism I'd never seen. She'd often been angry with me, but this was different, as if I were just another woman trying to slight her.

'It suits you,' I said to placate her. 'Things ought to go to the people who can wear them.'

'If I've any use for it where I'm going,' said Kate, then she flushed.

'Of course you will. More than you have here.'

'We'll see.'

'Remember that dress of mine – the pink silk? Wasn't it awful?'

She smiled briefly. Then she looked hard at me. 'You've a bit of colour today. You must get yourself out, Cathy. Away from here.'

'That's what Mr Bullivant says.'

As soon as I said it I remembered I must never say that name to her. But instead of growing angry she looked at me steadily, puzzling me out.

'It wasn't him, was it?'

'No.'

'I've thought so for a while. And you couldn't say his name like that if it was.'

'It was no one you know,' I said.

'You must forget it,' she said. 'I know you. You're always carrying things inside you, where they do no good. And you won't have me here to shake you out of it.'

'I know. You don't have to tell me.'

'It's better if I go,' said Kate. 'You don't think it but it is. With me here you'll stay the way you are for ever. Remember what I said when I'm gone, Cathy.'

For a moment something older and kinder than the Kate who was packing her box looked out of her eyes, then she slammed down the lid. 'I'll shut this up anyway – might as well. I've only my night clothes and my wages to put in it.'

'I've got you something,' I said. 'A present.'

I had it in my pocket, in a small box lined with midnight-blue velvet. I held it out to her. She took the box, but she didn't open it.

'Go on, open it now. I want to see what you think of it.'

Reluctantly she undid the little gilt catch and the box sprang open. The ring lay there, dug into the blue velvet. The colour slept inside the opal, but as soon as it was held up to the light it would catch fire.

'You can't give me this.'

'Yes I can. It belongs to me now.'

'It's your mother's.'

'No. She had it in her jewel box but it was never hers. It was my grandfather's – my other grandfather. You wouldn't guess it was a man's ring, would you? He had slender fingers, like my father. It was left to me when my father died.'

Kate took out the ring and tried it on the third finger of her right hand. 'It's too tight. My hands are ruined with work.'

'It'll fit on your little finger.'

She eased it over the knuckle and turned her hand round. The ring didn't look quite right there. The milkiness of the stone showed up the reddening of her fingers, and the gold band was slightly too narrow for her broad, shapely hands.

'Isn't it beautiful?' I asked.

'It is.' She examined it slowly, twisting it this way and that. The heart of the opal flashed as if it had been put away only yesterday. 'Some people say opals are unlucky, but I don't think so,' I said.

'You ought to keep it for yourself.'

'I'd rather think of it on you, going where you go.'

She looked at me and I knew she wanted it.

'Go on, don't be silly. I want you to have it.'

'Then I will. You're very good, Cathy.'

'No, I'm not. I'm not at all.'

She brushed my cheek with her hand. It was the clumsiest gesture I ever saw her make, and I knew we wouldn't kiss or cling to each other when she left.

'I'll wear it to keep it safe,' she said, 'but not until I've left here. I don't want any talk.'

'You'll come back to visit us, Kate. It's not so very far.'

Kate turned the ring again, her head bent over the stone. When she looked up at me she was crying. Her face didn't move but her tears slid sideways, covering her cheeks. I wanted to comfort her but I didn't think she wanted me to touch her any more.

'You'll come again,' I repeated.

'It's not likely, Cathy,' she said in a whisper, and she pushed away the tears with the back of her hands.

It had happened so quickly. We'd all had to go to Miss Gallagher's funeral, naturally. There were no mourners from outside the village, and it was mizzling gently. The vicar stood with his boots planted firm in the wet, heavy earth, and rocked back and forth slightly as he droned out the words of the committal. He'd known her well, he said, but I doubted it. The box with Miss Gallagher in it went down slowly, rocking in its bands until it bumped to rest at the bottom of the hole. There was a faint sucking noise as the coffin settled. People glanced furtively at the sky. If it rained any harder it would take the dye out of their black bonnets. Grandfather was gesturing to me. I stared back, unable to work out what he wanted.

'She's no family,' Kate hissed in my ear. 'He wants you to drop the first clod.'

'No. No, I don't want to.'

Rob stepped forward quickly and took the ornate little shovel the gravedigger handed him. He held it high and let drop pieces of earth on Miss Gallagher's coffin.

'You ought to have done it. It was you she loved,' Kate said.

Rob's hair was dark with rain. He had taken off his hat and was holding it in front of him. His head was bowed. The wind was getting up, sighing in the big elms at the corner of the churchyard where rooks nested. No one wept but there were coughs and sniffs which did for the sounds of sorrow. A group of boys kept jumping up to look over the churchyard wall. Sometimes the tops of their heads appeared, and their eyes, then they must have got together to hoist one boy high, because the top half of his body came clear of the wall and he stared across at us, collecting every look and word. When we'd gone they'd come in and look at the new grave, and one of them might be bold enough to stand for a second on top of its heaped earth and say to himself that he was standing on top of her. She'd never liked any boy, though it was Rob she'd hated.

As we turned from the grave and walked along the path towards the lych-gate Kate fell back from where she'd been at my side. Grandfather was giving directions about the grave. He was to pay for her headstone, because she'd had no money and the relations she'd spoken of couldn't be drummed up. Besides, she'd died on his land. She should have been left there, I thought. She would have sunk back into the earth quietly, without this show and the thud of soil on to wood. It was like Grandfather to order a coffin with brass fittings and a white satin lining. She'd had nothing as beautiful when she was alive.

Now Rob was walking beside Kate. They looked serious, calm and oddly alike, as if the same thoughts ran in their minds. I stood and waited for them, watching Kate's skirt sweep drops of rain off the long grass by the edge of the path, and Rob's boots walking in step with hers.

'Are you all right, Cathy? You look pale,' said Rob. Everything he said to me sounded false and unnecessary.

'I'm all right.'

'Well, it's over,' said Kate, 'and at least she's decently buried.' Then she looked at me quickly.

'When do they fill in the grave over her?' I asked.

'Once we've gone, they'll begin.'

'It makes it seem so strange, doesn't it, the noise of the earth on the coffin? As if she's really dead.'

'She *is* really dead,' said Rob.

'It's the rain,' I said. 'She didn't like it. That's why she wore her mackintosh. And now we go home and take off our wet things and she stays here and it doesn't matter because she can't feel the cold or the rain.'

'She's snug enough, anyway,' said Kate. 'That was a fine coffin your grandfather bought.' Rob laughed suddenly, a quick, unseemly explosion. The rain fell harder and it parted his hair and ran over his forehead like drops of sweat. Kate took a handkerchief out of her pocket, reached up and wiped his face, but as soon as she did it more rain ran down. I looked back across the churchyard but Miss Gallagher's grave was hidden in a fine mist.

'Let's go back to the house,' said Rob. 'There's some food.'

'Tea and sandwiches!' said Kate scornfully. 'Oh well, let her die as she lived.' Then she laughed. 'Would you look at that!' A fat squat duck was waddling down the muddy lane outside the church. Seeing us it stood still, then turned in purposefully and came up the church path towards us.

'You'd make a fine dinner, wouldn't you? I'll have you if you don't watch out,' said Kate to the duck.

'Break its neck and hide it under your skirt,' suggested Rob.

'I would, too. But not now, there's too many people about. We'll come back after dark.'

'I'll help you. I'll wring its neck for you,' said Rob, and he laughed.

'That's the best promise I've had from a man for a long time,' she said, and she laughed back at him while the duck shovelled about in the verges. Damp had curled her hair up under her bonnet, and brightened her colour, and for a second I saw her as Rob did, fresh and vigorous, the funeral rolling off her and forgotten. She always loved the rain and liked to be out in it, striding miles with her skirts kilted up above her ankles. Was it then she first thought of going, when she saw the fine fat duck waddle through the column of mourners? I stood stupidly beside them, disliking my own presence. My mourning was shabby and it smelled of dye and old sweat. My body had been thin and then fat and now it was thin again. Whatever it looked like I didn't feel as if I lived in it any more. I might have left myself there in the mist on her grave without knowing, like a caul in the rain.

'It's over,' I said, and they both looked at me as if they'd forgotten I was there. I can shut my eyes and see their two faces now, while I hear rooks and a hammer beating somewhere, and people's mourning voices starting to lighten as they moved away from the funeral and down the lane. Less than a month later Kate was packing her box.

Nineteen

'You can't stay in your room all the time. You must go out.'

'I don't want to. I like it here.'

'Come on, Cathy, we'll go shooting. You like that. We'll have pigeon-pie tomorrow.'

'No. I can't go out, not today.'

I hadn't been out since the funeral. I saw the outside world in slices from one window or another. Out there was a white, swallowing silence; in here, if I concentrated, I could wake up, dress myself, move about. Time moved oddly. Sometimes I'd be in a room and not know how I'd got there, or I'd be in the middle of washing, stroking the water over my arms again and again, and I'd know from the gooseflesh on my arms that I'd been there a long time. Here was my hand, with a fork in it, raising a brown bundle of fibres to my mouth. It was braised beef and I was eating my dinner. I must not look too long at anything or Grandfather would notice. Outside the window the arm of a bush tapped steadily at the glass, like a signal.

'Time I asked George Bullivant over to play chess. Should you like that, Cathy? Should you like a game?' Grandfather reached over and poured some wine into my glass. It was the colour of straw and it smelled of sweat. After the first sip I put down my glass.

'Take a glass of wine, Cathy. It will do you good.'

His dark eyes fixed me, attentive as a hawk's. He thought I was missing Miss Gallagher. He had the idea that women wanted other women about.

'Let me peel you an apple.' He picked through the fruit bowl to find me the best one. There were russets, beginning to wrinkle now, but still firm-fleshed. When Grandfather peeled an apple he turned the fruit into the knife-blade and brought off the peel in one long curling piece. I picked up the peel and shaped it back into a globe, empty inside. My apple had gone brown and I couldn't eat it.

Opposite me Rob swallowed off his port and reached for more.

'Haven't you had enough?' asked my grandfather.

'No, not yet,' said Rob, and he poured a deliberate stream of the wine, holding the decanter slightly too high so that we could see that his hands were perfectly steady and the port fell clear into the centre of the glass.

'It's hideous stuff, anyway,' Rob went on. 'You have to drink it fast if you don't want to taste it.'

'It's the last I'm buying. You'll pay for the next yourself.'

Grandfather's hand with the fruit knife in it drummed at the tablecloth, marking the linen where Eileen had webbed it with neat darns, years back. My hand jumped slightly with the drumming of the knife.

Upstairs Kate was walking about. These nights she sat up late, I knew, because I saw the yellowness of her candlelight seeping down the stairs. I didn't know it but she was already packing in her mind.

My grandfather touched my shoulder where the blades made wings. If I looked over my shoulder in candlelight I could see the wings pointing out of my skin. When they grew a little more I would be flying. Eileen used to say if a new-born baby could speak it would tell us what it was like to fly with the angels, but by the time the baby had learned to talk it had forgotten. Grandfather's hand stayed on my shoulder. He ought not to touch me, it might hurt him. Everything in me was sharp and burning. I twisted away, and he sat back heavily in his chair. Later I heard him talking to Rob over my head. Everyone was talking at me and over me and through me.

'Grapes. What about grapes?'

'She likes grapes.'

'The sun's quite warm enough if she wraps herself in a rug and sits in a sheltered spot. The fresh air would give her an appetite. Get some colour in her cheeks.'

'She hasn't been out since I don't know when.'

'It's the shock.'

'Seeing it happen.'

'I never realized she was so fond of the woman.'

'Still waters run deep.'

'Why doesn't she go out?'

'Kidneys. No, liver, that's the thing to give her.'

'Ought to have it raw.'

'Squeeze lemon juice on it and chop it fine and you don't taste it.'

'It's for her own good.'

'My mother swore by sarsaparilla. It cleanses the blood.'

'Who'd have thought she'd pine for her like this?'

'She looked very bad at the funeral.'

'Course, it's no life for a young girl. You've got to feel sorry for her.'

'And her colour – it's terrible.'

'Her skin's like candle wax.'

'You've got to get the blood moving.'

They weren't real voices, they were just the blood moving. If I turned my head too quickly it sizzled in my ears and made words.

'If you don't try, Cathy, I can't help you,' said Rob. But who was he to tell me when he'd been drinking again? I could smell it on him, not fresh drink but the smell of last night coming out through his skin. He didn't smell like my Rob any more.

'There's nothing wrong with me,' I said.

'You should eat. Why don't you go out? I'll go for a walk with you, just round the garden. We needn't go far.'

'I've had enough of walking. And I am eating. Look.' I picked up a knife and cut my tea cake into tiny squares. One by one I put them into my mouth and swallowed them. There was a salt slither of butter on my tongue, then the dryness of the cake. I had to think about each chew and swallow, but if I concentrated I could still do it. 'There.' I looked at Rob triumphantly.

'You can't have tasted it. Why do you eat like that?'

'I can't do everything for you!' I spat out. 'Haven't I done enough?'

But I could still be calm. For an hour or two I could stitch time together and keep my fear on the fringes of my mind. When Kate told me she was going the first thing I said was to ask her whether she had found a place yet. I told her she could be sure of an excellent reference. The day we sat in the attic and talked while Kate packed there was a little space between what happened and the reality of it. That day everything was easy. I sat and watched her pack and I gave her the opal ring. It was more than she expected, and she was ill at ease, not me. Kate didn't steal my mother's dress, so someone must have given it to her and I knew who. Sunlight blew in through the window and there was the kindness of its warmth on our skins, the first real warmth after the winter. I was kind with the ring. I looked at the shapes of the roof slanting away and thought I wouldn't be afraid to step out on to them, but I said nothing to Kate. I've always had a great sense of balance and I never minded the drop at my feet, no matter how high I was, as long as I had a foothold. When she'd finished packing and the lid of the box was down she went away to make some last visits in the village.

I said to Rob, 'I ought to go away, not Kate,' and he didn't tell me not to go. Instead he said, 'But where would you go?' and I looked at him, longing for him to tell me I must always stay, I was as much part of him as the blood running round his body. But he said nothing more, and only looked at me with the quiet wariness that pushed me even farther away from him.

Once I did go out. I walked as far as the top of the drive, where we had waited for Miss Gallagher to collect us in the trap to go and see Father in The Sanctuary. At first I was quite safe because I made a tunnel in my mind and walked in its safety, and whenever the sides wavered I plastered them together so nothing could come through. But when I was at the top of the drive I thought I was stronger than I was and I let myself slip into knowing how far I was from the house. The trees changed from themselves and became unreal as paintings. I put out my hands as if I was swimming. I looked round quickly, jerkily, at the trees, the wall, the gate, the sky. I could not see the house. Even if I ran I could never run in one breath. Gaps came in my tunnel faster than I could patch them together, and the world began to pour through. My heart was beating faster and faster and I could not breathe. The noise in my ears hurt me.

'You're all right,' I said to myself loudly and angrily, dragging in the breath for it. 'Don't be so stupid. Don't be such a fool. You're as safe here as you are in the house,' but this time it didn't work. I could not run, so I shrank into myself and curled up there on the drive and lay in a ball where nothing could get into me and then the world broke on me like a rough sea.

Rob found me. He had to talk for a long time before I knew it was him. I thought he was something happening inside my head. I don't remember what I said but I was crying and shaking. I'd never cried before although two people had died.

I wanted him to stay with me and hold me but he was frightened and he tried to pull me up and get me back to the house.

'It's not far,' he kept saying. 'Come on Cathy. Another step.'

He should have left me there. Nothing worse would have happened, and perhaps after a while I'd have uncurled and looked up at the branches tangling the sky and everything would have been back in its place: the wet oak leaves plastering my knees, the rustle of sparrows which had come out to look at me, the cool wind sifting my hair. I would have watched the sparrows bounce closer and heard nothing but their cheeping. I would never have been frightened again.

When we got back to the house Rob didn't want to be with me. I knew why he was afraid. He thought I was ill because of Miss Gallagher. *I'll deal with her*, I'd said, and Rob remembered it.

'Don't worry,' I said when we got to my room, 'I'll be all right. Just leave me for a bit. I'll rest.' I lay on the bed and let myself sink down as if I would vanish into the shape my own body had made over the years. I shut my eyes.

'I'm no good to you, am I,' he said, not making it a question.

I smiled. He was so wrong that there was no point in answering, but I could tell him that another time. I had to get him out of the room while I was still strong. I wanted him so much, but every time I tried to pull him to me it made things worse.

'I just make it worse. I make things worse for you,' he said, and he left a space for me to answer. But I couldn't say anything then. I was fighting too hard. I was in the ditch with my father, sweating and trembling. I couldn't have anyone near me who was afraid of me, and I knew I'd be better alone.

'I should never – ' he said, then he stopped.

'It's all right,' I said quickly. 'Never mind. It doesn't matter.'

That was when he went up the stairs and met Kate. I'm only guessing, but I'm sure of it really. I know how it happened as if I had been there, in Rob's skin. She came round the turn of the stairs with kindling in her arms and she saw at once from his face that something was wrong and he needed her.

They both had their secrets. I wonder if they've ever told them? Kate is the only one who knows where my daughter is buried. And Miss Gallagher's dead, knowing what Rob and I did at night in the narrow space of my bed. She took with her that tiny image of us twined and sleeping. Rob thinks he knows what happened in the wood. If I said again that she fell down before I had a chance to touch her he would want to believe it, but in the end uncertainty would creep back, a cloud growing to cover the day. I can't give him certainty because I haven't got it. I go back to the woods in my mind and I hear her voice. Did I touch her?

There wasn't a mark on her. Dr Milmain had to write down her cuts and bruises for his report, but they were made by bramble and stone, not human hands. It was just a weakness waiting in her body, and it could have happened at any time.

'We all carry our deaths around with us,' said Dr Milmain, 'but if we're lucky we don't know what they are.'

Everyone reassured me, but there's still a little gap that no one knows about except me. Sometimes it closes up so it's as thin as a hairline, then at other times it gapes wide, but it's always there. It separates me from people.

I don't think Kate would ever tell Rob what happened in the empty cottage with the syringe, or how that little female creature twirled slowly in her bucket of blood. I can trust her for that. I don't think Rob would ever tell Kate about the gap he senses although he can't see it: what happened in the moment before Miss Gallagher's natural weakness overtook her. But I also know that two people don't always need to tell things to one another. Secrets can cross from one person to the other without words, and suddenly you find that you've always known them. If a child was born from those two people, I wonder if it would be born knowing all their secrets, somewhere within it. Perhaps that's why I was born with such heaviness inside me.

I've always liked letters. I get so few of them. And then the sight of my name on the envelope makes me feel real. If the writer believes that I exist, why I must do. But this time it wasn't my mother's writing on the envelope, though I had half expected it since Mr Bullivant told me she was sure to write again. There was just my first name written there, 'Cathy', and that would never bring a letter safe from France. I fingered the envelope without opening it. The writing wasn't clear and black: it was the cramped handwriting they had never been able to do anything about at Rob's school. It was hard to read because he did not always form his letters in the same way. I would read it later, I thought. There were two cups on the breakfast table, my own and Rob's, one half-full and one clean. He must have gone out early, to the woods perhaps. He wouldn't be late back, because this was the day Kate was going and everyone would gather in the hall to say goodbye to her, then spill outside to wave for as long as the trap was in sight. I had planned to go to the station with her, and perhaps Rob had too. The house was quiet and the room was full of gentle sunlight. I heard a blackbird in the magnolia. Once it had stopped singing I'd open his letter.

He began it the way he used to open his letters from

school. Never 'Dear Cathy', but just 'Cathy', as if he were talking to me.

Cathy,

This is the fourth time I've started to write this, and whatever I write this time I'll seal and you will read it. There isn't time to write it again. I'm sorry. You know I'm not good at letters. Yours were always so much better.

Cathy, you'll be better without me. I know it. You don't believe it yet but you will. Remember what you said about the Callans? You said 'the barrenness of it' and I couldn't forget it, although I didn't see what you meant then. I thought you were talking about children, but it's more than that, isn't it? I can't bear to see you not eating and frightened to go out. I hate it when you're frightened. I used to be able to stop it but I can't any more.

I'm going with Kate. By the time you get this I'll have gone. She was going to go to Ireland but she's changed her mind. There's nothing for her there except another place, worse than this one probably. I think she only wanted to go because of

The next bit was scratched out with deep gouges of the pen and I couldn't read it even when I held up the back of the letter to the light and tried to read the words backwards.

Never mind. It doesn't matter. We're going to Canada. There are liners from Cobh. They sail from France, then they call at Southampton and Cobh. We'll sail to New York. I've got the money for the passage and some to live on until we get started, but don't worry, I've only taken what's mine. I've written to Grandfather to tell him.

I don't care what I do, I've got to get away from here. I know you don't feel the same. You ought to have this place, not me. It seems to belong to you more.

You know that Kate has a cousin in Canada. We'll start there, and I'll write to you. I must finish this now, because there isn't much time. I went to look in your room but you were sleeping. You looked so peaceful.

You'll be better without me, Cathy, I know you will. *Don't let Grandfather know what's in this letter*.

At the bottom he'd written *Remember our*, then put a line through it and scratched out what came after so it was illegible.

Twenty

'Canada,' said Mr Bullivant.

We were walking in the rose garden. I'd been pruning the roses that morning. Their stems were woody, and I wore my pigskin gloves against two years' growth of thorns. I cut hard back until I came to the greenish shadow of sap. Now another skin was hardening over the cuts I'd made, slanting just above the bud spurs. I'd been outside the whole morning, working until I'd cut away all the old spongy wood and raked the prunings into a pile. Later I'd fetch a barrow and wheel them to the ashy place behind the glasshouse where John made his fires. They were dry enough to burn at once. Fire would pour upward, thin and colourless in the spring sunshine, snapping with heat. Tomorrow I'd do more.

We walked on. The word 'Canada' expanded like a breath in the following silence. I looked out and away to the woods where they were covered in a grey-green haze, not quite leaf but a little more than bud.

'Which part of Canada? Do you know?' asked Mr Bullivant at last.

'I'm not sure what it's called, but I'll tell you what it's like.'

'Go on.'

'It's in the middle of the prairie. You can see the roof a dozen miles off, rising over the grass like a sail. The grass is taller than a man and when the wind blows through it makes roads wide enough for a wagon and horses to turn. The house is made of white board and the roof's red. You can see a thread of smoke as it comes out of the chimney, then it blows away to nothing. The wind's always moving, day and night, like a sea, and the house creaks and moves with it.

There used to be a turf house there before, a sod house they call it, made of the earth and crouched down low to it so you could almost walk past without seeing it. They have a fence round the vegetable garden to keep the fowls in, and you would never believe what they grow there unless you'd seen it with your own eyes. Their tomatoes are so fat they bend the vines down and loll on the ground till they split, and their potatoes are yellow-sweet and each as big as a fist. They never turn to mush in cooking. There are peas and beans and squash and berry bushes. What they can't eat or store they take to the cannery. In the winter the snow buries it all a yard deep so you'd think nothing would ever grow again, but the cold cleans the ground and as soon as it melts the sun's hot and the seeds crack open and start to grow. They don't have spring as we do. The soil's black and it crumbles sweetly in your hand, and it's so rich that if you put your ear to the ground at the start of the season you can hear the grass growing. If you stuck your walking-stick into that earth it would burst into leaf.'

'How on earth do you know all this? Your brother can't have written to you already. He's only been gone a fortnight.'

'Twelve days.'

'He might be in Ireland still, waiting for his ship. So what's this place you're telling me about?'

'It's what Kate told me. She made me half believe I'd been there myself.'

He hadn't said Kate's name. He'd talked as if Rob were travelling alone, from delicacy I suppose. But everyone knew. When I went to the village waves of whispers opened in front of me and closed again as I passed. I didn't care. Why shouldn't people know? I walked steadily. I had to speak to the Semple boys about some work that was needed on the roof. If I didn't arrange it, no one else would.

'Is your grandfather any better? I'll call on him as soon as he can have visitors,' said Mr Bullivant.

'He's not ill at all. It was just –'

'The shock?'

'Yes.'

Shock was one way of putting it. He was ill with rage. His skin was yellow with it. Then when his rage had burnt out he lay on his bed, tiny and malevolent, his hawk eyes masked as if another skin had grown over them. He looked at me with hunger.

'Ah, Catherine. You're still here.'

'Yes, I've been sitting with you. You've been asleep. Do you want some of this barley water?'

'Good God, no. It looks like an overnight chamberpot. I'm not ill.'

'I know you're not.'

'I'm angry,' he said. 'What did I bring her here for?'

I knew he meant my mother.

'To run away from me, that's what,' he went on, 'and to teach the boy to do the same. That fool doesn't know he's born, but he'll soon find out once he gets wherever he's going. Canada! Fairyland,' he said. 'He'll soon see what he's thrown away. For he won't get an inch of the land now, not if he crawls back through the snow on his hands and knees.'

'He won't do that,' I said.

'You'd know, I suppose. He's a stranger to me. You're all I've got now, Catherine.'

I said nothing. He began to eat the beef sandwiches I'd brought him, chewing them with quick, chopping bites at the front of his mouth. He had lost most of his side and back teeth but the front ones were good, small and sharp. His room faced north, and the light was sparse, crowded out by the tall furniture that he'd bought with the house. When I was little I thought a family might easily live in his wardrobe.

245

There was a badger-hair shaving brush on his wash stand, stiff with disuse, and water standing in the jug. He hadn't washed.

'I could eat another plateful,' he said, chasing the crumbs and pinching them between his fingers.

'I'll bring you some more. There's any amount of beef.'

'It's a fine life we lead, isn't it, Catherine?' His laughter cracked out. '*Any amount of beef!* Wait till that fool of a brother of yours gets to Canada. He'll be begging for beef in his sleep. Kate will be all right. She's not soft like him. She wasn't brought up between sheets.'

'I think she was, Grandfather. She brought her own when she came.'

'You know what I mean. Get those sandwiches and I'll tell you something.'

The kitchen was empty and clean, with the bleached dishcloths hung up to dry above the stove. Mrs Blazer would be sleeping. Without her afternoon sleep she was a dead thing by dinnertime. I cut the beef myself; the yellow fat and the rosy, marbled flesh. I made a plateful of sandwiches and a big pot of strong tea and took it up to him.

'You forgot the mustard. Beef's no good without mustard.'

'There was no mustard in the ones you ate before. But I'll fetch it if you like.'

'Never mind.'

Outside Grandfather's window there was a laurel tree which had grown up to hide half the window. He would not have it cut back. He seemed to like its dim, leathery leaves feeling at the glass, but to me they weren't like living things at all. I would have chosen something supple and tender to look at every day, like a birch or a beech. I said so.

'Don't be a fool, Catherine, you can't have a beech growing so close to the house.'

'Or wistaria.'

'That wouldn't live out of the sun. What's wrong with my laurel?'

'It's so stiff. The sun doesn't come through it. And it doesn't shake and make shadows when the breeze turns the leaves. That's what I like.'

I'd never talked to him like this before. Perhaps it was because he was lying down, or because I'd never spent so long in one room with him in my life.

He turned sharply on his pillow, raised himself on one elbow and said, 'That's what you like, is it?'

There was too much in his voice for the small conversation we were having. 'Yes,' I said, surprised. 'I like to look up at the sky through the leaves.'

He pushed the sandwiches aside and was silent for a long time while I looked out of the window. I thought he was falling asleep again, but then he said, 'She liked to look up at the leaves.'

'Who?'

'Cynthia.' Not 'your mother', not 'Cincie', not 'my daughter'. I'd never heard him call her by any name since she'd gone. I didn't know what to say so I said nothing, and in a while he went on.

'It's hard for a man to rear a child. He hasn't the feeling for it. She wanted soft things. Even when I was holding her she was wanting to crib herself round into something soft that wasn't there. The way a man's body is made, it's like a rack of ribs. It doesn't fit to a child.'

He was quiet again and I thought he'd finished. There was so much I wanted to know but I didn't dare question him. He was talking as freely as if I weren't there and he was alone inside his head.

'I had her from ten days old. Her mother seemed to be better. She sat up in bed and drank a bowl of milk with the baby folded into a shawl at her side. But the next day the rash started on her throat, then lower down and all over her body. She wouldn't let anyone see it until she was too weak to stop them. She put out both hands to push me off, and I let her. She talked all the time for two nights and then she was quiet. She'd forgotten that she had the baby. It didn't cry like a baby – it sounded like the door creaking, to and fro.'

He looked at the laurel leaves. 'The smell of her was terrible,' he said. 'It hit you as you came over the threshold.'

I thought of the baby: my mother. I knew he had brought her here alone, and no one knew anything about her mother, except that she'd died.

'She was the first to go,' said my grandfather. 'I couldn't keep her. But I kept Cynthia though there were women waiting to take her, thinking they knew more than I did. She was my flesh and blood. I gave her goat's milk. You've no idea what it is to sit up all night with a child, dipping your hand in goat's milk so she'll suck it off your fingers. Then I found she liked sweet things and if I let her taste a little honey first she'd swallow the milk. I could hold her in one hand with two fingers behind her neck to steady it. She would never sleep in her cradle. She wanted a body round her, so I had to sleep with her curled inside one arm and I'd wake to find she'd crept up close and her face was crumpled against me. I was afraid I'd crush her in my sleep, but I never did. Later, when she learned to smile, that was the first thing I saw: her face beside me looking like half the world because it was so close, and her smile.'

He stopped talking. I poured the tea and handed it to him. It was as dark as he liked it. He swallowed and said,

'If you ever have a child that won't sleep, Catherine, though you won't if you go on the way you're going, take it out under the trees. When she cried I'd hold her in my arms and walk her under the leaves so she could see them spread out against the sky and moving. It always quieted her. She'd put her head back on my arm and open her eyes wide and I could walk her there for an hour or more without another sound from her. It was nothing much when I looked up to see what she saw, but it pleased her. Just the leaves. I suppose the sound of them quieted her too. She liked birches best, and then the horse-chestnuts.'

There was a sound in his voice I'd never heard before.

'Did you ever take us out under the trees when we were babies?' I asked.

'You! No. There was no call for it. You had your mother.'

He drank down the tea, his fingers agitated on the cup. 'And once was enough,' he said. 'It was enough.'

'Yes, I think he'd like to see you,' I said to Mr Bullivant.

'Good. I'll come.'

We walked on. There were weeds sprawling in the gravel and the grass was overgrown. Everything grew too fast: weeds, damp patches on walls and ceilings, the holes in the roof, the brambles in the woods, the debts that nobody mentioned. None of this would be Rob's now. There was no way of asking if it would be mine, but already I felt that it was. It was mine to work on.

'You must be very much alone,' said Mr Bullivant.

'Yes. Look, let's go this way.' The magnolia's buds were fat. I picked one off and sliced it through with my fingernail, to where the flower crouched, crumpled. I dropped it and pulled off another.

'Don't do that.'

'Look, this one's a bit pink. They're just as they will be.'

The exposed petals turned brown almost at once where they had been torn.

'It's getting old, this magnolia,' I said. 'That branch is coming down. It'll go in the next storm.'

'You must miss them. Kate too.'

They were suddenly as close as if they'd been standing on the path in front of us. Kate in her dark-blue work dress and apron, her arms folded, looking at me with the beginning of a laugh in the corner of her mouth, and the same laugh sliding into her eyes. There was Rob, stopped in mid-stride, his gun over his shoulder and his bright brown hair crushed down under his cap. He glanced back over his shoulder and walked on. They were like a great wind tearing at the sides of the house, like the storm four years ago when the windows had bent as if they were sucking in breath. Grandfather had jammed the big drawing-room window shut with a door-stopper and the wind hadn't got in. I forced my mind shut. As if the wind had dropped they hung suddenly still, shimmering a little, then vanished.

'If they were in the house now they wouldn't be any more with me than they are,' I said.

'How do you mean?'

'I wonder sometimes, if it's the people themselves who keep you company, or the idea of them. The idea you have of them.'

'I think that's true.'

'I know it is, for me.'

'So they're still with you.'

'Or still not with me. Perhaps they were not with me all the time, when I thought they were.'

'Because they kept things secret from you? You didn't know?'

'I don't know that there was anything to keep secret.'

'There must have been.'

'People do things suddenly sometimes. Out of nowhere.'

'Am I just an idea in your mind, then, Catherine?'

He was facing me. Although it was so early in the year he was already tanned. The sun had got into him in Italy and it was always half there, ready to be brought out again even here in April. He looked at me carefully as he always did, as if I were as much worth looking at as a painting. A bright spring wind blew clouds across the sun and away again, so their shadows flickered over us. 'You've got some colour,' he said.

'I was out all morning. There's so much to do. This place is falling to pieces.'

'Will it be yours? Is that what you want?'

'I don't know,' I said.

'I'm going away.'

'When?'

'Quite soon.'

'To Italy?'

'Yes, but to France first.'

'Are you coming back?'

'I don't know.'

'You can't just leave it. All that building. And the new orchard – your fountain –'

'It isn't going as I wanted it to,' he said slowly. 'I don't know why. If I were a painter I'd say I was overpainting – do you know what I mean? Stubbing out what was good in the sketches. But I'm not a painter. It was a wonderful idea but now it feels like moving things around for no reason. Soil and trees and furniture.'

'But it's going to be beautiful.'

'Very likely. But that wasn't the point.'

'I thought it was.'

'Part of it, perhaps. I wanted to explore, to find something that might have existed, to feel along the thread like a spider. Perhaps discover a landscape I could live in.'

'And you can't?'

'No,' he said. 'No, I don't think I can. I wanted to.'

'So you're going away.'

'I think so.'

'You'll sell up.'

'No. Not yet. Listen, Catherine. You could come too.'

The wind was loosening my hair and blowing strands across my face. The sharp sunlight scrubbed at my eyes. Down below us the tops of the woods were moving, ready to come to life like great arms that lifted me and held me in. The woods. The place of the hare. He knew nothing about me.

'No,' I said, 'I can't leave here. It's my place.'

'You'll never be able to keep it on, just you and your grandfather.'

'I can work. Besides, I can't leave him. Everyone else has gone, and if I left then he would have to leave too. I've had a look at the books while he's been in his room. We shan't be able to pay wages if things don't change soon.'

'He'll stay till the house falls in around him. He made it. It's his. He won't leave it.'

'Nor shall I.'

Our hands lay quite close on warm grey stone. We had drifted across to the terrace wall, looking out at layers of grey and green, stubby with buds and the raw, hurting sense of spring.

'You really are very like your mother,' he said, and touched my hand lightly, as if he were pointing something out.

'She never sent another letter, did she?'

'I could take you to see her.'

'No. Not yet. Have you ever been to Canada?'

'As it happens, yes. I seem to be haunted by your family wherever I go, Catherine.'

'What's it like really?'

'The part I went to was mostly forest. Wild, but not as things are wild here. Anything might happen. If you walk into the trees and turn around with your eyes shut you might lose yourself for ever.'

'It'll be like that here soon. Why were you there?'

'Oh, business. Railways. There's a lot of money to be made in an empty country.'

Twin steel lines glittered like fish as they disappeared into the forest. The train rounded the bend with a long plaintive whistle that there was no one within a hundred miles to hear. Its freight was money.

'I'd like to go there,' I said, 'but not yet.'

'Time might run out.'

'Why?'

'Things don't go on for ever, waiting till you want them. And the world's changing fast. All the things we're so sure about can vanish just like that.'

'I'm not sure about anything.'

'Except that you'll stay here.'

'Yes.'

'And when I next come, will the roses have grown right up the castle walls?'

'No,' I said, 'I'll prune them.'

I looked at his hand, which had been to Canada and to France. It had held my mother's. I looked at my hands, which had pushed at Miss Gallagher as she stumbled. Or had they? Had they touched her? I had no memory any more, only a puzzle of images, each one so bright I had to believe it as it burnt up in my mind. My body was thin now and full of hollows, but it had carried my child inside it. I had buried the hare but I was alive and my body was not a burial ground. I had worked two hours without stopping. If I looked behind me I could see where I'd cleared the ground. I would make myself strong.

Twenty-one

Ash Court was empty of Mr Bullivant. I was surprised how much difference it made. I'd got used to thinking of him there, building and planting, giving as much attention to a new type of kitchen stove as he gave to the carving of a balustrade. I missed the crackle of new plans in his pockets: plans not of things the way they were, but as they would be. He was back in Italy, they said in the village, trying to save the precious things in his villa against the war. No, he was in France. He'd volunteered though he need never have gone, seeing he was close to forty. He'd had to fight to make them take him, 'near as hard as he'll fight in France'. Then they laughed, because in the end a man was a fool to leave his land unless he was taken. France was far away and unimaginable, like the war.

'It's all nonsense,' said my grandfather. 'George Bullivant is on a hospital ship, lugging stretchers about. He wrote and told me so himself. He asked after you, Catherine. There's mud on your forehead.'

I rubbed it off. I'd been chopping turnips, but half of them were rotten with frost. My hands stank with their slime. They were chapped too, and there were itchy sores on the middle fingers of my right hand which wouldn't heal.

'He's gone to Gallipoli,' said my grandfather, 'the more fool him.'

'I'll go and wash.'

Mrs Blazer came in with a dish of mutton stew. She still slept in the house, but you couldn't have said we employed her any more. She had her keep from us, a share in whatever there was. We'd pared life down to manage without money. I could skin a rabbit now as easily as I could undress myself. We ate pigeon-pie baked with apples stored in the loft until they wrinkled into intense, nutty sweetness. We ate rabbit and rabbit and rabbit. Roast rabbit, potted rabbit, rabbit stew. We didn't buy and sell any more: we bartered, exchanging a load of firewood for honey on the comb, and a bushel of apples for a length of calico. We were lucky.

Mrs Blazer traded like a market woman, using our house as her supply base. She kept goats in the paddock, starting with a pair. We had milk and cheese, as much as we wanted, and she sold the rest. Their milk was sweet. 'It's all in the feed. Everything they eat comes through to the milk,' she said. She knew a man who kept a market stall in town. He sold remedies, simple things like horehound pastilles for coughs and Goalings Syrup for gripe. And other things too, she said, nodding at me, kept under the red-and-white checked cloth and slipped into women's hands after they'd added a whisper to their request for 'something to settle this stummick that's troubling me'.

'They'd have called him a wizard when I was a girl,' said Mrs Blazer.

He sold her goats' milk for her, under a sign we'd painted to his direction: 'Cleans the Stomach and the Complexion'.

'D'you think that'll sell it?' I asked.

'Course it will. You wouldn't credit how many people are troubled with their digestions, specially these days.'

She wrapped her goats' cheeses in comfrey leaves and heaped them under a second sign: 'Fine Sweet Cheese to Slip Down Easy. Build up your Best Boy when he Comes Home'.

She grubbed up handfuls of wild garlic from the neglected paddock so the goats wouldn't eat it. She was old but she was young too, more vigorous than ever. I saw shadows of the tough, free-stepping girl she must have been once, before kitchens swallowed her. 'There's no call for a goat to smell goaty 'less you keep them dirty,' she said. She taught me to make bread, punching down the dough in a big earthenware bowl and setting it to rise under a clean damp white cloth. But she hated the flour we had now, coarse stuff that looked as if it had grit in it or worse, and made a loaf that wouldn't rise no matter how you kneaded it.

We fished for carp and shot duck on the lake at Ash Court. Mr Bullivant had made his lake before he went. He'd left enough money to keep everything immaculate as a stopped clock, but once the war took hold you could buy everything but men to work for you. One by one men had leaked out of the village. Not many went from choice, but some did. It's hard now to remember how it was then. I only knew one well, and that was George Semple, but I couldn't say what it was that made him go. Then they brought in conscription and the hunger of the war began to close in on the village. Suddenly all the things that had been difficult became easy: men who'd never been five miles from the village had their travel warrants issued and they were gone. Men who'd always worked alone, ploughing with a cloud of starlings for company, now marched and drilled and slept in a flock, like starlings themselves. And the things that had been easy were difficult. It was hard to get up and put on your working boots and go to the job you'd been doing all your life.

The Tribunal was set up and whatever reason a man pleaded for exemption, they'd knock it back at him again, blinding him with quick office words as he stood there in his Sunday clothes twisting his hat in his hands. The men who'd hoped to melt into the land were winkled out and conscripted. It made an empty quietness in the village, as if it was always haymaking with the men gone to the fields and the sun moving along whitened doorsteps while a baby wailed.

One June day I went out with my gun at dawn. There was a

smell of fox round the hen-run, but nothing was harmed. He must have come padding round the wire, busy and quick, not wasting his time when he saw he'd get nothing. Mist lay on Mr Bullivant's lake. A duck took off, running across the top of the water before he whirred into the air. My gun followed his flight and as soon as he was over the marshy end of the lake I shot him and he dropped plumb into the meadowsweet. I waded through the black, boggy ground. The reedmace quivered stiffly in the shallow water at my side. The duck had made a hollow in the mud where it fell, and there was a light sweet sound as I pulled it out, like the pulling of a tooth when it hangs by a thread. The mist was changing to pale blue, thinning as if cream were being skimmed out of it. The noise of the gun rippled outwards like sun's heat, clearing the sky.

George Semple was dead almost before people had begun to believe this war would lead to dying. I met him in the lane before he went, on a dry November day which was so still it felt warm. The war had been going on for three months. He was walking one way and I the other, but the day was perfect and as we stood there its perfection was borne in on us like a scent, light and evasive on the air. The ground was printed with exact shadows, and the air was sweet and a little fermented, like an apple that had lain in long grass for a week. Brown oak leaves rattled lightly in the hedge, and the sun fell on us, low and slanting. Through the hedge we saw the ridges cut deep in the ploughed field, made deeper by the late afternoon sun which was turning the earth damson in the shadows of each ridge. George had been ploughing there till yesterday.

'I'm off,' he said, 'off tomorrow.'

'Where?'

'Slinsden first, to the barracks. Then for training.'

'Just you? Not Michael and Theodore?'

He shook his head slowly, amused. 'No, not them. They won't go till they get a shove.' He laughed, because that was never going to happen. 'They think I've been a fool to myself,' he went on, and reached out to pick a spray of rose-hips. The hips were slim and a perfect dark red, slightly over-ripe. Their flesh would be mushy, and the seeds dark yellow. He held them and looked at them abstractedly. 'Pretty,' he said. 'Maybe they're right. I wonder if they have such things in France.'

I thought of mimosa and my mother, and the navy swell of a warm sea in winter. She was safe where she was. And now here was George going to France before me.

'I don't know,' I said. 'I expect it's like here.'

'Maybe. You know how you think there's nowhere like your own place. But I'm sure they think the same.'

Our words pattered like dry berries in the quiet dust of the lane.

'I can't remember such an autumn,' I said. 'Usually it's a sea of mud here by now.'

'Yes, there's a seam of clay across here. Comes up every year and you can squeeze water out of it like wringing a cloth. Mucky stuff.'

There was no mud now. My boots were coated with silky dust, and the hem of my skirt was white too, white as harvest. The hollow of the lane held fragile warmth. If we stirred it would be gone.

'Better be going,' said George. 'Ma's made a steak pudding, seeing it's my last day. If I'm not back in time the others'll eat it for me.' He grinned. His eyes were the palest blue, like starch-water. Neither of us moved. The lane tunnelled away beyond us, turning corners he'd soon turn too.

'So many berries everywhere,' I said. 'It's going to be a hard winter.'

'Not where I'm going. France – it's hot there.'

'Are you glad to go?' I asked, but it was the wrong question.

He shrugged. 'Find out when I get there, shan't I?'

'Yes, of course.'

'Best be going, then.'

'Enjoy the steak pudding,' I said, and that was the last time I saw him.

Theodore would never have volunteered, nor would Michael. There was something set in them against it, though they never said what it was. 'I'm not such a fool,' said Theodore once, before George died, when his letters from camp were talked of round the village like an achievement everybody shared. But he said it as if it were code for something he couldn't express. He had that fine feeling for words which would make him use none rather than the wrong ones. He would tell me of things I ought to know, a broken field drain or a blocked ditch. He talked to me as he used to talk to Rob, as if I weren't a woman to him any more. I liked it.

The second year of the war, after George had gone, he taught me to plough. 'Go gentle,' he'd say. 'No need to rush it. This field'll be here tomorrow, and the day after.' When Theodore ploughed, a long, sure seam of earth opened behind him, ripping and crumbling like a wave as it breaks into foam. The fresh earth showed colours which dulled almost immediately, as the colour dulls on a fish when it's caught and landed. It was chocolate and bramble and iron-blue, then the wind dried it and it was plain brown earth. Seagulls followed us, swooping low so I saw their pale green eyes looking emptily into mine as they sailed a tight turn above the plough. It was slower when I ploughed. The blade jagged at the soil and the mare dragged heavily, baffled. I looked back and saw the ugly line of the furrow.

259

'Let the mare go to her work,' said Theodore. 'She knows how, only you won't let her.'

I tried again. It was on the second day that I caught the rhythm. The mare relaxed, trusting me, and the plough ran deep and straight.

'Now you've got it,' said Theodore, and at once I lost it as the plough juddered. But I got it back again. I was ploughing, turning the earth so it could ripen in the frost. But the mare was old. We would get one more season of work out of her at most.

'If he hadn't of gone to Canada he'd be driving the plough. Think of that now. You'll not have had many letters with the war,' said Theodore.

'No, not many.'

'He'll have got a place of his own by now. Land's cheap there.' Theodore probed by statements, not questions.

'Yes,' I said, 'there's plenty of land out there.' I didn't tell him that Rob had none, as far as I knew.

'It'll have some kind of foreign name, the place he's living at.'

'It's called Rivière-du-Loup. That's where he was when he last wrote. It means Wolf River.'

'That'd be the Canadian language.'

'It's French. He's in the part where they speak French.'

'They got wolves there then, I suppose. He'll like that. Plenty of shooting.'

'Do they shoot wolves? I don't know.'

'Couldn't have wolves running around the town.'

'No.' Wolves running, heads down, on the icy tracks of a sledge. He wrote that the river froze solid in winter, first a mush of ice, then big slabs, then an iron road you could drive across with a sledge and horses. He said nothing about Kate. He hoped to go to Quebec and get a job there for a while before going on westward, but he was learning French first.

The kind of French he'd studied at school was worse than useless. He was sharing a house with a trapper who came into town for the winter to drink away his profits. The noise went on all night sometimes. There was only one page of writing. I held the letter in my hand and thought of how far it had come, but even its long journey couldn't make it anything but dead in my hand. Grandfather read it and then it was left lying open on the sideboard. When I next looked I couldn't find it. I began to wonder if I had made it up: the horses galloping on the frozen river, the trapper insensible with alcohol, my brother learning French in a room from which he could hear wolves howling. I took my atlas and worked west through the place names. Glace Bay, Halifax, Quebec, Trois-Rivières, Montreal, Sault Ste-Marie, Thunder Bay, and then the map broke up into a thousand lakes without names. I wondered how far Rob would go. Would he get beyond the towns to where there wasn't any language spoken at all?

'Hard when it's your own flesh and blood, in another world as it might be,' said Theodore. He tossed aside the crust of his bread-and-cheese and a seagull plunged down the air, feet first, and stabbed at it. The bird looked big and evil, its feathers oily, its beak a razor. Like this it would come down on the head of a drowning man at sea. I knew that Theodore had forgotten Rob now. He was thinking of George, ploughed into earth none of the Semples had ever touched, earth whose colour and texture was unfamiliar.

Do they shoot wolves? I don't know.

But they shoot men every day.

'Best be getting on then,' said Theodore.

The Semples' chapel minister was said to be against the war, but no one walked those miles over the fields to find out if it were true. Then the tribunals started, with Livvy's father one of the local dignitaries on the board. Livvy had no brothers, so it was easy for him to write those words that

261

meant a man went or stayed. Livvy rolled bandages two days a week; she had married a Staff Officer. She smiled when we met, but she was a young matron now, not a mermaid.

'They can't take all three of 'em from me,' said Mrs Semple, who had no patriotism in her. Her boys were what she cared about. The village had always thought she cared for them more than was decent. 'She'd step on a dead man's face to get to one of her boys.'

Grandfather showed me a correspondence in *The Times*. A woman had written in to say that she had sent every one of her six sons to the war.

In these times a mother's heart, wrung as it is with sorrow, beats high with pride and the knowledge that among all those fine young men her own flesh and blood is marching. Mothers of England who have given and given and given again, our sacrifice will never be forgotten.

All the next week people wrote in to say they had sent more. Six was nothing; here were eight, or ten. Impossibly the figures piled up like the huge weight of cabbages at a village show. The crowning letter came from a mother who had eighteen close male relations at the front, and the correspondence closed.

'There you are,' said Grandfather, folding up the paper. 'We might show this to Annie Semple, eh? Do you think it would do her good? Well, we've no one to send, have we, Catherine?'

'You'll manage,' said Theodore to me. 'You're coming on. Only for the mare's lameness, you'd be fine. What'll you do?' He was really asking me what money we had. I knew how little it was and how much it had to do. We'd be lucky to buy another plough horse.

'You're going then,' I said.

'Got to,' said Theodore. 'Me and Michael both. Ma's

terrible, I wish you'd look in and see her when we're gone. Pity she never had a daughter, times like this.'

'She didn't want a daughter. You three were all she wanted.'

It was true. She'd gloried in them from when they were babies. She loved their maleness: the creak of their boots as they came in, their hair dark with sweat at the roots, their sudden scuffling fights, their appetites.

'Quakers don't have to go. They can join the ambulance service,' I said.

'I dare say,' said Theodore, 'but it'ud be a bit late to be turning Quaker now.'

Rumours were coming back of what they did to conchies, how they made them run all night naked on freezing beaches near Scarborough, how they put them up for shooting practice or sent them over the top without guns. I wondered if Theodore had heard those rumours too.

'What did the Board say?'

'Stood us there,' said Theodore, 'and read out our medical reports. Michael was six foot in his stockinged feet when he was measured. "*Magnificent specimens*", that's what they called us. We didn't tell Ma. You'll keep things going here, then.'

'I'll try.'

'Take it slow. You don't want to lose heart with rushing at it.'

I knew about taking it slow now. I even chewed slowly, tasting each morsel, while the surface of my mind grazed at peace. At night I was often too tired to dream. Muscle by muscle I fell into sleep like someone swallowed by deep water, and in the morning I began the day as soon as I woke and worked through it steadily, my hands on the ropes. On Sundays I crouched by the fire like a dog, watching the flames for hours, too stupid to read.

'He's getting old,' said Theodore. He meant my grandfather.

It was true, and though it hadn't happened suddenly, it was suddenly final and there would never be any going back on it. He got up late and went for long shambling walks in the woods, poking at things with sticks. He was like a fire banked up for the night: if you broke the crust there was heat hidden there, but more and more often all I saw was the dulled surface of him, giving out nothing. At first I'd wanted him to notice everything I was doing. I thought he'd be glad of it. I'd come back and tell him how I'd cleared a ditch, or learned to use the double-handled saw with Theodore, but he was irritable, as if the reality I described had nothing to do with him. He could not believe in the world he found himself in, with all that huge struggle come to nothing but an old man in a leaking house, wife, daughter and grandson gone, granddaughter working as hard as any Shawl Ellen in skirts that showed her legs. I watched him disappear into the woods, his head bowed and his stick ferreting.

But he talked to me now, at night after we'd eaten, when there was one candle on the table, or only the firelight, and we sat with a bowl of nuts to crack and a glass of wine. He poured out my wine faultlessly, so that it swelled to the brim but never spilled. He poured me one glass, then another, and pressed me to take more.

'Take another glass of wine, Catherine. You must keep up your strength.'

In the mornings my head felt light and distant, with an ache in it which soon worked off in the cold air.

'There are only the two of us,' he said once. 'We must –' and then he mumbled some words I couldn't hear.

'What did you say?'

He sat bolt upright, his heavy-lidded eyes shooting out their fire again as they rarely did now.

'Only the two of us. We must –'

He stopped again. I swallowed my wine, looking away to help him.

'CHERISH!' he shouted. 'One another!' and he looked at me like a hawk about to plunge on my heart. But I knew him now.

'Yes,' I said, and I put out my hand and laid it over his. It was warm: that surprised me, how warm it was.

We ate our nuts. 'Did you walk in the woods today?' I asked.

'I walked to Silence Farm,' said my grandfather. 'Why, I don't know. A fool's errand if ever there was one.'

The path was quite overgrown. I wondered how he had got there, thrashing down dry hemlock with his stick, forcing open the tangled field gate.

'No one's been that way for a long time. I saw a stoat kill a rabbit on the path in front of me as if I weren't there. Didn't see what it was at first — just the shape of it whipping at the creature's throat. They've an instinct, you know, Catherine. They can sense the blood under the skin. Do you know, I half believed it would go for me too.'

'How were they, at the farm?'

He picked up his knife. 'Is there no fruit? You ought to have fruit. No, I didn't go in. *This the war, that the war.* You know how they are there, half-starved for company. She'd choke you to death on cake if it'd keep you there talking another quarter of an hour. I came back through the woods.'

I'd seen him, walking slowly home, feeling ahead of him with his stick. 'There'll be fruit tomorrow,' I said. 'I gave six geranium cuttings for some dried figs.'

'Good girl.'

I walked to Silence Farm. Oh no, I didn't go in. I came back through the woods. He was mostly alone, as he'd always been.

I hoped that sometimes he looked up at the bare branches and saw them suddenly clothed, I hoped that he listened and heard the tender rustle of leaves, so new they were still damp and crumpled from the bud. I hoped that he felt a sudden weight in his arms and looked down where the baby stirred and looked up, noiseless with wonder, into the spreading hands of a horse-chestnut.

It was the fourth winter of the war. The mare was dead and, though I'd hired a horse for ploughing, most of the land lay fallow. I'd had to let First Field go. There were eight goats now, though, and trade in the market was good. I had repaired the fencing round the paddock, and planted a new herb garden with pennyroyal and purple sage, spearmint, rue and rosemary. The wizard planted his own herbs but he always needed more, and we could make up bunches for market. I caught myself thinking how I would show it all to Theodore when he came back. It was impossible to believe that the men they said were dead were really gone, without a corpse to kiss or a funeral where we could see them folded neatly away into the soil. It was a trick, a magic hand wiping the landscape clean of young men. They had walked over a hill and vanished, so suddenly that they might come back just as they left, walking quietly along the lanes, a little older and more deeply tanned, speaking a few words of a language we didn't know. Before the mare died I thought I heard Theodore once, close behind me, clicking his tongue in the way she liked. She turned her head as if she heard it too.

'It's not now we'll feel it,' said Mrs Blazer. She swilled boiling water and soda round a milk-bucket, then tossed it out in a long arc on to the grass. It stood on the grass for a few moments, then was sucked away. 'It's when this war's over and they don't come home. That'll be the breaking-point.'

'If it's ever over.'

266

'There's a hole in the wire there. A fox'd get through that.'

'It's too small.'

'Don't you believe it. They can stretch themselves out like water when they want to.'

She went indoors to make tea for us. She'd made oat biscuits too, with the last dark smears of honey scraped from the comb. We were going to eat them with a bit of cheese. My mind ruminated on food as I knelt by the chicken-wire, plaiting one brittle strand into another. The wire was old and it broke easily. The work was too tricky to do with gloves on, but the wire hurt my fingers. There was blood coming up under the thin surface of my damaged skin. If I had a handkerchief, perhaps I could wind it round so the fingers were protected . . .

I heard boots crunch on the path. Too heavy for Grandfather. I looked up and he was standing there. My hands went out as if to push him away, as if he were the fox.

'Hello,' he said. He smiled, not quite looking at me. He was wearing dark clothes of a cut I didn't know. Town clothes.

'You've come back.' I was cold from kneeling on the winter grass and I stood up slowly, rubbing little flakes of rust off my hands.

'I didn't write,' he said. 'I thought it was best not. I thought you might not see me.'

'Where's Kate?' He'd taken off his hat and his hair was squashed flat. It was shorter than it had ever been and not conker-brown any more, just an ordinary brown like anybody's hair.

'Kate?' he asked, his eyes blank for a second. 'Oh, she's not with me. I haven't seen Kate for a long time. She married, you know. A widower. They have a son now.'

'*Married?*'

'Yes. Well, why not? She could have married ten times

over in Canada. There aren't enough women there. And he had some money.'

'Did he?'

'Well, not all that much, I don't suppose. But it was a lot to Kate. I went to her wedding.'

'You went to her wedding?'

'Yes, why not?'

He picked little grains of frost out of the rotting fence-post. His hands were fine and soft, quite different from how they had been. My own looked rough beside them, my fingers thickened with work.

'What have you been doing?'

'Oh, all sorts. I worked in an office for a while, selling insurance.'

'Insurance!'

'Good God, Cathy, don't sound so surprised about everything all the time. Yes, I sold insurance.'

'I wouldn't have thought you'd go to Canada to sell insurance, that's all.'

'It's a big thing there. All the farmers need it. They pay into policies against drought and so on.'

I wasn't convinced. It came out too easily, as if it were something he'd read about rather than done.

'Were you doing well?'

'Pretty well, I suppose. Aren't you going to ask me in?'

'You don't have to be asked.'

'I think I do.'

He stood there, his eyes uneasy but insistent. I kept looking at his hands. They had touched me: for nearly four years I hadn't thought of how they'd touched me. But he was like another person in another skin, paler and softer than it had ever been. The slightly ill-fitting smartness of his black clothes, and the hat pushed jauntily to the back of his head, were stranger than Canada. He was here but it was too sudden and in my mind he was still far off in that little snow-buried town.

'Come in then,' I said, 'but we won't tell Grandfather yet.'

'Why? Is he ill?'

'No, not really ill. But you'll see a difference.'

It was like the dreams I hadn't let myself dream. He sat at the kitchen table, drinking tea. Mrs Blazer took away his cup and filled it before he had finished drinking. Dark patches flared in her cheeks and her hands flustered, eager to be doing but not sure what to do.

'Is there any cake?' asked Rob, sure that there was and it was only a question of which tin he should choose from. Pound cake or seed cake or gingerbread cut into squares with an almond sitting glossily in the centre of each piece. Once he'd known the rhythm of her baking and now he was going to pick it up again like dropped stitches.

'There's no cake,' said Mrs Blazer. I saw her fingers yearn to feed him. 'But we've some oat biscuits.' She pushed the warm tray across to him and he took one, bit into it, laid the biscuit down again.

'Try it with a bit of goat's cheese,' she urged him, but he crumbled the biscuit away between his fingers.

'We can't get the ingredients,' I said, 'with the war.'

'Count ourselves lucky we don't live in town. They're queueing for margarine there, nasty stuff that it is,' said Mrs Blazer, 'and jam with wood chips in it for strawberries. Least what we've got here is clean.' Rob got up and ran his knuckle down the row of pale green enamelled tins where she'd kept her baking. The little tin for shortbread, the big square one that was meant for weddings and christenings. They rang with an empty music under his hands.

'I see what you mean,' he said.

'Things are different in Canada, I dessay,' said Mrs Blazer, allowing a hint of criticism into her voice. 'Shops full to bursting.'

'With tallow and beaver skins and dried bear meat,' said Rob, 'but I'm here now.'

Are you, I thought. Under the table I nipped the pale flesh of my fore-arm and made a little sting. It hurt. Rob smiled at Mrs Blazer as he ran a finger under his collar, loosening it. It was a cheap collar, shiny where it shouldn't be, but clean. It would have been washed over and over. I remembered Rob spoiling his starched white collars and chucking them on the floor while Kate chided him for his extravagance. He took other people's time for granted then. Something had gone wrong; badly wrong. He was anxiously clean in his dark suit, and all the bloom of confidence had been knocked off him.

'You'll be hungry,' I said. 'I'll bring you some hot water and you can wash while I go and tell Grandfather you're here. He'll need a little while to get used to it before he sees you.'

It was late. We'd dined together, Grandfather and Rob and I, becalmed around the table. Grandfather's hands shook a little more than usual, but that was the only sign. I saw the effort of will he made to stop them trembling while he poured the wine. The first thing Rob had said to him, forestalling him, was, 'I'm on my way to France. I'll be gone tomorrow.'

'What, dressed like that?'

'Of course not. I've got to be trained first. Artillery.' But he said it at random, as he had said insurance, as if it might not be true.

'Are you really going?' I asked him later, when we were alone in the hall, with the fire at our faces and the cold at our backs. Grandfather had gone to bed no later than usual, saying good night as if Rob had been gone for days, not years. I knew he would lie awake for hours, watching the laurels push at the window, listening for voices.

'Yes, I'm going.'

'But it wasn't true about artillery, was it? You just said it.'

He stretched. 'Where's the sense of a commission? Might as well go in as a private. It's all the same once I'm in the machine.'

'But you can't bear people telling you what to do. You wouldn't be pushed around as much if you're an officer.'

He shifted restlessly. 'Everyone gets told what to do. Doesn't make much difference who's telling you.'

'You could have stayed in Canada. No one would have known where you were.'

'Oh well. It seemed to be the thing to do.'

'That never bothered you before. Not when you went off with Kate.'

He looked at me. 'Don't go for a fellow, Cathy.'

I took the poker and stirred up the fire. 'I cut these logs,' I said, 'and brought them in.'

'It'll be yours, of course, this place. Don't think I don't know that. I haven't come back to take it away from you. Is that what you think?'

'Of course not.'

He leaned forward and thrust the poker deep in the fire to heat. His hair was dry at the ends, badly cut and shabby brown.

'Why did you come back then?' I asked.

'To see you, of course,' he said, and took out the poker. Its end glowed red and then dulled over. He wrote his initials on one of the logs that was drying in the hearth. The first downstroke burnt deep but the rest scarcely charred the wood. 'I wanted to see you before I went to France.'

'You might not get sent to France,' I said. It was too easy, all this. All he had to say was the word France and we would melt before him, forgetting or not daring to mention what he'd done. 'They don't take everyone.'

He looked round, his eyes blank with surprise. 'Of course they'll take me.' He sounded like a man who'd walked for days to the edge of a cliff, bracing himself to look down, only to find the drop no more than a few feet which a child could jump. For a moment we were together, looking into the chasm of what he wanted. Not to think, not to decide, just to go blindly with a force as impersonal as the wind.

'Don't go,' I said quickly. 'I don't think you're well. You look awful. Livvy's father is on the Tribunal, he'll fix something up for you. You could get a staff job.'

'Livvy's father! He won't have any great love for me.'

'She's married.'

'Everyone's married. Kate, Livvy . . . What about you?'

'You know I'm not,' I said. Suddenly I noticed how my feet were planted firmly apart, warming themselves at the fire. I'd got out of the habit of noticing how I stood or sat. And my face was weathering too. Soon outdoor work in the winter would make the colour on my cheeks break into thread veins.

'Funny thing, I always thought George Bullivant would have you. What became of him?'

'He's an orderly on a hospital ship.'

'Good God. Who'd have thought it?'

Rob was silent, dipping the poker in and out of the flames.

'He didn't have to go, he's over age,' I said.

'Very commendable, then,' said Rob.

'Don't talk like that!'

'Like what? Why?'

'You sound . . . I don't know. Sour. As if nothing matters to you. Don't be like that.'

'You've certainly changed,' he said.

'How?'

272

'You see things.' He spoke dismissively, as if what I had been was better than what I now was.

'I've had to keep things going.' It didn't sound like much when I heard it through his ears. Others could go to Canada or fight in France: I would keep things going.

'I can see that.'

He sat heavily, gazing straight ahead. I was longing to go to bed; every fibre in me ached for sleep. But there was a look on him I'd never seen before, like a disappointment.

'Did you really go to Canada?' I asked suddenly, before I knew I was going to ask it. He swung round sharply.

'Don't be an idiot, Cathy. How on earth else could I have sent you those letters?'

'You could have got Kate to post them for you.'

'You don't know Kate if you think she'd do that for me.'

'I don't see why not. She did worse.'

'She went away, that's all. She never said she was going to stay here for ever.'

He talked as if 'here' was as unimportant as the Canada I no longer believed in. Where had he really been? Perhaps he'd sailed with Kate, then come back and struggled as a clerk in some city, London or Manchester, in lodgings where the landladies liked him for his voice and his manners until he ran short of money.

'Aren't you tired? I've made up your bed.'

'No, I'm not tired. Besides, I don't seem to sleep very well – it must be all this travelling –' He shot me a look, half-teasing, then he asked, 'Will you stay up with me, Cathy? I don't like sitting alone.'

'What do you do when you're not here?'

'Oh, there's usually a chap to have a drink with,' he said evasively. I seemed to see a small room with furniture that smelled of new varnish, and my brother sitting on the edge of his bed, absolutely still, frowning at his boots. Suddenly, decisively, he got up and walked straight out of the door without looking back. In the public house there would be a couple of chaps who half-knew him by name.

'We could play cards,' I suggested.

'No. Let's talk. You can tell me everything that's happened.'

'That won't take long,' I said. I had always let him look into my life through my eyes, but now there were things I had to keep from him. The long, mostly silent evenings with my grandfather had made a confidence between us which would not survive my talking about it to Rob. And there were a thousand details that could mean nothing to anyone else: the tar-washing of the apple trees; the way the Victoria plum had broken its branches with fruit last summer and we had scoured the countryside for sugar to bottle them ... There were two bottles left, the big oval plums swimming in transparent syrup in a dark cupboard ... The night the fox got into the hens and the morning a heron rose from its nest not fifteen feet from me while I fished in Mr Bullivant's lake ... The tasteless bony flesh of the carp ... The day I had roped myself to the chimney and let myself down to look at the place where the tiles had come off in the gale. The rope had dug in tight to my waist and the world swung under me as I lost my balance, caught it again, hauled myself back up to the attic window, hand over hand ... He hadn't been there.

'I'll tell you something. I met the brother – Dodie. Kate's uncle. The one who helped carry Joseph down the stairs.'

'Did you!'

'Yes, he's still there, in this little house in Dublin. He has the table scrubbed white and he drinks half a pint of porter every afternoon. Just half a pint. He still never goes out, you know. God knows what he lives on. There's a neighbour who brings a dish round in a cloth at midday. He went upstairs when he saw me, but he talked to Kate.'

'So you saw the stairs where the arm —'

'Yes. I couldn't help looking at the floor, in case there was a mark.'

'Was there?'

'Of course not. Kate says he scrubs the flags every day. Can't bear anything dirty near him. I suppose that started after all the business with Joseph.'

'Fancy you actually seeing him . . .'

'Mm. It *was* a bit odd.'

'Theodore's dead,' I said abruptly, 'and George.'

'I know. I heard it in the village.'

'Did you stop there first? I thought you'd come straight here.'

'There was no one around. I should think I know more people in France than here, these days, dead or alive.'

He stood up and looked restlessly round the hall.

'Remember how we danced?'

'Yes.'

'Those orange trees still going?'

'No, they died last winter. We couldn't spare the fuel to heat the conservatory, and the frost caught them. I cut them hard back but the stems were brown all through. Don't tell Grandfather.'

'He must have noticed, surely?'

'He might have done. But he might have forgotten again,' I said.

'He didn't seem gone in the head at dinner.'

'He isn't. It's hard to explain.' I thought of how the baby he'd reared by hand was more real to Grandfather now than the woman who was somewhere in France or her son who sat, a shadow, opposite him at the dinner table. And yet Grandfather and I had swum into focus for one another, when for years we'd been shadows to one another, feared or ignored.

'It doesn't matter,' said Rob. 'Listen, Cathy, I'm going to give this as my address. Is that all right?'

'Of course it is. This is your home. You'll come back here when you get leave.'

He touched my wrist. I looked down at the fingers which seemed to insinuate themselves into my flesh as if they belonged there. If I wanted he would come upstairs with me and sleep with me as if he had never been away. He wanted things not to have changed, because something had hurt him when he'd been out in the world, killing the glow that had been on him like the glow of a child that has always been loved. But he hadn't always been loved, except by me.

I thought of the Canada I'd made for him in my mind: the house set in long swells of corn which beat like surf to the threshold, and Kate sitting on a patch of grass, a zinc bath on a stand in front of her, and a plump, wriggling child on her lap. It was always a boy. Kate scooped out a handful of water and splashed the child until he screamed in ecstasy. The warm wind blew over them, drying the child, lifting Kate's hair, rustling the corn. Now Rob wanted to come back to me as if none of that had happened. And none of that *had* happened.

'You're right, I suppose I have changed. We've all had to. Things have been so different with the war,' I said, and I watched his fingers, just perceptibly, lift. His face was still close to mine and I saw the familiar way the line ran from the corner of his mouth to his nose. Yes, it was already deeper, just a little. He reminded me of someone, or something that had happened before. Suddenly I had it. I saw my father lying under the sheets in The Sanctuary, so close I could have touched him, with that same hurt shadow in his eyes.

'Don't go,' I said again, almost against my will, as if it were something I had to say. But he was quick. His gaze moved against mine and he knew that I no longer wanted what he wanted. He'd never ask again. The home he'd come back to didn't exist, any more than the house in the cornfields.

He smiled and stretched as if he were ready for sleep, and said, 'Oh, I have to go – I'm ruined for home. Isn't that what they say?'

Twenty-two

'I still think we should fetch Harry,' said Mrs Blazer.

I stood up and peered again into my grandfather's face. It looked no different to me.

'Listen to him breathe.' I listened. There was a rasp in it, louder than before perhaps, but then his breathing had been harsh and hoarse for days. He'd been caught in a sudden slash of cold April rain: a few moments later the sun was out, making the drops glitter like knives. But it wasn't enough to warm him.

'See his colour now. There's been a change,' Mrs Blazer urged. There was duskiness gathering on his face. Round his lips and nostrils the skin was as dark as a plum. She'd wanted to fetch Harry Shiner since yesterday; Harry, she called him now, though to me he was the wizard. And we'd had Dr Milmain out twice, though how we were going to pay his bill I couldn't imagine. But I could imagine his anger if he found out we'd let Harry Shiner near my grandfather. *Old-wives' tales and cottage cures and superstition. They'd still be hanging witches if we let 'em.*

'All right. But no one's to know he's been here. Tell him that.'

'Oh, he'll say nothing. He's the soul of silence,' said Mrs Blazer proudly, as if the wizard were her belonging.

My Grandfather's head jerked sideways as if someone had slapped him. He lay so still he seemed to have stopped breathing, then just as I got up, panicky, the bubbling creak began again in his chest.

'That's congestion,' said Mrs Blazer. 'It's lying on his lungs.'

'All right. Go and fetch him. Get him to come quickly.'

If he died, I thought, I wouldn't even remember the last thing we'd said to one another. Something about beef-tea or bed-bottles, it would have been. Then he'd lapsed back into the sleep that stuck to him like glue. While Mrs Blazer was out, perhaps I could open the window. She wouldn't have it opened, not a crack, because it would be the death of him. But it was May and the air was so tender that there were birds singing even in Grandfather's laurel tree. I'd been in the room so long I couldn't smell his sickness any more, but my head ached with it. I crossed to the window. I was only going to open it an inch, but as the sash started to move and new air blew in I pushed it up with all my strength and the dirty glass gave way to a panel of clean, sparkling air. A bumblebee droned close, swerved at the invisible barrier, lifted itself into the laurel's yellow-green fresh leaves.

'Cathy.'

I turned. He'd rolled towards me. His eyes were wide open, wider than I'd ever seen them, like a baby's eyes.

'Did you get your brother his coat?'

I didn't know he even knew about the coat.

'Yes, of course,' I said.

'I never saw it.'

'The Army and Navy make up parcels for France. They sent it straight out to him as soon as they got the order.'

'Good.' After a while the bubbling wheeze grew louder and I saw he was trying to laugh.

'No coat if he hadn't —'

'Hadn't what?'

'Gone in as an officer. No coat for private. Good thing changed his mind.'

'Yes, it was.'

I'd spent on the coat the money I'd put aside to hire horses. Now I'd have to see what price I could get for timber this year ... There wasn't much else left to sell ... except land.

'Good coat.'

'Yes it was. The best. Superior Quality British Warm.'

He was sweating heavily. Was that bad, or good? People sweated when their fevers broke. It had a strange, childhood smell to it, teasing at me. Then I had it: pear drops. We'd have to change his bedlinen again.

'Do you want the bed-bottle, Grandfather?'

'No. Water.'

He couldn't sit up to drink it, but we had a feeding-bottle with a spout that Livvy had sent over. She was a VAD now, working in the convalescent hospital. It was good of her to think of us. Her groom had bent down, po-faced, handing me the feeding-cup without getting off his horse. How was it she had kept her groom? He was a fine strong young man, fit to be fighting. I put the spout to my grandfather's lips and he sucked noisily, his eyes closed with concentration. There was a little brandy in the water, to keep up his strength, and a spoonful of honey. The liquid began to run out of the side of his mouth. He'd gone to sleep again, and the prow of his nose was sharp and white in his darkening face. I wondered how long it would be before they came. It wasn't market day, so the wizard would be at home. He worked long hours making up his remedies, Mrs Blazer said. There was a skill to it like nobody knew. And then the sweets, which made good money in the greyness of the war: candied angelica, crystallized violets, peppermint drops. He could always get sugar from somewhere. If you wanted beauty as well as sweetness there was honey water and elderflower water, and eyebright cream to make the whites of tired eyes as clear as a child's.

'You ought to try it,' said Mrs Blazer. 'Shall I bring you home a sample?'

He'd gone a long way now, deep into his sleep. The

summer air moved around the room, flickering patterns on to the walls and drying the sweat on his face. It couldn't do him any harm, and I was very tired, too tired to close the window. I curled my feet under me in his big, uncomfortable armchair and shut my eyes. I heard the swifts skirling under the eaves.

When I woke they were both bending over my grandfather's bed, one at each side, Mrs Blazer and the wizard. His broad back faced me. He was a big man, not as I had imagined, broad-shouldered and narrow-waisted, his hair so black it had blue in it. And young: I'd thought he'd be old. But when I turned I saw he was not so young. Fifty, perhaps, or more. He was a walking advertisement for his own remedies, his skin supple, his eyes clear and pale in his dark face, his hair still thick and glossy. His eyes shifted around the room, taking it all in, fixing on nothing. He rummaged in his pockets and brought out a brown paper bag, untwisted it, shook out a few white lumps.

'You melt this, see, over a flame. Would you have a little dish, and a lamp? Then he'll breathe easy.'

Mrs Blazer took the white stuff reverentially, and hurried away.

'We've been rubbing his chest with eucalyptus balsam to help his breathing,' I said. 'I thought you might bring some remedy he could swallow.'

It seemed to me that if you went so far as to call in a wizard, he ought to do something more than you could do yourself. Perhaps there were other brown paper bags rumpled up in his pockets.

'There's no need for medicine,' he said.

'But he looks worse to me. That's why we sent for you.'

'Come here.'

He had a strong animal smell, like the fresh sweat of a

281

horse mixed with herbal mustiness. His body was huge and safe at my side.

'Now if you look down at him, see those little speckles round his mouth and nose, coming up under the skin.'

They seemed to spread as I looked.

'Skin's got that plum-colour since this morning, has it? You'll see the blue coming stronger now.'

Yes, it was stronger. It was the blue of bruises around his lips.

'He's quieter than he was,' I said. 'Is that a good sign?'

'He'll go out easy,' said the wizard. 'Sometimes you see 'em thrash like they've missed their tide, but he's caught his. Knowing what I know of him, he had his mind made up.'

What do you know of him, I thought. Only his reputation. A hard man. The man from nowhere.

'He'll be finding them already,' said the wizard.

'Who?'

'The ones he wants to find. Dessay you'll know who they are.'

'So you won't give him anything.'

'Give him a little water if he asks. But I think he won't ask.' He bent over suddenly, and took my grandfather's wrist, counting his pulse just as Dr Milmain did.

'Want to feel it?' he asked me.

'No.'

'Starting to flutter now; a bit of him's still caught here. You were dreaming when I came in.'

'Yes, I was.'

'What was it about then?'

'A dance we had, a long time ago. Only it was all different.'

'How was that?'

'There were two dances, one in one hall and one in another.' I didn't want to tell him any more.

282

'Good and evil, eh?' said the wizard. 'Was that it?'

'How did you know?'

'I cast dreams, didn't she tell you?'

'Then you know what I did.'

'Maybe.'

Mrs Blazer came back with the lamp, the flame turned down as low as it would go and a little tin dish balanced above with the white stuff beginning to swim in its own grease. As the lumps melted a smell of roses curled into the room. Dark red roses, red almost to blackness and fleshy at the base of their petals, with drops of dew standing on them. I looked at the wizard.

'Attar of roses,' he said. 'You have to take a field full of flowers to make an ounce of it. I don't let it go to everyone, but Mrs Blazer has promised to pay me well.'

I opened my mouth to say we had no money, then I saw how she looked at him, smoothing down the folds of her apron over her belly. She was old but she was young too, just as he was. The smell of roses opened out into the room.

'He's going,' said Mrs Blazer suddenly and sharply. My grandfather's face was a wreck now, only the nose standing out on it. For a second he seemed to want to rear himself up and catch his breath, then he sank back. The lamp burnt but he was going. I had my arm behind him, and his nightshirt was wet and cold with sweat. His head lolled into my shoulder, the whole head rasping, not just his breath. Mrs Blazer put a wet flannel to his lips, then wiped the sweat from his face, but it sprang out again, as if every pore of his skin was weeping. The wizard turned up the flame of the lamp so the stuff bubbled and the fume of roses mixed with the May air blowing in through the window. Then black slime ran out of his mouth. He coughed once, struggled and then he seemed to tear free of himself, leaving his mouth wide and empty as a cave and his body slipping down my shoulder and back on to the pillows, which wheezed softly with escaping air as if he were still alive.

Twenty-three

It is winter in the house. The floorboards creak overhead as if someone is walking up there in long deliberate strides. Suddenly there is silence. The footsteps have risen into the air, skimming it as they ride from room to room. Dust angels stir in the corners, then subside. I don't open many doors. It's not necessary, and I don't want to see the damp patches growing on the walls like watercolours. There's a trapped, musty smell which would go if I opened up the rooms in turn, throwing up the sashes and lighting fires. But there's not enough fuel, and why should I air rooms for people who are never coming back to them?

Kate has sent me a photograph. She sits with a child slipping off her lap, a hefty boy who looks as if he is already fighting his way out of her arms. His brows are drawn together as he scowls into the camera. All Kate's features are mixed up in him, but he is not an attractive child. He hasn't inherited Kate's long eyes, and when I look closely Kate's own eyes look narrower and more ordinary than I remember. Perhaps the boy takes after his father, who stands beside Kate, his spade-shaped face impassive, one arm resting on her shoulder as if he owns her. And Kate sits bolt upright as if she is proud of the possessing hand, the dark-clothed man who is hers as much as she is his. I wonder. The Kate I know would whisk out of his grip in an instant. This Kate is heavier, and she wears a hat that looks more like a testament of respectability than an ornament. The photograph is hand-coloured, and Kate's face is a startling china pink. I peer close to see if there is a ring on her hand, but she's wearing gloves. Behind this little family the Niagara Falls thunder. Kate, chair, child, husband and all look as if they are about to topple off the edge of a precipice and disappear in a cloud of spray, leaving Kate's hat bobbing on the turmoil of the waters. But it's only a photographer's backcloth, draped out in some airless room, smelling of dust.

Another photograph fell out of the envelope when I opened it. It's an amateur snapshot, over-exposed, showing a whitish house with windows like tiny staring eyes. On the front porch there stands a sideways Kate, one hand on the door handle in proof of ownership. At the edge of the photograph there is the corner of another, similar, whitish house. They live in the fast-growing town of Forêt Noir, where Kate's husband manages a timber yard. The little boy is called Paul and he is stuffed into a waistcoat and jacket that are a tiny replica of his father's clothes. His arms stand away from his body stiffly, and his legs look unchildlike, as if a little old man has perched himself on Kate's lap. How old would she be now – about thirty-five? She might have many more children, but somehow I feel that she won't. The three of them look as settled as a story which has already been written.

I don't suppose Paul is ever allowed to play in the timber yard, tossing up handfuls of white, resinous sawdust and riding the logs as if they were bronco horses. One day, Kate writes, they plan to make a trip back to the old country, but she doesn't say which old country that will be. I am sure she won't come here. Paul won't want to meet the grown woman who once sat on his mother's lap, and Kate won't want her widower to see her narrow attic room with its looking-glass making faces at him.

She asks after Rob and my grandfather as if they are still alive. I can't bring myself to write back for a long time. She is the last person in whose mind they are living, eating, sleeping, quarrelling, still capable of change. My letter will end that:

286

even in Canada they will be finished and fading. I wait, letting the words I will write drum over and over in my mind. Perhaps Kate ought to know how things had happened. But then I re-read her letter and realize that she has only written to me because she wants to stamp on to the image we have of her the icons of her house and her child. She has probably written the same letter to the little house in Dublin where what remains of her family lives and has enclosed the same two photographs, the proofs of her new life. It is the sending of that letter that is important to her, not any answer I might send back. In the end I write briefly, telling her that Grandfather has died, and Rob is missing, believed killed.

Missing, believed killed. Believed by whom? It takes a long time for belief like that to solidify from whirling grains of hope, fear and speculation to a slow giving up. He died little by little in my mind. At first I was sure he was hiding out somewhere behind the lines, holed up with an injury or loss of memory. The front was another Canada, and one day he'd appear when I least expected him, telling me nothing of his past, giving me nothing but the fact of his presence.

Nothing told me he was dead. I can't look back on that ordinary day and make it extraordinary. It was a clear late summer day, that last day he was seen alive, the day on which I have to presume he died. He walked out of the world while I was picking apples. My hands moved from branch to basket, drunken wasps throbbed inside hollow windfalls, and I thought of nothing but checking the apples for blemishes, and how many baskets I had picked. It was a calm, satisfying day. The Michaelmas daisies stood still, waiting to glow at dusk as if they were lighted from within. There wasn't a tremor in the air as I lugged the first basket to the orchard gate.

There wasn't a shred of his clothing left, or of his flesh.

There was only the coat, because he hadn't been wearing it. It was sent back to me muddy, smelling of wool that has been packed when damp, and of wood smoke. There was nothing in the pockets. I shut my eyes the first time I felt deep into his pockets. When we used to walk side by side I would put my hand into his pocket and our fingers would meet and twine there. I felt the ridge of the seam, and the silky, expensive lining fabric. They had given me my money's-worth with that coat. There wasn't even the tiniest hole through which something might have fallen.

Weeks after the telegram and the official letter I had a letter from someone who knew him. They'd been at a rest camp together and he'd played chess with Rob every night. It was summer, so they played until the light went.

We never had a candle because of the moths. It was only when someone lit a lamp that we'd realize it was quite dark.

There'd been a concert and Rob had sung a song in French.

It was the kind of tune you catch yourself whistling all the next day. I meant to ask him to write it down for me, but then our orders came and we were sent back up to the line, so it went out of my head.

It was a nice letter, though he didn't know any more about how Rob had died. The war was over by the time he wrote.

It seems such terribly hard luck that it should happen just then. I lost the chess set when our trench was shelled, or I'd send it to you.

I'd read in the newspaper how our men played chess using bits of paper for pieces. These were better than wooden pieces because they could be swept up into a pocket in an instant when orders came. The men did not need to have the real thing. If 'Queen' was written on a piece of paper, then it was a queen and it could ramp triumphantly over the other pieces, destroying them. I thought of Rob playing chess with Edward Manston in the greenish twilight, with the white pieces still showing clear while the players had to fumble for the black.

I'll be able to go and see his grave if I want, only it won't be his grave but a representative grave where they've reverently lowered a lump of flesh that is supposed to approximate to Rob and all the others who can't be traced by so much as a button. I shan't go. Better to think of the ditches lined with cow-parsley and Rob knocking off flower heads with his stick as he strolls down the lane to turn in. I see him look up suddenly, startled to see me. He's brown again from living outside for months; his freckles are like the speckling on a hen's egg. His hair has grown and it springs up, full of life.

'Cathy!' he says. 'Whatever are you doing here? You'd better get home, you'll be frightened.'

He knows I'm frightened of everything: Grandfather and Miss Gallagher and the boy in the wallpaper. But I'm not any more. I look back at the long lines of tents which make up the rest camp, and the men lounging their way to bed or queueing for the cocoa and biscuits organized by the YMCA. Then I blink and the field clears and grows green. The pale yellowish oblongs left by the tents show for a moment, then vanish in a wave of bright new grass. It's up to our ankles, then our knees. There are dog-daisies in it, and corn-cockle, and the ripe tips of the grass tickle our legs. Rob's wearing his Norfolk jacket again, the one I haven't seen for years, and his dirty hands move deftly as he plaits a tiny trap for field-mice. Not to kill them, he tells me, just to let them run in and out. I bend over to have a look. There is the little hole for the mice to go in, and crumbs of the biscuit I've brought in my pinafore pocket, to tempt them. It is such a satisfactory little mouse-house that I can't believe the mice will be able to resist it.

'There!' says Rob, triumphantly, holding it out to me, and I take it very carefully and balance it on my palm, turning it round while I become a mouse in my mind, brushing my way through the plaited entrance.

Suddenly we both stiffen. A voice caws from far off, near the house:

'Cath-eee. Rob-ert.'

'Get down,' says Rob. 'She'll never see us,' and we fold ourselves down into the tickling, rustling grass, slowly so that we won't attract her eye by a sudden movement. We are close together, facing one another, the flower heads and grasses blowing above our heads. This is exactly like being inside the mouse-house, I think.

'She's just shouting. She doesn't know where we are,' he says reassuringly.

I can smell his hair, hot from the sun, and his sweat, and the overheated wool of the Norfolk jacket. This is our house. I nip off some tiny pimpernel flowers which are growing close to the ground, and spread them out on my lap. The breeze passes over us without touching us.

'We could stay here for ever and she'd never find us,' says Rob. 'No one will ever find us here.'

'I've brought you a letter,' says Mr Bullivant. He has walked over, because there aren't any horses at Ash Court now. When people in the village heard he was coming back they thought it was all going to start again, the building and planting and landscaping, with Ash Court buoyed up on its tide of money. But he's selling up and going away.

'We're always hearing about hard-faced men who've done well out of the war,' he said, 'but I'm not one of them.'

He is five years older. He's held the hands of dying men

while vomit and salt-water slopped around the decks. But the worst, he says, is the men who want to die and can't. He still sees them gibbering at him out of torn faces, or just their eyes, black with anguish, the pupils dilated, staring when the man was long beyond speech.

'We ran out of everything. Chloroform, bandages, dressings, wound-drains. They say it was better managed in France but I'd like to have seen it. And some of those army surgeons are incompetent brutes at the best of times. They wouldn't bother to hide it in front of an orderly – didn't think it mattered. Only sometimes, if they heard me speak, they'd look at me queerly. I've seen them take a man's leg off when it could have been saved with careful nursing – but there wasn't the nursing to be had. And then it'd haemorrhage anyway, three days after the amputation. And the man'd stare at you as his blood came rushing out, too frightened to ask if he was dying. One of them kept apologizing because his blood had spattered all over the next stretcher and soaked the man lying in it. He was still saying he was sorry when he died.'

There are crocuses up now, and aconites. He comes every day and we walk endlessly while the months of the war unscroll from his memory into mine. Gallipoli – the most futile campaign of them all. The hospital ships lying low in the water from their burdens. The chaos of stretchers and wounded men and orderlies mopping up pools of blood and faeces and vomit. The constant hiss of steam from the field-hospital sterilizers, and the long lines of men waiting to be operated on, while surgeons bustled among them sorting out the hopeless from those who were operable.

'They'd talk to them as if they were still on parade, even when they were dying.'

'Did you talk to them?'

'Oh yes. All the time. It's very frightening to die in a place you don't know, with strange people around you. At least, it is at first. When they're very bad it gets so it doesn't matter. I liked to know their Christian names. They have wonderful flowers there in spring, and sometimes the wind would blow the scent over the dressing-tents and those who weren't too far gone would turn towards it, sniffing for it like dogs. No matter how much water we carried round there were voices begging for it all the time. We couldn't keep up with them.'

'Do you remember those narcissi you used to have – great bunches in every room?' I ask, and he nods.

'They were always my favourite flower. I don't know that I could stand them now. I should always be smelling gas gangrene coming through them.'

'You couldn't start the building again?'

'No. I'll take the paintings with me. They're the only thing worth having out of all of it.'

He'd said he wanted to visit my grandfather's grave.

'It's in the churchyard,' I say, 'just inside the wall, about as far from the church as you can get.'

'Won't you show me?'

I hesitate. 'I don't go there very often. The last time I went someone had put a jamjar of snowdrops on his grave. They think I neglect him.'

'Do you?'

'Oh no. It's just that I don't like going there.'

You can see Miss Gallagher's grave from my grandfather's. Drops of water run down the rather showy black marble headstone which he paid for.

Eunice Maria Gallagher
A Faithful Friend

It is the sort of inscription one would put on a dog's grave, but the headstone is much admired and I know there is a feeling that I should have done something equally impressive for my grandfather, instead of the plain grey granite which bears the date of his death but not of his birth. We never knew it. When I came to draft the inscription I realized how many gaps there were.

'You could pay Annie Semple to tend it,' says Mr Bullivant. 'She'd be glad enough to do it.'

'Open your letter,' says Mr Bullivant. 'I'm tired of bringing you letters which you never read.'

The pale spring sunlight makes me squint. My mother's strong black handwriting looks clear, but is in fact quite difficult to read. It is a cool, small letter set in the middle of a big creamy sheet of paper.

Pre-war quality: she must have kept it.

Dear Catherine,

If you would like to see me, you might come here now that the war is over. Write, and I will send you directions. It's not such a bad journey.

I should like to see you,

Your mother,

Cynthia Quinn

'I wonder why she signs herself with my grandfather's name?'

'It's hers too. She doesn't use her married name.'

I go back to the letter.

'Douarnenez. Where's that?'

'It's a little fishing village in Brittany. She's living a couple of miles from there. She has some friends who've bought a farm; not to farm, of course, but to live in. They're painters. She's renting a cottage from them.'

'You mean she's moved for good?'

'I shouldn't think so, but she's there for now.'

'Have you been there?'

'Not to see her. But I know Brittany; I've been there to buy paintings. You'd be surprised how many painters have lived there at one time or another.'

'What's it like?'

'Oh, poor. At low tide there are women swarming all over the rocks, mussel-picking. They tuck up their long black dresses and the girls jump from rock to rock. They need good balance, because mussel-shells cut like razors if you fall on them. The tides go out for miles. There's plenty of fish, so no one starves.'

'Whatever is she doing there?' I have a sudden, flying vision of my mother in black, sure-footed, leaping from rock to rock as the tide swirls in along the sand-channels. She jumps like a goat and her basket is full of fresh, succulent mussels.

'She's very fond of these particular friends,' says Mr Bullivant, 'and they're very fond of her.'

'Have you bought their paintings?'

He hesitates. 'Well, no. They're not my type of thing.'

'You mean, not much good?'

'I'm not saying that. You'll probably meet them, so you can judge for yourself. Why don't you go and see?'

'I haven't the money,' I say, 'really. We have nothing.'

'I'll give you the money.'

'Can you afford it?'

'Yes. I've sold the fountain. They're coming to cart it away tomorrow. The buyer is delighted with himself: he thinks I don't know what it's worth. He could hardly control his excitement when he came to see it. I took a hundred pounds from him, and he couldn't get the money out of his pocket fast enough. So here you are.' He takes an envelope out of his breast pocket. There are twenty big white five-pound notes in it. He counts off ten and holds them out to me.

'You'll be able to stay some time if you want to.'

'Where are you going?'

'Back to Italy.'

I take the money, fold it and tuck it into my skirt pocket.

We have reached the hen-run. Several of the hens have come out to peck at grit in the sun. They stop and look at us with the self-righteously busy stare of hens. Soon they'll be pecking up groundsel and coming in to lay. The slightly acrid smell of hen droppings wafts from the coop. It is all so familiar. My hands know every fence post: where the wood is smooth, where it's splintery. My hands know the warm fullness of finding an egg in the straw. The paddock grass still has its wintry yellowness, and it's empty now.

'We kept goats there, all through the war,' I say. 'That's how we got our milk.'

'Did you?'

'Mrs Blazer did. But she took them with her when she went to live with Harry Shiner.'

'Good God. She must be sixty.'

'Maybe more. But he wanted her, you could see it. And off she went. She sends me rosemary water to rinse my hair, and goats' cheese. She thinks nobody'll have me if I don't look sharp.'

'Is that what I can smell? The rosemary on your hair?'

'It might be.'

'Living with Harry Shiner. They put up with that round here now, do they?'

'He's a wizard, so no one'll cross him.'

'I like the smell,' says Mr Bullivant. 'It seems to go through you. Not sweet.'

'Like the lemons.'

'Yes. When I think of you – when I thought of you – it always had that sharpness, like lemons.'

He looks at me as if I am a solid, continuous thing in his

mind, to think of and to come home to. He makes my darkness shaded and beautiful, lit by the lamps of the lemons.

'There's a lot of things about me you don't know,' I say hurriedly.

'Of course. Of course there are. We can't hope to know everything about one another. I went to your grandfather's grave, you know. And that woman's – what's her name – the woman who used to look after you –'

'No, that was Kate. She was the one who looked after us. Miss Gallagher taught me.'

'Miss Gallagher. That was it. What an extraordinary woman she was. I always used to wonder what on earth your grandfather saw in her, to have her always in the house.'

But he speaks as if it really doesn't matter, and we walk on.

'There are graves here too,' I say. 'All old houses have them.'

'Whose? Do you know?'

'A hare Rob shot. And a baby who died a long time ago.'

'It's the same with my house in Italy. You can't live on a piece of land there without knowing there are layers of people who've lived there before you. Their houses, their fires. Their bodies I suppose. But usually I don't think of it. You said you'd come and see my house there, do you remember?'

'Yes.'

'France is on the way to Italy.'

'But you're here.'

'Not for long. I'm finished here.'

I look round at the empty paddock where grass and weeds will spring up again as soon as the days grow longer. Without the goats they will grow uncontrollably. How can I keep pushing back this tide of green? Bindweed is waiting to twine its way up the rose bushes and squeeze them to death. One fragment of white bindweed root, dropped into the earth, will grow into a thick green snake in weeks.

'You couldn't find the graves now,' I say. "They are quite overgrown.'

The house is fighting me too, gently but with great force. It doesn't want to be a house any more. It swarms with life. It has become a place for starlings to nest and rats to scuffle: a habitation of owls. When I went into my grandfather's room his window was black with leaves. There are so many empty rooms, but I'm not sure that there is room for me in any of them. The drive where my father picked out stones to divide good from evil is packed with moss now, and the stones cling to one another. They have grown together. This is the dream of a man who came from nowhere with nothing. It needn't be mine.

'Tide's coming in.'

'Is it?'

'Come and look.'

I kneel up in bed, dragging huge pale flounces of eiderdown with me. The light on the wall ripples. There is almost nothing else in the room but the bed, made of old black oak, high and hard and broad, with its bolster like a dead body and its stiff twill sheets. But the eiderdown is a dream of satin with panels of lace, oyster-coloured and delicious as water on our bare skin. I am sure it is the secret self of our landlady. I noticed how she stroked it without looking down when she showed us the room. She is tall and spare and firm-faced, always dressed in black. She cannot imagine what we are doing here, but she is glad of the money. She is widowed and she has a foolishly blond son of about eighteen who just missed the war and seems determined to be idle for the rest of his life in celebration of this.

'He puts his boots out for her to polish, did you see?'

'Yes.'

'I'd throw them out of the window if I were her.'

You could just about throw a pair of boots into the sea at high tide. The house stands on a little grassy rise, hedged by tamarisks which are all blown one way by the wind, like greyhounds. The garden is full of sand. We lie in bed and hear them talking, not in French but in Breton. We cannot understand a word. It's like listening to seagulls. The tide came up at ten yesterday, filling the bay and changing the light in our room until I felt as if I were curled up inside a sea-shell, listening to the noise of the waves. We get up too late.

We miss half the day. Mme Plouaret tells us so every morning. 'You have lost the best part of the day, M'sieu-'Dame.' And her son lounges in the hearth, grinning, as she ladles out bowlfuls of hot milk to make our coffee.

'Come and look.'

He's blocking half the window. He has pulled on his red dressing-gown and when he turns round I see the firm, careful knot he has tied in the sash. It makes me want to laugh. And as if he senses it he gives me a smile that makes his eyes shine. It's hard to say what this smile is like. It's not timid; he isn't afraid of anything I am or might do. Yet it isn't bold either. It's the kind of smile you hardly ever dare let appear, except to a small child who will smile back as immediately as a reflection in clear water, so immediately that you want to cry.

I like to watch him wash in the morning, ducking his face right into the bowl of water and rubbing vigorously at the short hairs on the back of his neck.

'What are you laughing about?'

'Nothing.'

'There's a boat – look – wonder where it's going?'

'It'll be one of the fishing boats.'

'I don't think so. Wrong shape. But it's so far out I can't be sure.'

'Let's go down to the quay when they come in, and get a lobster.'

'D'you think she'd cook it?'

The window sill is low. He hasn't fastened the shutters and they blow to and fro, to and fro, though the breeze is mild, not like the wild day nearly a week ago when we arrived. I have never been so sick in my life. Sick on the boat, sick on the little train with its wood-slatted seats and stink of cigarettes and sausage, sick again on the jolting cart that brought us here. It was dark by the time we arrived and I could hardly stand against the rough warm wind.

'We'll have to stay here for ever, there's nothing else for it. I can't possibly go back.'

The sea grows bluer each day. But it doesn't last, Mme Plouaret keeps assuring us, there'll be a storm soon. You can't play about with our sea here. She tells us about the hungry teeth of the Point des Espagnols and the Point du Raz, and how many men and ships they have caught. Last year an old woman was blown over the edge of the cliff while she was gathering gulls' eggs. Behind Mme Plouaret's back George winks at me.

'Gulls' eggs!' he exclaims politely. 'I don't think I've ever tried them. Are they good?'

'You've missed nothing,' she says grimly, seizing our bolster and thumping the life out of it.

'How she loves disasters,' he says later, when we are back in our room. He cups my kneecap in his hand, then bends down and licks the skin.

'I can taste salt, must be from when we were bathing yesterday.'

It's cold and the sea pulls hard, bearing out Mme Plouaret's warnings of rip-tides and currents. But at low tide there are big pools which the sun warms. We walk round the headland on firm, biscuit-coloured sand, past caves and mussel-clustered rocks and shallow rock-pools, to a big pool we have found where the water is deep enough to swim. But you have to be careful. The tide sweeps in and if we were caught we would never climb those cliffs.

I haven't seen my mother yet. It's not far, just around the next headland, on the next bay. We could walk to it at low tide. But there's no hurry. She doesn't know I am here. One day slides into the next, and the promised storm holds off. It never seems hot, because of the wind, but my arms are tanned and my face is quite different when I bother to look in the glass. Already my hands are growing soft, losing their callouses, splinters and raw places. But it's only for a little while, I think. I've grown to like the way my hands know how to work.

The dunes trap the heat. We lie out of the wind, choosing our hollow carefully so we are sheltered but still able to watch the tide coming up. When we talk our words stay close instead of being whipped away on the wind. I dig a hole for our bottle of wine, wedging it in cold, unsunned sand. We eat bread and cold bacon, and occasionally there's a muslin square with red gooseberries wrapped in it, or a piece of cheese. It's impossible to keep sand out of the food, and everything we eat has a slight grittiness which we wash away with the wine. At night, when I take off my clothes, thin streams of sand fall from them. We never meet anyone.

'Oh, we get a few visitors. Painters. But they don't come, since the war,' says Mme Plouaret. 'There's no money.'

Old women in rusty black dresses crouch in the fields, scratching at rows of potatoes. There don't seem to be any young men around, except for Jean-Marie.

'They go away. And besides, the war . . .'

One morning I go to the baker's with Mme Plouaret and see the respect with which he greets her. She is a rich woman for these parts, with her big, scoured house and the rent of two cottages. She works, works, works; she never stops working. Jean-Marie is her only luxury. God knows what she thinks of us. Her eyes veil themselves and she says nothing. Jean-Marie is a hopeless fisherman, but his mother sets her lines unerringly, as if she's already struck a bargain with the fish. She's the first to detect the far-out metallic seethe on the sea that means a shoal of mackerel. We see her rush down to the rowing-boat which she drags across the sand in minutes. She leaps in and rows sturdily out to pull in mackerel after mackerel after mackerel, so many that she just lets them flop like oily rainbows in the bottom of the boat until they die.

Killing them would be a waste of valuable fishing time. What we can't eat straight away, she smokes in a little lean-to shed. Nothing is ever wasted.

'If she netted an albatross she'd eat it,' says George.

We seem to have plenty of money here. Our English money changes into thousands of francs, and a few sous buy what we need each day. We could live here for months. If we took a cottage, we could get fish, bread, cabbages. One day we're going to Italy, but not yet.

'Come on, let's go for a walk.'

He's restless today. Something stands between him and what he sees.

'I don't like that whine in the wind,' he explains. I listen. Yes, the wind's getting up. It does sound like someone moaning, far off, so far off that you could ignore it if you chose. The horizon is brilliantly clear. I pull on my cotton stockings and the cotton dress which is exactly the same colour as the convolvulus clinging to the sandy paths. My hair is sticky with salt and I can put it up without even looking in the glass. Everything's so easy here. Mme Plouaret has gone out, so for the first time Jean-Marie serves us with coffee and new rolls. He has fastened a clean white cloth around his waist, no doubt in imitation of some waiter in town whom he admires. His nails, however, are black. Jean-Marie's hair is much too yellow – surely no adult has hair like that? It flops over his pale forehead so he can't see, and he has a permanent twitch from flicking it back. He tells us about a *caporal* from the next village who lost both legs when a shell fell into his trench.

'He was washing himself, imagine. When they found him he still had the soap in his hand.'

'Remarkable that he had any soap at all,' agrees George.

The *caporal* has just been sent home from the military convalescent hospital. There was an official welcome.

'And he's going to get married next year, think of that.'
But he speaks with a child's curiosity which has nothing
salacious in it. He hands us our coffee with a flourish. His
mother made the coffee before she left, so that he would
have nothing to do but warm it up, and this he has failed
to do. If you met Jean-Marie on a train you'd place him as
a barman who has been got rid of by a succession of em-
ployers. He has all the mannerisms of a busy man, but he
never does anything. He watches our every mouthful,
hungry not for the food but for our difference. It's off-
putting, and although I'm hungry I eat only one roll.
George wraps two more in a napkin and smiles at Jean-
Marie.

'You'll be hungry later. What about a long walk? I think
this weather's going to break.'

'There's a storm coming,' Jean-Marie assures us, nodding
his yellow head.

At low tide it's much quicker to walk round on the sand. The
wind is whipping crusts of foam off the top of the waves, but
the tide is down and we walk fast, leaving a long line of
footprints on the clean sand. My hair is coming out of its
knot already. It streams across my face, half-blinding me. We
are close together, our arms hooked, my head down so the
wind won't blow sand into my eyes. Suddenly I feel his arm
jerk. He stops.

'What is it?'

'Look.'

I shade my eyes. There's something glistening on the sand
a few hundred yards off, like a grey rock or an upturned boat.
Two gulls which are sitting on the wind just above it begin
to scream at the sight of us.

'What is it?' I ask again.

'Come on.'

We are running. The thing is big, as big as a boat, but it's not a boat. It's a smooth, shining wall of flesh.

'Is it a whale?'

We come up to it where it lies on its side, beached, its big ribby tail dug into the sand. It is about eight feet long, its grey-black skin drying already in the wind and sun. For a second I imagine us raising it, dragging it back into the water, pouring water over its back, watching it hang still in the waves then suddenly convulse with life. But then I realize that it's already dead.

'It's a porpoise.'

I walk round to its head. The cloud of gulls overhead shrieks at me. The porpoise is theirs. They have been at it already: they've had its eyes. There's no sign of how it died.

'What do you think happened to it?'

'I don't know. Perhaps a big wave . . .'

'But there haven't been any. It's been calm.'

'Sometimes they go in the wrong direction and keep on going. They run themselves up on to the sand.'

I wonder where the porpoise thought it was going. What was it like, that moment when the bright sea slopping over its eyes went suddenly grainy and began to hurt? Or perhaps it happened in the night, last night when there was a track of moonlight over the sea, leading nowhere. The porpoise has lost its beauty as quickly as a pebble which dulls when it is taken out of a rock pool. Already its skin has stopped reflecting the light. It is grey and hard. It looks like meat, lying there waiting to be cut up. I can see Mme Plouaret picking up her skirts and racing over the sand towards it with her sharp little knife in her hand. Soon the flies will come.

'Perhaps it will float out on the tide.'

I hope it will. I hope it will go back to where it came from, to the deep water. Even there crabs will burrow under its flesh as it rolls, and the fish will eat it. There's no getting away from it. And in the earth, worms. Its sheen is fading as we stand here.

We walk on, to where my mother is busy with something else, not knowing we are coming. I see her on the doorstep, shading her eyes with her hands. She is waiting for the baker's cart, not for us. She wears a mauve-and-white striped skirt, and a rather severe, high-necked white blouse. The fashion has changed, but I cannot change her. On her feet there are small workmanlike black boots, like the boots Mme Plouaret wears to market.

'Of course she has no money now.'

'Hasn't she?'

'Only what she earns from her stories.'

'I didn't know she wrote stories.'

'Yes. For children. She publishes them under another name. They're supposed to be quite good. These friends she's staying with — they illustrate them for her.'

She is shorter than I am, just a little. George has told me that.

'An inch or two. There's not much in it.'

But then I am tall for a woman.

I am making my mother up. An oil lamp hangs over a scrubbed table. My mother reaches up and pulls up the wick with a pair of blackened tongs. Then, carefully, she trims the wick. The lamplight shivers and begins to burn clear. We face one another across the table. My mother puts her elbows on the clean white wood and rests her chin on her folded hands. I have her face, and she has mine.

'Well,' she says. 'Here we are.'

I am making my mother up. She is my child, my sister. I lean close to George, and he feels me shiver.

'Never mind,' he says, 'there's nothing we can do now.'

'No.'

'Best not tell Mme Plouaret, though, or she'll be serving porpoise for supper.'

I laugh with pleasure. He too has seen her tiny assiduous figure swarm over the body of the porpoise.

'Quick. The tide's coming in.' It is very close now, sly and innocent, licking the sand. Ahead of us there are the rocks we must get round before it comes. Behind us the gulls sink down and settle.

The sky is full of hurrying clouds, thin strips like torn-up paper.

But my mother isn't in the cottage. Its door is open in the way they leave doors open here, because there's nothing to steal. We look in. The walls are apricot, glowing, the colour uneven as the cheek of a ripening fruit. There's a table covered with papers, held down with stones, and a jar of cornflowers stands in the middle of them. There's a big silk shawl thrown over a wooden settle by the wall. Black silk, with yellow iris splashed over it. There's a small iron stove, not lit. My mother must cook here. I never saw her cook.

'I remember that rug,' says George. 'She had it on the floor in her villa.'

It's Chinese, I think. Yellow and black like the shawl, too beautiful to walk on. It covers the whole of the far wall. There are no pictures, which surprises me. If I were alone I'd read through her papers, wrap her shawl around me, stroke her Chinese rug. Or would I? If I were alone I would never have come here. I would still be waking in my iron bed in the old night nursery, with Rob's coat around me like a shroud. I shiver. I can smell the mud on it, even here.

On the little dresser there's a round loaf of bread, the same bread as we eat each morning in Mme Plouaret's house. I don't know why this should surprise me as much as the absence of pictures, but it does. My mother eats, and cooks, and uses the privy in the battered shed that leans against the cottage wall. Her room looks as if she's only left it a minute ago. Perhaps she's still here somewhere. There is a narrow wooden stairway in the corner of the room.

'That'll go up to the sleeping-place,' says George. 'These cottages are all the same.'

'Can we look?'

'Why not?'

I go up the ladder. My head comes out level with the boards, and I look around. Light comes in through a narrow window cut into the side of the cottage. The sea leaps in the distance. The whistle of wind sounds louder here. I bunch my skirt up and scramble into the room. It's easy. The spurs of the ladder stairway are secured to the floor and worn to a dark shine where generations of hands have grasped them. Thousands of quick touches have put that polish on the wood. My mother's touch is part of it, too. Her hands, like everyone else's, grasp and move on.

It's a plain narrow room. Hardly a room at all. I can't stand up straight. I am directly under the roof, and if it rained I'd hear each drop spatter. Seagulls scream, inches away. They'll be floating round the cottage on their way inland from the coming storm. Through the window the sea heaves, grey and white as the storm blows up, wilder and wilder. There's a narrow bed tucked close to the wall. My mother has thrown back her bedclothes and humped them up to air. White sheets, white bolster, a big shapeless white *plumeau* that she has shaken into a cloud. Bending my head, I go over and sit down on the mattress. My mother has a box chest by her bed, with a candlestick on it, a book and a deep-blue glass bottle of perfume. I pick up the book. It's in French, stories by a writer called Anton Tchehoff. So my mother reads in French at night, not English. Page seventy-nine is turned down. I weigh the book in my hand, not reading it. My French isn't very good, not good enough. I put it down and pick up the bubble-shaped bottle of perfume, take out the glass stopper and breathe in.

It's my mother. Not flowers or musks but her. Her skin, her hair. The way those tiny crisp curls round her forehead would tickle me when she bent down to kiss me. It fills my throat and I can't swallow it. I put the stopper carefully back into the bottle, sealing up her perfume. The wind bats at the window and the gulls scream. I shut my eyes to the white sealight and lie down. I have my face in her pillow, where she lies. Without opening my eyes I reach out for the *plumeau* and drag it around my shoulders. It is as light as snow. This must be how a plant feels, wrapped in snow. Snow is better than frost. Frost scorches, but snow protects, though we call it cold. I think of Christmas roses sleeping, flowering under a crust of snow.

My mother's smell is all around me. The wind beats and beats like a heart on the window. I think the *plumeaux* they have here are filled with feathers. The best ones are tiny white feathers, the down of the bird. They trap heat so that even in the middle of the harshest winters you sleep warm. My brother had a coat that weighed so heavy it must have bowed his shoulders as he stood on guard at night, straining his eyes into the humped region of nightmare where shell-craters bulged as the flares went up. His coat could not keep him warm. They sent it back to me but when I knew after a long silence that he was dead I could not bring myself to throw it away. I could never get the damp out of the cloth, no matter how much I roasted it by the fire. The heat of my body would not pass into that coat. It was winter in the house and in my body which could not warm anything. In the end I knew I had to get rid of my brother's coat. I took it off one morning and rolled it up and tied it tight with twine. I went out to the orchard carrying it, and I buried it under the conference pear tree. They are big pears, some of the best we have. They look like drops of rain in September. I dug a hole and buried the coat. First the hare, then the little female thing, then Miss Gallagher and my grandfather. The coat was the last thing I buried. I should have known as soon as I opened the parcel it came in that there was no use in keeping or wearing my brother's coat. It belonged to the earth, with him.

I've stopped imagining ways he might have died. It doesn't help. I can't go there with him. But I still wonder how hard it was. Did he walk, then crawl, and then shrink back to nothing but a cry in the darkness? Nobody came. I would have come. Nothing would have stopped me. But I was picking apples in the orchard I'd made mine, carrying baskets of them home to store in the house that was mine too. I'd left no room for him.

There were always the two of us. There are two of us now. He hears our mother's heartbeat, just as I do. A hard bump, then its echo. Her flesh fans out the sound into our soft bodies. He heard it before me. He feels the warmth of her and smells her skin. He will leave her body before I do, and he'll be there, waiting for me, making sure I'm never alone. We slipped like fish over the lip of our mother's body. He waited for me. He waits again.

The white down covers us both like a wing, and the noise of the gulls and the approaching storm covers the sounds I'm making.

George doesn't come up the ladder to look for me. After some time I push away the *plumeau* and get up. My mother hasn't got a looking-glass, so I wipe my face on the sheet and push back my hair. On the floor in the corner of the room there's a white china jug and bowl, with some water still in the jug. I dip in my handkerchief and wash my face with it, then I recall something Kate used to do when we had fever and I let the water drip on to the insides of my wrists. Each drop cools me. Where did Kate learn all these things? She was a child when she came to us. Fourteen is nothing, though to me she was a woman. It was from Kate I learned how to be a woman, though I didn't know what I was learning. I see her hands, working. Her voice, telling me of things she saw that no child ought to have seen. Then her laugh and the mocking smile in her long eyes. It doesn't matter how many respectable photographs Kate sends me from Canada, I shall never believe in them. I'll always see her alive, laughing at everything, moving with her own sure grace.

The floor creaks. These cottages are built to lie low to the earth, to resist the wind by yielding a little each time it blows. Downstairs George is seated comfortably at my mother's table, reading. He looks up and smiles.

'It's one of her stories,' he says. 'Quite good, I think. Are you all right?'

'Yes.'

'Doesn't look as if she's coming back just yet, does it? Shall we go up to the house and have a look? Even if she's not there, Marc and Isabelle ought to know where she is.'

Outside the wind snatches at my skirt. Sand is blowing up from the low dunes and whisking across the grass. No one will hear us coming.

'I'll just use your mother's privy,' says George, and disappears. I might as well use it too, I think, considering all the bushes I've had to crouch behind since we came to France. When I go in I can smell his urine, quite strong but not unpleasant. It's strange to live so closely with him, but I am getting used to it more quickly than I would have thought possible. The privy has a big wooden seat over a hole. The walls have been washed white years ago, but the whitewash flakes wherever I touch it. There is dark-red valerian growing

311

out of the top of the wall, where the light comes in. My mother has spiked sheets of paper on to a nail. There's writing on one side: her manuscripts I suppose. I like the mixed smells of earth and carbolic and urine and the sea. I tear off a piece of paper.

And then the nurse blew out the candle so all Emily saw was the glow of the fire.

'That's not the end of the story,' said Emily. 'Tell me the re

I wipe myself with the paper.

Rain scuds in from the sea. Bars of rain move fast, gaining on us as we run towards the farmhouse. The door is open.

'Go on,' says George. 'We'll get soaked if we stay out here.'

We step through the low doorway, ducking our heads. There is no one in the long narrow kitchen which runs back into shadows. A heap of fire sends out petals of flame, and a black kettle has been pushed to one side of the hearth.

'They'll be here soon.'

Wind funnels through the doorway. I watch white curtains of rain shudder as they rush in from the sea. Then I see a figure, head down, hurrying to get out of the rain. A woman. The wind buffets her clothes as she runs the last few yards up the path. She stops in the entrance, not seeing us. She bends down, unlaces her boots and kicks them off.

We stand still in the shadows as she comes in, pushing back the hair which has blown all over her face. I notice her hands first, mud-stained and as broad as mine. Then her face. The hair she smoothes isn't black any more. It is grey, grey at the roots. The grey is pushing up into the dark mass she wears knotted at the nape of her neck.

She is smiling to herself. She reaches into her pocket and tosses something into the air. There is a flash of yellow. She presses her thumbnail into its skin and I catch the small explosion of volatile oils.

The air floods with summer. Against a screen of leaves the lemons hang, dipped in shade. It is noon. The sky burns white and no one moves. I hear the croak of a frog huddled by the water tank, the stir of a bird in the leaves, a shimmer of cicadas in the valley below the lemon grove.

She turns, her eyes lively, friendly. They don't see many people here. Then she stands quite still.

'Catherine,' says my mother quietly. One hand goes up to her hair, holding it back. This is my mother. For a moment my beautiful mother with her long white fingers, her hair like ink, her perfect, averted face stands between us, filling the space across which we must touch. Then I blink and the slide of my tears across my eyeballs washes her away. Here is my mother.

I look at my mother's face, her lively eyes still and watchful, her body a strong column in its dark dress, her face which is not beautiful at all but is like my own.

My mother stands facing me, waiting to see what I'll do, or say.

Again, like a flood of icy water, I see her not staying by me, not watching my body grow tall alongside hers, not measuring my head as it comes to her shoulder, her chin, her eyes. I see my hungry body fitting itself against my brother's. I see the long dark corridors where I ran as a child with Kate's stories flapping at my heels. I see the body of a dead man break into flower, and the trees of home swaying like arms that have laid down their burdens. I see Miss Gallagher's lips moving in greedy speech and my brother hurling a hard-boiled egg like an arrow against death.

The wind howls but my mother is near to me, next to me, her eyes only inches from mine.

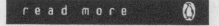

HELEN DUNMORE

MOURNING RUBY

'Moments that bring the reader to tears ... a fascinating – often brilliant – novel'
The Times

Rebecca was abandoned by her mother in a shoebox in the backyard of an Italian restaurant when she was two days old. Her life begins without history, in the dark outdoors. Who is she, where has she come from, and what can she become? Thirty years later, married to Adam, she gives birth to Ruby, and to a new life for herself. But when sudden tragedy changes the course of that life for ever, and all the lives that touch hers, Rebecca is out in the world again, searching ...

'Bold and unusual ... miraculously written, Dunmore's drama of loss and regeneration pieces together shattered lives' *Daily Mail*

'Emotionally restrained, beautifully observed' *Daily Telegraph*

'A tale of unbearable tragedy ... prose and plot-lines as taut as hawsers. Dunmore is the most gifted novelist of her generation' *New Statesman*

'Beautifully told, intricate, powerful' *Independent on Sunday*

HELEN DUNMORE

HOUSE OF ORPHANS

Finland, 1902, and the Russian Empire enforces a brutal policy to destroy Finland's freedom and force its people into submission.

Eeva, orphaned daughter of a failed revolutionary, also battles to find her independence and identity. Destitute when her father dies, she is sent away to a country orphanage, and then as servant to a widowed doctor, Thomas Eklund. Slowly, Thomas falls in love with Eeva ... but she has committed herself long ago to a boy from her childhood, Lauri, who is now caught up in Helsinki's turmoil of resistance to Russian rule.

Set in dangerous, unfamiliar times which strangely echo our own, the story reveals how terrorism lies hidden within ordinary life, as rulers struggle to hold onto power. *House of Orphans* is a rich, brilliant story of love, history and change.

'Part love story, part tragedy ... Dunmore on dazzling form. Everyone should read her work' *Independent on Sunday*

'Outstanding, a sheer pleasure to read. Dunmore is a remarkable storyteller' *Daily Mail*

'Every character is richly drawn and makes for compelling reading ... top-quality fiction' *Daily Express*

'Richly ambitious ...there isn't a dull page. A remarkable achievement, firmly establishes Dunmore as among the best living novelists' *Scotsman*

He just wanted a decent book to read ...

Not too much to ask, is it? It was in 1935 when Allen Lane, Managing Director of Bodley Head Publishers, stood on a platform at Exeter railway station looking for something good to read on his journey back to London. His choice was limited to popular magazines and poor-quality paperbacks – the same choice faced every day by the vast majority of readers, few of whom could afford hardbacks. Lane's disappointment and subsequent anger at the range of books generally available led him to found a company – and change the world.

'We believed in the existence in this country of a vast reading public for intelligent books at a low price, and staked everything on it'
Sir Allen Lane, 1902–1970, founder of Penguin Books

The quality paperback had arrived – and not just in bookshops. Lane was adamant that his Penguins should appear in chain stores and tobacconists, and should cost no more than a packet of cigarettes.

Reading habits (and cigarette prices) have changed since 1935, but Penguin still believes in publishing the best books for everybody to enjoy. We still believe that good design costs no more than bad design, and we still believe that quality books published passionately and responsibly make the world a better place.

So wherever you see the little bird – whether it's on a piece of prize-winning literary fiction or a celebrity autobiography, political tour de force or historical masterpiece, a serial-killer thriller, reference book, world classic or a piece of pure escapism – you can bet that it represents the very best that the genre has to offer.

Whatever you like to read – trust Penguin.